The Creation of Marla Adams

A Mystery Thriller Set in South Texas

Patrick Hanford

SAVOY
HOUSE

Savoy House Publishing

PatrickHanford.com
Savoy House Publishing

SAVOY
HOUSE

This is a work of fiction. Names, characters, places, and events are creations of the author's imagination or are used fictitiously and are not to be construed as factual. Any resemblance of events, locations, organizations or persons, living or dead, is purely coincidental.

If you enjoyed the book, please leave a review on Amazon. Books may be ordered through booksellers or by contacting Savoy House Publishing at the website address above.

ISBN: 979 8 985693935 (paperback) 979 8 985693928 (ebook)

Book Cover by KJ Waters Consultancy (KJWConsultancy.com, and Jody Smyers Photography (JodySmyersPhotography.com)

Other Books by Patrick Hanford

Fabricated Lies
Coming Soon: *Necrotic Survival*

What readers are saying about *Fabricated Lies*

"*Fabricated Lies*' is a fast-moving, captivating cat and mouse murder mystery. I had trouble putting it down because I had to know who was really pulling the strings behind these brutal Chicago murders." K. Hagen, Amazon Reviewer.

"There is action at every turn. This book is one adrenalin rush after another. And the author does a fantastic job of keeping the suspense ratcheted up." RJ McKay, Amazon Reviewer.

"This book reminds me of the great police and gangster movies of the 60s, where the action was always on. It's one of those books that you sit to read for half hour and next you know two hours have passed and you are still caught up in the adventure." tbrmorgans, BookBub Reviewer.

"The book is fast-paced and the storyline is intriguing." Hailey, Goodreads Reviewer.

Mystery without murder?
Might as well tell the Texas wind not to blow.

Chapter 1

A flashing streetlight threw crimson red across John Walker's face, revealing a thickened scar, forehead to chin, and a whitened cornea. He glided between century-old buildings toward the only Catholic Church in town with a steeple towering toward the heavens. A soft glow projected through the belfry and leaked from the windows of the facade. The midnight chill sheared through the empty streets of Hildebrandt, Texas—and him. It resolved his purpose to take what's his.

Across the street, Officer Marla Adams was alone in the police station working the late shift. Cool night air flowed through open windows. In full uniform, with hair pulled into a tight bun at her neckline, she stood six feet from a 17-inch monitor sitting on her desk with her right hand near her holstered pistol. Her sea-green eyes concentrated on the white screen, with numbers decreasing every second. The monitor buzzed, and a timer in the bottom corner spun in milliseconds. She drew her pistol and dry fired. When her gun clicked, the timer stopped at 507 milliseconds. "C'mon, faster. I can get to five-hundred." She did it again, and again, and again.

A gunshot outside snapped her back to reality. Grabbing the 9mm magazine from her desk, she loaded it in her pistol, racked it, and rushed outside. Donnie Lucio's dilapidated pickup truck backfired at the stop sign. She's heard his truck backfire a hundred times before.

Across the street, Walker watched the officer stand in the open doorway of the police station until she returned to the warmth of the building.

He turned his attention toward the church and walked by a plastic sack spinning aimlessly just above the concrete. Flipping the collar of his wool overcoat up as icy air dove down the back of his neck, he passed to the side of the church and drug his fingernails over brick.

Between the ornately carved front doors, a vertical sliver of light shined on his face. It took a few seconds to jimmy the lock. The hinges creaked as the doors opened. He came to take what's his.

The St. Juan Diego Catholic Church aimed to save two hundred and fifty-five sinners at each service, except he was not there to be saved. He glanced over the empty sanctuary with a vision blurred from alcohol. The church stood empty, not a soul inside. Just him.

He stumbled over a heavy cardboard box near the door and landed on his hands and knees. Quickly standing, he kicked the box to the corner. Black stenciling trumpeted HOLY BIBLES across the top.

Trying to clear the cobwebs in his brain, he wiped his hand across his face before picking up his knife. "Shouldn't drink this much when I got business."

Bleakly lit stalactite chandeliers hung from a high-pitched roof over the pews. The ceiling across the nave all the way to the altar held a replica of Michelangelo's Sistine Chapel.

Stained glass windows stood high on the walls filled with biblical figures.

Dark stained pews sat empty, nailed down in perfect order. His echoing footfalls resonated as he stepped forward. His hand tried to wiggle each pew. *Where is it?* His finger touched a small cross carved on the arm of the twelfth pew. Walker twisted the point of his knife into the wood. "Here." He slipped a Maglite out from his overcoat pocket and bent down on his knees.

His head spun like a bowling ball. Closing his good eye for a few seconds, he opened it again to wavy lines. His hand rubbed the wooden floor. "Where is it?" he called out to emptiness. The flashlight scanned under the pews. There, a board slightly different in color and one edge jagged. He stuck the knife between the boards. The nails creaked with resistance, revealing a hole wide enough for a small box. Reaching in, he felt a metal box and smiled. Pulling it out, he flipped the latch up and opened it. The inside was as empty as the church. He flung it against the wall.

"Drop the knife," a voice from behind the stranger demanded. "Why are you here?"

Walker's light switched off. He laid the knife down and asked without looking, "Do I need permission to be in a church?" His fingernail raked across his facial scar again.

A voice bellowed down the nave. "I asked, why are you here?"

Walker's overcoat hid the holster on the right side of his belt as he turned to see who was behind him.

A weathered-faced man, broad, with a long black coat and a wide-brimmed hat, winced at the deformed face. "Are you looking for this?" He held out a Bible toward Walker.

"You the preacher?"

"Hardly."

Walker sat on the pew while his fingertips felt the rough diamond cut pattern on the pistol handle. He contemplated killing in a church but wasn't ready to commit to hell just yet. "I felt bad about what happened at the bar tonight. I needed to come here and pray before my work tomorrow." Twisting back toward the altar and cross, Jesus stared down at him. He glanced at the Bible in the man's hand before noticing the opened box next to the front door. "Did you just take that from the box and walk over here?"

With the Bible held out in front of him, a deep bass tone roared like Moses commanding his flock. "I saw you drinking to excess, lying, and telling stories." The weathered man shook the Bible at Walker. "And sex with that girl."

"I did not have sex. The woman came over and sat next to me. I gave her a twenty, and she slipped her hand under the table." He raised his left hand in the air. "Promise, I did not know that was her husband at the other table." He needed to lean sideways to slip the gun out of the holster. "I'm John Walker, and I know who you are." He rubbed the thick scar on his face. "I'm here for my property."

The brooding man hovered over the man. "Walker? That's not your name." A heavy hand pushed Walker's shoulder down. "Looks like someone sewed your face with a fishing hook."

"Don't worry about my face." It would be an odd angle if he tried to pull the gun out of the holster while sitting. Instead, his right hand slid down the pant leg and wrapped around the handle of his KA-BAR army knife. "I might end my business here before tomorrow." His left hand swung wide across the pews. "Show me the coins." His brain spun from the alcohol.

The weathered man leaned closer. "Walker? No. I see...McCleskey."

"You don't see shit. Hand them over."

"Those are not yours. You left them, gave them up. There's nothing here for you."

"Listen, bud." Walker's left thumb rubbed across the keloid again. "I beat the shit out of an idiot in a bar an hour ago. You want some of that trouble tonight?"

The front door banged against the box of Bibles. Frigid air tunneled down the aisle, swirling dried leaves at the entrance. Standing quickly, Walker raised the knife in his right hand, then spun. His feet stumbled for balance. The blade swung toward the weathered man's chest, stabbing the center of the Bible.

"You have more sins than just tonight. You need to pay for them all," the brooding man said.

"You need to give me what I came for." Walker pushed his coat behind the holster. A fist the size of a brick slammed against his temple. He shoved his attacker away, and the man fell with an echoing thud onto the wooden floor.

The weathered man's voice roared out again. "You should listen a little better to what God tells you."

"Look at my face. God doesn't talk to me." Walker slipped the pistol out of his holster and stood over the man. "You think God talks to you? Those are little voices in your head."

A boot jammed into Walker's knee. The pistol clattered to the floor.

White light flashed. A gunshot bellowed from the church.

Marla stepped outside again and watched Donnie's truck taillights disappear down the street.

Chapter 2

Seven-fifteen in the morning, Detective Crosby Adams entered the Catholic Church looking like a sun-kissed Adonis. Dressed in a heavily starched, long sleeve white shirt, Wranglers, and western boots, he held his beige felt Stetson in his hand while boot heels resounded down the Catholic Church's center aisle.

Officers dusted for prints, and cameras flashed toward the victim, blood, and shell casings. Each burst of light gleamed off Crosby's face. He closed his bloodshot eyes for a second while trying to cover the stale beer breath with spearmint chewing gum. He never slept well when Marla worked the night shift.

Crosby addressed the cameraman, "One vic, right?"

"So far."

He glanced at the coagulated red glob on the floor, and a Bible with a KA-BAR knife stuck through the center. Spattered blood spread across the nave and pews, ending with a dead man lying sideways and wrapped in a sheet with red wine poured over it. After slipping on blue Nitrile gloves, Crosby bent down and touched the sheet where the bullet entrance wound penetrated the upper left mid-pectoralis. "Possibly a 9mm, or a .38. Too big for a .22 caliber, too small for a .45." Reaching across to the back, he felt an exit wound at the upper scapula. Not a straight face-to-face shot. "The sheet had no bullet hole, so he was shot before wrapped up." He doubts a bullet in this location would have killed the man.

Crosby pointed to the tangled mess in the corner of the church. "And those are his clothes over there?"

The officer stopped taking pictures, nodded, and replied, "We believe so, sir. No ID, no wallet."

Marla's shift ended at seven, but instead of going home to shower and grab a change of clothes, she walked to the church. She nervously pulled her hair back into a tight ponytail, then released it to fall back behind her neck. Her hand brushed Crosby's shoulder, exposing a thin gold band on her left ring finger. As she leaned forward, a wisp of hair fell in front of her face. She whispered in his ear, "Did you forget about the beer can in your truck's cup holder? I opened your door to get rid of it, and next to the empty can was your new bottle of OxyContin I picked up from the pharmacy yesterday. It's almost half gone."

He stood. "I've got it under control."

"Too many, and don't drink in your truck."

"The pain is worse in cold weather. And when you're not in bed with me."

She scoffed and looked to make sure no one was listening. "Half gone in twenty-four hours? We don't need another," she tilted her head, "incident, my love."

Glancing at the blood and vomit surrounding the body, her stomach twinged from a coppery-acid stench wavering in the air. She pulled an inhaler from her pants pocket and inhaled deep after a spray.

"Is he the only victim?" Marla asked.

"Single vic," Officer Larry Keyman said, returning from down the hallway. His gloved hands held a tall wastebasket with an empty wine bottle and two feet of clear vinyl tubing. "Found these in a closet."

Marla raised the crook of her elbow to her mouth and coughed. "Blood splatter and puke all over the floor. It's a frickin' ass mess."

Officer Logan Searcy, Marla's younger brother, said behind her, "Very observant, sis." His pencil wiggled between two fingers. "I'll write that down as your official observation of the crime scene. You state that this is a frickin' ass mess."

"Shut up, Logan," Marla said. "Had enough of your crap already this morning."

Logan's pencil tapped the small gold pistol pin on the flap over her left pocket. "Don't get so all high and mighty with me. You ain't such a fast draw." His smirk revealed a need for a dental cleaning. "Pops can still beat you. He was feeling bad at the competition last month." The pencil tapped a second pin on the pocket flap. "And this little gold shotgun? Big deal. So, you can shoot a bunch of clay pigeons in an open field. What about a man? Ever shoot a man with a shotgun? Messy."

"No, as a matter of fact, I haven't. Why don't we go outside and let me see if I can hit a dumbass pigeon running on the ground instead of in the air?" She snatched the pencil from him and grabbed the back of his neck. The point of the pencil pushed under his chin. "Fast enough for you, brother dear? A sloth could beat you."

Chief of Police Edwin C. Searcy's cowhide vest zipped halfway covered his gluttonous belly. He stepped between them. "All right, children, enough. Don't make me stick you in separate corners."

"Pops, just keep this maggot away from me," Marla said.

"Don't call me Pops while I'm on duty. I'm Chief or Searcy to everyone, including you."

"Sorry, *Chief*."

"Is that the new vest you tanned, Chief?" Logan asked. "I'm likin' it."

Marla's palm rubbed the tip of her nose. "Brown nosing again, Logan?"

Searcy looked down at the vest. "Yeah. Finished it last week." With his hands shoved in the vest pockets, he turned to the victim. "He's wrapped up as tight as a naked tamale with a bottle of hot sauce poured on him."

"Red wine, not hot sauce," Marla said.

Crosby crossed the church and stared at a stained glass window with a round hole in it. He turned back to the blood splattered pews and stood as close to where he thought the victim would have been. He estimated the angle of the shot from the bullet hole in the window. The victim hovered over the shooter, lying on his back.

Searcy slipped on gloves and then pulled his pocketknife from the leather sheath on his belt and opened it. "Has forensics taken enough pictures so I can cut the sheet off this guy and see what's underneath?"

"Chief," Logan said. "Might want to use scissors. Don't want to cut him accidentally." He chuckled. "That might hurt the evidence."

"Your jokes are deader than this guy. I'm cutting the sheet." The knife sliced through the sheet in seconds.

Red wine and dried blood stained the upper half of the body, the rest as pale as paper.

"Does anyone know who this is?" Crosby asked again.

Searcy peeled off the gloves and dropped them next to the body before he stood and pulled a small spiral notebook from his shirt pocket. He flipped through six pages before stopping. "He's an outsider, a visitor. I checked the hotels close by, and the manager at the Blue Ridge hotel said this guy fitting his description checked in yesterday. Paid in cash. The vic told him someone stole his wallet, so he didn't have a driver's license."

"Fingerprints will confirm the identity, but that might take a few days," Marla said.

Forensics continued dusting, swabbing, and clicking their cameras like paparazzi. The dead man's pale face illuminated whiter with each flash. A bloody shoe print smeared the floor near the body.

"Do we have a weapon?"

"A Glock with two bullets shy of a full magazine. Found both casings." Larry pointed at the empty yellow circles on the floor. "Bagged and in the evidence box."

"Any witnesses come forward?"

"No, sir. Nobody yet," Larry said.

Searcy snapped back. "The church has a brand new priest. Members have already called me. How did they know about this so early in the morning?"

Logan chuckled again. "They were probably across the street at the bar."

Crosby gazed around the inside. "First time for me in a Catholic Church. Got some fancy stuff in here."

Larry pointed to the back wall. "The priest's name is Father Jules, and he's the one who called 911. He is in his private chambers over there. I talked to him for a while. Said he came here a few weeks ago. Told him to sit tight."

"Well, Hell's Bells. Get the priest out here and talk to us," Searcy said.

"Pops, you shouldn't say hell in church," Marla said.

"Why?" Searcy raised his hands in the air. "Our pastor says it every week. We're all going to hell if we don't stop sinning. And don't call me Pops in here."

Crosby slipped a pencil from his shirt pocket and crouched down to the victim's head. "Does the priest have an alibi?"

"Whoa there, cowboy." Searcy nudged Crosby's shoulder. "He's not a killer."

"You know this, Father Jules? You vouch for him?" Crosby sounded surprised.

"Met him at the bus station when he arrived in town. I went in to visit with Missy, the ticket agent, and saw him standing against the wall with a single black overnight bag. We got to talking, and I gave him a ride to the church. Seemed real nice."

"See this," Crosby used his pencil to stretch the dead man's mouth open, "scrapes and cuts on his lips. Couple of loose teeth." Crosby leaned in closer to the head. "It looks like the tongue is cut. Must have gotten into a fight."

"He must have gotten into a hell of a fight years ago, judging by those scars on his face," Marla said.

Logan held his arms out wide. "Don't say hell in church, Marla."

"Shut up. Pops said it was okay."

Crosby's gaze shifted under one pew. "What's that?"

Searcy bent down. "That's called a Chalice. How did *it* get there?"

"Chalice? Like a church wine cup?" Crosby left it on its side. "Need to bag it and get those bags wrapped around the hands. Doesn't look like a scratcher, but he might have if he was dying."

"Chief." Logan tapped his shoulder. "Look at the box of Bibles near the front door. There's a bullet hole at the bottom of the box."

"Good catch, Logan." Searcy patted his back. "Everyone missed it. Take the box to forensics. It would be nice if we had a bullet matching the pistol."

"Probably stolen," Crosby said.

Searcy swung toward the chamber's door. "Bring that priest over here."

"Officer Adams?" Larry asked.

Crosby and Marla turned to him.

"Now that's funny." Logan pointed at both of them. "Oh, Officer Adams---and the two of you spun around. Maybe we should go back to Mr. and Grumpy Adams."

Marla slapped her holster. Logan jumped. She snapped at him, "I could drop you before you blinked."

Father Jules appeared out from his office and followed Larry. The fatherly-aged priest rubbed his hands together, eyes bloodshot from crying.

Marla stuck her thumbs under the belt and whispered to Crosby, "Is he sad because he has a dead man in his church, or the crowd and the tithes will be a little thin at the next mass?"

"Father, when did you arrive at the church?" Crosby asked.

With a hint of an Eastern European accent, he said, "About an hour ago. I always come at 6:30 every morning. I have much work to do." His hands slid through his full head of black hair. "And now this. God has not prepared me for this."

Crosby observed every movement, hands through the hair, feet moving, leaning first on one side and then the other. The priest was of medium height, with broad shoulders. "Father, do you come to church every morning?"

"Yes, every morning."

"Did you come through the front door and see all this?"

Father Jules crossed his chest while glancing at the body. "No, not that way. I come in through the side door of my office. This is what I do every morning. Later I opened my door, walked past the altar, and that is when I found the man on the floor. "

"You're new, right? A few weeks. I can't place your accent."

"I am from Eastern Europe, Montenegro." Father Jules spotted the bent chalice under the pew. "Oh, no. The chalice. It is desecrated." He reached under the pew, held it tight to his chest, and then out toward Searcy. "No, I don't want it if it caused this man to die." He pulled it back from Searcy's reach and wiped the chalice bowl across his robe. "No, it belongs to the church. I must send it to the bishop and let him consecrate it again."

Marla held out her hand. "Sorry, Father, but we need that back for evidence."

Searcy mumbled, "So much for fingerprint protocols."

Chapter 3

The squad room bustled like confused ants. After Marla drove home, showered, changed clothes, and grabbed a quick bite, she sat at her desk. Crosby leaned in behind her and watched a local bar's front door surveillance video.

"I've watched this twice." She ran it back. "Earlier that night, the murder victim had entered the bar, and three hours later, he came back out, or rather, staggered out. Definitely drunk. A few seconds later, Father Jules followed him out the door."

"Interesting. Why would a priest frequent a bar?" Crosby gently laid both hands on top of Marla's shoulders. "Is there any video of the parking lot?"

She tapped his fingers, leaned her head back, and smiled. "Hands off, Officer Adams." His hands slid off her shoulders. "You can touch me all you want at the house, but not here. With these rodeo clowns, I have a hard enough time being the only filly in the stable." She pointed at the monitor again. "There's the vic walking to a car. It looks like a Ford Escape."

Crosby dropped his hands to his sides. "Can't see the license plates."

"If it's a rental, we might backtrack and find the renter," Marla said. "Name, address, driver's license, and credit card would be on the contract."

"Did he fly in and rent at our airport, or did he rent in some other city and drive here?"

Marla zoomed in on the car. "It would take too many phone calls to contact every rental agency who rented Ford Escapes in the last two weeks."

"I could get Logan to start the calls."

Sitting at his desk, Logan yelled in his landline receiver, "No. You can't do that. I have seven more months on the rental contract. We can't leave in a week." He slammed the phone down. "I'm going to James Kinsey's sheep ranch and knock the shit out of him."

Marla paused the video and turned her chair toward Crosby. "You want Logan, my idiot brother, to be the Hildebrandt Police Department's spokesperson to all the San Antonio auto rental centers. You need to rethink that idea."

"He does excellent work when he puts his mind to it," Crosby replied.

"The only reason he has a job here is because he rides Pop's coattail."

Marla pushed the play button again. The priest exited seconds later but turned away from the Ford. Moments after the priest left, a girl came out through the door and ran toward the car as it drove off.

"Do you recognize her?" Marla asked.

"Not sure, with bushy hair covering her face." Crosby moved to the side of the desk and sat on the edge. "This Ford Escape was not at the church when we found the vic. Where's the car? And where did Father Jules go after he left the bar?" Marla added while she turned the monitor off. "I wonder if there is any surveillance video from the church?" Marla asked.

Crosby crossed his arms. "Good question. I'm guessing no one here has ever needed to ask before."

Chief Searcy walked by them. Marla asked, "Hey, Pops. Does the Catholic Church have surveillance?"

"Marla, I told you not to call me that at the station." He looked behind him, making sure no one heard him. "It's Chief or Searcy to everyone here, including you. And no, I don't think the church has outside surveillance." He went into his office and closed the door.

Marla shook her head and stared at Crosby. "We don't know much about the priest."

"I called Carla in the mayor's office. The priest was truthful. She told me he came from a small country in Eastern Europe called Montenegro."

"Don't know where that is," Marla said. "We need to ask him what brings him to the greater metropolis of Hildebrandt, Texas."

Crosby's cell phone rang in his coat pocket. The words Medical Examiner were on the screen. "Officer Adams here...Yeah? ... Tomorrow, got it." He slid his phone back into his pocket. "Need to go to the morgue at the Bexar County Medical Examiner's office tomorrow at noon. The ME said some strange things were going on with the body. That will give us time to ask the priest a few more questions."

"Well, that's just perfect," Logan said. "Chief, don't we have the outdoor shooting competition today?"

"Don't have time for games."

"Sure we do." Logan glanced at his watch. "Those two don't go to San Antone until tomorrow. We're waiting on forensics. That will take one to two days. We got time this afternoon.

Searcy waved his hands in the air. "Not enough for everyone to compete. We need all day for the competition."

"Chief, you are the best we have. You have won every time except..." he tapped the golden pistol pendant on Marla's shirt, "when little Miss Sis beat you because you were sick." Logan turned to the crowded squad room. "Anybody want to challenge the Chief in the shoot-out competition?" His hand swept the room. "See. No one is interested. Now that you're feeling fine, I want to watch how much slower Marla the Magnificent is against you." His finger aimed for the pendant again. "You are going down, Sis."

Marla grabbed Logan's hand, twisted left, and swung Logan around with his arm behind his back. "Why don't you be the one nailing the targets to the poles and see how close I can get to your head at twenty-five feet?"

"You two, shut up," Searcy said.

"For once, Logan is right. I have a couple of hours to kill." Marla pushed Logan away. "I'll be at the range in fifteen minutes. Bring enough ammo."

◆

Four miles outside of Hildebrandt, Marla was the first to arrive. Her pickup stopped in front of a bland, square building housing the indoor shooting range. Behind it lay five acres of flat emptiness. To the right, a hundred yards away, a row of firing booths stood with a twenty-foot wall of dirt behind various metal targets. To the left was a skeet shooting area with a small wooden tower.

Tapping the code on the door, she entered the shooting range with her Glock 17 holstered at her side and a shotgun in her left hand. In the lobby, a musty sulfuric odor permeated her nostrils and lit up her brain like crack to an addict. A familiar acrid taste crawled across her tongue; to some people, it was bitter; to her---sweetness. Her right hand grasped the countertop edge, then leaned forward. With her eyes closed, she watched holes fill the center of a paper target.

A lock snapped behind her, and the target disappeared from her mind. She placed the shotgun on the countertop and watched the front door swing open. Searcy entered first, holding his standard police issue, Remington 870 shotgun, and set it on the countertop next to Marla's shotgun. Logan, Crosby, and several others followed behind Searcy. Logan carried two grocery sack-sized reusable bags full of ammo and targets and put them on the floor close to two empty boxes marked Chief and Marla left from the last competition.

Searcy pointed at her shotgun. "You brought the Winchester Model 97, didn't you?"

"Sure. Can't remember the last time I missed a pigeon, clay or not, with the 97."

Being relatively new to the Hildebrandt PD, Larry leaned toward Crosby and asked, "What's so special about her gun?"

"The Winchester 1897 shotgun, sometimes known simply as Model 97, or trench gun, or riot gun, is a 12-gauge shotgun with a short 20-inch barrel. It became popular in World War 1, spraying death in trench warfare and later stopping bank robbers and gangsters in the 1920s and 30s. Do you remember townsfolk talking about old man Harris at the hardware store?"

"Yeah, sure. Remarkable stories, but didn't Harris die a few months back?"

"He was a Texas Ranger in his day. One of the best, and he carried that shotgun everyplace he went. Probably slept with it. Marla was Harris' favorite officer. I swear he wanted to marry her, except he was almost sixty years older. He gave it to her as a wedding present."

"You're saying it's not a good choice to be facing her while she holds the 97? Must remember that."

Logan stepped between Marla and Searcy. "We go by Hildebrandt PD rules with three competitions, one with shotguns and two with pistols." Logan grabbed the sack handles with 12-gauge shotgun shell boxes inside. "Everyone to the trap range."

The early morning crisp air gave way to the afternoon warmth. A golden sun arced high into the panoramic cloudless sky. Almost every officer in town and a few other high-ranking spectators sat on the bleachers.

Crosby leaned next to Larry. "At the card table next to the shooter's spot are ten boxes of 12-gauge shells." Crosby pointed toward the edges. "At each side, twenty-five feet away, spring-loaded, clay target throwers pitch targets left or right in the air at different speeds; fast, faster, slower, random, everywhere. The shooter stops after two misses."

"Two misses?" Larry scoffed. "That shouldn't take but a minute or so."

"Yeah?" He patted Larry's back. "Did you bring snacks? Between these two, we'll be here a while."

Searcy broke open the first box of shells, then loaded his Remington shotgun. Resting the gun butt under his armpit and across his forearm, he remembered last month's competition with Marla. Afterward, he could have fried bacon on the shotgun barrel.

Searcy fired his eighty-sixth shell and watched the second clay target spin untouched to the ground. He unloaded his gun and shook his head. "I shouldn't have missed that last one."

Marla nodded. "Nice shooting, Pops. Eighty-four is excellent." After loading her gun, she called out, "Ready."

She stopped after hitting eighty-five targets with no misses. She didn't step aside. Instead, she loaded six more into the chamber.

Larry asked, "What is she doing? She won."

"Showing off. Marla likes to slam fire the 97."

"What?"

"Slam fire is something her shotgun can do. Hold the trigger down, fire and rack. She can unload the six shells in a few seconds." He pointed to the clay target throwers. "Both will throw three as quickly as possible. You'll find out why you don't want to be on the wrong end of her 97."

Marla drew the butt of the shotgun to her shoulder, aimed at the sky, and called out, "Ready."

Six targets leaped off the throwers, and six targets shattered in mid-air.

Larry wiped his forehead. "Oh, Mother of God. I...no one has a chance against that. No one."

All the people returned to the building and piled into the lobby, mumbling who shot better, Searcy was faster, Marla didn't miss a single one.

Logan flipped up a light switch. Behind a plate-glass window, rows of ten shooting booths for short-range practice were lined up like a horse race starting gate. Each booth had white plastic walls with a waist-high, hinged table to hold guns and ammo.

To the side of the lobby, a placard on a bulletproof metal door read:
EYE AND EAR PROTECTION REQUIRED
CLOSE FIRST DOOR BEFORE OPENING SECOND DOOR.

Logan raised his hands for silence and then announced, "Marla won the skeet round." He nodded at her. "Congrats, Sis."

"Hmm. Thanks, Logan."

He placed a box of ammo and a single empty magazine into each box with their names. "Pistol competition rules are simple with two matches. Both of you have a standard-issue Glock 17 pistol. The first round is with a full magazine. At the buzzer, you fire all seventeen shots at the standard round target twenty-five feet away. Scoring is the total points on the target. Bullseye is 10, then decreases to 9, 8, 7 in the black. Hildebrandt rules apply. Anything outside the black circles doesn't count."

"Come on, Logan," Marla barked at him. "Everyone knows the *Hildebrandt rules*."

"The second comp is my favorite, the fast draw." Logan held a new target in the air. "At the buzzer, you draw and fire once." He pushed his finger on the round target on the page. "You must hit a black circle for your round to count."

Marla stared at her father like a boxer at a weigh-in. She nodded and grabbed her box and two targets off the table.

After slipping on the safety glasses and ear protection, Searcy opened the first door to the firing range, then the second, which buffered the gunfire noise. He stopped at station six and emptied his box on his table.

With her protection on, Marla followed and closed the second door. A satisfying scent of burned fireworks filled her lungs. She had loved the smell since the first time she fired a gun in elementary school. Through the window, her eyes stared at Logan as her fingertip streaked a line across the window grayed from years of accumulated gunpowder. She stopped at station four and laid her hardware and targets on her table. She clipped a target onto the mobile carrier and pushed a button. The electric motor ran until it stopped at twenty-five feet.

Logan called out from the speaker, "Everyone ready?"

The buzzer sounded.

Marla quickly stuffed the magazine with seventeen bullets, shoved it into the pistol grip, snapped the slide closed, and aimed toward the target. Her index finger slid to the trigger. In a single second, the hair on her nape tingled, and a rush of adrenaline soared from her brain to her finger. After seventeen blasts, the slide kicked back and locked. The corners of her lips crept up when Searcy's gun fired once more, then stopped. *He's slower.* She felt satisfied and placed her pistol on the table.

Marla focused on her target with holes in the center, then his, while the whine of the carrier motors brought the two targets closer to them.

Searcy counted quickly and called out, "I've got 157."

Her target had six holes in the bullseye, eight in the 9 ring, and three in the 8 ring. "I count..." She counted again. "Damn, 156."

Searcy stepped over to her station and took the target from her hand. "Almost got me." He flipped the target back on her table, took her pistol, looked at both sides, and then pushed the slide lock down. It snapped closed. He aimed the gun toward the back wall and pulled the trigger.

"Don't dry fire my gun," Marla said.

He laid the gun on the table. "Making sure it was okay." He shook his head and returned to his station.

Marla pitched the used target into the trash can and then pushed the magazine catch on the Glock. The empty mag dropped on the table. After loading her next clean target and pressing the twenty-five-foot distance button, she loaded one cartridge into her pistol and holstered the Glock. She glared at the bullseye.

The score was even with one win each. After several officers made phone calls, more people packed into the shooting range lobby waiting for the fast draw. Half the people stared at the slow-motion camera screen while the others watched the two for the live show.

Like a racehorse wearing blinders, tunnel vision drew her eyes toward the black bullseye. The A/C kicked in. Frigid air crawled past her trigger finger.

Logan called out, "Ready." He pushed the record button. The camera stood equally behind the shooters with both right arms fully visible.

Marla's ears searched for a sound; her eyes pinpointed at the bullseye. Her fingertip itched. She held her breath.

The buzzer's blast broke the silence.

Two explosions sounded as one.

Marla holstered her pistol and touched the return button for the target. It took too long to reach her. Like a car door slamming shut, the electric motor banged into a stop. Her finger touched the indentation with a single black hole at the two o'clock position of the bullseye. She pushed the earmuffs off her head to the back of her neck and charged toward the lobby.

Searcy followed and stopped next to Marla. He patted her shoulder. "Remember, it's just playtime."

She shrugged his hand off her shoulder.

Logan pushed play. Time in hundredths of seconds rolled like a speeding odometer.

After the buzzer blew, two hands clasped their pistols. It looked simultaneous; fingers wrapped around the gun handles, elbows bent back, guns rose from the holsters, arms straightened, gun powder spewed from muzzles. Two matching explosions, except one was faster, a single flutter of a hummingbird wing between the two shots.

No one moved when Logan pressed replay. With both shooters back to the slow-motion camera, a small round shock wave spread out from the muzzles like rings of water. Time stopped.

Both arm motions were identical.

Both guns fired with Marla three one-hundredths of a second faster.

Chapter 4

Logan stopped in front of Mr. Kinsey's clapboard house. A dilapidated sheep-holding area stood to the side of the house where a man held a shotgun in his right hand. Logan slammed his truck door closed and charged toward the house.

"You can't do this," Logan yelled.

"I can do anything I want with my property. I got a buyer, and he wants it by next month."

Logan stopped. "You're selling? I'll buy it. Told you a long time ago I would."

Kinsey shook his head. "He's buying all my rentals. You don't have that kind of money."

Logan pointed at the house. "Still selling weed and pills? How much is in your house right now? You could get twenty years for what's in there."

"And I'll drag you with me. You're not Mr. Clean."

✦

Crosby and Marla drove to San Antonio. Construction on I-10 narrowed the three lanes to two, then one, and the speed dropped from seventy-five to five.

"There are too many cars on this damn highway," Marla said. "I could never live here."

Crosby changed lanes to pass another tractor-trailer carrying a large bulldozer. "There's a lot of concrete here."

She pointed to a Walmart parking lot full of cars and pickup trucks. Every fuel pump had cars waiting in line. "They probably sell more gas in a day than all the gas stations in Hildebrandt in a month."

They passed the exit to Loop 1604, noticing the speed of the cars on the bridge was zero.

A few minutes later, Crosby's gray Dodge 3500 Ram truck with a Hildebrandt police star logo on the door pulled in near the back entrance of the County Medical Examiner's office. The Forensic Crime Lab shared the other half of the building. Crosby and Marla opened their truck doors to the aroma of smoked sausage and brisket. A food truck had stopped at the back corner of the parking lot with a bright sign on the side that declared MACKEY'S BBQ IS THE BEST IN TEXAS. A line of employees ready with paper plates and plastic utensils in their hands must have agreed.

Crosby asked one woman in line, "Something special going on?"

"Once a month, the ME buys us lunch." She grinned widely and pointed at the trays of brownies. "Those are as soft as a cloud. Only the second time they've been here this year. Pick up dessert before they're all gone."

Marla headed toward the back entrance. "Remind me to come by here during lunchtime when we don't have business."

Crosby stopped next to a young Hispanic man, spaghetti thin, who wore a tall chef hat and a long apron with the name FLOUR DELIGHTS across the top. His grin matched the employees. A six-by-six-foot sign behind him had pictures of pastries. "*Podemos tener un brownie?*" he asked.

"*Si, Senor,*" Crosby said.

A pan of warm brownies cut in squares sat on a stainless steel table. He grabbed one and pointed at Marla. "I've heard of this place. It's won multiple State Fair awards. Want one?"

"No, yes, no. I'm getting ready to see a dead body. No food."

"Too bad for you." Taking the last bite, he pointed back at the cheerful man. "*Fantastico.*"

Crosby's hand pushed on the door marked 'Employees Only.' Their footfalls echoed down the quiet hallway with white walls and a tiled floor. They stopped at a solid metal door with MORGUE written in large letters.

Albert Einstein's clone, wearing green scrubs, came down the hall with uncombed white hair and a shoe brush mustache. He held a large plastic cup with a lid. The plastic straw pierced the center of the mustache. He sucked on the straw until it gurgled, then dropped the cup into the waste-basket.

Marla smiled. "Dr. Berghoff, I presume." She glanced down at his blue surgical gloves and waved her hands. "I'll pass on the handshakes."

Dr. Berghoff chuckled. "Sorry, habit. I wear gloves all the time here. Change them, of course, but still, you know. Are you the two officers from Hildebrandt?"

"Yes, I'm Crosby Adams, and this is Marla Adams. Thank you for meeting with us."

He motioned for them to go forward. "Shall we?"

He pushed the automatic door button on the wall, revealing the morgue with stainless steel walls and freezer doors. Marla coughed from the heavy disinfectant odor. She grabbed two masks off the desk, flipped one to Crosby, and covered her mouth. "Brownies outside smell better than formaldehyde inside, or whatever that is."

Journey's song, "Don't Stop Believin'," bounced off the walls.

A long, black zipper bag lay on a stainless steel table a few feet from them. He pointed at their masks. "I've completed the autopsy, so those aren't necessary."

Crosby raised his eyebrows at Marla. "Okay." They gently pulled their masks off.

"After a short while, the smell disappears."

"I doubt that," Marla mumbled to herself. "What did you want us to see?"

He unzipped the bag to the neck. Marla couldn't help but stare at the ever-present extended facial scar now split wide open. The body looked eerily asleep with ashen gray skin and pale purple lips. He picked up a plastic bottle next to the body and poured several small pieces of metal into his gloved hand. "This is shrapnel from a bomb or a grenade. It was still embedded in the skin." He placed them back in the plastic bottle and screwed the lid closed. "Whoever sutured the wound didn't take the time to clean it well." He touched some of the other facial wounds. "Not from acne or pockmarks. These are shrapnel scars. My guess is a quick surgery on a battlefield." The doctor unzipped the bag down to the victim's mid-chest. The chest wall had a large irregular scar, two taser marks, and a recent bullet wound. "After being taken back to a MASH unit, the surgeons cared about saving his life, not so much about the cosmetic repair." He touched the wide scar on the left side of the chest. "Although, under the skin, there was no wound in the muscle or chest. It looks more like a botched job of removing a tattoo or a growth on the chest years later." He then pulled off the left outer ear of the dead man and revealed a flat, round hole. "He had a prosthetic ear."

Marla quickly buried her face into Crosby's neck. "Now you know why I didn't want a brownie."

"But let's get to why he is here." Dr. Berghoff pointed just below the victim's neck and said, "Two small puncture wounds indicate taser marks. And the victim drowned."

"No way, Doc." Crosby pointed at the chest. "What about that bullet hole in his chest? Besides, they found him on the church floor. Not anywhere near the lake."

"The wine bottle and the clear tubing in the wastebasket," Marla said. "Remember, you found his mouth all busted up."

"Outstanding, officer." The doctor swirled the ice and cola around inside the cup. "The bullet that hit him yesterday in the right side of the chest missed all vital areas." He pointed to the head with the top half of the skull cut off and the brain missing. "The crack in the posterior cranium made him unconscious, but that was not what killed him."

"It wasn't necessary to show that to me, Doc." Marla's stomach rumbled.

He pointed to the mouth. "Looks like something hit him here once or twice. There are small lacerations to the lips, and the front teeth are shifted back slightly, probably from a fist hitting him. The tongue is a different matter. It's split down the middle, front to back. The hard palate, pharynx, and trachea have lacerations as well." He pointed at the clear plastic tubing. "This had been shoved down his throat while he was alive. The lungs are full of wine and blood from the lacerated tongue." He held his finger up in the air. "Oh, this is interesting."

"Like none of this is so far?" Marla squeezed her eyes shut for a few seconds.

He unzipped the bag down below the concave stomach. The trunk was cut from manubrium to symphysis pubis with a thick white thread tying the center line back together again. "Found a few more shrapnel pieces near the aorta. The man was lucky he lived."

"This is what you wanted us to see?" Crosby asked.

"Excuse me, no." Dr. Berghoff handed Crosby two gloves and motioned him to put them on. "Help me roll him to his side."

The body was heavier than Crosby expected as he rolled him over.

"This is what you should see. I've seen a lot of bodily trauma in my years, but never this. Someone took a big knife and cut these numbers across the back, 37. There was a small amount of blood in the subcutaneous fat and skin, which means he only bled a little from the carving. This happened after he was dead."

"Do the numbers mean anything to you?" Crosby asked.

The doctor shook his head. "No."

"Got a time frame for this?" Marla asked.

"Still has a small amount of rigor in the large muscles. The fingers, toes, wrists, you know, smaller joints, have loosened. Mmm, my guess, early morning hours."

"The bar video showed he left just after midnight," Crosby said. "If he went to the church right afterward, that would fit."

"But where did Father Jules go?" Marla asked.

"Good question. Time we visit him for questioning." Crosby turned back to Dr. Berghoff. "Hey, Doc, was he moved? You know, picked up and brought into the church, died lying on his stomach, rolled over. Stuff like that."

"The postmortem hypostasis shows purple discoloration on the posterior neck, back, and legs. The pressure points of the back of the head, buttocks, calves, and heels all show he died and stayed on his back. His liver, spleen, intestines, and heart show blood drained posterior. I must conclude, he died where he laid, on his back." He snapped his gloves off and pitched them into the wastebasket. "Take your time and look all you want. I've got everything I need for my report." He hit the open button on the wall, and the steel doors opened. "Got to go to my office and finish the last report. Girl with a broken neck. The police report said she was on a motorcycle without a helmet. After that, I'm heading out to a conference."

"What if I need to call you next week?" Crosby asked.

"Call my cell. I'll answer if in range."

"In range? Where's this conference?"

"Same place every year, Death Valley."

"Is that a joke?" Crosby asked.

"Pathologists love it there. You should come with me sometime. Excuse me," he pointed down the hall, "broken neck."

"This guy is muscular, at least five feet ten." Marla zipped the bag back over the victim's head. "That's enough for me."

"Two hundred pounds. It would require someone fairly strong to force a tube down the man's throat while alive," Crosby said.

"And Father Jules is not that big," Marla replied. "Five-seven, five-eight. Can't tell his weight with that robe on."

"Cassock," Crosby said.

"Excuse me?"

"Cassock. It's called a cassock, not a robe."

"How do you know that? You're not Catholic."

"I'm a cop. Cops got to know stuff."

"I think the formaldehyde is soaking into your brain." Marla dropped her mask on the body bag. "Let's go see the priest and ask him some basic questions."

Crosby pitched his mask on the bag as well. "I wonder if the food truck is still out there."

Chapter 5

C rosby slipped the Stetson off his head and pulled on the metal back door of the police station. The false ceiling with fluorescent lights threw paleness down the hall. A lieutenant pointed at Crosby, "Chief wants to see you. Watch your back. He's on a rampage again."

"Thanks, seen it before." He wound around the corner to the frosted glass door with CHIEF etched in the glass. Searcy was standing and screaming. Crosby took a deep breath, knocked, and cracked the door open.

"Damn it, I told you, I don't know anymore. This will take time. It hasn't even been a day since we found the body."

Indistinguishable words mumbled from the telephone.

Searcy's knuckles pushed down against the desk. "Mayor, I know what I'm doing. I've seen dead people before." He slammed the phone down and looked at Crosby. "What the hell did you do? Mayor Pichler is up my ass." He sat down hard in the overstuffed chair. "He's trying to cover this up."

Crosby closed the door. "Don't think the mayor has anything to do with this murder." He placed his hat on the chief's desktop.

"How the hell do you know? Besides, what are you doing interrogating Father Jules? He's a priest, for Christ's sake."

"Marla and I stopped by and just asked him a few questions. How did you find out?"

"Father Jules called the mayor after you left. The mayor's office helped the church complete the immigration papers to get him here from Monte Carlo. The church direly needed a priest since the last one died from a heart attack. And don't forget, the mayor is Catholic."

"Montenegro." Crosby shook his head. "He came from Montenegro."

Sliding the bottom drawer out, Searcy pulled out a bottle and two small glasses and slid them across the table. Whiskey sloshed inside the bottle. Searcy filled the two glasses. "Monty Hall, Monte Carlo, Montenegro. Wherever it is, it's somewhere far away. Don't ask him any more questions."

"Wrong. I got lots more to ask. I need some proof of who this priest is. All this is suspicious with a new priest at the church where a murder occurred. Are you sure he's a priest? Did the victim know him? Is that why he's dead? No, I've got lots of questions."

The whiskey shot down Searcy's throat. "Drink that."

"No. Promised Marla no more."

"Yeah, I've heard that before." Searcy reached for the glass and slammed the other shot of whiskey down. "The priest is off limits."

Logan knocked on the office door. "I need the rest of the day off. Having problems with the landlord. He wants us to move out next week, and Cindy and I must look at some rental houses."

Searcy waved his hand at him. "Go. Get out."

Crosby's cellphone rang in his lamb's wool vest, "Adams here...that was fast...and...who...you're certain...I was at the ME this morning, but I'll return within the hour." He shoved the phone back into his pocket. "That was Forensics. The bullet in the box came from a registered gun of a Private Investigator. Marla and I are heading back to the same building we were at a few hours ago. Should have stayed in San Antone."

Searcy stood. "A PI. What the hell are you talking about?" His butt crashed back into the chair. "The victim was a dick? Damn."

"What's a PI doing in Hildebrandt?" Crosby asked. "You know something you're not telling me?"

Searcy slid the drawer open and placed the bottle and two glasses back in, then closed the drawer. "No."

Leaning back in the chair, Searcy pointed at Crosby as he opened the door. "Call me as soon as you find out anything."

❖

Crosby and Marla returned to San Antonio. While driving, his eyes bounced from the windshield to side and rearview mirrors. Traffic is worse. "How much further?"

Marla tapped the screen on the dash. "GPS says just under five miles."

Twenty-five grueling minutes later, they arrived at the BCCIL, Bexar County Criminal Investigation Lab, which is on the other side of the Medical Examiner's building. They opened their truck doors to a waiting man at the front entrance who wore a dark suit and a smile.

Their doors closed, and the truck alarm chirped. They stepped in tandem toward the man.

"Officers Adams and Adams?" the man asked with his hand extended. "Yes."

They all shook hands and then entered the building. "Mr. Adams, there is someone you know at the lab, correct?"

"Yes, that's right."

"While you are waiting, may I offer you coffee or sweet tea?"

Crosby smiled and said no. Marla did the same. The three walked down a hallway to the Firearms Section, where the room was abuzz. The right side of the room had a man looking at a computer monitor with a picture of a bullet with striations. Crosby called out like he was still in a fraternity, "David Weidman!" Crosby held out his hand. "How in the hell did you graduate? You never studied."

The two graduated with a degree in criminology at the University of Texas. David didn't want to wear a ballistics vest or carry a gun; instead, he headed for the safety of a crime lab. He motioned for both to come over. After man hugs and backslaps, Crosby introduced Marla to him.

"Great to see you, Crosby. How long has it been? Four years? Anyway, I heard your department sent in a bullet, so I took it and ran it through ASAP." David twisted to Marla and chuckled. "Did Crosby ever tell you about the time we got caught sneaking into a sorority window?" He laughed out loud. "There was no doubt we were going to be expelled."

Crosby tried to hold a smile back while cradling David's chin with his hand. He looked David straight in the eyes. "She doesn't want to hear about any of that stuff. Tell us about the bullet. That's all, just the bullet."

"Sure I do." Marla smiled. "I'll call you later this week, and you can give me all the details."

"Okay, perhaps not that," David snapped back. "But at least she needs to hear about the Coke machine we stole and put cans of beer in it." He leaned into Marla. "We sold beer all night long out of our room for weeks. Someone ratted us out after we ran out of beer. Luckily, it was empty, so they gave us a 'demerit' for having a coke machine in our room."

Crosby pointed at David. "The man is delusional, psychotic. Obviously, he had terrible hallucinations while at UT."

"Oh, and in the middle of the night, when we got hungry and flat broke, skinny little Crosby would sneak through the bathroom window in the cafeteria and steal a box of donuts. They never caught on." His smile drifted to somber. "And then, you know...the bad thing happened."

Crosby shook his head and put his hand out like a stop sign.

David continued. "It was almost midnight cramming for a test the next morning, and we were starving. We left the dorm to get more donuts and turned the corner when two girls walked by the cafeteria, smoking. There were orange cones around a gas meter, and we smelled gas. I stopped and started backing up. Crosby ran toward them, wrapped his arms around them, and tackled the two girls. The explosion burned him, and he was in the hospital burn unit for a month. The two girls survived with a few scratches. He was a hero."

Marla turned her head toward Crosby, then back to David. "He never was that clear about the burn scars." Her fingertips gently stroked Crosby's chest. "Just that it was an accident at the university."

"Enough ancient history. Tell me about the bullet," David quipped back.

"A murder in a local church," Crosby said. "Two bullets fired. One went through the vic's chest and out a window. We lost that one, but the other lodged in a box of Bibles. You have that bullet and, hopefully, the matching gun."

"Bibles? Oh man, don't piss off God." David chuckled and pointed to the monitor. "We have a match. It was clean and easy." He pointed at the screen with three bullets side by side. "The left is a bullet we fired in the bullet recovery tank. The second is the one you brought. The third is from the NIBIN, the National Integrated Ballistics Information Network, hoping to find an ID for a specific gun already captured. It popped up matching a gun originally owned by Roberto Sardino. This gun."

Crosby moved the mouse across the striations of both bullets. "How did you get the first bullet from his gun?"

"I dug a little further, and the reason NIBIN had a bullet in their system is because Private Investigator Roberto Sardino was killed with his own gun three years ago. Initially listed as a homicide but later changed to suicide. Once the bullet is in NIBIN, it's in forever. Obviously, this man is not your killer. Did your victim have any ID on him?"

"No ID, no money, no keys," Crosby said. "someone took everything from his pockets. How did the victim get this gun?"

"I called the sheriff's department from the county of where the pistol originated. After they cleared it from criminal activity, they planned to sell his gun and others at an auction." He looked up at Crosby. "That didn't happen. The police station's evidence room caught fire, and everything burned to the ground, except all the firearms were missing."

"Arson attempting to cover a robbery," Crosby said.

"So, this gun is stolen property," Marla said, "and we will never know why the victim had the gun."

Chapter 6

A yellow morning sun bleached the limestone walls of the Adams house. Light penetrated their living room bay window. Marla stood with eyes closed, wearing Crosby's green pajama top above smooth bronze legs. Cool air flowed through the screen past the open front door and brushed against her naked thighs. She sighed and felt the warmth of the rising sun across her face. Green hills saw-toothed in the distance. A red-painted barn stood on thirty-five acres of dew-crowned grassland. She breathed deeply while two deer pranced in front of the house. "Good morning, deer." They have no fear. She wondered how every animal in the county receives notice of opening day of hunting season. Through their antlers?

Bare feet stepped behind her. "Good morning to you too, dear."

She looked behind her and smiled. "I was talking to Bambi outside."

"And I was talking to Marla inside." Bare-chested, Crosby wore the other half of the green pajamas. Hyperpigmented burn scars rippled across half his chest and back. Crosby held a coffee mug in front of Marla. A spiral of steam rose.

"Thank you," she said.

He grabbed a brown medicine bottle from the coffee table, opened it, placed two oxycodone tablets in his mouth, and sipped from his coffee mug.

She inhaled the flavorful vapor as her hands wrapped around the mug. She sipped. "Mmm, perfect. Thanks." She glanced at his cup with no steam. Leaning forward, she smelled his coffee.

"Nothing added," Crosby said. "No whiskey this time."

"How many are left in that medicine bottle?"

"The correct amount. Two twice a day, that's all. No alcohol."

"You promise?"

"I can promise you this." He took her cup and placed both onto the coffee table, then slid his hand up her hip to her back, revealing the only clothes she had on was the satin top.

She smiled while her palm brushed against his thigh. Her thumbs hooked inside his waistband and lowered the back of his pajamas. He kissed her neck. In a fluid motion like gentle waves on a beach, their lips locked together, and the two slid on the couch.

Two bangs on the front door startled them. Marla rolled on the floor and tried to cover up.

"Anyone in there?" Searcy called out. He banged two more times on the door.

"Jesus," Marla said. "This early?" She pulled the pajama top down as low as it would go. "Pops, what is it?"

The screen door squeaked open. Searcy's beer belly hung below the belt and strained the buttons of the newly pressed police shirt. A thick, black utility belt with a sidearm holstered wrapped under his voluminous waist and another on a shoulder harness. A bright chrome badge hung on the shirt—an outfit he hadn't worn since the July 4th parade. His right hand held a double barrel 12-gauge shotgun. Sweat beads lingered on his forehead.

"Pops, come in." She gently took the shotgun from his hand while gazing at his thinning comb-over and unshaven face. "Let's leave this outside." She snapped it open and ejected the two shells.

"Searcy, you OK?" Crosby asked. "You look like you ran from the station to here."

Searcy wiped his cuff across his forehead and tracked past the couch. "I couldn't sleep thinking about this dead guy. What was he doing in town? Was he watching someone who caught up with him and killed him in the church? And then it happened out of nowhere. Someone shot my front window." His boots clomped toward the kitchen. Grabbing the carafe, he poured coffee into a mug and took a sip.

"Pops? Someone shot at you?" She handed the two shotgun shells to him. "I...uhh...took these out."

He stuck the two shells into his pocket and then grabbed the cold toast from the top of the toaster and shoving half in his mouth. "Yeah. I ran out and looked, but it was still dark. Couldn't see shit out there."

Crosby returned from the bedroom wearing his wranglers and a t-shirt with Marla's jeans in his hand. She slid them on and then put her hand on Searcy's back.

"Pops, are you still taking all your medications?"

He sipped his coffee. "Yeah, yeah. No problem."

She picked up her phone on the kitchen countertop. "Let me call Doc Brown, get you in, and check you over."

Searcy slammed the mug on the counter; coffee exploded across the white Formica top. "I'm just mad there's another murder in this town. It was a nice, quiet town. Now, this. A bullet through my window. Nothing's going right. Damn squirrels messing with my stuff. I don't like strangers in my town." He slung the half-eaten dry toast in the sink. "I'm going to drive around looking for anything conspicuous. Recheck the church for something." He pointed at Crosby. "What the hell *is* that priest doing? I need some answers from him." His hand pounded the screen door open like a fullback stiff arms a linebacker. He grabbed the shotgun leaning against the outside wall and charged toward his pickup.

Marla held the two shells in her hand. "I'll give these to him later."

Crosby poured his coffee in the kitchen sink. "Be ready in ten minutes. We need to see the priest before Searcy goes ballistic on him."

◆

A cool breeze slapped Marla's face as she exited their house. Crosby was ahead of her by fifteen feet. Red mud covered his Dodge truck quarter panels. Gentle breezes whispered through weeping willow trees along the long-curved driveway to the main road. A quick push on the start button cranked the diesel engine. "I know Searcy has a lot on his mind, being the Chief of Police and all, but what kicked off this morning's rage?"

"He's an emotional guy, always has been." She coughed several times.

"You alright?"

She pulled the inhaler from her shirt pocket, sprayed it twice in her mouth, and inhaled deep. "It's his town. You understand that. He wanted to be a cop in a small town forever, and since we moved here, he has taken ownership of just that."

Crosby put the gear shifter in drive and coasted past the gate. "Didn't like him coming to the house with a loaded shotgun."

They turned down the dirt road toward SH 216.

"Neither did I," she replied.

A few minutes later, Crosby opened the church front doors. It was Wednesday morning, and the church furniture had returned to normal except for the yellow crime scene tape. The sound of footfalls from their boots announced visitors. Father Jules came out of his office to the right of the altar and closed the door behind him. A smile crossed his cheeks, his hands clasped in front of the black cassock.

"Morning, Father Jules," Crosby said. "We'd like to talk to you a little more about the homicide. I'm sorry if you felt uncomfortable yesterday last time we talked. Heard the mayor was unhappy."

"I must apologize. The mayor came by almost immediately after you left, and I only mentioned it in a very small fashion."

"That's right. He did," Mayor Pichler said as he closed the priest's office door and held out his hand, as all politicians do.

"Mayor?" Crosby shook his hand, followed by Marla. "We are not here to cause any problems. We just need...a few questions... clarification on a few things. Some help in the murder case."

"Glad to hear." The mayor patted Father Jules on the back of his shoulder. "We need him here taking care of church business, not worried about your police business."

"Yes, sir. I understand," Crosby said.

Mayor Pichler held out his hand again. "Good. I'll be on my way." He firmly shook both of their hands like he expected their vote in the next election.

Father Jules waited until the man left. "I am always here to help the police in any way I can. Would you like to come into my office?" His hand swayed to the right. He opened the door, revealing a modest cherry wood desk sitting in the center of the room, and two bookshelves lined a wall with a full-length mirror next to them. Twenty-four by thirty-inch unframed pictures lined another wall, and a large mural of the *Last Supper* covered the entire back wall.

"Very Catholic, Father," Marla said. "Is this a typical representation of an office?"

"Each one is different. To his own taste, you see."

Crosby's hand brushed across the paintings. "These aren't painted on the walls. They feel smooth."

"No, no. These are vinyl reproductions. You see, printed at a vinyl wrap company. Like what you see on cars and trucks for their business."

Marla's hand rubbed across one. "It looks like actual paint. Where did you buy these?"

"Down the street at the store called Wrap It Up."

"That is my father's store," Marla said.

"Yes, Chief Searcy is exceptional at copying a picture from a book I showed him."

"Did he do the ceiling, too?" Marla asked.

"Yes. He was extremely helpful."

Crosby gazed at each wall. "There are four pictures. Why them?"

Father Jules rubbed his hand over the first one. "Each one is significant to the Catholic Church. This one is *David and Goliath*. Everyone knows the story of David's bravery." He stepped to the next one. "This is *The Brazen Serpent*. Moses erected Nehushtan, a serpent on a pole, to protect Israelites from a plague."

"Who is the woman?" Marla asked.

"Her name is Judith. She saved her kingdom by killing a vicious warlord."

"And the last one?" Marla asked.

"Ah, yes. *The Punishment of Haman*. The King hung him from the very gallows Haman built for attempting to kill Queen Esther."

"Seems there is a lot of violence in the Bible," Crosby added.

"The Bible depicts good and evil. You should come to church on Sundays. I can teach you many things from the Bible."

"Enough history for now," Crosby said. "Father, were you here at any time during the night of the murder in this church?"

Father Jules sat down in his dark leather chair. "No, I was at my house, asleep."

"Anyone with you?"

"With me? No, I live alone. I am celibate."

"Asleep?" Crosby asked, "We have a video recording of you at the bar the same night, and you walked out less than a minute after the victim left. Did you follow him?"

"I was there trying to save souls. I often go to the Crescent Bar but usually leave before midnight. After that, people are too drunk to remember anything I say."

"Were you there while the fight was going on between the victim and another man?" Marla asked.

"I did see what happened. The man was sitting at a table alone, and a girl came and sat next to him. He handed her money, and she scooted close to him. A minute later, her husband stopped at the table and started arguing with the man..." he used his fingers to trace a cross over his chest, "the now deceased. A few punches thrown, mostly by the deceased. He left afterward. I didn't see me trying to save any souls after that, so I left. I went to my house and to bed."

Crosby stopped next to a bookshelf and slid a book forward. "Husband? How did you know it was her husband?"

"Both had wedding rings on, and the man yelled at her like he was her husband."

"You know them?" Marla asked.

Father Jules shook his head. "No, that was the first time I had seen them."

Crosby flipped pages in the book. "Do you have video surveillance here at the church?"

"There are old cameras on the eves. I don't believe they're connected to anything. But then again, I never really looked. Of course, there are no cameras inside. Everyone deserves their privacy when they pray."

"When did you come to this church?" Marla asked.

"Two months ago." Father Jules stood from the chair and coursed around to the front of the desk. "Be careful; some of those books are quite old."

Crosby closed the book. "Where were you before here?"

"Montenegro."

"Why would someone from Europe move to a small town in Texas?"

"A calling. The Lord called me to come here...and because of the civil unrest back at home."

"Civil unrest? Like what? Guess I have little knowledge of eastern Europe." Crosby leaned in and stared at a large brass key on the third shelf. "Interesting key. It looks like a key from a castle or an enormous lock."

"It is from my house. I found it among the ashes. The only thing I have left from there."

"I'm sorry for what happened to your home. Did they find who burned your house?" Marla asked.

"Yes, they received what they deserved and will not have the chance to do that again."

Crosby held the key up to the light. "Must have had an enormous door for such a large key." He turned toward the priest. "Do you have any paperwork that I may see about your education, priesthood?" Flipping the key in the air, Crosby missed the catch, and it dropped to the floor. The whang of brass echoed in the room.

"You want paperwork. I have miles of paperwork, but what you want is there." He pointed to a frame that hung on the wall. "This is my *celebret* from Theological Bible Seminary in Montenegro."

"What was that word?" Crosby asked. "Let me pick that up."

"The word is celebret, or as you would call something like a diploma." Father Jules' hand pushed Crosby to the side with more power than a priest would be expected to have. "No. I will get the key." He raised the cassock above his shoes and bent to his knees to pick up the key; it exposed his exercise pants and ankle high boxing shoes with a green V across the sole.

When Father Jules bent down, Crosby flipped through papers on the desk and found a picture of a quaint house with a tall leafy tree to the side. He took a picture with his phone.

Father Jules stood and arranged the key on the shelf precisely as it was before.

Crosby asked, "Is this your house in Montenegro before it burned?"

The priest grabbed the picture off the desk. "Please, do not take things from my desk."

"I'm sure everything is on the up and up," Crosby continued to stand close by the priest,

"The seminary you went to would have records of you being there, right? I'll need an address and a phone number."

"Am I a suspect in this murder?"

"No. Sorry, I went on a tangent there for a moment."

"Father," Marla asked. "Is there a place to exercise in the church?"

"Exercise? No, why?"

"You're wearing exercise pants and boxing shoes."

Chapter 7

Padding across the parking lot, Crosby pointed the fob at his truck. It chirped.

Marla's fingers aimed for the door handle. "Relaxed fit," she said.

"What do you mean?" Crosby asked.

"He's wearing exercise pants and ankle high shoes boxers wear in the ring under that cassock. What do you think?"

"Don't like it." Crosby climbed into the truck and closed his door. "I'm not Catholic, but how many priests wear gym clothes under their cassocks? Does he seem like a pacifist to you?"

"Right. Start it up." Marla closed the door. She locked her seat belt while the diesel engine hummed. "Is there more than one seminary in Montenegro?"

Crosby turned from the church parking lot. "Good question. Let's look it up at the station.

Ten minutes later, Crosby's truck pulled under the metal roof at the back of the police station. They entered the squad room, and Crosby diverted toward his desk. Marla stopped at the picture of the unknown victim hanging on the 'Active Investigation' corkboard. Bloodied, torn lips with teeth broken from a fist or the tube shoved down his throat. She had never seen such violence, such hatred so close to her. She touched the long thick scar and remembered Dr. Berghoff holding shrapnel in his hand at the autopsy. Her fingertip almost felt the ridges on the picture. Staring into his frozen dead eyes, his voice called out to her, "Marla?" He repeated, "Marla."

"Marla," Crosby said. She spiraled back toward Crosby, waving his hand at her. "Come over here and look at this."

Two drawings of older men were on Crosby's monitor.

"I typed in Father Jules and what popped up were two priests from France born in the 1800s, but Jules is their first name, not last."

Marla shrugged her shoulders. "Maybe our priest's first name is Jules, like Mother Teresa or Cowboy Bob. Never thought to ask." She rapped on Crosby's desk twice. "I'm going back to his office and look for a full name."

"Inside the office? Not sure if that's a good idea."

"Don't give me any crap. If I want crap, I'll go talk to Logan." Her demeanor loosened. "While I'm checking on the priest..." she playfully tapped her fingertip on Crosby's chest, "see if you can find a seminary in Montenegro. After that, head for the diner. I need some decent coffee."

Half a block from the police station, Marla detected the only car in the parking lot of the church belonged to Father Jules.

Marla jogged across the street toward the front door. She glanced under the eaves for a camera, and there were none. After entering the church, she snuck down the outer aisle of the church toward the altar. The partially open priest's office door allowed music to escape. The song was not a church song; instead, a battle song, an unrecognizable military song, and Father Jules sang along word for word in a foreign language. Her finger touched the door and inched it open. His cassock hung on a wall hook, and a clerical shirt lay over the chair's back. On the floor, his shoes lay on the sides with a green V on the bottom. Father Jules stood wearing a wife-beater t-shirt and exercise pants in front of the full-length mirror. Powerful trapezius and latissimus dorsi muscles bulged while lifting large hand weights above his head with ease. A dark round scar on the right deltoid caught her eye. She had seen that before, a healed bullet wound. His biceps flexed fully with the weights. He put the weights down, stood in front of the mirror, and watched himself as he punched several quick jabs with his fists and a roundhouse kick.

Marla held her breath as she watched. *Nope. Not looking like a passive priest to me.*

Father Jules stopped and stared into the mirror, then took the shirt from the chair, moved backward, and disappeared from her view. He grabbed the knob and yanked the door open, revealing an empty sanctuary. The side door pounded open. Rushing back to the mirror, he touched the left upper corner, revealing CCTV images of the back parking lot and both sides of the church. He panned the camera across the parking lot.

Marla leaned against the outside wall. Above her, a camera hung from the eve. Its internal motor whined and panned right from the side parking toward the front corner of the church. *Guess they do work.* She stood perfectly still under it and watched it slowly turn toward a row of four-foot-high bushes along the side of the property thirty feet away. She had always been the fastest in the fifty-yard dash at high school, six seconds, but that was years ago while wearing shorts, a tank top, and track shoes. Today, she had an armor vest, tight pants, black leather boots, twenty extra pounds of equipment around her waist, and a lingering cough. That would be an extra two seconds, she thought. Eight seconds was a long time. *I could snap the camera off the stand and end this dilemma.* The motor started again with a slow turn away from the bushes. *Go now.*

Father Jules panned the camera back toward the front; birds fluttered away from the top of a tree. There were broken branches on a bush that were not there before.

✦

A cheap brass bell dinged above Marla's head as the front door of the diner opened. She scanned the red vinyl booths filled with people. Black and white tile squares covered the floor while Texas swing music crackled from the overhead speakers. On each end of the half-circle counter, fresh out of the oven, warm slices of apple and coconut cream pie sat on glass shelves. Fathers and sons perched atop every round stool with their upside-down western hats sitting by each owner's left hand, except for one teenager who still wore his baseball cap.

Walking behind the stools, Marla's hand slid across the top of the boy's head, scraping the Texas Rangers cap off his head. "Caps off inside, Billy," Marla said. She dropped it next to him on the counter.

"Yes, ma'am."

The father smirked. "Told you someone would do that."

Crosby's Stetson sat upside down at the end of the table. He leaned back in the corner booth and smiled. Steam swirled above the coffee cup and fought valiantly against the ceiling fan draft.

In the next booth, two elderly ladies from the Catholic Church sat across from each other. He snickered at their gossip about the priest; his jet black hair, short sermons, too many "Hail Mary" penances, and he constantly flirted with the widows.

Marla slid in across from Crosby and leaned back. "This priest is buff, muscles on muscles, pumping heavy hand weights. He made a few Bruce Lee moves in front of the mirror." She coughed twice and took a labored breath. "There's an old bullet wound scar on his left chest. Initially thought this medium size man couldn't take on the victim, now I'm not so sure."

"You run a 5K before coming here?" Crosby asked.

She pulled an inhaler from her shirt pocket and sprayed it once. "This damn duty belt weighs three hundred pounds. Cargo pants and a heavily starched shirt along with an armor vest that shoves my breasts behind my lungs don't help." She snagged his water glass and, in three gulps, emptied it. "The camera on the eve is live, and it followed me. He almost caught me."

She coughed several times. "Damn weeds. I can feel the swelling build in me." She pulled out an EpiPen from her cargo pant pocket, jammed the needle through her pant leg, and clicked. Twenty seconds later, her heart rate hammered, and her breath cleared.

"Better?"

"Got another on me if needed. Go ahead. What did you find?"

"Looked up Montenegro." Crosby dropped his leg down under the table. "It's a small country surrounded by Bosnia, Kosovo, and Albania, on the northeast coast of the Mediterranean Sea and east of Italy's boot heel. There's a small Catholic Seminary west-southwest of the Capitol."

"You and Google become close friends?" Marla pulled a sugar packet from the holder. A waitress slid a coffee cup and saucer in front of Marla. "Thanks, Becky."

Crosby looked at her cup. "That coffee is white."

"Right, a little coffee in my warm milk. Becky knows how to make it for me."

"Thought you drank black coffee."

"You are never around me when I drink coffee in the afternoon. Black and strong first thing in the morning, light and easy the rest of the day." Marla poured the sugar into the cup and stirred a spoon around a few times. After a quick sip, she asked, "Does this seminary have an 800 number to call?"

"No phone number, no website."

"Probably built five centuries ago and never took the time to add a phone. No website? Bet they don't have electricity either."

The brass bell above the front door rang again. Crosby ducked his head. "Today just went to crap."

Miss Hildebrandt of 2014 entered wearing a windbreaker with the Channel Ten logo and her shoulder strap purse draped to her side. She held a microphone like she was ready to sing on *The Voice*. A cameraman followed behind her. A light clicked on from the top of the camera. Her eyes lasered on the two police officers in the corner booth and scampered in front of Crosby and Marla before they could move.

Marla focused on the unusual six-inch deer antler prong hanging off the side of Rebekah's purse attached to a quick release key chain. *Is that her weapon of choice?*

"This is Rebekah Farmsdale reporting from San Antonio's Premier Channel Ten news. Officer Adams, what can you tell the public about the awful murder that happened at the St. Juan Diego Catholic Church in Hildebrandt this week?"

She aimed the microphone toward the table. Crosby and Marla sat still while looking at Rebekah.

The newscaster brought the microphone back and spoke, "Officer Adams, would you give an update for us?"

Crosby sipped his coffee before asking, "Which Officer Adams are you talking to, Rebekah?"

Rebekah's hand dropped to her hip, the microphone behind her back. "Come on, Crosby. You can't *still* be mad at me. Just talk; you're on camera."

He sat up and cleared his throat. "All information must be kept in confidence during an investigation."

"So, you admit that there was a murder in town?"

"I am not the official spokesman for the police department."

The bell over the front door rang again, and Chief Searcy entered the diner. His eye caught the camera and lights in the corner.

"Go ask the Chief," Crosby pointed at the door. "He would be able to answer any questions you have."

Rebekah spun around.

"Time to go," Searcy said and rushed out the door. Rebekah and the cameraman followed.

Marla's eyes focused on Crosby as she sipped her coffee. "I enjoyed that." She put the cup back down on the saucer. "And why are you still mad at her?"

His fingers rubbed his eye sockets, and he sighed heavily. "She dumped me for the captain of the football team at the high school prom."

"You're still mad about that?"

"No, of course not. Rebekah just won't let me forget she dumped me. You're a cop. You've been living here in the great town of Hildebrandt for a few years. Why don't you know all this?"

"Don't remember ever seeing her anywhere in town. Does she live here?"

"No, San Antone. Went to a university and stayed."

"Big move, thirty miles."

"Some people are dying to get out of Hildebrandt, and others just die here."

"When did she move?"

"She left Hildebrandt after the football player left town."

"And remind me where this alleged good-looking football player is now?"

"In prison. I arrested the guy for trafficking, and she has never forgiven me for *that*."

A text message on Crosby's phone dinged. "Logan ID'd the victim. Searcy wants us back at the station and asked us to bring them burgers and fries."

Chapter 8

In the squad room, waiting for their food, Officer Logan Searcy sat at his desk while Chief Searcy worked in his office. The ceiling fans spun a lazy whirl, forever suspending dust in the air. Sunlight bounced off the partially open Venetian blinds.

Logan sat in his office with his laptop opened in front of him. Google Earth had zoomed in on Downtown Birmingham, Alabama. On a narrow street, a five-story building had apartments on the top floors and three businesses on the first floor. The middle storefront had CROSSED KEYS INVESTIGATIONS printed in large, white letters across a plate glass window. A small square yellow and white logo was in the corner. Mike's World Famous Pizza and Calzones Restaurant were on one side of Crossed Keys and Peter's Royal Palace of Antiquities on the other.

Logan tapped the Birmingham PD number on his phone and stretched the truth just a little bit. "This is Hildebrandt Chief Investigator Logan Searcy. I need to speak to your Chief."

A few seconds later, a voice on the other end said, "Hello. This is Chief Johnson."

"This is Chief Investigator Searcy in Hildebrandt, Texas. Thanks for taking my call."

"Always ready to help a fellow officer. What can I do for you?"

"I'm looking for information on a company called Crossed Keys Investigations."

"Crossed Keys? Yeah, I know the business, or rather, him."

"Him? What do you mean?"

"Did you look up the business on Better Business Bureau or any other site before calling here?"

"No. I'm trying to find if there are any priors, arrests about an employee working there."

"That explains it." Johnson cleared his throat. "Crossed Keys Investigations had a long history of poor BBB ratings. The FBI raided it last week for alleged bank fraud and money laundering, along with twenty other federal charges. Unfortunately, someone must have tipped them off because there were no employees, no files in the office, and all the bank funds transferred to off-shore accounts two days prior. Big story in the Alabama news circuit for several days."

"A week ago? I talked to an employee yesterday, Abriana Mastrofrancesco."

"Send me the number, please," Johnson said. "Not sure who would still answer the phone. APD will investigate that later today. I would suggest you call the FBI, though I doubt they'll tell you anything."

"The website shows there are fifty PIs employed."

"No. Not true. Only one."

"One? Are you sure? The website said fifty."

Johnson chuckled. "Right. If it's in print, it's true. The entire business was a scam. Allegedly, over one hundred million dollars ran through that business in the last decade. The owner fled, and the FBI is looking for him."

Logan leaned back in his chair. His hand brushed across the back of his neck. "I know exactly where he is."

Johnson didn't reply for a few seconds. "How would you know that?"

"Is his name John Walker?"

"Yes. Where is he?"

"He's in cold storage in San Antonio."

◆

Searcy glanced at a news flash on his computer. He touched the recorded link from seven o'clock that morning, and Channel Ten news reporter Rebekah Farmsdale announced FedEx reported one-hundred-thousand oxycodone tablets stolen at the San Antonio International Airport.

"Logan? Come in here." He ran the video back to the beginning and showed Logan. "I wonder who FedEx was supposed to deliver that package to?" Searcy asked.

"Not my house," Logan said. He went back to his desk with an over-expression of tapping his watch when Marla entered the squad room with the food bags. "Thanks for coming in, Sis. Traffic problems between the diner and here?"

With a quick draw, her finger pointed at Logan's head. She mouthed, "Bang."

Crosby called out to Searcy, "Rebekah Farmsdale from Channel Ten News is looking for you, Chief." He placed two sacks on Logan's desk.

Searcy logged out of his computer and went into the squad room. "Just finished watching a recorded announcement on my computer with her reporting stolen oxy tabs at the airport." Searcy shook his head. "She needs to stay in San Antone and out of my town."

Logan ripped his sack in half, unwrapped the burger, and took an enormous bite.

"Good God Almighty," Marla said. "You are nothing but a slob. How in the hell can I be related to a caveman?"

With a mouthful of burger, Logan smiled. "I'm hungry." He shoved six fries into his already full mouth.

Marla turned toward Searcy. "This is your son. Would you *please* teach him some manners?"

"Too late for me to do anything about that now." Searcy pulled out his burger and fries, then laid all of it on the flattened sack. "Get on your computer." Marla entered her password and the screen lit up. Searcy pulled up the news flash about the stolen oxycodone tablets.

"Damn, a drug robbery at the San Antonio airport?" Crosby asked. "What happened?"

"Not sure if during loading or unloading," Searcy said.

"The DEA will be all over that," Marla said.

"Should be," Crosby said.

In two minutes, Logan finished his burger and fries, wadded the paper and sack in one large ball, and shot it in the air like a basketball toward the wastebasket against the wall. He missed by more than a foot.

Crosby snickered and turned to Logan. "Are you going to tell us who the victim is?"

"Just got this put together a half-hour ago," Logan opened his laptop. "No one else has seen it." He reached across and connected the computer to a projector. "Close the blinds." Dust particles flickered like fireflies in the projector's light. The picture on the white wall showed the victim's dead face. The scene chilled the mood.

Marla felt someone behind her. She spun around, and Father Jules stood, leaning against the doorway. He asked, "Mind if I listen?"

Searcy said, "Police business."

The priest stepped forward. "I feel very bad about the death inside my church. I want to help any way I can." He pointed at Crosby. "I noticed Officer Adams carrying food sacks into the building, so I followed."

Logan asked, "Are you spying on us?"

"There's a murderer in town. I'm just keeping an eye out for anything unusual—different."

Marla broke the ice of bilateral suspicion, "Come in, Father. Have a seat. I'm guessing being a priest, you are good at keeping secrets."

Searcy called out to Logan, "Go ahead."

"San Antonio Crime lab ID'd the fingerprints and sent the info to me about an hour ago. They belong to a William McCleskey who legally changed his name to John Walker, a white male, age fifty-two."

Searcy sat up in his chair. "Who did you say?"

"John Walker, no middle initial."

Searcy slowly nodded and leaned back. "Okay, John NMI Walker."

Logan changed to the next slide with Crossed Keys Investigations website on the wall. "This business is out of Birmingham, Alabama. On their website, the business is extensive, with over fifty PIs employed and licensed in almost every state. I called the company, and all I got was a recording that the number was no longer in use. Thought that was strange, so I went back to the site and tapped the contact us link. Lucky for me, the contact name at the bottom of the page was unusual: Abriana Mastrofrancesco. I cross-checked the name, and there is only one in the U.S. It took a while, but I found her cellphone number." Logan tapped the key on his laptop again, with the disfigured image of Walker appearing again. "Called the Birmingham PD, and he was on the run for alleged money laundering."

"When I called the woman, she didn't want to tell me any info about Walker until I sent her a picture of him dead on the floor of the church. The lady became belligerent, threw wild accusations at me, and then hung up. I tried calling back several times, but no answer. I think she's personally connected to Walker. I Googled John Walker in Birmingham and got this." Logan tapped another key on the laptop, revealing a photo of Walker's official military induction before the disfigurement. "Walker was a 1st battalion, 6th Marines veteran who lived in Birmingham, widowed. He's not on any social media sites."

"You got all that in a day?" Marla asked. "All right, little brother, I'm impressed."

Crosby leaned in closer to the screen. "I know this man." Crosby pulled his phone out and thumbed through his pictures. The image on the phone had Walker and Crosby standing next to each other and smiling. "This is Major John Walker, retired," Crosby said. "Three times decorated; two Silver Stars, a Bronze Star, and four Purple Hearts. I remember him as the keynote speaker at a law enforcement conference almost ten years ago. He must have received the facial wounds after this picture. Hardly recognizable."

"John Walker." Searcy leaned back in the chair and crossed his legs. "What the hell is a decorated, retired major doing in Hildebrandt?"

Marla looked around the room; the priest had left.

Chapter 9

After dinner at Jack's Steakhouse, Crosby and Marla sat on bar stools at The Crescent Bar and Grill. Light jazz music whispered from a portable stereo behind the bartender. Pictures of him at famous scenes, the aurora borealis, Vatican, Eiffel Tower, Machu Picchu, and Angkor Wat, hung on the wall.

"Moon," Crosby said to the bartender.

"Officer Crosby Adams," the bartender snapped back.

"Moon, did you travel to each of those places, or did you Photoshop yourself into those pictures?"

Moon wiped down the bar counter. "Geez, never thought of that. I could have saved myself a ton of money. Thanks, Crosby. Need something?"

"Give me a Coke."

"Cosmo, please," Marla requested.

"You two need to change up your drinks. Same order, except you used to put Jack in that Coke."

"Jack and oxycodone don't mix well."

"Okay," Marla said. "I'll take a Jack and Coke without the Jack, and he will take---"

"The Cosmo?" The dishtowel flipped over Moon's shoulder. "Coming right up."

"Moon, how long have we known each other?" Marla asked.

"We met two days after you met Crosby. It was the worst day of my life. If only I had met you before he did." He leaned toward her and whispered loudly. "Leave him and make me the happiest man in Hildebrandt."

Marla smiled. "May I ask you a personal question?"

He dug a plastic scoop into the icebox and poured the ice into a glass. "Do I need my lawyer?"

"You know why everyone calls you Moon?" Marla asked. "Somewhat insulting."

He shook his head as his infectious smile showed perfectly bleached white teeth. "Not at all. Look at me, round face full of acne scars. I came up with the name myself. I decided Moon sounds better than Limburger Head or Divot Face or SpongeBob."

"You named yourself Moon?"

"Sure, Moon's a good name. What about Moon Zappa, or the Man on the Moon, or Warren Moon?"

"Hence, the name of the bar, The Crescent," Crosby said.

"Better to be forward than let some schmuck come up with something worse. I don't mind being forward. Do you mind if I am forward with you, Marla?" Two drinks clop on the bar. "Need something else?"

"Like?" Crosby sat straighter and tried to look bigger. Marla half-smiled at both men.

Moon wiped a hand towel across the bar. "Pot, blow, pills, guns."

Crosby relaxed and sipped his Coke before saying, "I would not be surprised."

Moon raised his eyebrows for a second and asked while looking straight at Marla. "Okay, how about carnal satisfaction?"

She slowly spun her glass and smiled. Her hand flipped her hair back and then looked at Moon. "How about you tell us about Father Jules."

"Denied again." Moon sighed and shook his head at Marla. "He's been here almost every day since he hit town. He walks from table to table and sits at some for a while; others he stands."

"He talks to the regulars?" she asked.

"Sure, someone orders a glass of wine for him, and he sips on it for an hour or so. When the wine is gone, he leaves."

"Was he here when the victim was here?" Crosby took another sip of his Coke.

"Yeah. Never sat together, but the priest kept glancing at him."

"What caused the fight?" Crosby asked.

"Women, it's always women. Lizzie, being who she is, decides to piss off Mitch. It's so easy. He's a very jealous man, even came at me and told me to back off from her. He thought I was hitting on her when I asked what they wanted to drink. I'm a bartender, for Christ's sake."

"You mean Mitch and Lizzie DeVries," Crosby asked.

Moon tapped his finger twice on the bar. "The definition of an unstable couple."

"Tell us about the fight," Marla said.

"Lizzie sat down next to the stranger, stuck her hand under the table, between his legs, and started rubbing. She licked his facial scar. Sick woman there. She wanted to make sure Mitch saw it. Hell, everybody saw it. Mitch walked to the table, chest flared, and said something. The guy stood and bunched his fists. Mitch had no chance with two quick blows to the face and once in the stomach. The guy had to be ex-military or a boxer."

"Think Mitch is the type who would take revenge?" Crosby asked.

"Jealousy can get you in deep shit, man."

"Are Mitch and Lizzie regulars?" Marla asked.

"Yeah, two, three nights a week."

"Father Jules said he didn't know them, but you said they're regulars," Marla remarked.

"They are, but they usually come in about one in the morning. Stay for two drinks and leave near closing time."

"Why early this time?" The ice in Crosby's glass clinked as he drank the last of his Coke.

"Not sure. Might have finished their drug runs early." He turned his attention to Marla. "May I freshen that Cosmo for you? I do like intoxicated women."

"Father Jules, what did he do?" Crosby asked. "One more, please."

"Another, Crosby," Moon smirked. "I don't know. I *am legally* allowed to stop anyone from having too many drinks."

"Thanks. I promise to take it easy."

"Well, that's what I like. Fine upstanding police work here in Hildebrandt. Another cop refusing to mix alcohol with his opioids." Moon slid a square cardboard coaster under Crosby's glass. "If that copay for the oxy is too high, I might get you a better deal."

"I have no doubt you could do just that. Back to Father Jules, what did he do?"

Moon shook the cocktail mixer. "Sitting two tables over, he watched like everyone else." After pouring the red solution into a new martini glass, he pushed it toward Marla. "On me." He slid the soft drink to Crosby and patted the countertop. "Two bucks for the Coke. The guy walked toward the door, and Father Jules caught up to him. They both said something, and the guy pushed the priest backward. He almost fell down."

"They talked? How long?" Marla asked.

"Few seconds."

"When did Mitch and Lizzie leave?"

"They argued at the table, then he huffed to the bar and ordered two drinks, and when he wasn't looking, she ran out the door. My guess? To chase after the guy and piss off Mitch."

A bright light exploded from the front door as two ladies walked in. "Moon, honey. Please bring us..."

"Gotcha, Michelle. Be there in a sec." He looked back at Marla. "If you need something, *anything*, ask me." Moon sucked in his belly. "Anything."

He poured two Chardonnays. "Got to go." Moon walked to the table with the newest customers. Michelle clutched his arm, and he sat next to her. She squeezed his bicep and giggled.

"What do women see in him?" Crosby asked. "This is a man that could win People Magazine's 'Most Ugly Man Of The Year' award."

"Oh, I don't know about that." She sipped the Cosmo. "Kind of cute what he does."

"Cute? He's ugly."

"In a cute sort of way."

"You better not let him hear that. I *know* he wants you."

She sipped again as her eyelashes fluttered. "Wants me to do what?"

Three girls in crop tops and tight exercise pants walked in. The brunette called out with three fingers held in the air. "Moon, baby. Three Michelob Ultra's, please."

Michelle pecked Moon's lips and let him go. He returned to the bar.

Crosby pulled out his phone and showed Moon the picture of the house he took in Father Jules' office. "Ever seen this place?"

Moon pulled his glasses from his shirt pocket and slipped them on. "Hmm. Perchance. Surprised you don't." Moon handed the phone back to Crosby.

"Me? Why?"

"It's been a few years since I've been on that side of town, but it looks like the old Pearlman house before they moved to their new digs with tennis courts and a swimming pool paid for from wind turbines on their land."

"Dave Pearlman?"

"That's the place. They left the old house and moved about two miles from the southwest corner of their land to the northeast corner."

"I need something from you, Moon," Marla said.

"Finally wore you down. Anything for you."

"Are you familiar with the name Roberto Sardino?"

"Roberto Sardino? Yeah, sure. He was a PI who mostly worked in the Dallas and New Orleans broken marriage racket. Made a bundle. We buddied up at the Mardi gras a few years ago. Hell of a bead thrower. Got all kinds of women to show their tits. Sorry to hear about the suicide. Doesn't seem right. Always happy around me."

"Is there anyone you don't know?" Crosby asked.

"Hmm, maybe a few people in India."

"I'll take another coke," Crosby said.

Marla raised her shoulders. "He's my designated driver. One more Cosmo, please." She lifted her almost empty glass to Crosby. "And then you take me home."

Moon poured the rest of the red mixture into her glass. "You're supposed to say that to me, not him." He gathered three beer bottles and popped the caps off. "And don't forget to tip."

Chapter 10

Marla awoke at the sound of an alarm chirp outside the house, followed by a truck door opening. Her hand slid over the gamut of cold sheets. Crosby wasn't there.

From their bedroom window, a pale whitewashed moon hung high in the western sky. She slipped her nightgown on over her head before leaving the bedroom, and headed for the front door, only to stop when she found the kitchen light on and the coffee pot percolating. Crosby's pill bottle stood on the counter with a small piece of paper next to it. She shook the bottle once, and it felt the same as yesterday. The note in Crosby's handwriting read, *Back in an hour.* Blackie, Crosby's horse, whinnied outside near the front door.

The eastern morning dawn was peaking above the horizon through tree branches. She tip-toed to the front bay window, bent down on her knees, drew the bottom edge of the curtain slightly to the side, and watched Crosby retrieve his Stetson from the dashboard before easing the truck door closed. He placed the hat on his head before zipping up his shotgun vest.

Blackie stood still next to the truck with the reins resting across his neck. Crosby grasped the saddle horn while his boot slipped into the stirrup, then with a quick motion, he mounted the horse and took one last look at the dark house. Marla released the curtain and lunged backward. Crosby kicked Blackie's haunches, and the two launched forward. She pulled the curtain back again and nervously watched Crosby ride away as the horse ran past the barn toward the hills. Marla moved off her knees and sat on the floor, dazed. It was the first time he didn't tell her good morning or goodbye. She raced back to the bedroom.

As Crosby crossed over the hilltop to the edge of the fence line, he pulled the reins, and Blackie turned toward the creek's rushing water. He felt a million miles away from where he needed to be and what he should be doing.

An image jumped into Crosby's head. Water flows down a creek behind overgrown trees and scrub brush and wraps around the back and sides of his childhood house. Crosby feeds the chickens, his last chore before supper. His father, a Texas Ranger, monitored the Rio Grande River crossings of desperate men called drug mules. He came home the same time every evening at 6 PM to a house with a loving wife placing a hot meal on the dinner table and young Crosby waiting and ready to eat. Each day Crosby's father repeated his actions; he entered the house, hung his hat and gun belt on the hat tree next to the front door, kissed his wife on the nape, and hugged his son before he asked the same rhetorical question, "Who's hungry?"

Blackie snorted and bent down toward the water. The image disappeared, and Crosby dismounted, letting the horse drink. The back of his riding glove touched a tear at the corner of his eye. He patted the horse on the neck as the memories of his childhood returned.

He remembers the smell of his mother's cooking on the stove. In the front yard, Crosby played catch with his dog. His stomach growled from hunger. It was an hour past time for his father to return home from work. The house phone rang. Crosby glanced down the dirt path toward the main road again.

He ran into the kitchen when he smelled burnt chicken and dumplings through the open kitchen window. Standing next to the fridge, his mother blew cigarette smoke straight ahead. Her eyes stared at the turquoise phone on the wall while her finger continuously wrapped and unwrapped around the coiled phone cord. Three bent cigarette butts lay in the ashtray on the kitchen table. It was the first time he had ever seen her smoke a cigarette. The dumplings boiled over the edge of the pot. He eased past her and turned off the stove.

Crosby watched dirt swirl in the air as a pickup truck trailed off from the main road toward their home. It wasn't his father's. Instead, another pickup with two Texas Rangers stopped in front of the house. His mother dropped the cigarette on the floor and stepped on it.

Crosby never saw his father again. His mother died six years later from running out of tears and too much alcohol.

Crosby's phone rang in his pocket and snapped him out of his reverie. He glanced at his watch: 7:10 AM. The call was precisely when they said it would be. "Adams here." He listened for a few seconds and ran his hand up Blackie's mane. "I'm alone. Had to leave the house so Marla wouldn't hear." He patted Blackie's neck as the voice spoke for a long time. "Listen," Crosby said. "I don't have the time for that now. We have an ongoing murder investigation here in Hildebrandt. Let's do it in three or four weeks." He scraped his boot across the grass and then paused while he listened to the voice on the phone. "Why now?" The voice became louder. Crosby swung around and moved away from the horse. "If I do this, it has to be as real as possible." He adjusted his hat and tapped his shirt pocket. "What you want is dangerous." He slipped an oxycodone out from his pocket and chewed the pill.

Marla dismounted Daisy next to Crosby. "What is dangerous?"

Crosby disconnected the call and shoved his phone in his front jeans pocket. His arms swung wide in the air. "All this. All this is dangerous. Investigating a homicide is dangerous."

"Don't you bullshit me." She punched two fingers against his chest. He didn't budge. "You snuck out of the house and rode down here to avoid me. Why?" Her hand patted his shirt pocket. She held out her hand. "Give them to me."

"Give what?"

"Give me the pills in your pocket."

He dug two fingers into his pocket and pulled out three pills. Marla took them and pitched them into the creek. "Is that all?"

His brow furrowed at her. "Yeah, I think so."

"You think so? You know the arrangement with Doc...and me. Pills are taken only at the correct times of the day, not whenever you think it's a good idea." She patted his two shirt pockets and felt nothing. "If I have to strip you down and search your clothes, I will. So, help *you*, God, if I find one hidden pill, it's going to be a long, cold, naked walk back to the house for you." She held her palm out, ready for the rest. "Any more?"

He dug into his jeans pocket and pulled out two more pills. "That's all, I promise." He placed the two in her palm.

While staring at him, she pitched the pills into the water. He closed his eyes for a few seconds.

"Don't do this again, or I will call Dr. Sanborn and cut you completely off. Now, tell me... WHY did you sneak out here?"

Chapter 11

C rosby popped his head past Chief Searcy's office door. "New info on the Walker case."

Searcy held the office phone receiver to his ear and held back his anger. His eyes shifted toward the open door. "I promise, mayor. We are doing everything by the book." He disconnected the call, closed the laptop, and nodded toward Crosby to come in. "Walker? Okay, what?" He pulled the bottom drawer from his desk open and placed a bottle of bourbon on the desktop.

"No," Crosby said. "Not doing that anymore."

Searcy reluctantly put the bottle back. "I enjoyed you more when you drank."

"I didn't, and Marla sure as hell didn't." Crosby sat down in the chair across from the desk. "Think the priest is not as clean as he wants us to believe. Walker last reported into Crossed Keys Investigations two days before his death. He pulverized Mitch DeVries in the bar a few *hours* before his death and argued with the priest at the front entrance of the bar and then they both left, almost simultaneously." Crosby leaned back in his chair. "Walker is dead, and the priest has no alibi. We can't find Mitch or his wife. Conceivably, they saw the priest kill Walker, and now they're on the run, or the priest killed them to keep them quiet."

"Too many other things to think about," Searcy said. "Do you think Mitch DeVries is a drug dealer? Get more info on him. Seems the likely perp. Jealousy is a powerful motive."

"What happened?" Crosby asked. "The other morning, you barged into our house with two pistols and a shotgun, thinking the priest had something to do with the murder. Now, it's like you never said that."

"What in the hell are you talking about?"

"You don't remember coming to our house?"

"Hell no."

Crosby sat back against the chair. Can't argue with a man who says he doesn't remember. "I'm leaning toward the priest. He had a picture of David Pearlman's old house on his desk. Got to be a reason for him having a picture of an abandoned house."

Searcy slapped his thick paws on the desk. "You think the priest is a killer? Wrong. Get all you can on this Mitch character, then bring it to me tomorrow morning. We'll discuss Father Jules later."

"Let me work on the background of the priest first. I think there is..."

"No." Searcy slammed his fist on the desk. "DeVries first. Find where he is and ask him for an alibi for that night. Why is he not in town? Something is damn sure going on, and I don't like it. This is more than a pissing match between DeVries and Walker." Searcy patted the closed laptop. "Walker might be dirty as well, but it's feasible someone killed Walker in self-defense. Too many other suspects need to be cleared before we slander priests."

"Let me have an hour on the priest," Crosby said.

"No." Searcy stood from his chair. "Mitch DeVries is number one." He pointed toward the door. "Out, now."

◆

Crosby's truck sat three hundred yards from the farmhouse. Shooting stars filled the black night, icy fire sprinting across obsidian heavens.

Marla sat in the passenger seat and asked, "Why do you think Pops wanted us to emphasize on Mitch and not the priest?"

Crosby rolled his window down and lifted his binoculars to his eyes. "I don't know. The man is smart. I'm sure he has his reasons."

The priest's car sat in front of the house. A flashlight beam skimmed inside.

"Why is the priest there? No one lives in that house," Marla said. "I ran off a homeless couple last month with a small fire in the middle of the living room cooking beans in a can. All that dry wood could have turned uncontrollable in seconds."

Crosby watched through the binoculars again and said, "Searcy said not to follow the priest, but something is wrong with this guy. Who is he going to meet in there?" Crosby lowered the binoculars. "He's not doing last rites."

"Should we go in?" Marla asked.

He shook his head. "Not enough reason to."

Father Jules headed into the kitchen. The cupboards were gone, revealing large rectangles of unpainted drywall. Broken drinking glasses and rusted utensils littered the countertop. Beneath the countertop, all the doors to the lower cabinets were missing. Father Jules bent down on one knee and shined the light on the shelving. The cassock stretched; a thin layer of mud covered half of the green V on the bottom of the right shoe. Putrid odor pushed him back with animal feces scattered across the shelves. He covered his mouth and nose with the cassock sleeve again, reached over the feces, and slid a small section of the back panel to one side.

There, concealed in the wall, sat a single metal cash box. He pulled it out, set it on the floor, opened the latch, and flipped open the top. The flashlight shined in the container. When he removed a 9mm pistol and placed it next to him on the kitchen floor, a single coin slid across the bottom of the box. Four bundles of 100 Euro bills laid in the box, each with a 10,000 Euro currency strap around it. He flipped the edges of the bills past his thumb, smiled, and placed the pistol back into the box, snapped the latch shut, and carefully replaced it behind the false back, careful not to move the feces.

"Forty will get me another one-twenty." After kissing the fourth bundle, he dropped them into his satchel, stood and then pulled out a handful of birdseed and mixed nuts from his pocket, and poured half on the shelves and the other half across the countertop.

Outside, Crosby's truck idled. His binoculars skimmed across the front and side of the house as he looked for something to happen, no shadows, no movement from the windows. A flashlight beam stretched from the open front door to the porch. Crosby pointed at the house. "He's coming back out."

Father Jules opened the front door of his car, flipped the satchel onto the passenger seat, and sat down behind the wheel. He started the engine and patted the satchel twice. The car shot down the dirt road and disappeared behind tumbleweeds and thick scrub brush. Crosby put his binoculars down. "We should follow him." He started the engine.

"Wait," Marla said. "You follow him, and I'll check out what is so interesting in the house."

Crosby's truck lumbered down the road toward the priest. She rushed toward the window of the blackened house and bent down on one knee. After listening for movement, she rubbed a round spot of grime off at the corner of the window. She couldn't see anything. Had the priest met someone? Was he waiting for her? Shoot first and leave her to die.

Marla stepped around a patch of mud toward the door. A deep hollowness filled her ears when her boot hit the wooden porch. With the front door closed, the knob spun loosely in her hand. She could kick the door in and yell, "Police!" That might produce a reply of bullets.

She walked around to the back of the house and tried the kitchen door, but it was locked. The last time she was here, vagrants ran out a doorway from the side of the house. Quietly moving around the house, she stopped at the side door and turned the knob. A shiver ran up her neck as the door creaked open. The last Stephen King movie she watched had creaking doors. She snapped her flashlight on and called out, "This is the Hildebrandt Police. Anyone here?" There was no answer. The dried wood flooring snapped and crackled with each of her boot steps. Unhinged bedroom and closet doors laid on the floor with bent spoons, syringes, and burnt matches scattered about.

Stepping over the doors and into the den, she glanced inside. The house was a basic design; two bedrooms, a bathroom, a den, a dining area, and a kitchen. Small, everything small. She scanned the light beam around the den and dining walls. Torn black sheets partially covered the windows. Fast food trash and sleeping bags laid in a corner of the dining area. Black soot and spiderwebs lined the inside of the fireplace. Her hand waved over the burnt ashes. Everything felt cold.

She aimed the light beam at the center of the empty den; muddy shoe prints with a V in the center trailed from the front door toward the bedroom. The shoe impressions traveled from the first to the second bedroom.

The prints faded toward the single bathroom in the house, with the door still hung on its frame. She pushed it open only to have it bounce against the vanity—unable to open all the way to the wall. The top half of the faucet laid in the sink. Black mold flourished in the toilet bowl. A rust ring circled the bathtub drain. On the floor, a round white pill caught her eye near the corner of the vanity. She picked it up. One side was scored, a line down the middle to snap in half, and the other had 30 printed in the center. "Oxy. I wonder if this is from the airport heist." She glanced behind her and stuck the pill in her pants pocket. "The priest?"

The sound of rattling flatware came from the kitchen. Marla whipped out the pistol from her holster, pointed straight ahead, and crept closer to the kitchen. Her throat tightened. The noise clinked again. She thought it sounded like a spoon in a cereal bowl moving around. Again, a clatter. Something fell on the floor. With two quick steps, she entered with her flashlight and pistol aimed straight ahead. "Police, freeze." Two squirrels on the kitchen countertop turned, cheeks stuffed with mixed nuts, and froze. Two seconds later, they scurried away through the broken window. She breathed deep and coughed again. "Damn varmints."

She noticed the missing cupboard on the wall and all the lower cabinet doors. On the countertop, animal feces and crushed nuts intermingled between the broken glass and metal utensils. Marla holstered her pistol and tried to cover the rancid odor with her nose buried into her elbow. Her fingernail flicked a fractured piece of a pecan across the countertop. She pulled her inhaler out of her pocket and shot a spray into her mouth. *Why was the priest in this filthy place?*

Her flashlight beam swept across animal feces on the bottom shelves. She knelt to check a board slightly off-center. While reaching for the back wall, the wooden floor creaked behind her. It was an odd angle, pulling her hand back and reaching for her gun. She turned to see the butt end of a pistol swinging toward her head.

Chapter 12

M arla felt her head pound like a hammer on an anvil. She wrestled an eye open. Her flashlight beam aimed away from her. Pushing up with her elbows and then hands, she sat with her legs crossed. Her head spun. She touched a golf ball sized lump on the back of her scalp. "Damn, that hurts."

Fear struck her. Was it there? Her hand brush over the pistol still in her holster. Whoever hit her didn't take her weapon. She checked for the pill in her pocket. It was gone.

◆

Downtown San Antonio, Father Jules' car turned on a side street and pulled into an angled parking spot. A flickering green neon sign above the door introduced Paddy's Irish Pub to the public. Jules' car alarm tweeted, then he raised the satchel strap over his head and across his shoulder.

Crosby parked on the side of the street. With his binoculars, he watched Jules pull open the front door. He placed the binoculars on the seat and picked up his phone.

Marla's phone rang. "Hello?"

"Find anything?"

"Someone sucker punched me on the side of my head with a pistol."

"Are you alright?"

"Alive."

"See who it was?"

"No, but I found a pill on the floor. Looks like an oxycodone. Could be from the airport heist."

"Do you think the priest had anything to do with it?" Crosby asked.

Marla flinched when she rubbed her scalp. "Where are you?"

"I'm here in downtown San Antone at Paddy's Pub, a real shithole bar. The priest walked in with the satchel."

"Are you going in?" Marla asked

"No, he would recognize me and blow this to hell. I want to know what's in that pouch."

"You think he's there to sell the oxy?" Marla asked.

"It's feasible Walker was onto him, and I think Father Jules killed him."

"A stretch yesterday, but more likely today."

Crosby drove past the pub. "I'm heading back to Hildebrandt. While he's here in San Antonio, we need to check out his office. Want me to stop by the Pearlman house and pick you up?"

Marla looked around. "Need to get out of this creep zone, ASAP. I'll call Logan and have him drop me off at the church."

❖

Father Jules stopped next to the back door of the bar and knocked twice. A small window on the door slid open, then closed. The door opened with men talking loudly behind it. It was for illegal off-site betting. Each time he came there, it reminded him of the scene in *The Sting*. CCTV monitors broadcasting horse races hung across the upper walls. With his black cassock still on, Jules turned to the cashier with black iron bars between him and a man on the other side. "Tonight is British racing, right?" Jules asked.

"Welcome back." The cashier glanced at the wall clock. "Post in about four minutes."

"Forty-thousand Euro on Crosstown Radio, on the nose." Jules dropped on the counter four bundles of bills with a 10,000 Euro currency strap around each.

The cashier's eyes looked above his half rim glasses to the priest. Without expression, he took the bundles, slid the straps off, dropped the bills in the currency counter, and watched it quickly flip the bills until it stopped, then wrote a note on a slip of paper while he asked Jules, "Forty-thousand in Euro on Crosstown Radio to win, right?"

"Right," Jules said.

The cashier twisted his head around and spoke to a man behind him, "Forty big in Euro." The man stared for a few seconds at the priest on the other side of the cashier bars, then nodded. The cashier turned back to Jules. "Conversion is one-to-one. Hard to get this back across the water. Are you okay with that?"

"Sure, hurry up."

The cashier looked at the clock. "Just made it by less than a minute."

"Right. Hand me the ticket, please," Father Jules said.

After he stuffed the paper in his pocket, he crossed over to the small bar. "A pint of Harp."

The bartender pushed his glasses back up his nose and gazed at the white tab on the man's collar.

"Going to a costume party tonight," Jules said. "I'll take that pint, now."

The bartender tipped a glass under the beer pull. "Seen you here before wearing the same outfit. Going to the same costume party?"

Jules took the glass and sipped the golden liquid. "Sure, same party. It's a running joke." The bell clanged for the race to start as he watched the CCTV monitor on the wall.

Jules stood at the cashier's window ten minutes later and slid his ticket back to the man behind the bars.

The cashier took the winning ticket. "I'm giving these back to you. Remember, I said conversion is one-to-one."

"Right," Jules said.

The cashier slid the cash across the counter. "Forty thousand in euros plus twenty thousand in dollars. Congrats on the big win."

"Thanks." Jules dropped the bundles in his satchel.

"Need help getting out of here with that much cash?"

"No. I'm a freaking priest. Who's going to rob a priest?"

The cashier scanned the crowd. "Just about anyone in here. Be careful, sir."

Jules opened his pouch, revealing a small caliber pistol. "I'm going out the same way I came in, the front door."

◆

Marla stood at the curb of the abandoned house and watched Logan's pickup slow down and stop in front of her. She pulled on the handle, but it didn't open the door. The passenger side window rolled down.

"Looking for a new place to live, sis? Bet you could get this real cheap. How about I loan you twenty dollars so you could buy it today?"

Marla's fingers wrapped around the door handle, ready to pull. "Unlock the door, Logan."

The window rolled back up. A few seconds later, the lock clicked opened, and she quickly snapped the door open. The truck rolled a foot forward.

"Oops, sorry. My foot slipped on the brake pedal. Okay, you can get in, now." The truck moved another foot. "Oops, sorry, Sis."

Marla pulled out her pistol and aimed it at the back tire. "How about I make sure the truck doesn't move again?"

"All right. Just joking with you. Get in."

She holstered the pistol and cautiously entered into the truck.

"Why are you out here?" Logan asked.

"The priest came to the house, and I checked it out after he left."

"Find anything?"

"Besides a gun butt to my head?" She shook her head. "Squirrels and their shit."

"Where to, Sis?"

"Take me to the church. Crosby is meeting me there, and you head back to the station and check who owns this dump; the Pearlman's, the bank, or a new owner."

"I can do that," Logan said. "Afterwards, I'll come back and watch the house to see if the priest returns."

◆

Crosby and Marla cut through the church, past the altar, and knocked on Father Jules' office door. No answer. He motioned toward Marla. "Let's go."

"Don't get us in trouble. We don't have a warrant."

"Just going in looking for the priest. I need to confess something." Crosby twisted the doorknob. "Father Jules, are you in here?" After a quick nod, Crosby whispered to her, "He might be unconscious in there. We should look behind the desk or in the desk drawers for him. Crack open the side door and watch for him in case he comes back."

Marla grinned at him. "Damn good thing your wife can't testify against you."

Crosby opened several drawers with nothing but office supplies in them. He opened the bottom right drawer of the desk and paused. "Interesting."

Marla turned toward him. "What is?"

"A bundle of Euro bills, a map of Montenegro with a hotel circled in red, and a plane ticket." Crosby looked at his watch. "He has a flight leaving at 11:40 tonight under the name of Benny Simic."

"He's going to Montenegro?" Marla asked. "Why would he travel back to Montenegro?"

"Cover tracks? On the run?"

Tires ground on the parking lot pavement. She closed the side door. "He's coming. Let's go."

A few minutes later, the deadbolt unlocked, and the metal side door opened. Father Jules entered from the parking lot and quickly locked the deadbolt. He sat down in the chair, dropped the satchel next to the legs of his chair, and thought about the bet. Once a month for the rest of the year could get him enough cash for what he is after. A knock on the front office door startled him.

"Father Jules, are you in there?"

He opened the door and Crosby and Marla stood at the entrance. With his hand on the doorknob, Father Jules answered, "Yes, of course. Come in." A quick glance down the nave confirmed the church was empty. "Please, sit down." He closed the door. "Can I help you?"

"We were wondering if you could come to the station and say a prayer for an inmate tomorrow morning?" Crosby asked.

Marla leaned toward Crosby and mouthed out, "What?"

"He's heading to prison for a long stint. You know, give a blessing for his last meal here and safe passage."

"Oh, I see." Jules sat in his chair and pushed the satchel further under the desk. "I would very much like to, but I must travel tonight to another church. Of course, I will be back for the Sunday mass."

"Gone? Where? If you're flying, the police department can have anything heavy or bulky sent at no cost. We can say it's police business."

"Thank you, but not necessary."

"Not going too far?" Crosby asked. "Could you come by tonight before your trip?"

"Tonight?" Marla whispered to Crosby as she placed her hand on his forearm.

Jules glanced at his watch. "I could come by there now if you feel that may help."

"Can't right now; bringing in new prisoners. I know it would be late, but how about in an hour?" Crosby pointed to the ceiling. "You could come by and bless his material things and pray for a safe trip. We have a small religious room where people can pray and contemplate the bad stuff that happened to them."

Marla squeezed Crosby's forearm and coughed once.

Jules smiled as he glanced at his watch. "That is an unusual request, but yes, of course. However I can help, I will."

"All right." Crosby smiled. "Thank you for all you do for Hildebrandt, Father."

◆

Marla climbed into the pickup while Crosby stayed outside and dialed a number on his phone Marla had never seen. He leaned against the truck bed. "Have a lead on the oxy pills. A priest in Hildebrandt... Right, the same church where the murder took place... What do you want me to do?... Would have to take him before he boarded ... Understand... He may be hiding it, sold it, taking cash and fleeing. I don't know... That's a long way away. You sure you want me to do that? DEA going to reimburse me as soon as I return? My credit card won't handle much more." He glanced at Marla. "Would need to have her to come with me... She won't know why until she needs to ... Understand, sir."

Their truck doors closed. "What in the hell was all that with the priest?" Marla asked. "What prisoner? We don't have anyone transferring."

"Right. I want to be at the airport before the priest arrives. This way, he's not hanging around the airport too early and see us."

"Okay, but why? Nothing we can do to him unless we arrest him, and there is nothing so far that warrants an arrest."

"I want to keep a close eye on him," Crosby said.

"We'll lose sight of him when he goes through TSA."

"That's not a problem. We can get past TSA with our badges. Where's your passport?" Crosby asked.

"Next to yours, I think. We've only used it once when we honeymooned in the Caymans. What is going on?"

"We'll need to change out of uniform." He started the truck engine. "Ready?"

"Why do I need my passport to watch him get on the plane?"

"Were you a girl scout? Be prepared and all that stuff."

"I was not a girl scout, and I am not prepared to use my passport." She knew nothing of Europe or Asia. She would have to search the travel channels or YouTube for this place. "I'm not going to some hellhole or stand on the edge of the earth for this guy."

"We're not going anywhere... just... be prepared."

"Are you telling Pops what you're doing?"

"*We*. It's we, and no. Jules already hit up the chief and the mayor about our questioning him. Don't want this to get back to Jules before he leaves."

"Who were you calling?"

"A friend. I need to inform Nancy at the station about Father Jules." Crosby picked up the police radio microphone and called, "Grand-mamma."

Grand-mamma was the police call name for Lorena Paulensky. She had four kids, twelve grandchildren and had worked at the HPD since she was twenty-eight years old, forty something years ago.

"Here," she said.

"Tell Nancy I'm calling her on my cell phone in a minute."

"She's right next to me. Want to talk now?"

"No. Not on the radio."

"10-4."

When Crosby called the station, Nancy answered the phone. "Hilde-brandt police. How can I help you?"

"It's Crosby. I need a big favor from you. When the priest comes over in about an hour and asks to see a prisoner, don't act surprised. Just tell him the prisoner was transferred at the last minute."

"What prisoner? We have no one in the back."

"I know, but I have a sound reason."

"Crosby, I shouldn't lie to a priest. That's like lying to God."

"Probably right, but it's just a little white lie. How about I bribe you with two dozen brown eggs from my chicken coop?"

"Those eggs are fantastic. Okay, I'll do it."

Crosby hung up and glanced at his weather app on his phone. "Supposed to be chilly. We might need a coat."

"Inside the airport?" Marla asked.

"Pack a coat," Crosby said.

"Pack?" Marla pushed his shoulder. "What is swirling in that brain of yours?"

An hour later, Crosby sat at the gate with a newspaper in front of him. Marla wore a floppy hat that covered her head and as much of her face as she could. She felt ridiculous in this spy game.

Father Jules carried his satchel across his body and stood in line, ready to board. Within minutes, the announcement for first-class passengers blasted from the speakers overhead. They watched him scan his ticket and disappear down the jetway.

Marla stood. "He's on. You ready to get back home?"

Crosby folded his newspaper and dropped it on the seat next to him. He walked toward the counter. Marla stood still. He flashed his ID at the airline employee, and she returned an anxious smile.

Crosby turned back toward Marla and motioned for her to come next to him. "She needs your passport."

Marla slowly slipped her passport out of her back pocket. "I'm not too keen on this."

Minutes later, they sat on the opposite end of the plane from Father Jules. "Have you thought about how we're going to talk to these people in Montenegro? I don't think anyone there speaks Texan."

Crosby held his cellphone up in the air. "Google Translate app."

Chapter 13

Nine hours later, the plane's wings bounced as the wheels screeched across the Charles De Gaulle International Airport runway. The captain thanked everyone for a pleasant trip and hoped they'd return to Iberia Airlines again. Marla adjusted her watch.

Father Jules deplaned long before they did since he flew first class. Marla exited the jetway to a beehive of passengers.

"My first time to Paris, France." She looked up at the ceiling. It's a beautiful skyline. All the magazine and snack shops. "Oh, look, French bathrooms." She wrapped her hand around Crosby's arm and smiled. "Thanks so much for such a wonderful time in France." She let his arm go. "What in the hell are we doing?"

"I've been thinking. We need to get to the seminary before Jules does."

"Got a faster plane than him?"

"Got a diversion."

Across the airport, they arrived at their next gate. Father Jules sat between two families with unruly children. His satchel rested on his lap with the boarding pass on top.

"Could not have asked for anything better." He pointed to her head. "Stick that floppy hat back on and bump into one of those children. Fall to your knees and quickly stand and walk away. Don't let him see your face."

"And what are you doing?"

"When he stands, I'll take his boarding pass off his satchel."

"You're stealing his boarding pass? I'll visit you in prison every Wednesday."

Minutes later, Jules stood in front of the ticket desk, waiting for a new boarding pass while Crosby and Marla hurried through the jetway. They found their seats and watched as the door closed and latched without Father Jules on the plane.

Marla laid her head on Crosby's shoulder. "Didn't see the Eiffel Tower. You'll have to bring me back. I love you..." she raised her head, "...but if you get me thrown into a foreign prison, I will never, ever forgive you."

❖

A winter festival booked all the vehicles at the Podgorica International Airport. Not a single car left to rent. The only thing left was an off-site facility on the south side of town. After a lengthy discussion through Google translate, Crosby and Marla pretzeled themselves inside a rental vehicle only slightly larger than a circus clown car. Crosby pushed back against the seat until it stopped; his shins still touched the dashboard as he turned the steering wheel between his knees.

"I'll need a sauna and a massage after this," Crosby said.

Marla sat back with her knees up to her mid-chest. "I feel like I'm visiting Doc Sanborn for my annual physical. Let's get out of here. The sooner we go, the sooner we can climb out of this sardine can."

The road south of Podgorica narrowed to the width of a licorice stick with abundant towering trees on both sides. Trees so thick a herd of buffalo could hide. Crosby shifted into another gear as he turned on a sharp curve. A tour bus coming toward them took most of the road. Crosby swerved as tree branches scraped paint off the side. The front tire hit a pothole, and the whole car rattled.

Marla's head hit the roof. "We should have upgraded for a car with suspension."

"I should have brought my Ram truck," Crosby quipped back light-heartedly.

After thirty minutes of roadside dodge ball, their car passed a sign: Lake Skadar 1km. Crosby's side of the road opened to a restaurant and parking area. Several people were eating under an awning.

Thirty-five minutes later, the road straightened, and a sign said Beranvat 5km.

In town, people wore heavy coats and exhaled clouds of condensation. Bicycles swarmed the sidewalks and streets. A green road sign had a building with a short steeple and an arrow pointed left. Crosby down-shifted and turned. The steering wheel rubbed his knees. Rows of clown sized cars filled almost every parking space at the seminary.

"Not expecting this at all. It looks like a fortress or a cathedral with enough cars to fill a Walmart parking lot." Marla gazed at the tall roofline. "This place is bigger than the Alamodome."

Crosby pulled into a parking spot and stopped. When Marla opened her door, an icy burst of wind shot up her long, dark blue dress. She rubbed the sleeves of her sweater, then pushed the small shoulder bag around her waist. "Should have worn ski pants instead of this dress."

"You'll blend in better with the dress."

"My legs feel like a two-stick popsicle."

Crosby smirked. "Don't get me thinking about your legs."

She smiled back. "We're going into a church or some kind of religious place." She pointed up to the sky. "You need to watch your mouth," she tapped him in the groin, "and both heads."

They rushed to the front doors. *Teoloska Biblijsko Sjemeniste,* Theological Bible Seminary, was etched into the dark wood above the archway.

"How did you talk me into this?" She patted Crosby's butt, then pushed her hair away from her face. "Ready."

Crosby pushed on the double twelve-foot-tall wooden doors that looked a century old. They swung open like riding on air. A massive groin vault ceiling stretched across the church all the way to the altar. Enormous Gothic light fixtures hovered over congregational pews full of people. The organ pipes bellowed and echoed off ancient walls while a young man sang in a foreign language from the altar. Another young man in a cassock walked past them with his arms swinging to the music like a maestro conducting a symphony.

"This looks like Sunday morning service, except it's not Sunday," Marla said.

"I think we could fit our church in that corner over there." Several doors lined the hallways to the left and right. "Come on, this way," Crosby said. "No one will see us. Everyone is looking at the altar."

A voice behind them called out. "*Oprostite tko ste vi.*"

Crosby spun around and grinned as wide as he could. Both hands held up head high. "Sorry." An older man, maybe in his fifties, stood firm, with arms crossed, in a standard black cassock, and said, "*Tko si ti! Zasto si ovdje!*"

Crosby looked at Marla with a blank stare.

"Use your Google app."

"Oh, right." He pulled the phone from his pocket, tapped the app, and said, "Hello. We are tourists and want to see your beautiful building." Crosby pushed the speaker button, and the app translated.

The man lowered his hands, shook his head, and spoke. The Google app translated. "We are having religious services. Return tomorrow."

Crosby spoke into his phone. "May we stay if we donate?"

The man looks confused.

"A church offering."

He smiled at Crosby and Marla while pointing his finger at a silver platter.

"An offering?" Marla asked. "Do you have any Seminary Rewards on you?"

"I believe he wants Euros." Crosby pulled out a crumpled wad from his front pocket and separated them. "All I have are fives and tens. What have you got?"

"Me?" She moved her head side-to-side slightly and chuckled toward the man. She spun back to Crosby. "All I have are twenties and hundreds."

"Great. Use that."

"And how much is a twenty in euros?"

"Like twenty-five dollars." Crosby smiled at the man waiting next to them.

She reached into her shoulder bag and dropped a twenty on the platter.

The man stared at Marla.

"More?" she asked and then dropped another on the platter.

The man smiled, waved goodbye, and left down the hallway.

"Tell me, was the Google app free? It cost me sixty bucks."

"Come on, let's go before someone else wants money."

"What's upstairs?" Marla asked as they hurried down the hall.

"Not sure. Can't be anything we want. Business offices should be on the first floor."

Each black cherry stained door held clouded glass inserts. The first door to the left had *WC* etched on the glass. Holding his phone to the sign, Crosby pushed Google Translate again, Toilet. "Hey, just like our church, first door on the left," Crosby chuckled. Next room, *Financije*, Finance; next, *Prihvancanje Sjemenista*, Seminary Admissions; next, *Datoteke*, Files.

"Got it. Follow me." They entered and quietly shut the door. A row of gray metal filing cabinets stood at attention against the wall.

Marla trailed to the back of the room and looked at the side door with a transparent glass insert. "Every office is lit up and has a side door that looks the same with the glass inserts. I can see every office from here down to finance." She turned the knob and opened the door. "These offices are lined up like ducks in a pond."

Crosby aimed his phone at the lettering on the file cabinets. "What?"

"There's a door connecting each room with clear glass. I can see from one end to the other. Finance, Admissions, here..." Marla spun around, "...and whatever is next door, except that room is dark."

The organ stopped. Marla touched Crosby on the shoulder. "Church service must be over. If it's like home, there will be a mad rush out the door and head to Dairy Queen."

"I don't think they have a DQ."

"Best reason not to move here," Marla said.

Crosby slid a metal drawer open and flipped through the tabs, "There is only one Simic." He opened the folder. "This is a picture of Jules taken several years ago." Someone slashed a black line across it with the word *ODBIJEN*. Crosby tapped the app again. REJECTED. He stuffed the file into his coat pocket and slid the drawer back. Voices down the hall were coming closer.

Marla watched two black shadows pass by the front door. The doorknob turned to the room they were in.

"I prefer not to sit in a Montenegrin prison for the next thirty years," Marla said.

"Promise, you won't."

"Yeah? Why's that?"

"We'll both be murdered within a week," Crosby said.

"Let's get out of here." She cracked open the side door. "We go all the way down to finance, then out to the hall."

The admissions front door opened, and the man who extorted the forty Euro from her entered. Marla quietly closed the side door.

With the File Room front door half-opened, a man called out into the hallway. Crosby tapped mute and read the phone screen. *Thank you, sir. I will call you tomorrow.*

She whispered to Crosby, "Change of plans." She crawled to the other side of the room and opened the door to the next dark room.

The man heard the side door open and spoke.

Crosby's screen read *Zorana? Is that you?*

Crosby whispered, "Whose office is this?"

"We could retire with the amount of gold and silver in this room." Marla took the nameplate from the desk and read it, Rector Sudvaric. Marla shrugged her shoulders and angled it toward Crosby. "What's a Rector?"

"It's the guy who runs the seminary. Like an apartment manager."

"Where did you read that?"

"I'm a cop. Got to know stuff."

"Well, I'm a cop, and I know we have got to leave now," Marla said.

"Quick, under the table," Crosby whispered.

The man opened the side door, scanned the room. "Zorana?" After no reply, he closed the door.

"Oh, Jeez, that was close." Marla pointed to the front entrance. "Need to go." They crept out, and Crosby quietly closed the front door. A young man in a black cassock walked toward them. Marla looked down, trying to avoid eye contact. "If he taps me on the shoulder, I'm punching him in the face and running like hell."

Crosby waved and said, "*Zdravo.*" He twisted back toward Marla and the entrance. "Let's go."

"Now you speak Montenegrin, too?"

"Googled a few words on the plane."

"Fine. Google, I'm going to kick your ass all the way back to Texas."

Chapter 14

F rigid air swirled through the heater vents under the dash of their car. Marla cupped her hands over her mouth, trying to warm her fingers. "Didn't think about gloves." She rubbed her palms together, then stuck them under her arms.

Almost fifteen minutes later, their headlights focused on a yellow curve sign. Two small motels stood at the top of the hill, one on each side of the road. The heyday for either was decades ago, now displaying weather-worn parking lots and faded paint. Crosby downshifted. Marla's eyes widened.

"We're here," Crosby said.

"Here, as in, here to stop and check the tires before we go to our hotel?" She shook her head as the car slowed. "No. Not here. We need to go to a pleasant hotel with a bathroom and not a one-hole outhouse."

"Remember when we were in the priest's office, and he circled a place across the road on the map? This is the place and will be the best spot for us, across from him."

His hand rested on the gearshift knob. Marla wrapped her hand around his and said, "Tell me it's the one that should be condemned and not the one that should be bulldozed."

Crosby said nothing and turned the steering wheel left.

"Oh, Jeez." Marla released Crosby's hand. Her finger rubbed away wet mascara from under her eye. "I might sleep in the car."

"You want to sit in this thing all night with your knees up to your chest?"

"No. I want a hot bath with room service and us cozy under the sheets."

The car stopped in front of the office glass door. "How about a warm washcloth and a cola from the outside vending machine?"

Crosby pulled open the door for Marla. Her lips tightened as she held back a cough. Wishing this was all a joke, she hesitated a few seconds before entering past the door. A gray cloud of stale cigarette smoke permeated the office. The check-in desk looked like someone had beaten it with an ax and nailed it back together fifty years ago. Behind the desk, a plump middle-aged woman sat on a single metal chair with a cigarette between her fingers and eyes fixated on a 19 inch black and white television screen.

Crosby's hand hit the desk bell with an underwhelming, tinny ding. He spoke into the Google app on his phone. "Do you have any rooms?"

The woman stuck the cigarette between her lips, aimed the remote at the television, and lumbered to the desk. "Da." She pulled the cigarette from her lips and flung the butt in the corner of the room, then coughed a few times until a mucous plug gurgled into her throat. She pushed a printed piece of paper in front of him. The registration card had Croatian and English text. The woman spat into a handkerchief, then smiled, exposing the few teeth she had left. "*Ona je jako lijepa.*" Crosby's phone translated. "She is very beautiful."

Marla stared at the woman, then closed her eyes for a second before opening them again. Crosby smiled back and nodded.

He held the phone close to her. "You need more than one night with her. I will give you the honeymoon suite."

He laughed, grasped Marla's hand, and held both in the air, exposing wedding rings. "Married."

The woman regretfully nodded and wrote on a paper, 25 E. She held up a finger, then her hand. Stepping away for a few seconds, she returned with a bottle of red wine and wrote 9E.

Marla gripped Crosby's forearm. "We... you don't need that in the room."

He nodded at Marla, then shook his head toward the woman. He gave her twenty-five euros and then took the key.

Crosby slid the key into the deadbolt lock and jiggled it until the bolt snapped open. He opened the door, flipped the light switch on, and stepped back for Marla to enter. The odor of must and mold hit her full-faced while six-legged insects scurried under the bed. A pink and green floral blanket barely covered a full-size mattress with no headboard. Two well-used pillows were turned vertical, like someone had sat on the bed, leaned against the wall, and watched television.

Marla threw a few verbal barbs at Crosby. "Honeymoon suite? For whom? The cockroaches?" She passed the bed and stuck her head into the bathroom and gazed at a single sink with a stained bathtub and no shower curtain. She dared not lift the toilet seat. She didn't want to know.

◆

Bundled in their beanies and heavy jackets, Crosby and Marla walked along the beach and held hands while foreign sand crinkled under their shoes. A cold breeze cut through them. Colored clouds pushed the Montenegro sun down toward the Adriatic Sea, with seagulls drifting high above them. People walked down the long pier two hundred yards in front of them while icy waves crashed upon the posts below.

Marla watched an airplane roar over their heads toward Western Europe until it faded into a black dot. She snuggled close to Crosby's arm. "Not sure this was a clever idea, walking on the beach. Must be forty-five degrees outside." She drank the last of the hot tea in her plastic cup, trying to chase the chill off her back. She watched Crosby chew an oxycodone tablet before finishing his water. "And I'm also not surprised this seminary is not anywhere near a city, but I was hoping it was closer to the airport. Took almost an hour in that little car."

"With a worn-out, four-banger engine, the car topped out at 65 kilometers an hour or about 40 miles an hour." Crosby chuckled. "Might have gotten here sooner riding Daisy and Blackie."

She swung her arm wide. "I think the room we got had to be built the same year as the Seminary."

"It's a one-star dump, but it's across the road from where the priest, or Benny Simic, is staying."

She tilted her head against his shoulder. "I was hoping for an elegant hotel built this century."

"Cheer up. Today is supposed to be the hottest day of the week," he said. "The weather app says heavy snow tomorrow."

"What the hell are we doing here, Crosby? A million miles from home and no authority."

"The priest killed Walker. I feel it." Crosby pulled her shoulder closer and kissed her cheek. "There is no way this guy is who he says he is."

Marla pointed toward a rock formation. "What's over there?"

"The cave? A few boulders, maybe some soft sand."

She raised her eyebrows and smiled. "And a little privacy."

Crosby looked around to find they were the last on the beach. The horizon had consumed half the red sun. "I'm pretty sure it's illegal to drop your pants on the beach."

"There is no way I am taking my clothes off and lying on that musty mattress at the motel." She wrapped her arms around Crosby's neck and pressed her lips against his. Her body inched closer, arms squeezed harder.

Thirty-five minutes later, they slipped their clothes back on.

"I've worked up an appetite. Let's get something to eat," Crosby said.

They stopped at an intersection with two restaurants. No cars sat in front of the Jelka Cafe. On the left side of the road, the Crvena Riba Cafe had three vehicles in front. "Let's go there."

Crosby and Marla sat at a small table next to a front window as snowflakes floated to the ground. Across the street, a restaurant employee swept the snow away on the outside patio. A single patron stepped around the man to one table. Across from Crosby, Marla moved their knives and forks to the corner of the table. Crosby glanced across the street again. The man sat alone wearing his coat while an outside propane heater poured warmth down on top of him.

"It's almost like he wants someone to watch him eat outside in this weather," Crosby said.

After they finished their meal, Crvena Riba's owner stopped at their table and asked in broken English, "Was good, yes?"

"Yes, wonderful," Marla said.

"You are tourists, no?"

"Yes, of course."

"I am owner. My name is Kadic. What yours?"

"Mmm...Dick and Jane," Crosby said.

Marla curled her eyebrow up. "Who?" Crosby shrugged his shoulders.

"Dick and Jane, you must try Rakija."

Marla lifted her wine glass. "This is enough for me."

Crosby continued to watch the man across the street.

"No, no. You must." Two fingers snapped toward a waiter, and he brought three shot glasses of yellow liquid. "This is Rakija. You must taste."

A quick glance from Crosby, "No thanks."

The owner slid a chair to their table. "You are guest in my cafe. I insist. Good for you."

"What is it?" Marla asked.

"Is good."

Crosby sipped it while watching across the street. "Tastes like peach schnapps."

"No, no. We must see each other and drink. Look at me," the restaurant owner said.

Marla locked onto Crosby's eyes. She mouthed for him not to drink it.

"Of course. What next?" Crosby asked.

"We look at each other and drink."

The three glasses clinked, the owner's eyes shifted back and forth to each of them. "Ziveli."

Crosby and Marla sipped.

"No, no. Everyone say, Ziveli, then drink."

"Like Salud or cheers," Marla said.

"Yes. You finish glass."

"Ziveli," Crosby sipped his.

"No, no. You say *Ziveli*, then clink glasses. Finish drink, we do again." He snapped his fingers again. Three more shot glasses appeared. "Say and clink. Do again."

Three glasses clinked. Crosby repeated, "*Ziveli*," and drank half of the liquid. A fur ball of alcohol and oxycodone grew in Crosby's head.

"*Predivan*. I come back, we do again." He left as he said, "Two more glasses."

Marla's hands cradled his face. "Crosby? No more. Okay?"

"Sure." He finished the glass. "No more. Is this flavored Everclear? Got to be over a hundred proof."

A waiter slid two full shot glasses onto the table. Marla's hand pushed them to the corner of the table. "No, we don't need anymore." She glanced across the street at the man's table. He was gone.

At the other end of the restaurant, behind the counter, the owner held a receiver connected to an ancient wall phone. He whispered in Croatian, "I kept them busy. Did you leave?"

The man replied in Croatian, "Yes, thank you. I owe you one."

The owner replied, "You owe me half, and you pay me tonight, or I call the policija."

Marla grasped Crosby's arm. "Come on. We need to get out of here."
She pitched a hundred Euro note on the table, hoping it would cover
the tab. "Can you walk?" She called out to the crowd. "Anyone have any
coffee on their table? Anyone speak English?" Marla spun back to the table
and noticed an empty shot glass. "Oh crap. Crosby, why did you drink
that?" Crosby's head bobbed from side to side, his hands slid across the
table. "This is going to kill you. Damn, got to do it." She grabbed the
fork on the table and flipped the handle toward Crosby. "Don't bite me."
She shoved the handle in his mouth and pressed down on the back of the
tongue. People sitting at their tables jumped back as vomit splattered on
the restaurant floor. "Sorry, everyone, had to do it."

She grabbed him, pulled his arm around her neck, and drug Crosby's
near-dead weight toward the front door. Eyes from every table locked onto
them. His boots slipped and slid under him as Marla all but drug him to
the car.

After she stuffed him in the front seat, the man across the street called
out behind her, "Need help?"

"No," she said.

"I help you."

Marla turned halfway around to a man with a knife pointed at her. "I
don't have time for this. Get out of here."

He took a step closer. "Your money, now."

Marla closed the door and marched straight toward the man.

"You give me money or I..."

Marla grabbed the man's wrist, spun around, and snapped it over her
knee. The blade clanked on the ground. She kicked it under the car as the
man ran away, holding his wrist.

She floored the accelerator, and the car whizzed down the road. Crosby
gurgled while his head lay against the window.

She kicked their motel door in and rolled Crosby onto the bed. His
breaths were shallow and infrequent. Marla slapped him twice across his
face—nothing. His heart and breathing stopped. "Crosby, don't die on me
in this shithole." His face swung left and right with her slaps.

"Breathe, damn you."

She climbed on the bed and straddled him. The heels of her hands
bounded down on his chest in rhythm, putting the CPR refresher train-
ing she got at HPD six months ago to good use. She called out loud,

"1,2,3...Come on. Do it. Breathe, damn it." Her eyes welled; her hair bounced with each compression. "1,2,3..."

She opened her purse, emptying the contents onto the bed next to her. She tore his shirt open, grabbed two EpiPens, and ripped off the covers. Two-handed, she plunged both against his chest wall. Two clicks. "They work on me in thirty seconds or less. Just do the same."

Her hands pushed ten more times on his chest. She screamed, "Breathe, damn it. Breathe, Crosby." Ten more. "Goddamn it, Crosby." She counted out ten more times.

She stopped, grabbed a Narcan nasal spray, shoved the tip into his nostril, and squirted. Twenty more chest compressions, nothing. She repeated the second Narcan. She pulled out her last two EpiPens from her purse. "You're going to be like popcorn in the microwave." The two pens shoved against his chest, they clicked.

Crosby's eyes exploded open—pupils surged wide. He gasped a deep breath in. His heart sprinted.

Exhausted, Marla still straddled him with her hands on his shoulders.

"What happened?" Crosby mumbled.

She rolled away and grabbed a pillow.

He bounded off the bed and paced the floor like a captured animal. "I don't understand what happened. What happened? Tell me what happened?" Five steps forward, five steps back. Rinse and repeat a hundred times.

Marla squeezed the pillow into her face and sobbed.

Chapter 15

P odgorica airport terminal was one of those Eastern European attempts at modern architecture, one story box, metal, flat roof, about the length of a chip shot for Phil Mickelson.

Crosby and Marla sat in standard airport-blue plastic seats. Dark glasses and a plain black beanie cap covered Crosby's eyes and head despite being dark outside. "Thanks for saving my life last night."

"Take your damn pills for your pain, but I will kick your ass if you ever drink again." She wrapped her hand around his arm. "I can't imagine life without you. Promise me, no more alcohol."

He knew its best to change the subject than answer her. "Not real fond of wearing this thing on my head and the puffy lime green nylon coat."

Marla wore sunglasses, an 'I heart Monte' beanie, and a coat they bought at a tourist store. She tapped him on the arm. "Don't think you'd blend in with the Stetson, Tony Lama boots, and shotgun jacket."

A large plate-glass window separated passengers from the visitor's secure side. They watched a twin-turboprop plane creep forward, then stop—the engines shut down. A jetway ambled forward, engulfing the plane's side door. A few minutes later, thirty-three people entered the terminal with Father Jules, aka Benny Simic, the last. Draping the satchel strap over his shoulder, he wore the same sweater and jeans he had on from the beginning of his trip.

Crosby stood and adjusted his beanie over his forehead. "Let's go to the car and wait for him outside."

Simic pulled a small suitcase behind him, strolled to the terminal's car rental desk, and checked in. Moments later, Simic stopped at the back of a car, lifted the trunk lid, and dropped the satchel and suitcase inside.

Crosby said, "His car looks bigger than ours—and uglier. Who paints a car puke green?"

Marla shrugged. "Guess it's who you know. Bet it has suspension."

Simic's car started smoothly. The car turned from the airport parking area onto the main road, with headlights bright.

"So far, we're good. Simic is on the same road heading southwest toward the seminary and the Adriatic Sea."

Crosby looked in the rearview mirror. "Not much traffic, but at least there are a few cars on the road. He shouldn't spot us."

Crosby couldn't keep up with the car on the narrow two-lane road. "He must know this road well. He's taking these curves faster than I want."

Marla pointed at the sharp curve in front of them. "Watch out. That car is drifting over in our lane." The right wheels bounced from the asphalt to gravel. Marla felt the car slide. "Don't kill us in Transylvania or wherever this is."

Crosby's boot slid across the accelerator to the brake pedal. He hit it too hard, and Marla's head banged against the side window. He looked ahead and watched Simic's car disappear around the next bend. "I'm slowing down. We can catch up to him in Beranvat."

Thirty-five minutes later, Crosby negotiated the narrow road between cars to his left and tree branches to his right. On the edge of Lake Skadar, the restaurant and shop had a few cars in the lot with more boats docked on the waterside. Marla pointed at Simic's green car in front. "There he is."

"I shouldn't turn there," Crosby said. "He might recognize us."

Marla waved her hand toward the water. "Cross the bridge and find a hiding spot on the other side. If we're right, he'll want to be at the seminary tomorrow."

Several people in wet suits and heavy jogging outfits walk along the side of the lake while others play volleyball or Frisbee. "This could be a picture of a 1960s American tourist stop, except it's forty degrees colder here," Marla said.

"Be right back. Need to pee." Crosby climbed out of the tin can and headed for the trees before making a phone call. "In Montenegro at a bait shop halfway between the airport and the seminary... He could be... Not sure if he has oxy with him."

Almost twenty minutes later, Simic's car crossed the bridge. Crosby turned the ignition key, and the engine cranked a few times before it started. He glanced at Marla. "We don't need to get stuck here in a car that won't start. Triple-A doesn't come out this far."

Simic drove into Beranvat and turned left off the road to the Crvena Riba Cafe instead of his hotel.

"We're not going back in there," Marla said.

◆

With his coffee mug in his hand, Searcy stood in front of the evidence wall and looked at the picture of John Walker. He sipped his coffee and turned around. "Where in the hell are Marla and Crosby?"

Logan leaned against his desk and slid a toothpick across his lips. "Gone. Heard they went on vacation."

"There's no vacation in the middle of a murder investigation. Get Marla on the phone."

"Just when you need them the most, Chief, they skip out on you." Logan stood straight. "Not professional."

"I said," Searcy's hand shoved Logan's shoulder backward, "get her on the damn phone."

"Yes, sir, Chief." Logan bent across his desk and grabbed his phone. "You should drop them and make me chief investigator. I can find who did this."

"Shut up." Searcy slid his mug across Marla's desk. "I'm going back to the church to talk to Father Jules."

Logan said, "I went by there this morning. No one knows where he is."

"Gone? I might know where to look." Searcy charged out past the back door. Reaching into his truck, he pushed phone search on the dashboard screen, "Call Father Jules." It rang with no answer. "Damn it. Where are you?"

Searcy turned down a dirt road toward the same abandoned house where Jules hid the money. He stopped the truck, rushed out, and shoved open the front door. Wadded sleeping bags and spent syringes lay piled in the corner: animal droppings and broken pecan pieces laid in the kitchen sink. The bathroom door was open and pushed against the vanity. His hand swiped years of dirt off the mirror and gazed back at his reflection.

An airplane engine approached, a crop duster roared and dropped aerial herbicide over the field behind the house. Voices outside the broken bathroom window caught his attention. Searcy tracked through the kitchen, and opened the back door.

Three young boys were sitting on a pickup truck tailgate, laughing, and drinking beer.

"You boys don't look old enough to be drinking beer."

The three scooted off the tailgate.

Willie Cross said, "No, sir. I mean, yes, sir."

Searcy grasped the edge of the truck bed. "Willie, didn't you graduate last summer? And Ethan Dutton, you graduated a few years ago." Searcy turned to the third boy. "Danny Schmidt, you might not finish high school hanging with the older boys."

"Yes, sir." Danny held the beer bottle behind him.

"How's the football team this year? I mean, if they kicked the quarterback out of school for drinking, that would make a tough year."

"Yes, sir," Danny said.

"How about you pour the rest of those beers on the ground and head back to school?"

"Yes, sir, Chief," Danny said. "We can do that. Thank you."

Searcy patted the boy's head. "Don't suppose you could tell me who got that six-pack for you, could you?"

The three looked at each other and then at Searcy. Willie said, "Chief, we, uh, we just found them." They flipped their bottles upside down, and beer foamed on the dirt.

Searcy stepped in front of Ethan. "I bet your mamma doesn't know you're here. I mean, her being busy teaching at the high school. It might be an embarrassment for her to find out." He placed his hand on Ethan's shoulder. "Who bought the six-pack for you?" Searcy noticed several empty beer bottles under a tree about twenty feet away. "Looks like you boys have been here before. How many beers have you found?"

They put the empty bottles back in the carton. "You want us to take this to the garbage?" Willie asked. "We can do that for you."

"Well, that would be right nice of you, but don't think it's such a fine idea for you carrying a six-pack of beer bottles, empty or full, in your pickup. And let's hope we make it to the playoffs this year."

Danny scraped his boot across the dirt and said, "Chief, I should get back to school. The day before a game, we have extra practice."

"Well, how about you jog back to school and work on those passes? I'll watch Willie and Ethan clean up every bottle out here, put them in garbage bags, tie them up, and leave the bags in the kitchen. If the two of you can do that, I'll forget about all this.

Chapter 16

A blast of ice-encrusted air slapped Crosby's face as he opened their motel door to the outside. A gray haze of a full moon peeked behind thin clouds. Their room light gleamed across soft snowflakes floating effortlessly to the cold ground. Marla's skin shivered as she squeezed past him. She wiped off the white crystal sheen coating their clown car's windshield with her bare hand.

His hand gently touched the back of Marla's neck and he kissed her. "Thank you for...."

"You owe me a real European vacation." She quickly brushed her hair away from her forehead. "Won't be missing this one-star rat hole."

"Simic's two-star motel isn't much better. The sun will be up soon."

A light flicked on from a motel room across the street. Crosby motioned for Marla to close their door. Simic slid his glass door open. Wearing his cassock, he stepped outside, opened the back car door, and pitched his satchel on the backseat.

"He has a sliding glass door? We have cardboard for a door," Marla said.

"He's not looking around. I don't think he knows we're here."

They stood motionless while Simic's car started with white condensation blowing out the exhaust. It turned onto the road and shifted gears every few seconds.

"He has to be heading to the seminary. Let's go," Marla said.

The cold engine ground slowly as Crosby's foot pumped the accelerator. The engine started with a whimper.

Marla pulled the passenger door closed. "Does this Hot Wheels have a heater?"

"Think so, but only works in the summer. For the winter, we have a/c."

With Crosby's foot to the floor, the engine sounded like a muffled golf cart.

"Bet he has a heater," Marla said.

Ten minutes later, Simic turned onto the long driveway of the seminary. A few hundred yards back, Crosby stopped at the edge of the road. A thin blanket of snow covered the ground. Marla stuck her icy hands under her armpits.

Simic's car left a single set of tire tracks on the illuminated parking lot. It stopped close to the front entrance. He climbed out, surveyed the grounds before opening the back door and reaching for his satchel. Yellow candlelight escaped when Simic pushed the enormous front doors open.

"We should leave the car here, on the road," Crosby said. "Don't want to leave tire marks across the parking lot."

"Agree. We can walk along the side and not leave obvious shoe prints," Marla said.

At the seminary entrance, Crosby pushed the enormous doors open and they entered. The pews and altar were empty this time. Down the hall, voices spoke Croatian. A light shined from the clouded glass insert past the Rector's front door. One voice was Simic. Marla motioned to follow while she crept into the admissions office next door. The room was dark.

Through the side door window, Marla pointed at a man dressed in a white cassock and hood. She whispered, "The name plate had Rector Sudvaric on it. This must be him."

Sudvaric's hand rested on a bundle of money sitting on the desk. More words exchanged. The voices became louder, interrupting each other, then stopped. He raised his hand off the money, and Simic placed the bundle in his satchel. Simic punched his finger in the Rector's chest. When he slapped at Simic's hand, Simic shoved him back. The Rector grabbed Simic's collar and ripped it down his chest, exposing a square tattoo on his right pectoralis, half yellow and half white. Simic snatched the satchel and rushed out of the room. Rector Sudvaric rubbed his forehead and mumbled words, then rearranged everything on the desk to its proper place.

After closing the door, Marla and Crosby heard footfalls clambering up the stairs.

"What now?" Marla asked.

"We need to find out why Simic is taking money from this place. Let's go upstairs and ask."

"Ask? How? You know Montenegrin?"

"Remember?" He held his phone in the air. "Google Translate, and they're speaking Croatian." Crosby tapped the app and showed Marla the screen. "He says a sentence or two, and the app converts it to English. And vice versa."

Upstairs, there were four doors. Crosby's hand grabbed the top of the handrail while listening for noise. Crosby whispered, "There's light under the third door."

"We're up this far. Might as well commit the full felony," Marla said.

Crosby knocked on the door.

The Rector's head poked around the partially open door. "*Tko si ti? Sto zelis?*"

Crosby's phone translated, "Who are you? What do you want?"

The door opened more. "I speak English."

"We're Americans," Marla said over Crosby's shoulder. "We know Simic is doing something wrong. Can you help us?"

The Rector opened the door wide. The white cassock laid flat, unwrinkled across the bed. He was shirtless and bore the same square tattoo on his chest, the left half yellow and the right half white with a central crest. He slipped a white t-shirt over his head, then asked, "Are you from Hildebrandt, Texas?"

Crosby and Marla looked at each other, then back at the man. She smiled and nodded. "Yes. May we come in?" They entered into the room and Crosby closed the door.

"What's with the yellow tattoo? Both you and Simic have one," Crosby said.

"It represents naivety and stupidity. How do you know about his tattoo?"

"How do you know about Hildebrandt?" Marla snapped back.

"I received a request in the mail for documentation of Simic's confirmation, a celebret."

"That would be from us," Crosby said. "Our office sent it."

"Are you investigating him?"

"Yes." Marla straightened a picture on the wall of the Pope in Vatican City. "We could use your help."

"What can I do for you?"

"Why is Simic extorting money from the seminary?" Marla asked.

"He's not. He's extorting me. Why do you care?"

"We think he may have killed someone in Hildebrandt."

"Doesn't surprise me. You have no authority here. Whatever I say to you is not repeatable. Agreed?" Marla and Crosby nodded. The Rector crossed his arms. "There were four of us, and we did something I'm not proud of decades ago. Now he threatens to expose me if I don't send him money every month."

"Tell me more." Crosby sat down on one of the two wingback chairs behind the door and next to the window.

"I don't know you well enough to tell you everything. What I can say is Simic, myself, and another worked together on a... project. Afterwards, we split up to meet later, which never happened. We were nearly caught and paid a dear price by hiding over the years."

"Did you rob a bank or kidnap someone? What could be so bad you have to pay Simic to stay quiet?" Crosby asked.

He cleared his throat. "How do I know you won't use this information against me?"

"We're after what Simic did in the United States. Unless you committed murder, whatever you did is past the statute of limitations." Marla said.

"I can't say. I'm a Rector, and if Simic released my past, I would lose this job."

"How did you get this job?" Marla asked.

"After what we did, I went home to Cincinnati and married my high school sweetheart. A month later, I caught her in someone's bed, so I left after I nearly killed the guy."

"Are you a fugitive?" Marla asked.

"Not sure. I left the next morning and flew to my ancestor's country here and changed my name."

"What *is* your name? Both names." Marla said.

"You don't need to know."

"I can ask around and find out soon enough," Crosby said.

The Rector grasped a handful of Crosby's shirt, twisted it, and jerked him forward. "You don't want to mess with me, not even in a place of God."

Crosby's hands shot up in surrender mode. "Right. My apologies. I'm in a foreign country and need to be nice." The Rector released the shirt.

"Back to the story," Marla said. "You and your buddies split up after doing something wrong."

"I never thought of them as buddies, only fellow workers who shared an apartment and a bad idea."

"What happened?" Crosby asked.

The Rector shook his head.

"Why is Simic here?" Marla asked.

"Money."

"How did he find you here?" Crosby asked.

"I might have mentioned my family came from Montenegro. Months after I came to the seminary, I receive a letter from Simic asking for help. He said our old boss found him and wanted payback. He needed money. So, I helped."

"You helped him. Why is he extorting you?"

"He's just a bad person. Said he would tell the bishop what I did if I don't send him two thousand Euro each month."

"That's a lot of money. Where do you get that much?" Marla asked.

"Nothing repeatable."

They both nodded again.

"There are several successful wineries and sheep ranches nearby." Swinging a chair around, he sat down. His gaze dropped to the floor. "We have a public church in the seminary. Many seminaries do not, but this is a small town with the only Catholic Church in fifty kilometers. Part of my job is collecting the tithes and offerings. I decrease the money by five hundred each week. No one has any idea."

"Did Simic attend the sanctuary?" Crosby asked.

"No, of course not, but I forged certificates that said he did."

"He said he had a celebret from here," Marla said.

"When I saw him a few months ago, he said he was going to a small town to be a priest, and he needed to know some protocols. I taught him enough to be mediocre."

Simic shoved the bedroom door open and stood at the doorway with his torn cassock pinned together. He leveled a pistol at the Rector. "Who are you talking to?"

Rector Sudvaric shifted away from the door, keeping Crosby and Marla hidden from Simic.

Simic spoke in Croatian. "I know there are foreigners in town. Are they here to see you?"

"No one is here." He pointed at the radio. "I turned it off when you barged in."

"That was in English."

"I keep in practice. May return someday."

Simic waved the pistol barrel in the air. "I'm tired of this. It cost me a lot of time and money to come back here. I'm going to take your cut."

"And how are you going to do that? You know where the bag is?"

"I'm close. Expect to have all of it soon, except for the one piece you kept. It might have my fingerprint on it, so hand it over."

"That... you will never get." The Rector's eyes shifted toward the window.

Marla shoved the door, and Simic stumbled. The Rector threw a punch, knocking Simic to the floor. The gun fired.

Crosby and Marla ran out of the room and down the hall. At the end of the hallway, Crosby looked both ways. "Go left. Everybody goes right."

They turned into a room and closed the door. Stacks of kitchenware, pots and pans, and utensils were piled in the room. Heavy footsteps came closer. A shadow crossed the space at the bottom of the door. They both stood motionless and watched the shadow creep across the floor.

Simic's boot kicked the door open. He swung the pistol left-to-right. A frying pan slammed against his chest, and he dropped like a stringless marionette.

"Now what?" Marla looked around the room and found a ball of twine. "This is not much, but we can hog-tie him before he wakes. Won't hold him forever, but we can get out of here without being seen."

Crosby grabbed another piece of twine. "Looks like the twine I used to cook pork loin."

Marla pulled Simic's hands behind him. "Go check on the Rector. I got this."

Crosby ran to the Rector's room. He lay splayed across the floor with a bullet hole in his chest. Blood poured down the white t-shirt onto the floor.

With Crosby's help, the Rector sat up against the edge of the bed. "Anything I can do for you?"

The Rector gasped for air and pointed toward a cedar chest at the corner of the room. "Inside..." He coughed up a plug of blood and mucus. "Small black bag."

Opening the top of the chest, Crosby pointed. "Here?"

The Rector nodded. "Don't let Simic take it."

Crosby rummaged through the clothes. He held a small black felt bag in the air and looked back at the Rector. "This bag?"

He whispered, "Open it."

Crosby opened the bag, a Vatican City gold coin dropped into his palm.

Rector Sudvaric slid sideways and hit the floor; eyes frozen open.

Marla came back to the room and stared at the dead man on the floor. "We have to wipe down this room for our fingerprints." She grabbed the bottom of the cassock and wiped knobs and pictures.

A minute later, footsteps bounded up the stairs. Crosby put the coin and black bag in his pocket and opened the window. "You first."

"Don't be so chivalrous," Marla chuckled. "Ladies first and all that baloney?"

"Hey, I'm just trying to be a nice guy."

"Thanks, but you first. And if you break a leg, quietly let me know."

Crosby grabbed a small box from the dresser, and dropped it out the window. It disappeared into the deep snow. "Let's hope it's deep enough."

Chapter 17

Marla and Crosby walked in-step on the beach wearing knit beanie caps and most of their clothes from their carry-on bag. The Adriatic sea was deep lapis blue streaked with the gray of a moonshine. Saltiness filled the air while small waves rushed the beach every few seconds. She hung on to his arm for warmth.

Marla adjusted the watch on her wrist. "It's 10:40 PM here and mid-afternoon at home. I should call Pops and get more information about this fake priest. Simic had to have killed Walker in the church. His violent nature showed in the rage Simic exhibited tonight. The real question is why."

"And what about Rector Sudvaric's coin?" Crosby asked. He pulled out the black felt bag holding the coin from his pocket and held the coin between his fingers. "Looks like an image of a Pope and he has on a skullcap." He read the inscription on the front, "PIVS XII PMAN XX" Flipping it over, he read, "CITTA DEL VATICANO LIRE 100."

"Vaticano sounds like the Vatican," Marla said. "Didn't the Vatican used to make their own money?"

"Think they still do. This one has the year 1958."

"What's so special about it?" Marla typed in Vatican gold coin 1958 on her phone. "Wow. It's rare. Only three thousand made. Pope Pius the twelfth is on the front and his crest is on the back. It's a one hundred lire gold coin worth over a thousand bucks now."

"A thousand?" Crosby asked. "Sudvaric was embezzling thousands of Euros from the seminary. What's all the commotion about over a single thousand dollar coin, and why hide it?"

"Who knows, but Simic's willing to kill for it."

They paused at a small beachside cafe with a television on the wall. On the screen showed a picture of a smiling Rector Sudvaric.

Marla glanced at Crosby, then back at the television. "We wiped down the Rector's chambers, but we have our fingerprints all over the first floor."

"Hopefully, with a hundred other people's prints."

"Get your phone out and translate what they're saying."

Crosby opened the app. The newscaster's speech translated into words on his phone. They read the screen. "If anyone has information about Rector Sudvaric, please contact this number on the screen." The newscaster looked into the camera. The people in the café mumbled to each other. "Once again, Rector Sudvaric was found in his second-floor bedroom, dead from a gunshot to the chest. An outside camera captured a video of a green car parked near the front doors, and a man wearing a black cassock walking into the building." The video zoomed in to a blurry blob.

Marla whispered in Crosby's ear, "They've got Simic walking into the building, but it's too fuzzy to tell it's him." She stared at the screen. "Anything about a couple walking up?"

The screen changes to the townspeople speaking. Afterward, Crosby puts his phone in his pocket. "Nothing about," he glanced around them and murmured, "a couple."

"Simic won't show his face during daylight. He must be in his green car hiding," Marla swept her hand wide in the air, "somewhere out there."

"Right. Somewhere."

"Could we get lucky enough and have the Montenegrin Rangers or Mounted Police capture him?" Marla asked.

"I don't think they have Rangers here."

"Nothing like the Texas Rangers? Another reason not to live here."

Crosby tapped Marla's shoulder. "We should get to the airport and be on the flight back to Texas tonight," Crosby said. "I'll go online and buy two tickets."

"I'm all for not stepping foot in that room again," a shiver ran up her spine, "waiting for God-awful bugs to crawl on us another night. What if Simic wants to hop a ride on the red-eye? He doesn't need to know we were here."

"Good point. Let's check out his room. If his passport is there, he'll be back to get it tonight. We'll wait for him and then flatten his tires. That would make him miss the flight."

"And if the passport is not there?"

"Don't want to think about that."

◆

Crosby downshifted the transmission and then doused the headlights. Their car rounded the corner with Simic's motel room light on and his green car parked in front.

Marla pulled a pocketknife out and snapped open the blade. She pointed at the bushes past the motel. "Stop over there and let me out. Keep the motor running. Shouldn't take me long to flatten a couple of tires."

Crosby stopped the car. "He'll know someone's following him. Slashed tires don't happen by accident."

"Someone tied him up, so he knows something is awry." Marla said. "Hope he doesn't add up our involvement." She quietly closed her door and trailed around the bushes. Her chest tightened, and she coughed several times into her bent elbow. The entire building was dark except for the light from Simic's room. The dark parking area had no outside lights. She bent down and rushed to the right side of his car.

Simic's glass door slid open. Wearing the sweater and jeans again, he drug his carry-on bag behind him outside. Marla crawled around to the front of the car while Simic stopped at the left passenger door, opened it, pitched his bag onto the seat, and closed the door. He stared out at the road. Fifty feet away, a line of white smoke streamed up in the air from behind the bushes. An engine hummed. The road was as dark as the motel. He looked left and right for any headlights. Across the street, at the other motel, sat a few parked cars. His shoes crunched across snow-crusted gravel as he strode toward the bushes.

Marla peered around the front of his car. She couldn't call out to Crosby. She texted, GO NOW. It bounced back as *message sent failed.*

Simic stood a foot away from the back corner of Crosby's car. White mist billowed out the tailpipe. He rushed to the front door and flung it open--- the vehicle was empty. There were no papers, clothes, or information in the front or back seat. He glanced back at his room to see the door open, lights on, and his car parked in front. His eyes widening, he sprinted back into his room. Someone had emptied the satchel on the bed. Bundles of money, car keys, and plane ticket splayed across the unmade bed. He shuffled through the contents, spreading all evenly with one item missing. His passport was gone.

The bathroom door was open, and the light was on. Simic knew he'd shut it off. Moving back from the bed, he called out in Croatian, "Come out from under the bed. I have a gun."

He noticed the square alarm clock was missing from the nightstand. From the reflection in the bathroom mirror, his eyes caught two hands swinging the clock toward his head.

Marla stepped forward from behind the front door, swung the clock with all her might, and hit Simic on the back of the head. He dropped face forward, blood splattered from his nose across the floor. She ran from the room and shot past the bushes to find Crosby waiting for her in the vehicle. "We got to go." She looked back at Simic's room, then Crosby. "How did he..."

"How did he not see me?" Crosby replied. "I saw him coming, so I got out, walked around the bush, then back to the car when he ran to his room." He waved his hand at her to get into the car. "We need to go."

Marla pitched Simic's passport in the bushes and squeezed into the vehicle. Crosby hit the gas before she closed her door. He flipped the headlights on and charged down the road.

Simic rolled to his hands and knees as blood poured from the back of his head and his nose. "I'm going to kill whoever that was." He pushed his hand against the skin to stop the flow; it didn't help. Outside, a motor revved. He sprinted out the door with blood covering his shirt and face and opened the car door, pulled out the pistol under the seat, and fired twice at the taillights.

Crosby asked, "Did you flatten his tires?"

Marla's lungs spasmed with hard coughs.

"Marla? Did you cut his tires?"

"No. Didn't have time." She coughed again. "He was right on me. If I cut a tire, he would have heard it."

Crosby glanced at the rearview mirror. Two headlights were closing in from behind. "He's coming."

Marla shifted and looked behind her, then spun around. "He'll catch up to us before we get to the airport."

They passed a road sign, Lake Skadar 5km. "He'll catch us before we make it to the lake." Crosby glanced at the rearview mirror again. The headlights had enlarged. "My guess is about the time we hit the curves near the lake."

Simic focused on the two taillights in front of him while his hand rested on the pistol in the passenger seat. His vehicle zipped by the Lake Skadar sign. The red lights disappeared around a curve. His car drifted down to the oncoming lane and hugged the corner like a race car. The taillights reappeared closer than before.

Crosby glanced at the headlights, then turned a hard right at the next curve. "We have maybe a minute before he's on us."

"Got an idea." Marla clambered to the back seat. She unzipped her bag and rolled down the window. "This won't stop him, but it might slow him some."

After another curve, Simic was close enough to read the license plate number. "You are dead. Here me? Dead." He swiped blood off his nose and lips before swallowing away the metallic taste. His index finger played with the trigger guard of the pistol. "Dead."

Marla threw a pair of pants out the window. It floated in front of Simic's car. She dug into the bag and pitched a running shoe out the window, ricocheting off the windshield. She felt inside the bag and smiled. "Got something for you, preacher man." She held her curling iron in the air. "Never had a chance to use this." It bounced on the pavement and hit the left headlight. She whooped, "Strike one!"

Crosby glanced at the car behind him with one headlight and smirked. "Top-notch aim. Do it again." He turned left on another tight curve, and passed another sign, Lake Skadar 2km.

Marla shoved her bag out through the window. It bounced on the pavement and knocked out the other headlight. Simic's car went dark.

Crosby looked at the rearview mirror. "Great job."

The road evened out, and Crosby shoved the accelerator to the floor. The dark restaurant appeared on the other side of the bridge. There were no cars or boats.

Simic's vehicle slammed into the rear end of their car, smashing the right taillight. He fired the pistol through his windshield and shattered their back window. He aimed the gun out the side window, drifted left, and struggled to get a better angle on the driver.

Marla flattened out in the small seat. "Not expecting bullets." Another bullet shot through their open back window and blew a hole through the windshield. Crosby jerked the wheel right, then left.

"My bag is gone," Marla yelled. "Got your bag of clothes and one more of my shoes. That's all the weapons I have back here." With her head down, she flung her shoe out the window.

The bridge was a few hundred yards away. Simic's car rammed into their back end again.

"Sit tight." Crosby slammed on the brakes. Marla rolled against the back of the front seats.

Simic watched the single taillight turn bright red. Tires squealed in front of him. He jerked the steering wheel hard right, missing the edge of the oncoming bridge. The car bounced across the grass and onto the beach, where the tires stuck deep into the sand. He pounded the steering wheel and watched the single taillight pass over the bridge.

"Are you alright?" Crosby asked.

Marla sat up and swept her hair from her face. "I think so." She pushed Crosby's empty bag away from her. All his clothes had spilled out on the floorboard. "What are we going to do about the car?"

"Don't know."

"The trunk looks like The Hulk pounded it a dozen times." She climbed over the passenger seat and sat down next to Crosby. Her fingertip touched two bullet holes in the windshield. "How are we going to justify all this to the police?"

"We don't have to return the car until tomorrow." He pointed to a hotel by the beach. "Let's leave it there and call for a taxi to the airport. By the time they discover we're late turning it in, we'll be back in Texas."

"Let's hope there's no extradition for not having rental insurance."

The car limped off the road to the entrance of the hotel and stopped at the far corner of the lot.

Marla pushed on the door with her shoulder, but it was stuck. Leaning back, she kicked the door open, rolled out, then butt-pushed the door closed, but it creaked back open. Gentle sounds of repetitive waves rolled over the beach. Fresh air filled her lungs and tasted good. It was an unexpected pleasure to breathe deep without a residual cough. While hiking down the rock stairs to the sandy beach, she yanked her phone from her back pocket. "You call for a taxi, and I'm calling Pops. He can research this guy while we're in the air." Marla dialed the number.

Searcy answered before the first ring ended. "Where are you and why is your truck at the airport?"

"How did you know that?" Marla asked.

"Did you forget, every police vehicle has a GPS monitor on it?"

Marla mouthed toward Crosby, *Damn.*

"Pops, we need more information on Father Jules. His actual name is Benny Simic, and he's not a real priest. I think he killed Walker, but we need to find the reason he came to Hildebrandt."

"You think our priest is the killer? You need to tell me where you are."

Marla shook her head. "Pops, you pick the funniest times to ask the funniest questions. It doesn't matter where I am. I need the info, quick."

"Don't hang up. I have new information. Are you sitting down?" Searcy said.

"No, we're walking on the beach." *Damn, didn't mean to say the beach.*

"What beach? I need you back here, ASAP."

"We can be back tomorrow. What's the information?" Marla asked.

"There's been another murder."

Chapter 18

A s the pilot slowed the Embraer 175 engines, the plane shook in response. Crosby's seat vibrated like a massage chair five-thousand feet in the sky. He held the gold coin between his fingers. Marla glanced at it.

He flipped it over in his palm. "Citta Del Vaticano on the back and a man on the front?"

"You think it might be one of the Popes?"

"Looks like it." He placed it back in the black bag, then into his pocket. His hand touched the cool window next to him and looked down below the wing at a straight line of headlights aimed toward San Antonio. Out past the highway, hundreds of pinpoint lights scattered across the blackness. He pointed at a small mass of lights. "I think that's Hildebrandt."

Marla crossed her legs toward Crosby, pressed her shoulder against him, and leaned forward to look outside. Their fingers interlocked on the armrest. From the other side of the plane, a passenger raised the window shade. A yellow hue rose above the horizon and shot warmth inside the bulkhead. The aircraft floated slowly lower, veered left, and revealed a bustling airport below them.

A little more than an hour later, Crosby's gray Dodge Ram pickup crossed over the cattle guard at the JK-4 Ranch, where sheep, lambs, and goats dotted several acres. Yellow crime scene tape encircled the small house and shearing shed. Searcy stood near the house, watching them pull closer and stop.

Marla instinctively tapped her holster as she trailed around the truck. Rumors always flew that James Kinsey, owner of the JK-4, was involved with the cartel.

"What happened?" Crosby asked as he closed his door.

"Where were you two?" Searcy asked.

"A couple of days at the beach," Marla said.

"We had a murder in town, and you left?"

Marla covered with, "I think what you meant to say was 'You left town, and we had another murder.'"

Searcy waved his hand toward the shearing shed. "Disturbing. See for yourself."

Past the wooden door, splotches of blood-red sand covered the floor. A cold campfire had partially burnt branches in the center.

"This is the scene." Searcy pointed to the floor, and all three bent down. "The bloated bodies have been removed—but imagine this. Two dead sheared sheep are lying next to a burned-out campfire with bellies sliced open and guts pulled out." Searcy pointed to the other side of the blackened wood, "The vic was lying here, stretched out on the ground, his abdomen split open top to bottom, and intestines pulled to the side and cut off, just like the sheep except his head bashed in with a blunt object and his throat slit."

Searcy pointed to the blood-splattered wall. "Not sure if it's human or sheep. We'll find out later. My guess, he was already dead from his throat cut. From the angle of the head wound, the killer hit him after James was flat on the ground." He shook his head in disgust. "Brutal."

"What about the house? Anything out of place? Ransacked?" Marla asked.

"We found a garbage bag full of oxycodone ripped open with pills on the floor, and ten pounds of weed," Searcy said.

"The stolen oxy?" Crosby asked. "You think he's connected to a Cartel?"

Searcy shook his head. "I've never been able to catch cartel mules here."

Marla asked, "Isn't Logan's landlord this guy? I remember him saying Kinsey was forcing them to move out of their rent house."

"Are you saying Logan has something to do with this?" Searcy asked.

Crosby glanced at the tools and equipment hanging on the wall in its correct place. "Doesn't look like a scuffle. Do you think Mr. Kinsey knew the person?"

Searcy said, "James had the same three men come back every year for the shearing season. But he had struggled with getting paid for the wool this year. Perhaps they robbed and killed him."

"You know them?" Marla asked.

"I know everyone in this county."

"Where do you think they are now?"

"My guess is back across the border. We'll never see them again."

Crosby knelt next to the campfire. "Sticks propped up like a teepee. The fire didn't burn well." He reached over and touched the partially burnt wood. "Under the sticks were burned intestines like a ritual. Not sure whether it's the sheep or human remains in the fire, but that slowed the fire down. It never got hot." He pushed the charred intestines to the side. Crosby stood again, "Why would someone build a fire next to a dead man and two slaughtered sheep?"

Marla shook her head. "Pops, anything else cut out from the sheep?" Marla asked. "Heart, liver?"

"No. We sent the animals to the Vet. After his examination, he incinerated them. The victim went to the Bexar County Morgue. That reminds me, Dr. Berghoff said he's finished with the autopsy and wants to see both of you at 4 PM."

Crosby chuckled. "Looks like we get to go back to your happy place. Want to stop and get a sausage plate before we go?"

Chapter 19

A few hours later, Crosby pulled into an angled parking space on the street behind the police station. Marla followed him through the back door. They walked down the hallway into the squad room. Marla headed for the coffeepot, and Crosby aimed straight for Searcy's office, and between the open blinds, caught the chief sitting in his chair yelling at no one. He slammed his fist onto the desktop and stood.

Crosby thought, *who the hell is pissing him off? Like it doesn't take much.*

Searcy leaned into the speaker on the office phone. "Listen to me, Mayor Pichler, I am in control of this. We do not need the Texas Rangers taking over this town. It would scare the hell out of everyone. Why don't you worry about the budget or the Summer Sausage Festival, or the... I don't know, anything but my business?" Searcy pushed the disconnect button on his phone.

Crosby knocked on the door.

Searcy rubbed his forehead. "What?" He looked at the door and motioned to Crosby. "Come in."

"Chief, I have something I would like for you to look at." He pulled the felt bag from his jacket pocket and opened it.

Searcy peered at him over his half-rim glasses. "What is that?" He held his hand out. "Let me see."

Crosby dropped the gold coin into his palm. "Ever seen one of these?"

Flipping the coin between his fingers, Searcy asked. "Where'd you get this?"

"Gift. Someone gave it to me."

"It's not American. Where's it from?" Searcy asked.

Crosby wasn't ready to say where he obtained it. "Not sure. Italian?" He dropped the empty bag on the desk.

"I know an antique coin dealer in San Antone." Searcy slipped the coin in his shirt pocket. "I'll call him and get an answer for you." Searcy stood and pointed out the door. "Logan said he has something. Let's find out what he has."

The squad room had pictures of Walker, Kinsey, dead sheep, and Mitch and Lizzie DeVries tacked on the corkboard.

Logan tapped his finger on the images on the wall. "Walker and Kinsey are dead," he turned toward Marla, "and no, I didn't kill him."

"Don't you rent your house from him?" Marla asked. "Weren't you yelling at him a few days ago about having to move out? What was that about?"

"So what? I'm not going to kill a man over rent." Logan continued. "The DeVries are missing. Per DMV, they sold their car in San Antonio the day after Walker died. I called the used car lot, and they paid cash for it."

Marla poured coffee into her insulated mug. "We should go by there and check out the car."

"Too late. The dealer had already detailed the car and gave it to his daughter in high school."

Marla sipped her coffee while walking to her desk. "We need to find out if there is a connection between Walker and Kinsey. Two murders in a week will rattle this town."

"Kinsey moved here about ten years ago," Logan said. "Had transients work on his ranch. He owned several properties in town." Logan stopped and stared at Marla.

She held her hands in the air. "You said you didn't kill him."

Logan turned back to images on the wall. "Widowed a few years ago. Two girls, both married and moved away."

"Have we contacted them as next of kin?" Marla asked.

"Both said good riddance and hung up on me," Searcy said.

"Damn, I forgot to make a call." Logan grabbed his phone and dialed a number. He held his hand over the phone and murmured into it. "Hi, Tony. Did you find out anything?"

"Not a good idea to be making secretive calls." Marla said.

"Right, thanks." Logan said on his phone. "I owe you big time."

Logan put the phone on his desk. "We're on the wrong connection. It's not Walker and Kinsey. It's Walker and the priest. I just talked to Tony Sanchez at the Texas Department of Public Safety office. They have a registry of all the PIs in Texas, and Walker does not have a Texas license. I called the Alabama State Board this morning, and I'm waiting for a return call to tell me what year he registered there."

Marla sipped her coffee, then asked, "So what's the connection?"

"We all know about Major Walker's heroics. I had a feeling Walker was not as clean cut as some think, so I called a buddy who's a big shot in a PMC, a private military contractor. After Walker's honorable discharge from the Marines, he joined a PMC and went to Albania, hence the scars. It borders Montenegro, where Father Jules is from."

Marla and Crosby's eyes met.

Logan pointed at the Walker photo on the wall. "That's too much of a coincidence to be a coincidence."

Chapter 20

After the discussion in the squad room, Searcy stood. "Good work, Logan. Keep looking into Walker's business with the PMC and his possible connection with Father Jules in Montenegro." Searcy pointed at Crosby and said, "You and Marla, go recheck the DeVries' apartment. They could have snuck back and gathered clothes. After that, don't forget Dr. Berghoff wants to see you in San Antonio at four o'clock."

Yellow crime scene tape flapped in the wind in front of the DeVries' apartment. Crosby squeezed under the police tape, unlocked, and opened the door, then went inside. Marla followed. The air was stale and heavy.

"Looks like they skipped out of town as quick as possible and left enough paraphernalia to run a small cocaine store." She said. There were no changes from the pictures previously shown at the station. "Can't remember if the mirror, scale, rolled dollar bills, spoons, and lighters are in the same place."

"I'll take the bedroom," Crosby said. "You sweep the kitchen and fridge for any fresh food."

The unmade bed had dirty clothing spilled across it. The closet had a few wire hangers hung on the rail, with dust bunnies collected on the floor. Crosby pulled out each of the dresser drawers, revealing most clothes gone. The toilet water had a slow swirl. He jiggled the handle, and the water stopped. The sink and tub were dry. He grasped the towels in several places, nothing wet.

Marla flipped the lights on in the kitchen. She noticed a freshwater drop on the countertop and a spoon next to an open one-pound bag of sugar. Her fingertips touched the warm coffee carafe. A fresh yellow banana skin, minus the banana, rested next to the sink. A clunk came from behind the pantry door.

Marla crept to the wall. "Police, come out with your hands up." Marla's fingertips touched her holster. "Come on, out with you."

The knob turned, and the pantry door creaked open. A woman stuck her head out and put her hands above her head. "Whoa, Officer. We didn't do nothing wrong."

Marla grabbed the woman's arm, twisted it behind her back, and pushed her face down on the countertop. "Why are you here?"

She tried reaching for Marla's hand on the back of her neck. "Nothing."

Crosby walked into the kitchen. He recognized her. "Damn, Caitlin." He took her free hand and placed it flat on the counter. "What are you doing here?"

"I'm sorry. Okay? Let me go."

Marla looked to Crosby. He shook his head and said, "All good."

She released the girl.

Jimmy leaned out from the pantry with his hands held high. Caitlin spun around to him. "Put your hands down, idiot. Nobody's going to shoot you." She looked at Crosby and shrugged her shoulders.

"Why are you here?" Marla asked.

"It's a place to sleep."

A few minutes later, the four of them were sitting at the kitchen table. Caitlin explained their hard life was getting harder. No one will hire a junkie, two junkies. "I didn't think anyone would come back here for a long time, so we crashed here for the last couple of days. It's safer than under bridges."

Crosby's phone rang. "Officer Adams."

"Dr. Berghoff here. I have finished the autopsy, and you have a serial killer. Need to come see what I have for you."

Crosby mouthed the word Berghoff at Marla. "Thanks, Doc. We'll be there within the hour. I'm looking forward to it."

The doctor laughed. "Yes, I thought so."

Marla stood and pointed toward the front door. "Both of you need to leave. You can't stay here. This is a crime scene."

"We got no place to go. Can't we sleep here tonight?" Caitlin eyed Crosby. "I mean, we got some pretty good history between us, right Crosby? One more night." She pointed to the kitchen. "We slept on the floor last night. We'll do it again and won't mess with anything. I promise. Jimmy and me, we'll leave tomorrow."

Crosby rubbed the back of his neck and glanced at Marla. "They've already been here for a few nights. One more?"

Marla headed toward the door with her hands up in capitulation. "We need to get to the morgue. Let's go."

Crosby's truck left the apartment building parking lot and stopped at the red light. He felt her waiting for him to explain.

"I've known Caitlin since she was in elementary school. Her older sister ran away, and we never heard from her again. Caitlin discovered marijuana at thirteen. She dropped out of middle school and bounced to every late-night party in town. I arrested her on her sixteenth birthday."

"So, you arrested *another* schoolmate and sent them to jail. You are going to be really popular at the next high school reunion."

"Well, I sort of arrested her." The light turned green. "I was her main character witness and told the judge she's fixable. He sent her to drug rehab for three months. She cleaned up, was a waitress at several places in town, and stayed out of trouble for years."

"What happened?"

"The police found her sister inside a dumpster in Hollywood. Needle marks on her arms, legs, toes, neck, everywhere. They said she was a five-dollar prostitute with numerous arrests. Caitlin couldn't take it. She dive-bombed hard." Their truck crossed the intersection. "I think she still has a chance."

"Let's hope so," Marla said.

"We have an appointment back at San Antone." Crosby turned the truck onto the highway. "We need to talk about Jules, or Simic. What are we going to do about him?"

"We know he killed a man in Montenegro, but it would take months to get anywhere with that."

"Right," Crosby said. "That certificate he has on his wall is fake, but not sure about warrants or subpoenas in another country. Who is going to investigate all that?"

Marla scooted back in her seat. "If we implicate this guy, then that shows we were there. There are a few laws we probably broke, leaving a scene of a crime, taking evidence, and stealing records, to name a few."

"What about evading arrest? Skipping the country? And don't forget about the car we totaled." Crosby tapped the steering wheel. "We are backed into a corner on this."

◆

Crosby's truck stopped at the back of the building. He cleared his throat and asked Marla, "Okay, ready?"

She held a mask in her hand. "Ready."

At the morgue entrance, Marla took deep breaths like a snorkeler would before a deep dive. She hoped the mask would cover the odor, except formaldehyde, rubbing alcohol, and whatever else seeped through the mask with ease. She squeezed her eyes closed for a second, then quickly glanced at Crosby. He opened the door.

"What have you got, Doc?" Crosby asked.

Marla doesn't want to look. Once again, another body laid on the steel table with a white sheet over the lower half, except this one looked more like a dark red balloon ready to pop than a human. Once again, Dr. Berghoff had sliced open the chest and sewed it back together with a ¼ inch white cotton cord from neck to groin. And once again, acid gurgled like boiling witch's brew and climbed up Marla's esophagus.

Large forceps big enough to help deliver a calf were next to the body. The doctor took them and pointed at the head. "As you can see, he died from a fatal cut to the throat." He moved to the head of the table, and with the forceps, picked up the sawed-off skullcap. "A single blow to the head with a blunt object fractured the skull. The brain didn't bleed much. I suspect he was already dead when hit on the head."

"Doc," Marla said. "It's not necessary to show all this to me. I can read your report tomorrow."

"Taser marks on the chest, just like your last victim." Dr. Berghoff pinched the side of the nostril with the forceps in a way that would make anyone alive cry in pain. "Look at the nose, mouth, and neck. Blowfly maggots."

"Not necessary, Doc. I can read reports just as easily."

Crosby smirked and patted the back of her shoulder. "Hang in there with me."

"Blowflies can smell death a mile away. Within minutes, the female lays eggs. In a day, a day and a half, the eggs hatch. The first stage of maggots arise one to two days after that. The victim's stomach was sliced open with a sharp instrument, the edges of the skin were clean and straight, and a third of the small intestines were pulled out and cut." He tapped the forceps on the scaphoid abdomen. "I've closed the cavity but took pictures. You can see them over there if you want."

Marla rubbed her brow with the back of her hand. "Thanks for, uh... closing that up."

"I'm thinking bratwurst and sauerkraut tonight," Crosby patted her mid-back. "Sound good, Marla?"

Dr. Berghoff rubbed his finger across the victim's forearm. "Veins are noticeable now. The skin is blistering, breaking down. The color turned from white to green to red."

"Estimated time of death?" Marla asked.

"Being outside, weather changes, temperature night and day, blowfly larva, other stuff—three to five days. I think this happened in the evening because the victim had a coat on. I checked the weather reports over the last week and the mornings were cool, the afternoons were warm, but the evenings brought a chill enough for a coat."

Crosby said, "Father Jules could have been after the oxycodone and killed Kinsey before he went to the airport."

"You think he was involved in the stolen drugs from the airport?" Marla asked.

"Just throwing possibilities out," Crosby said.

Marla cleared her throat. "Is Logan mixed up in this? Walker and Jules could have known each other. Kinsey could have witnessed the murder. Did Logan know this?" She rubbed her shotgun pin on her shirt pocket. "He acts like he doesn't know the priest."

Dr. Berghoff cleared his throat.

"Sorry, Doc. We're throwing out ideas."

"That's perfectly fine." He handed Crosby blue surgical gloves and motioned to him to slip them on.

"Doc? What exactly do you want me to do?" Crosby asked.

"Don't worry. I'm finished." Dr. Berghoff pointed to his shoulder. "Arthritis. Some days it flares for no reason. Be so kind as to roll the body over on its side, please."

Crosby reluctantly slipped the gloves on and pushed the cadaver's shoulder and hip up and over. The stench from the decayed body increased. His lips tightened under the mask as he held his breath.

The doctor pointed at the victim's back. "There are numbers again. The killer cut into the back." He pointed with the forceps. "Cut across both scapulas is the number 35." He looked at Crosby. "You may put him down."

"Is it thirty-five or two separate numbers, a three and a five?" Marla asked.

"Excellent question, but I'll leave that to your department. Sorry, but I must clean up and get to Dallas before the opera tonight." He chuckled, "My wife would kill me if I missed that."

"Doc, Dallas can be a four-hour drive on I-35."

The doctor pointed up in the air. "Private airplane."

Chapter 21

B ack in downtown Hildebrandt, the sun hung just above the two-story buildings. The sidewalk had diamond cutouts in the concrete, with fifteen-foot trees standing tall in each hole. Birds chirped on top branches while cars trolled for empty parking spots. Crosby and Marla scooted across the street. Even with a mild Texas winter, sweat collected between Crosby's neck and collar.

In the corner of Cup Of Joe's Cafe, a teenager played country music on her acoustic guitar. Marla marched to the counter and reviewed the liquid menu items on the blackboard. "Hi, Misty. I'll take a small cafe mocha."

"You want whipped cream on it or the lactose-free stuff?"

"The cream from a real cow and put a little bit of extra chocolate in it, please."

Crosby angled his head at Marla like a confused dog, then announced loudly, "I'll take a medium black coffee."

Misty's 'May-I-Help-You' eyes gazed at her customer. Her smile widened as she asked, "Just coffee? Want room for cream?"

He shook his head in short, rapid movements. "No, thanks."

"How about a shot of espresso or caramel, just for fun?"

Marla stepped in front of Crosby, "Misty, you know Crosby. He doesn't like that poofy stuff. Do you have any coffee leftover from yesterday or, better yet, the day before? He'd rather have that."

They sat at a small table and looked up at the television hung on the wall. Everyone focused on the screen. Rebekah Farmsdale from San Antonio Channel Ten News reported information about the second murder and the Hildebrandt Police Department's refusal to give her information on the rumors the killings were connected. Marla looked across the crowd as all heads turned toward Crosby and her. "Sorry, folks. I got nothing."

Crosby slipped an OxyContin from his shirt pocket past his lips. A quick sip washed it down his throat.

Marla flashed her eyes toward him and then whispered, "No more today. Understand?"

Two tables over, Nicole, a pre-k teacher, asked, "Marla, do we need to worry?"

Shaking her head as she sipped her coffee, Marla's hand waved the question off. "No, I don't think we have anything to worry about...right now. Just be watchful and know your surroundings, like any other day of the week."

"I should start carrying my pistol in my shoulder holster instead of my purse," Nicole said. "I can get to it faster."

"Thank God for Texas women," Marla whispered to herself, then put her coffee cup down. "Don't get ahead of yourself, people. No one needs to open carry their pistols."

One table over, a heavyset man wearing overalls and a plaid shirt twisted his chair toward Crosby. "Should I put my shotgun back in my truck?"

Another asked, "Why are the police holding back information? I like Rebekah. She's a local girl, and if she asks for something, she should get it. The news station should know everything."

She whispered to Crosby, "Time to go."

Back in the truck, Marla blurted out, "Crosby." Her firm voice demanded an answer. "How many have you had today?"

Crosby stared straight ahead. "Not sure. I don't count. I just take them when the pain comes."

"Do I need to call Dr. Sanborn and tell him to slow you down?"

"I watch how many I take. The burns, the scars; they still hurt. You don't understand."

Marla's elbow hit the side of the door. "I understand." She wiped a thin layer of dust off the dashboard. "But you must be careful with that stuff. You're a police officer, and if you discharge your gun, you won't pass a drug test."

Crosby's voice raised as he turned a corner. "I don't take *this stuff* to get high or a buzz. I take it to stop the pain."

"I know it's addictive. You know it's addictive. Grandmothers get hooked on oxy. Why not you?"

"I got it under control. I can cut down anytime I want to. You want me to live in pain every day?"

"No, and another thing, don't drink with that in your system. We've already seen bad shit happen when you do that. I don't carry enough Narcan and EpiPens on me for your next cardiac arrest."

"I think we need to talk to Moon again. He knows more than all of us." Crosby's back burned against the seat. He could use another oxy.

"Drop me off at the Meals On Wheels office. Last month, I told them I would help pack the meals." She snapped her seatbelt. "After that, let's see Moon."

✦

People lined up like Ford assembly line workers placing their assigned items in the Meals On Wheels sacks. Marla glanced at the M-O-W printed in large letters on the outside wall. She opened the front door, and everyone waved and said hello. The only spot open was next to Rebekah Farmsdale.

Marla stepped in line and looked at her two boxes of vegetables. She stuffed an avocado and a banana in the sack. "Saw you on the news a few minutes ago. Pretty strong accusations."

Rebekah smiled while putting a protein drink into the sack in front of her. "Recorded it this morning so I could make it here today. Sorry, my boss tells me to push the envelope."

"Hmm. I haven't seen you here before."

"Right. I always went to The Food Pantry in downtown San Antonio near the Alamo. You know, the homeless shelter."

"Why the change?"

"The shelter was Mom's favorite. On the board forever and past president several years ago." She sighed heavily. "The last few months, her health had diminished significantly. M-O-W came every week and gave her food. Mom died a few weeks ago, so I switched."

"Do you drive here every week?"

"Not a problem. My house is right off FM 404." She snapped her finger. "Here in a flash."

"Your house? Not married?" Marla asked.

Rebekah stuffed a drink in the next sack and then passed it to Marla. "No. Can't seem to find anyone that doesn't want sex after the first handshake."

Marla scoffed. "Right. Men."

"You better hold on to yours," Rebekah said. "He's the only one in high school who didn't try to jump my bones on the first date."

Marla half-smiled. "And the second date?"

❖

A ray of sunshine as wide as an open door flowed into The Crescent when Crosby and Marla entered in. The door closed, darkening the bar except for the television monitor in the corner. They needed a few seconds for their eyes to adjust. On the back side, Budweiser lights hung over pool tables. Their boots knocked on the wood floor with each step.

Moon stood on the other side of the bar with a smile. "I was expecting you sometime today after finishing up at M-O-W."

They sat on the bar stools. "Yeah? Why today?" Crosby asked.

"I meant Marla," Moon said. "Her aura. I could feel the wish to see me again."

"Thanks, Moon." She glanced at Crosby. "He knows where everyone is." She pushed the peanut bowl away from her. "You got that feeling what I am going to ask next?"

"How about, do I know anything about anything since the last time you were here?"

Marla smirked at Crosby. "He's good. He has this bar, the girls like him, *and* he's a soothsayer." She looked back at him and asked, "Moon, if you are that good, then tell me if the Cowboys will win their division this year."

"I could, but then no fun in watching the games. Have you ever watched a replay of a game? No, of course not. Boring." He leaned toward her and whispered, "And I guarantee you will never lose money on the Cowboys again. In fact, I could make you forget all about the Cowboys."

"Moon," Crosby's knuckles rapped the counter. "I can hear you."

Moon wiped the bar top. "Sorry. Need something to drink?"

"Coke for me," Crosby said.

"And a Cosmo for the lady?" Moon quipped.

"Not now. I am on duty. Water, please."

Moon shook his head. "I feel a massive tip coming from this bar bill." He filled two glasses with ice and squirted Coke in one and water in the other.

Marla glanced at the screen hanging up in the corner. "Is that Eileen Lieb on television?"

Moon scoffed. "Yeah. She and her live-in, love-in are doing an infomercial."

"About what?"

"The Chili Cook-off in a few days."

Crosby glanced at the monitor. "Why advertise? The festival is always packed."

Moon rubbed a glass with his towel. "She wants to win."

"Everyone wants to win. I remember the two best ever. The moose meat from Alaska a few years ago, and the javelina last year. That is one of the ugliest animals, but the Bergen brothers made it so tender."

Moon slid beer glasses on a rack behind him. "She wants to win without meat."

Marla laughed. "Meatless chili. What's left, tomatoes, onions, peppers, spices?"

Crosby sipped his Coke. "You have to put meat in chili, otherwise, it's vegetable stew."

"She and Ron say they have the perfect recipe, and she's ready to kill for first prize." He smirked. "Not kill an animal, just the other participants."

"Don't need any more of that in town," Marla said.

"You never want to see her on the wrong side of the witness stand. As an attorney, she has committed her career to suing meat packers and ranchers. She's a vegan and hates anyone who eats meat. She said she could smell a meat-eater coming around a corner."

Marla chuckled. "I don't think we'll be inviting her over for Christmas dinner."

Moon pointed at the screen. "Ronald Abrams is a wuss. He snaps to attention anytime Eileen spits on the floor. She doesn't have a dog. Doesn't need one, not with her man-puppy gladly following her around."

"I thought he was a restaurant manager in town," Crosby said.

"Right. The two met at a charity function. I ran the bar. He was the manager at All Things Meat." He shrugged his shoulders. "He outbid her on five-hundred pounds of compost. Do you know what compost is made of? Grass, trees, leftovers, and piles of dog..."

"Moon!" Marla blurted. "I know what's in compost."

"Anyway, he came to the bar for a refill. She squeezed in next to him and stuffed a ten spot in my tip jar. She had the biggest smile I have ever seen on her. They forgot about charity activities and stood holding drinks and hands for the next hour. She told him he could have sex with her or eat meat. He quit his job the next day and moved into her house."

"A vegan and a meat manager, interesting combo," Marla quipped as she twisted toward Moon. "Back to why we are here."

Moon wiped his towel across the counter in front of them. "You need to check out Private Investigator Roberto Sardino's gun you found in the church, and Walker was not who he seemed to be. The three illegals at the Kinsey ranch are back in Mexico. The rumor is they saw the aftermath and high-tailed it toward another ranch they work at in New Mexico, but ICE agents spooked them at the same grocery store they stopped at near Laredo. My gut feeling? Air Force planes were overhead flying touch-and-go all night between East and West Texas that night, found them, and sent the ICE agents. They record everything under the planes. Who knows? They might have pictures of who was at Kinsey's ranch."

"Pictures?" Crosby asked. "You think the Air Force is recording everyone's movements on the ground?"

"Yeah, sure. Big Brother, I'm from the government, and I'm here to help. Do you trust them, and everything they say is the truth? They say the VA health system is the best in the world. How would you like to lie in a VA hospital bed for a week? They want to know what meds you're taking, how much booze you drink, how many cigarettes you buy, which car you drive, and how many hairs on your balls. The planes play laser tag on you when you walk out that door."

Crosby nodded slowly. "Uh-huh. Sure." He sipped through the straw again, then pushed the glass aside. "Do you think you can help get us in contact with the three illegals? Meet us at the border. They stay in Mexico, we in Texas, so we can't arrest them. If not face-to-face, do a phone call."

"That might cost you more than the price of a Coke."

"Moon, what do you want from us?" Marla asked.

"Not from you, from the building inspector. He's been dragging his feet and asking too many questions about my grill expansion in the back. There's big money in barbecued ribs."

"You mean, Mr. Hickman," Marla said.

"Yeah. Hickey has been riding me hard on all the building codes and crap."

"I could ask him to speed up his approval if we get to talk to the three guys," Crosby said.

"Okay, thanks. I'll arrange the meet in a day or two."

"I'll wait for your call." Crosby stood from the stool. "Time we mosey on."

"That's two dollars for the Coke?"

Crosby and Marla pushed the stools forward. "Put it on my tab."

"You don't have a tab." He watched the door close behind them.

They strolled across the parking lot to their truck.

"Are you going to ask Mr. Hickman to sidestep Moon's renovation?"

"No, of course not. I don't want the roof to fall in on me while I'm eating ribs."

The truck doors shut like a vacuum. The diesel engine cranked alive while the heater fan blew air on the windshield. Condensation peeled off from bottom to top. The police radio crackled. "Crosby, come in."

He snapped down the microphone button. "Here."

Searcy replied, "Got a missing person's report from Mrs. Cross. She hasn't seen Willie and his friend, Ethan Dutton, for three days."

"We know these two," Crosby said. "Both have Juvi records. Any idea where they might be?"

Searcy replied, "Head over to the Cross' house and talk to the mother."

Marla leaned toward the radio. "Pops, they hang out at the skateboard park and the video game store. We'll drive by those on the way over there."

Forty minutes later, with Willie nor Ethan found at the two places, they stopped in front of the Cross address.

A slightly overweight lady in a floral dress looking from a 1950s LIFE magazine stood on the porch and waved her hands like a ground crewman directing a plane on the tarmac. She called out, "Crosby, come in, come in."

All three entered the house, and Crosby shut the front door behind him. They stood next to the entrance of her small living room.

"Mrs. Cross, I don't think you've met my wife, Officer Marla Adams." They both nodded their acquaintance and shook hands. "You filed a missing person report this morning?"

"Willie is gone. I can't get him to answer the phone."

Crosby motioned to the chairs in the room. "May we sit?"

"Yes, of course." She fluffed two square pillows resting against the back of the couch. "Please find my Willie."

Crosby sat down next to Marla, and almost at once, a yellow tabby cat jumped into her lap. "How long has it been since you last saw him?" she asked.

She swept the back of her dress with her hands, then sat in a chair. "Three days. Willie has never been gone that long."

"He's disappeared for one or two days before?" The cat purred when Marla instinctively rubbed behind the cat's ears.

"Since Willie graduated from high school last summer, he and that vagabond, Ethan, have gone out overnight several times. Ethan is too old for Willie. He is three or four years older. Ever since Mr. Cross died two years ago, Willie has used Ethan like a father figure. Ethan still lives at home, no work, no school, no nothing. He's a bum. I would expect more from Ethan's mother, but she covers for them all the time."

"Why?" Marla asked.

"She's the high school principal," Mrs. Cross said.

"Any idea where he might be?" Crosby asked. "Is there a place at night they hang out?"

Mrs. Cross shook her head. "Ethan got him into drugs and drinking. I saw a tattoo on his wrist last week. I asked him why he got that ugly thing? Do you know what he said? Ethan got one, so he did too. Willie was such a nice boy before he met Ethan." Mrs. Cross's hands fisted, knuckles whitened.

"When is the last time you talked to him?" Crosby asked.

"The same, three days ago."

"We could use your phone and put his number in the FIND MY PHONE app," Marla said.

"No, that won't work. Willie turned that off so I couldn't see where he was going at night."

"What about Ethan's number?" Marla asked. "Let's try his."

"I don't have it. He would never give it to me."

"We'll put a BOLO on him," Crosby said.

"A what?"

"Sorry, it means be on the lookout. I promise I will call you first thing when we find Willie."

After all three stood, and the elderly lady escorted them to the entrance. Mrs. Cross took Marla's hand and attempted to smile, but the aged, sullen lips gave away her deep fear. Marla couldn't tell her everything would be alright, so she said nothing. Mrs. Cross slowly closed the front door.

Chapter 22

The alarm buzzed next to Marla. Blackness hovered outside her window. She tapped the snooze button and stretched her hand across the bed for Crosby, but it was empty. It was his turn to feed the chickens. Moments later, with a warm cup of coffee in her hand, Marla walked to the bay window where bright floodlights from the roof pointed down on a thin coat of ice-crusted grass. She sipped her caffeine.

Lights inside the chicken coop flickered with Crosby's movements. He eased down the wooden ramp as birds followed their Pied Piper and rushed past him when he pitched chicken feed on the ground.

She chuckled at him, then checked the weather app on her phone. It predicted a cool breeze and calm waters for the day. It's going to be a glorious morning for fishing, but there was no time for that.

She quickly changed into work clothes; old Wranglers, Redwing boots, a long sleeve t-shirt, her once favorite cotton plaid shirt with a nickel-sized hole, and a blue jean vest with a long forgotten stain.

Standing on the porch, she drank the last of her coffee and placed the cup on the railing. Gazing at the horizon, a morning freshness grew upward behind the ring of hills twenty-five miles away.

She jogged toward the barn while throwing a kiss at him standing next to the coop. He smiled and tipped his hat to her. She opened the barn side door, slipped her work gloves on, and enthusiastically ripped open a small hay bale, then pitched separate chunks toward the horses in their stalls. Daisy, her horse, stepped past the hay to Marla. She rubbed the horse's head. "Hey, girl. You hungry? You better join Blackie." The horse nodded and turned toward the hay.

She shoveled manure while the horses fed, then brushed the two the horses down.

Crosby joined her in the barn and slapped his gloves on his jeans. He held up a basket full of eggs.

"I think that fox problem is gone. We'll need to take some eggs to the station and pass them out. Everyone loves our eggs."

Marla put down the brush and smiled. "I've got a problem."

"Yeah? What?"

"After shoveling manure, I smell a bit rank. Need a shower before breakfast."

"Okay, I'll get the bacon and eggs going."

"I thought you might want to wash my back."

◆

Steam rolled over the top of the glass-enclosed shower. Marla pulled her hair above her neck into a loose bun, then pushed her back against Crosby's chest. Getting dirty at the ranch was always fun. Getting wet had a whole new meaning.

He flipped the body wash bottle upside down and poured a line across the top of her shoulders. His palms spread the soap over her back before slipping around to her stomach and breasts. She slowly turned around and tilted her head back. He kissed her. She kissed him back more robust than she had kissed him in months. Water drops beat around their melded lips. Her fingers ran slowly through his brown curled locks. She pressed her lips harder against his as her arms draped around his neck. Suds flowed down her body to her feet. Her eyes lit up. She felt his stiffness and smiled.

◆

With a towel wrapped around her head and another around her chest, she sat on the vanity stool at her bathroom counter. Lyrics to "Happy Anywhere" sung by Blake Shelton and Gwen Stefani repeated in her head. She smelled bacon sizzling from the kitchen. Her fingertip brushed across her lips, remembering his taste. On a small clock on the wall, the second hand ticked past 9:05.

Crosby's phone rang on the bathroom counter. Marla spun it around. Logan's name was on the screen. She touched the speaker button. "What's up?"

"Got a 911 call from Timothy Clark where Crawdad Creek enters the lake. Two teenage boys in trouble," Logan said. "Go now, and I can meet you out there."

"On our way." She yelled out, "Crosby! We got a call."

He ran back to the bedroom. "What happened?"

"Two boys at the lake. They might be Willie and Ethan."

◆

Five miles from their ranch, Crosby's pickup turned from the road to narrow asphalt, which quickly changed to mud and pebbles. The tires ground to a halt a few yards from a bicycle lying on the ground with the front wheel bent. A ten-year-old boy hiding behind a tree trunk waved to them.

Marla opened her door, jumped out, and ran to him. She knelt and asked, "Timmy, did you call the police?"

A tackle box and fishing pole sat next to the boy. He held his phone tightly and nodded yes. A voice from his phone said, "Timmy, are you still with me? The police will be there soon."

Marla gently took his phone from his hand. 9-1-1 was on the screen. "Officer Adams here."

The voice said, "Marla? Is that you?"

"Thanks, Janet. We'll take it from here. Send back up."

Marla looked at Timothy. "Talk to me."

Timmy's eyes bulged from fear. He pointed toward the water. "I was going fishing and I hit a big rock. I fell off my bike and then I heard yelling down at the creek. I'm scared."

Marla's hand rested on the boy's shoulder. "How many are over at the shoreline?"

"I didn't go down there. I wanted to leave but my wheel is broke. My parents are going to be so mad at me. This is my birthday present I got yesterday."

"What did you hear?" Crosby asked.

"Three voices. They were screaming."

The telling wind picked up with clouds blanketing the sun, a bad omen for a Texas morning.

Marla heard water splashes. She handed the boy his phone. "Get in our truck, lock the doors, lie down, and be quiet. More police will be here soon."

Crosby tapped the radio mike on his shirt. "Grand-Mamma. Send back-up to Crawdad Creek, ASAP."

"Got a call from 911," Grand-mamma said. "I've already sent it out."

They drew their weapons and ran across the muddy path toward the noise. Thick brush grew from the water along the shoreline. Small ripples rolled in. A small aluminum fishing boat listed heavily to one side–the stern in water and the bow resting on the muddy shoreline.

Marla caught a glimpse of two bodies wearing jeans, lying across the side of the boat, one on top of the other, neither moving. Ankles zip-tied and dangling from outside the boat. "Oh, Jesus." She motioned to Crosby she was going to the boys and needed cover.

He aimed straight ahead as he rushed to a burr oak tree. A wall of six-foot-tall Pokeweeds stood to his right. He tried to focus on who they were. Was it Ethan and Willie?

The stern of the boat slowly bounced in the water. Marla holstered her weapon, then ran into the water around the boat and pushed it further onto the shore. That's when she noticed neither of them had their shirts on. Something rolled back and forth in the boat as the ripples ebbed and flowed. She spun away. "No, God. No."

She ran back around the boat to the shoreline side, grabbed the male's shoulder and jeans belt on top, and pulled backward. Mud splattered when they hit the ground.

It was Willie with his ankles and wrists zip-tied and a noose tight around his neck. An extended vertical cut, from his right collar bone to mid-chest, splayed open his bloodied skin and showed muscle and ribs.

Marla loosened the loop around his neck, then checked for a pulse. Weak and erratic. She yelled, "Crosby, need help."

He ran to the boat as she started CPR. He pointed at the other lying over the side of the boat. "Is this Ethan? I'll pull him out and start compressions."

Marla waved her hand, then went back to CPR. "No need. Call for an ambulance. We can save Willie."

Twenty feet down the shoreline, a man wearing a hoodie over his head ran shoving head-high weeds away. Crosby yelled, "Police. Stop."

The man disappeared.

"You stay with Willie," Crosby said. "I'm following the perp."

She nodded an affirmative and continued CPR.

Crosby's boots sloshed through the mud and weeds. The man was ahead of him, zigzagging and slapping Pokeweeds away.

"Freeze. Police!" Crosby yelled. His shoulder scars ached like razor blades slicing with each step. His arms swung back and forth as he pushed the weeds from his face.

The man stopped and turned with a ski mask covering his face. His pistol swung above the weeds and fired.

Crosby dove to the ground and rolled sideways. His scars felt like concertina wire tightening around his torso. He jumped up and returned fire. The tops of pokeweed swayed back and forth as the sound of footfalls faded away. The man was getting away.

"Crosby, come in." The microphone on his lapel squelched.

He tapped the button on his muddied shirt. "Adams here."

Grand-mamma called out, "Marla said to get back to the boat, now."

He burst through the weeds, gun in his hand, ready to shoot anyone near Marla. She yelled for help as he sloshed through the mud.

Marla, still on her knees over Willie, gasped and coughed. "Help. I can't keep going." Her chest compressions weakened. Sirens wailed in the background. Red and blue lights swirled across the top of the weeds. She heard footsteps behind her and glanced at Logan running toward her.

His knees slid on the muddy ground next to Marla. "I'm here, sis. I gotcha." He took over the CPR.

"Thanks, Logan." Her wet clothes stuck to her skin, and boots full of water. Exhausted, she sat on the ground and pulled out the inhaler from her shirt pocket. It was wet with green slime on the side. Wiping the mouthpiece and wrapping her lips around it, she inhaled two puffs. It didn't help. She did it again. Her head spun.

Crosby pushed past the weeds and stopped next to Marla. "Are you okay?"

She laid down and rolled to her side. "No."

Logan kept pushing on Willie's chest and yelled, "Crosby! Check on the other one."

"No need," Marla sobbed.

"I have to," Crosby said back to her.

"He's dead."

Crosby looked inside the boat, then turned away.

Red and blue lights swirled in every direction. It seemed a thousand sirens wailed their presence.

Marla climbed back to her hands and knees, then stood and walked to the boat. Ethan's body lay halfway across the side of the boat. Water repeatedly slapped the outside of the boat's hull as bloody red water sloshed inside. Her entire body shuddered. She saw evil. The worst she'd ever seen.

Ethan's eyes were wide open, his upper lip lacerated and nose bloody. The boat swayed as a decapitated head rolled side-to-side. The swollen face screamed the horror it had seen. The killer beat him, strangled him, and cut off his head.

Snapping open her pocketknife, she held the blade against the zip tie that held Ethan's hands behind his back. It was the only decent thing left to do for him, but that would be tampering with evidence. Prints? DNA? She closed the knife and said she was sorry to the dead boy.

As if God wanted her to see what needed to be seen, Ethan's headless body suddenly slid backward off the boat to the ground with his bloodied chest splayed open, showing muscle and ribs, and the number 18.

"Oh, my God. You sick bastard."

Two EMTs took over the CPR from Logan. After they stabilized Willie, they rolled him on the gurney to the ambulance. She stared at the straight line cut across the right side of his chest. Was it a number 1? Did they stop the perp from carving an 8 or a different?

Logan knelt in the mud. His fingertips grazed across two boards nailed together in the shape of a cross. "Good God. This crazed lunatic was going to crucify Willie."

❖

A black sky enveloped Crosby's pickup as it passed their front gate. Tires bounced across the cattle guard. The wind had died, along with Ethan. His dreams had been ripped away by a madman, with Willie left fighting for his life in the ICU.

Crosby's hope emptied. He turned the steering wheel and stopped in front of their house. The engine idled as he sat with his head and hands on the wheel. The bright headlights on the garage door annoyed him. He turned the lights off.

Marla remained still, trying to find enough energy to open her door.

Crosby's hands slid to the bottom of the steering wheel. She laid her hand on top of his.

He inhaled deeply, then exhaled everything. "This is out of control." He cleared his throat. "Out of control. We need help."

She released his hand. "Pops said he doesn't want to bring in the Rangers." She quickly brushed hair from her face. "I know. You're right. He's being selfish, but he doesn't want to give up control."

When he opened the door before turning the engine off, the dashboard bell dinged. "Okay, okay." He turned off the engine and slammed the door closed. "This is not control."

Crosby entered past the front door of their house and unbuckled his duty belt. He swung it and let go as it bounced on the couch cushions. His jeans were wet to the knees. Boots, mud-covered. Both socks sunk to his ankles and itched from the green muck. He jammed a heel into the bootjack and slipped the first boot off with the sock still inside. He repeated the other boot with the same outcome.

Barefoot, he charged straight to the liquor cabinet. Two fingers of gold-colored tequila swirled at the bottom of the bottle. Crosby turned it upside down and let the liquid fill his mouth.

She ran to the kitchen and slapped the bottle from his hand. "Damn it." The bottle bounced across the floor, splattering liquid in every direction. "What the hell are you doing? I can't handle any more shit today."

She shoved him to the side and grabbed the two half-full bottles in the cabinet. Turning them upside down in the sink, she said, "No more. This is it. This house is booze free."

"What the hell is going on?" Crosby asked. "Willie strapped to a machine in the ICU with a tube stuck down his throat. Ethan Dutton died out there." He ran his hands through his hair. "Ethan is dead because we can't do our job."

"That's not true."

"Yes, it is. Some crazy is out there killing people we're supposed to protect—two boys, dead or almost dead. I grew up knowing Ethan's parents.

They lived down the street from me when I was in grade school. I'm a cop. I'm supposed to..." His arms wrapped around Marla. "My God, I'm supposed to protect them. How can I ask for forgiveness? It's my fault Ethan is dead."

Marla held him tight. She whispered in his ear, "It's not your fault. We saved Willie. We'll find this guy and put him in jail. I promise."

Chapter 23

A chill wrapped around Marla's bare shoulders. With her eyes still closed and remembering Crosby's soft touch last night, her hand flipped the sheet off her side of the bed as she sat up. Morning sunlight barbed through her hair. The smell of coffee roused her out of bed. She tied the belt around her short robe and noticed the kitchen lights were on. The floor was cool to her feet. In the kitchen, a carafe of hot coffee sat half full. Something that could pass for molasses or black glue poured into her cup. She watered it down and stirred in a tablespoon of sugar before the first sip. Three strips of cooked bacon sat on paper towels next to a glass of orange juice. Half an English muffin peaked over the edge of the toaster, waiting for her to push the lever down.

"Crosby," she called. No answer. "Crosby," she called again as she flipped on the living room lights. A white plastic cap and an empty oxycodone prescription bottle sat next to his iPad on the coffee table. She spun it around and tapped in his security code. A text from an unknown sender was open with no message in the body, only a title, *time.*

She moved to the bay window and sipped her coffee. His Dodge pickup sat next to the barn with interior lights shining through boards in the wall.

Inside the barn, Crosby felt comfortable. He shouldn't. Peeling off his coat and shirt, cold crawled over his back. He needed pain, excruciating pain. He wanted Willie's pain. Mrs. Cross' pain. Stabbing hay with the pitchfork, he threw it toward a horse stall. He did it again, faster and faster. Warm mist passed between his lips in the chilled air while flinging hay into the air. *Not the right time for this. Marla needs all the help she can get.*

The memory of water slapping the aluminum boat flashed before him, halting him. He closed his eyes tightly, trying to block everything. The sight and sound of Ethan's head rolling in the boat would not stop.

A cold shiver ran up his neck. He stabbed the pitchfork into the hay again, then leaned the handle against the post. His chest ached. His heart hurt.

Each time Crosby closed his eyes, Mrs. Cross begged him to save her son. There wasn't anything he could do. He imagined Willie lying on a hospital bed, gasping for his life and then his breaths stopped, eyes grew cloudy staring into death.

He took a long draw from the Coors Light bottle, swished it in his mouth, and spit it out. *I should tell them no.*

The horses stood in their stalls. "You guys are loaded for the day." He poured the rest of the beer on the ground. *Say no. Just say no.*

A text from Marla pinged on his phone. *Are you in the barn?*

He replied with, *All good, feeding the horses. Come check on me in fifteen.*

Crosby opened another Coors Light bottle. Willie flashed in front of him with tubes, a ventilator, and heart beeps from the monitor above the boy's head. Crosby's heart dragged the floor.

He replied to UNKNOWN, *Bad idea. Changed my mind.* He must keep an eye on Marla. She might get too close.

A reply came quickly. *Go to rehab, find the oxy, and finish your little town's problem.*

For the last three years, Crosby had to play a fine line between being a Hildebrandt cop and an undercover DEA agent, but a hundred-thousand missing oxy tabs changes everything.

Another text from UNKNOWN, *NOW. THAT'S AN ORDER.* It was in caps. He can't refuse it. Crosby took a large gulp, swished it, then spit it out. *A fine line, indeed.*

Crosby leaned against the post and drank more beer. When a buzz started in his head, he poured the rest out. His boot pushed the empty bottles close together. He typed *DONE* and pushed enter before hiding the phone behind the toolbox. He fell backward into the pile of hay and waited.

The horses whinnied. She listened for more and sent a text, *Are you alright?* His iPad pinged on the coffee table. *DONE.* She looked out the window toward the barn. "What the hell?"

She swung the front door of the house open. As she ran barefoot to the barn, adrenaline blocked the pain of the gravel against her tender feet with each step. Fear and a chilled morning shed what warmth she earlier had. The side door of the barn banged against the wooden wall. He was flat on his back.

"Crosby!" she yelled. Marla shoved the bottles away and knelt next to him. His breaths were shallow. She dug in his front pocket and pulled out the Narcan nasal spray he always carried. One squirt in his nose, and she leaned his head back for a few seconds. She called the police station on her cell, and before anyone said hello, she blurted out, "Crosby OD'd in the barn. Send an ambulance, now."

Twenty minutes later, Crosby was strapped on a gurney. The EMT said, "Marla, we have to get him to the ED. Dr. Sanborn is waiting for him."

"Sorry." Marla held his hand and kissed his lips. "You need help with this. Everyone at the hospital is going to help you."

"Changed my mind. I don't want to do this."

"Changed your mind about what?" she asked.

He tried to raise up as the straps on the gurney pushed against his chest. "Everything. I don't want to do this ...drugs... murder." He quit straining and laid his head back on the pillow.

"What are you talking about?"

The attendant pulled out a Narcan spray, stuck it in Crosby's nostril, and sprayed. "We need to get him to the hospital."

She nodded to the ambulance attendant. "He's ready."

Chapter 24

After getting Crosby admitted into the rehab center, Marla returned to the squad room. The last seven hours felt like a week. She gazed at the high school picture of Willie Cross hung on the wall next to Ethan Dutton. They transferred Willie to Bexar County Memorial Hospital. His brain held the secret to Ethan's killer.

Not enough sugar or caffeine could cover her heartbreak. Four cups of coffee made her head buzz like an overheated electric cord. Avoiding everyone staring at her, she poured black liquid into her insulated cup and sipped.

Rumors and gossip traveled at the speed of light in Hildebrandt, and the name on everyone's lips was poor Marla Adams.

Searcy, Logan, and two other cops stood next to the wall. Logan's finger tapped Willie and Ethan's image on the corkboard.

"Angels, they were not. A few weeks ago, I busted Willie Cross and Ethan Dutton for public intoxication outside the old Pearlman house with about a hundred empty beer bottles on the ground. Ethan's car smelled like a burning marijuana field. I picked both up for burglary at the Crescent last week. Moon said they stole some expensive Tequila." Logan pointed at the boys' crime scene pictures on the wall again. "Damn shame. Wonder when they knew they were going to die?"

"Shit, Logan. You are one cold bastard. These are kids," Marla said. "They didn't deserve this."

"Yeah? Ethan would still be alive if they were home at a decent hour instead of running around chasing who knows what at two or three or four in the morning, and Willie wouldn't have tubes sticking in him. What do you think about that, sis?"

Marla raised her middle finger at Logan. "This is what I think," she barked back.

"All right, first things first," Searcy said. "Everybody has heard about Officer Crosby Adams. He will be out in a drug and alcohol rehab unit for a few weeks. I don't want to hear whispers or anything about Crosby while he's gone. No funny looks at Marla. She did the right thing by sending him to dry out." Searcy looked around at each person in the room. "Any questions about that?"

Logan turned from the pictures on the wall toward his sister. "I didn't know he had a problem. What happened?"

Marla grabbed the stapler off her desk and threw it at him. He ducked, and it bounced off his shoulder. "None of your God Damn business. You got anything else you want to ask?"

Searcy waved his hands. "Enough. No more about Crosby. There's other stuff to worry about. We got three, potentially four, murders on our hands. Marla, I've made my decision. You take the lead."

"No. I don't want it. Bring in the Rangers."

"I want no one outside this station. This is yours, all yours."

With Crosby out of the investigation, Searcy threw Marla into a role she didn't want. Immediately, everyone asked her a thousand questions; her department, her town, her friends, and everyone in the station waited for her to miraculously produce the killer—today.

Outside, she leaned against a post holding an awning above the back door.

The door opened. "Marla?" Logan asked.

Standing straight again, she cleared her throat. "What do you need?"

He let the metal door close before he said anything else. "If you don't want to take the lead, I can take it."

"No."

"You should let me take this. I'm more than you think."

"More than what?"

"I've got ideas," Logan said.

"So, tell me these ideas?"

"Last offer. We share. I want to be a co-lead investigator."

"No."

"Then *you* should call in the Rangers? They'd send someone pretty fast, and you need help."

"Not my place."

Mayor Pichler stepped around the corner with his hands in the air. "Why not, Officer Adams?"

Marla stood straight. "Hello, mayor. Logan and I are discussing police business."

"I heard, and he's right. We should have the Rangers here."

"A formal request needs to come from the top, Chief Searcy. If I requested it, the Rangers would contact Pops and ask why one of his subordinates called and not him? They'd take it as the Chief was compromised. If guilty, he goes to jail. If innocent, everyone sees him as weak. He'd have to resign." She cleared her throat loudly. "Couldn't do that to Pops. He loves his job."

Mayor Pichler crossed his arms. "So, you are not calling?"

"No, sir. I will not."

"And what if I do?" the mayor asked.

"Pops is close to several city council members and my guess is they would be upset for you to do just that without their approval."

"Hmm." The mayor dropped his arms to his sides and stormed back around the building.

"Right," Logan said. "Need to lie back. That is, unless Searcy is..."

"What? You think Pops is in on this?"

"No. I mean, the academy taught us if you don't know who committed a crime, then everyone is a suspect until proven otherwise."

Marla clamped her hands onto her hips. "You think I'm a suspect?"

Logan waved his hand. "No, of course not. Forget what I said." He opened the door. "You do whatever you want."

"I want you to go back inside and comb over every detail."

After he left, her lips wrapped around the inhaler, and her finger pressed the top down. She coughed hard. She slammed the inhaler on the concrete. "This damn thing doesn't work. Might as well give a blind man a frickin' Ferrari."

She returned to the station building, swooped her hair back from her forehead, and grabbed the mug from her desk. After another sip of coffee, she stopped at the wall. "There has to be a connection between these four people and the numbers thirty-seven, thirty-five, and eighteen."

Logan called out, "They're sequenced."

"What do you mean?" Marla asked.

"Sequenced. Add the three and the seven, and you get ten. Add three and five, and you get eight. Add one and eight, and you get nine. You have three sequential numbers; eight, nine, and ten."

Officer Larry Keyman called out, "If you add all three of them, it's twenty-seven. Add the two and the seven, and you get nine again. Does nine mean something?"

Marla squeezed her eyes shut and rubbed her head. "Too complicated."

"No, I think Larry is on to something here," Logan said.

"Well, if you think there is, then I'm positive there is *not,*" Marla shot back.

"Numerology. The killer is throwing numbers at us. Well, actually, writing them down." Logan snickered.

Marla snapped back, "You are a piece of shit!"

"Sorry, I thought that was funny," Logan said. "You remember Helena?"

"Yes, I remember her. I thought she was the weirdest girl in school until you dumped her and picked up the next girl."

"Helena was into numerology. All that stuff about counting numbers in your name and birthday, and stuff." Logan typed on the keyboard of his desktop computer. "Here it is. Numerology. Okay, nine means teacher. Emotions are moody, bullying, and restless. Sounds like a killer to me."

"Does it tell us his address or his phone number?" Marla asked.

"Was that satire?"

"*Was that satire?*" Marla quipped back. "I cannot believe we share the same DNA. I will not run this investigation on your ex-girlfriend's crazy ideas." She slammed her mug down and looked at Larry. "I'm going back to the lake and look for clues. Larry, you come with me."

Chapter 25

The two rode in her truck toward the Crawdad Creek crime scene in total silence for the first ten minutes. Larry cleared his throat twice and watched from the corner of his eye as her foot pushed the accelerator pedal lower and the speedometer needle rose higher.

"Are you in a hurry?" he asked.

She glanced at him. "Have things to do today."

Larry patted the dashboard. "Logan's not a bad guy. He's just a little strange at times."

She turned the wheel, and the truck veered right onto a dirt road toward the crime scene. "Logan is Logan. He likes to stir me up, and for him, it's easy. He's done it since we were kids."

"Right, but he's still good. He's the one that busted that ring of convenience store robberies a few months ago. And, well, he also…"

She let up on the pedal. They slowed, the tires crunching across the gravel. "Don't get on my bad side, Larry." She turned toward the crime scene. "I've had a rough few days, and the last thing I need to hear is how great my shit brother is. God love him. I love him, but… never mind."

They stopped twenty feet from the water, then climbed out of the truck. "All the pictures have been taken." She waved her hand in a large swath. "Look for anything, touch anything we might have missed in the water, on the shore, where the boat was. Anything." She aimed her arm to the right. "I'm following the trail where the perp ran."

Marla zipped up her nylon jacket with POLICE in large yellow letters on her back, then slogged into the head-high weeds, pushing them away from her face as she walked. The Pokeweeds looked untouched for decades, except for this week's intrusion. Bending down, she didn't have a ruler, so she pulled a dollar bill out of her pocket and laid it down next to the two separate boot prints in the mud and took pictures. Were they Crosby's and the perp's? About thirty or forty feet in, she saw where Crosby had dropped, dodging bullets. After that, there was only one set of boot prints charging forward.

She followed the serpentine line of broken weeds and wondered if the guy had lost his direction. The muddy trail became soggier. The boot prints sunk deeper with each step before angling to the right. Pushing away the last of the Pokeweeds, a poorly maintained strip of asphalt appeared. On the other side of the road stood a fence, in worse shape than the cracked asphalt, with loose barbed wire and broken branches used for posts. She pulled out her phone, connected to the map app, and pinned her location. She typed in her notes, 'find owner, ask about motion detection cameras.'

Any chance of being lucky once in this cat-and-mouse game?

She bent down and felt two muddy tire tracks side by side. These were from a dually truck; the back axle had two tires on each side. This must have been where the killer hid his vehicle. She would need to check with the tax-assessor collector's office for the number of dually trucks registered in their county. With all the ranchers and farmers, she figured every fourth truck in town was a dually. Hell, Searcy, Crosby, and hers were dually trucks.

A spray of pebbles and dried mud spread across the asphalt where the tires traveled. *Watch for trucks with muddy wheel wells. That's probably every truck in town.*

Marla veered back down the muddy trail. A book and a broken cellphone laid on the ground. She bent down to the ground, picked up a stick, and flipped the phone over. The sim card was missing, and the screen cracked. Someone had stepped on it. Did it belong to one of the boys?

She scraped the mud off the top of the book, buried half in a puddle of water and soil, revealing HOLY BIBLE printed on the soft black cover. Opening the cover with the stick, St. Juan Diego Catholic Church was stamped on the first page. Marla took pictures, then pulled two clear plastic zipper bags from her pocket and placed the phone and Bible inside.

Another trail forked to the left and aimed straight toward the water. She pushed the broken weed stalks away and touched three different size mud-laden shoe prints. As she walked down the trail, she noticed the strides became shorter. Ethan and Willie weren't in a hurry to get to the water. She followed the prints to the end of the weeds. The tree where Crosby crouched down, covering Marla, was a few feet away. Definitely a shorter distance.

They had caught the perp off-guard in the act of killing the boys. With Crosby near the tree, the perp ran in a different direction than his straight shot to the truck.

"Marla," Larry called out to her. "Come look at this."

Still holding the evidence bag in her hand, she stopped next to him. "Whatcha got?"

Larry pointed at the line of boot prints toward the weeds. "Look at these aimed toward the weeds. Not full boot prints, but mostly the ball of the foot where he ran toward the weeds." He pointed to the water's edge. "These come from the direction out of the water to the shore. Rain and the edge of the waterline have washed out those prints."

"Yes, I noticed that too."

Larry stood. "Out there about ten or eleven feet... see that pole or big branch sticking out of the water?"

"Yes, but not following you."

"Remember in the report, a hole in the back of the boat and a rope tied to the bow? It wouldn't have floated."

"You're saying the killer was going to tie the rope to the branch in the water?"

"The killer didn't want the boat to float away. That's why he put a hole in the boat." Larry wiped his hands on the front of his jeans. "I have a pair of waders for fly-fishing."

"Of course, everyone uses waders when they stand in waist-high water," Marla said.

"This guy was wearing waders and went into the water."

"Crosby nor I got an adequate look at the man running. How do you know he wore waders?"

"Remember the boards laid out like a cross?"

"Sure."

"It didn't register with me until now. The picture of the boards had mud on them."

"Go on."

"At the bottom of the long board, there was a print of muddied small diamond shapes and wide lines. They help keep the sole of the boot anchored on a creek bed. This is a pattern from waders, not soles of walking boots."

"Why go to all the trouble of the branch and needing waders?"

"He walked out into the water and stuck that big branch down into the mud. I've been here before. The water is three or four feet deep and a foot of soft mud. Regular shoes or boots would stick in the mud like quicksand, but not waders. I'll bet he shoved that branch in the water and was going to tie the boat to it and let it sink while the two were hanging over the side."

"Do you remember the size of the hole in the back of the boat?"

Larry shook his head. "No. Not really."

"I don't either. Can't remember if it was small or large? Where's the boat now?"

"At the evidence building. The impound lot."

"Hole in the boat, an impromptu cross, a broken branch three feet in the water," Marla wondered, "why the elaborate scene?"

"I don't know, but you and Crosby surprised him and stopped him from finishing what he set out to do."

"Not soon enough."

"He wasn't hiding evidence." Larry shook his head. "He wanted us to find the two victims in the boat. He wanted us to marvel at his work."

She nodded. "And numbers carved on people."

✦

Marla's truck pulled in front of the police impound lot's wire fence gate. The evidence bags holding the phone and Bible laid between the two of them.

"Are you sending this to the Bexar County Crime Lab?" Larry asked.

"Yes, for fingerprinting and DNA."

She rolled her window down and aimed her ID badge at the guard. He waved her through. An electric motor clicked on, and the gate slid sideways. After pulling into the lot, the two hiked between rows of cars and trucks.

She opened the door to the single metal building against the back fence. Long fluorescent lights hung from the metal roof.

A man wiped grease off his hands with a red shop cloth. He had an ID tag with his picture and name pinned to his shirt. "You looking for the aluminum fishing boat from the crime scene?" He pointed to the corner. "That's a bloody mess. Need any help?"

"Thanks," Marla said. "We got it from here."

"Good. I got other stuff to work on."

The upright boat rested on wooden pallets. Marla placed her hand on the aluminum edge, closed her eyes for a few seconds, and wished it all away. She cleared her throat, tried to clear her head, then looked inside. The hull had a thin coat of dried blood. Ethan's decapitated head rolling from side-to-side flashed in her mind.

"There. Under the rear seat," Larry pointed, "the hole."

Marla reached under the boat and stuck her finger in the hole. "Broken metal pointed inward. That means someone had flipped it over and knocked a hole in it."

"He did this before he took the boat to the water," Larry said.

She looked around. "Find a hammer."

Larry moved from one pile of tools to another. He returned with a claw hammer and handed it to her.

They rolled the aluminum boat to its side. She placed the hammer head in the hole, but it was too small. "Had to be a sledgehammer."

"Hold on, "Larry said. "There was one next to the other tools. Be right back."

She touched the edge of the hole, hoping it would tell her who did this. Larry returned with the sledge. It fit perfectly into the hole.

"Does the killer have an obsession with hammers?"

"Why do you say that?" Larry asked.

"A blunt object hit Mr. Kinsey on the side of his head. Possibly a sledgehammer?"

"I can call around the hardware stores for purchases within the last few months."

"Check all the small towns in Bexar county." Marla's fingers rubbed the outside of the boat around the hole. "I don't see any other dents. One hit. He's strong."

Chapter 26

A light flickered through the bay windows of the Adams' house. Marla propped her feet up on the ottoman, and sipped Dr Pepper from a glass, frustrated, confused, and lonely. Her thumb changed the channel on the television remote.

Channel Ten News finished with their farm report, street repair schedule, weather, and San Antonio sports. Rebekah Farmsdale popped up on the screen for her Friday night's 'My Opinion' segment. She always overdressed for this thirty-second solo performance. This time she wore a cocktail dress that looked like it came from Neiman-Marcus or Gucci's high priced collection. Definitely not off the sale rack. She held a dozen papers in her hand as she told her cliff-hanging story about the murders.

"Something is going on in the town of Hildebrandt. In less than two weeks, there has been three murders with one person in serious condition at Bexar County Memorial Hospital in San Antonio."

Marla shook her head. "Say have been, not has been, girl."

"My sources tell me that at each crime scene, there has been mutilated bodies left for the police to find."

Marla sipped her drink and rested the glass on her thigh. "You like the words, has been."

"My sources reported a change in the lead investigator of these murders to a police officer with less than five years' experience. I wonder about the judgement of the police department."

"Oh, thank you for announcing that to everyone in Hildebrandt."

"My sources also reported a gruesome message left behind on the bodies."

Marla bolted upright in her chair and swallowed the rest of the wine in her glass. "No. Don't do it. Don't say it."

"At each crime scene, there has been a number carved in the body."

"Oh, son-of-a-bitch. No. Rebekah, stop, now."

Rebekah looked at her pages, then stared at the camera. "Different numbers carved with a knife into each murder victim–numbers thirty-seven, thirty-five, and eighteen. So far, they're a mystery." The camera slowly zoomed closer to her face. "Channel Ten News is reaching out to this person and asking him to tell us what he wants. These numbers must mean something special to The Number Killer."

Marla jumped from her chair and yelled at the television, "Don't give him a name!" She streaked her fingers through her hair. "Don't make him famous."

"I am willing to sit down with this Number Killer, and he can tell us what he wants. We, at Channel Ten News, want to help stop the murders."

◆

Instantly, Channel Ten's phone line became overwhelmed for the next three days. It seemed everyone in Hildebrandt, and most of Bexar County, had an answer, a request, or knew how to stop the murders.

"Arrest and put my worthless brother-in-law in jail, and I'll stop the murders."

"I need sixty-four dollars and fifty-six cents to pay my water bill. You pay that, and I will stop."

"I want to go to Fredericksburg and eat at the German restaurant."

"Give me twenty gallons of gas, and I can give him up."

"I saw him, brown hair, and kinda tall. Is there a reward for him?"

"I know who he is. I used to babysit that little boy. Can I tell you on television?"

"He's in my front yard. Hurry."

"I see this same car drive by my house every morning. Has to be him."

"It's my mailman. I know it is."

"It's kids, I tell you. These damn kids are driving golf carts on my street. You need to arrest all of them."

"I called earlier. I've seen it. You need to call me back. It's hard to believe that squirrels can do that, but I've seen it."

Chapter 27

M arla calls the station on her phone. "Grand-mamma, would you please take a minute from the call center and fire up a couple pots of coffee? I've got everybody coming in for an early meeting, and I want the children to stay awake while I bark at them."

"Well, of course, Marla. I do hope things go well for you."

"Yeah. Well, going to need everyone's help."

"You can count on me."

The sun was still sleeping at six in the morning. Searcy, Logan, and the rest of the Hildebrandt Police Force sat in the police station's squad room.

Logan swished the coffee in his Styrofoam cup. "Where is she?"

Searcy leaned against a desk. "She called me last night and asked me to get everyone here at six."

"On Saturday," Logan growled. "My kids have got sports this morning."

Marla opened the door and entered. She slapped a manilla envelope down on her desk while she held her coffee mug in the other hand. "We got a shitload of trouble in front of us."

"Well, good morning to you too, sis."

"Good morning, Brother. Now shut up and let me talk." She took a large swig of her coffee. "Did anyone besides me watch the Channel Ten news last night?" Each one stared at her with blank faces. "Rebekah Farmsdale did another one of her 'My Opinion' bits last night, and it wasn't pretty. This means confidential information leaked from this office. She announced to the public this was a serial killer, and he cut numbers into the victim's body. That info came from someone in this office."

"Now. Hold on," Logan sat straight up in his chair. "There were lots of people at the crime scenes of John Kinsey's ranch and the creek. What about EMS, fire department, even employees at the morgue?"

Several of the officers nodded in agreement.

Marla agreed, "You're right." She took another swig of her hour-old coffee. "Everybody here willing to take a polygraph test?" She placed the mug on the desk and crossed her arms. "I only want one question answered. Have you talked to Rebekah Farmsdale in the last five days?" She stared at Logan. "I don't need you to take the test. You are the worst liar in the world. I can pick out your lie before you finish the sentence." She grabbed the arms of his chair and leaned into him. "Answer me, little brother. Have you talked to Rebekah Farmsdale in the last five days?"

His fingernails dug into the Styrofoam cup. "I'm not answering shit to you. I know my rights."

"Your rights?" She released the arms of Logan's chair and got in his face. "Only someone who's guilty talks about their rights. Did you talk to her? Answer me. Yes or no."

Logan looked around at each officer in the room. All eyes were on him. His fingernails punctured the side of his Styrofoam cup, and warm coffee leaked out over his fingers. His eyes turned toward Marla. "No." His arm swung and aimed the coffee cup toward her. She slapped his hand before he moved two inches. The coffee and the broken cup spilled across his desk.

"You're still not fast enough, little brother."

"Enough of this shit," Searcy said. "Is that the only reason you wanted us here? Ask us if we talked to a news reporter?"

"No." She leaned away from Logan and slid images out of the manila envelope onto her desk. She approached the wall and pinned the new pictures of the broken branch in the water, the half-made cross on the ground, and shoe prints in the mud.

"Here, at the shoreline, are deep boot prints in the mud. Larry said something interesting about them." She turned back to the group. "How many here have fishing waders?"

Everyone except Searcy held their hand up.

"Chief, you got waders," Logan said.

"Me?" Searcy shook his head. "Don't think so."

"We went fly-fishing in Big Bend three years ago. Did you forget?"

Everyone could tell he was searching his mind. "Right, forgot. That was the last time I had them on. They're probably somewhere up in the attic." He rubbed his beer belly like he was seven months pregnant. "Why, Marla?"

"Larry has an idea. Go ahead, Larry."

"The killer was tying the rope from the bow of the boat to the large branch stuck in the mud several feet out in the water. He would need waders to get through the water and soft mud."

Marla took the picture off the wall and held it head high.

Larry pointed toward her. "That branch is still stuck in the water, but neither of us had waders to grab it."

Marla turned to Logan. "I know you carry waders in your truck. Go out there and bring the branch back to the station. We might get lucky, and someone's DNA will be on it."

Logan looked down. "I guess, but my gas tank is riding on empty."

Searcy raised his hand. "Good God. I'll get it."

Marla looked back at Searcy. "You would have to go back home and look for your waders before going to the crime scene."

"No. My truck rides high enough, and I can drive out in the water and grab it from the window."

"Don't get stuck, Chief," Logan said.

"The rain has probably already washed off any prints or DNA by now, but I'll be careful," Searcy said. "Come out with me, and we'll look around once more."

"Larry and I combed the area yesterday."

"Let me buy you breakfast and then we'll head out," Searcy said. "You want the branch, don't you?"

She finished her coffee and placed the cup on her desk. "All right, but I follow you in my truck. Got too many other things going on to ride with you."

◆

The bell above her head rang as she pushed the diner door open. The place buzzed with conversation, and hungry customers took every booth. She pointed to an empty one in the back, then slid between the table and bench. Searcy followed.

The waitress was two steps behind them and laid down a laminated breakfast menu. "Coffee?" she asked as she flipped the cup over and started pouring.

"Thanks, Ellie," Searcy said.

"Me too."

"Buttermilk pancakes with fresh blueberries is the special today."

Searcy sipped his coffee and then put it back on the table. "Sounds great. Add two sausage patties."

"Got it, Sweetie. And for you?"

"Sure," Marla said, "same thing."

Ellie spun around and marched back to the counter.

"You need to give your brother a break," Searcy said.

"Is that why you asked me to eat breakfast with you? He rides me like a red ass monkey in heat."

"Listen. You're the lead in this investigation. You need to use everyone in the department, and Logan has promising ideas. He can help."

"About one percent of what comes out of Logan's mouth is a promising idea. The rest of the time, he talks just to irritate me."

"I want you to use Logan more," Searcy said.

"Two specials." Ellie placed their plates of pancakes in front of them with blueberries and melting butter on the top. She slid a smaller plate of sausage patties over next to the cups. "More coffee?" She poured before they could answer.

"I tried to use him this morning. Send him out for the branch, but what did he say? Not enough gas." She cut the pancake. "Bullshit answer."

"I'll make sure he has gas in his tank. Ask him..."

"He's a grown man with a wife and kids. Buying their own gas is what people do. He doesn't need his *daddy* buying it for him."

He smeared the butter on top and then cut the pancakes in half. "Ask him again."

"This is my case, and I'll ask who I want for help." She slid out of the booth and stood. "You want him to do something, then you ask him." She trounced through the diner and out the door.

Chilled winds swept around her. She zipped her jacket halfway up, then climbed into her truck. She wondered what the hell these numbers carved on people meant. After starting the engine, she backed out of the parking spot and drove to the library.

The library mixed in numerology with astrology, tarot cards, spiritual maps, and other stuff she never wanted to read. She pulled a book off the shelf named DECODE YOUR LIFE WITH NUMEROLOGY, then flipped through the book's table of contents, Numerology 101, Master numbers, Birthdays, Numbers 1-9. She stopped and turned to page eighty-one, Numbers 1-9. The morning passed quickly.

Marla's phone buzzed in her pants pocket. It was the rehab center telling her their septic tank had clogged.

It was like getting out of school early or holding a get-out-of-jail-free card, except everything smelled like a pig farm. While the plumbing company repaired the system, everyone at the drug rehab unit earned a four-hour reprieve.

Family members sat in their trucks and cars in the parking lot and waited for their loved ones to come out the front doors. Marla leaned against her Dodge Ram 2500 4 door diesel pickup. Pride made her spend 15 minutes to run it through a carwash and towel dry it herself. "Not exactly spit-shined like Crosby would do it, but passable for a girl taking time off from work to see her man.

A smile stretched across her face as Crosby stepped outside and scanned the parking lot for her. They both ran and locked arms around each other's bodies. Her cheek rubbed against his smooth, clean-shaven face while her arms wrapped tight around his neck. Her lips plunged onto his. She stole his breath away as he lifted her and spun in a circle. To Marla, everyone else in the world disappeared.

It was almost 1 PM, and the next four hours would be theirs–no calls, no texts, away from the police station and Hildebrandt.

She leaned against him. "I've been working since five this morning. I waited an hour out here. I thought they weren't going to let you out."

"I missed you last night. Had to go to bed alone without..." he looks around and whispers, "you know, sex."

Her smile widened to an ache. "Well, I had to interrogate the Dallas Cowboys *tight* ends yesterday afternoon."

"Glad you weren't too lonely."

She wrapped her arm around his waist and hung on tightly as they headed toward his truck. "Speaking of that, we need to...take care of that problem soon."

"I was thinking the same thing." They walked with arms locked.

"Wait. Is there anything you want to bring?" Marla asked.

"There is nothing there I want. Let's blow this cookie stand."

As they headed to the truck, they talked about the house, the bar, the animals, anything but the murders. Their doors closed. Crosby started the diesel engine–he couldn't wait. His hands wrapped around Marla's face and pulled her to his lips. His hand slid down to her chest. She grabbed his hand and held it tight to her bosom.

"Soon, love. I got plans for you."

Crosby smiled and shifted to drive. He turned left on SH 216, and the diesel engine roared down the road.

Marla's hand stretched across the console and held his arm like a schoolgirl. "Where do you think you're going?"

"Back home, the ranch, the bed."

"Sorry, these four hours are mine... ours. I had to rush to put up our camping tent at the lake. Not the one night tent, the week-long tent, with a bed, music, and a cooler full of cokes and water. You're not allowed to do anything except take care of me for four hours. Turn right at the dirt road."

Lingering under cotton-puffed clouds, she watched buzzards hover across the open field. Something was dead, and the murders flashed in her mind. Her eyes squeezed shut, pushing it all away.

Her phone vibrated inside her sleeveless vest. *Not now.* She let it buzz.

Crosby turned to her. "You need to answer that?"

She dropped her head against his arm. "No. I don't want to. Not now. Not until I get my four hours with you." It vibrated again.

"Go on, answer it. It must be important," Crosby said.

She pushed against him, sat straight up, and answered abruptly, "Adams."

Dust swirled from the back tires as Crosby drove. He tried to listen to the jumbled voice.

She sighed. "Where?" She didn't move, with the phone stuck to her ear. "Yes, I can be there. Crosby is with me. He's familiar with the area better than anyone."

"Where, this time?"

Marla placed the phone back in her vest. Her spiritless face said it all. "A place called Devil's Horn. I think you know it."

"That was the place I led the DEA to the meth lab. A small shack with fifteen-thousand dollars of equipment, two generators, and over a hundred pounds of crystal meth."

"You never answered how you knew about that place? Especially since it was on the edge of the Hildebrandt limits."

"I... followed a suspicious person one day. Not much reason for someone to drive on private-owned land." He put his hand on her thigh. "What's there, this time?"

"Border Patrol raided that same shack with illegals hiding out. They found a sledgehammer and a hunting knife with dried blood." Marla took a deep, long sigh. She glanced at her watch, then patted his arm. "Searcy wants me to meet the agents there now. Won't leave us much time, if any, to ourselves."

"Do we need to swing by the station for evidence bags?"

She pointed toward the back of the truck. "You have some in the tool-box."

The diesel hummed as the truck passed three-foot-tall weeds along the bumpy asphalt. Crosby asked, "We have time for a quick break at Old Man Kinnebrew's abandoned house up ahead?"

Marla's eyebrows rose. Crosby pointed to the right at the house on a hill. She nodded with a smile. He veered right and then gunned the engine down the deeply rutted road. The truck's tires slid to a stop.

She flung her vest off, opened her door, grabbed one boot, and hopped while pulling it off her foot. He climbed over the console. She opened the back door and jumped on Crosby. Marla's fingers unbuttoned his shirt and rubbed her hand over his chest.

Fingers tugged on silver buckles. Zippers went down as flutters rose from her stomach to her head. She laid down across the bench seat. Crosby's hands slid her belt and the back of her pants down to the top of her one boot still on. Marla's breath heaved. Her smile strained with laughter; their arms meshed as he laid down on top of her.

Chapter 28

Three white GMC Yukon's with the well-known angled green stripe on the side flashed red and blue lights in every direction. Each one lined up like horses at a trough in front of a house. Half the shingles had blown off years ago, windows boarded up, and the front door with broken hinges attached laid over the entryway.

Crosby's truck bounced down a dirt road. A cloud of dust billowed behind. Tires crunched gravel until it stopped in front of the house. Crosby stepped out of the truck and brushed his hands over the front of his pants. His finger touched the zipper to make sure it was up. Marla pushed the pant leg down over her boot, then cut around the back to meet up with Crosby. Her badge hung on her belt. She patted his backside once as they advanced toward the dilapidated house.

Outside, four Border Patrol agents wore olive green, long sleeve shirts, cargo pants, and ball caps along with black military style boots. Each held an M4 rifle across his chest and glared in the distance. They nodded their hello.

Marla looked around into the vast emptiness. She walked toward the doorway and asked, "Expecting a counterattack?"

Inside, two other agents stood in the same gear while six underweight Hispanics, with hands zip-tied behind their backs, sat in a circle facing outward.

One agent smiled and stuck his hand out. "Joel Thompson."

The other said, "Mario Gonzalez."

After a round of handshaking, Marla asked, "Where's the evidence?"

"We swept the house for contraband and found a sledgehammer head and a knife in the dry toilet tank. People hide stuff in there, thinking we would never suspect to look. That's one of the first places we do. Anyway, the handle wouldn't fit in the tank, so I'm guessing someone broke it off, and we found it under a floorboard in the bedroom. The handle looks almost brand new. You might check the hardware stores around town." He shrugged his shoulders. "Didn't expect a bloody sledgehammer with hair stuck to it." He held his hand up. "Had gloves on, so I picked up all three and put them in the corner, over there."

Gonzalez said, "When we raided the house, they were compliant, sat down, and raised their hands in the air. I recognized a few of them. Not their first time caught. Joel thinks they crossed over to fatten up. They're ready for three squares a day, medical care, with heating and air conditioning for six months. Incarceration is part of life to them."

She slipped gloves on and opened three paper evidence bags. "No confessions about how the hammer or knife got here?"

Thompson replied, "None. Showed them the hammer head and knife, and no one became nervous."

Crosby studied each face. None of them seemed apprehensive. "Do you believe them?"

"They had heard about the murders in Hildebrandt and avoided town."

She placed the sledgehammer in a bag and then did the same with the knife. "Did you interrogate them about the murders or the weapons?" She dropped the broken handle in the third bag.

Thompson said, "Didn't know enough about the crime to interrogate. When I found the items, I radioed headquarters, and they mentioned you as chief investigator."

"Ask them if they knew Kinsey," Marla said.

Gonzalez asked, "*¿Alguno de ustedes conoce al señor Kinsey?*"

Wide-eyed, they all shook their head and spoke rapid-fire Spanish.

Thompson jumped in and asked them more questions with rapid replies. "They're saying the same thing; crossed the river at dawn, stopped here, and slept. They hide out during the day and run along Farm-to-Market roads at night." He smiled. "Each said they have a family at home that would verify they were in Mexico on the day of the murder."

"Thought you said they wanted to get caught. Eat, drink, sleep, be merry for six months in a safe place," Crosby said.

"Speculation," Thompson replied. "Some have family they want to see."

"Sure. I'm guessing each one knows some English, probably as much as me." Marla stooped down on her haunches and gazed at each of them. "Following the road, you had to pass by Kinsey's place. Would I find anyone's fingerprints there? Maybe someone forgot something and went back to get it."

One man started to talk. The one next to him yelled, "*Cállate.*"

She knew that word. "Why did you tell him to shut up?"

Gonzalez isolated the man and asked him more questions. After a few minutes of discussion back and forth, the agent returned. "He's a cousin to one of the laborers who sheared sheep at Kinsey's ranch. His cousin and two other laborers saw someone kill Kinsey. They waited until the killer left the ranch, then took off to a place near Hobbs, New Mexico to work."

"Know where his cousin is now?" Crosby asked.

Thompson translated, "*Donde esta tu prima ahora?*"

"He said no."

"Hmm." Marla sealed the bags. "How did you know they were hiding here?"

"They didn't know about the drones. We have one in this area, and the infrared spotted them running as a group last night."

"Drones. Eye in the sky." She looked at Crosby. "Maybe Moon was right."

Chapter 29

Logan climbed out of his pickup, closed the door, and pushed the lock button on his fob. The horn and flasher announced a false sense of security to the world. Sunlight pierced through the elm tree branches in his front yard. Butch, their pit bull in the backyard, barked incessantly, his way of saying hello. From outside, "Frozen" blared from the television. In his mind, he sang the words. Couldn't help it. After hearing the song a hundred times, he knew it as well as *America The Beautiful*, or *Star Spangled Banner*, or *On The Road Again*. He opened his front door to his favorite odor, transforming him into the happiest man alive. The aroma of chicken fried steak and fried okra engulfed the house.

He unbuckled his gun belt and placed the pistol in the lockbox. "I smell heaven."

Twin girls scream in unison, "Daddy's home!" They ran from the kitchen to the entryway.

"Daddy, we're helping Mommy with the biscuits. I put them in the pan."

"And I put butter on top of each one."

He rubbed their heads. "I bet they're going to be delicious. Let's go see Mommy."

The three marched in equal stride into the kitchen. Cindy wore a San Antonio Spurs t-shirt, skinny jeans, and flats. Standing in front of the stove, she turned a half-pound chunk of breaded steak over with a pair of tongs. Her lips arced into a wide grin. "Just in time." She puckered and waited for him.

He kissed her lips, then the nape of her neck. He winced when grease popped on his forearm. "Smells fantastic."

"You almost lost out. They wanted a peanut butter and grape jelly sandwich with red and yellow Gummy Bears on the side. Not sure how it will turn out, but we compromised by putting a Gummy Bear in each biscuit."

"I don't need bread when I got the best chicken fried steak in Texas on my plate."

Her smile diminished. "We're almost out of this." She pushed the baggie of marijuana to the side. "What about the rental agreement? Are we moving?"

He shook his head. "Nah. Everything is in escrow while they figure out what to do with Mr. Kinsey's properties. We have a little money. Maybe we could buy this house."

Cindy placed the meat on a platter and then on the table. "You know what you should do?"

"Hmm?"

"Call Marla and ask her to come eat with us. She's alone and worried."

He reached into his pocket. "On it."

Marla looked at her phone. The screen had Logan across the top. "Hello?"

"Hey, sis. Cindy cooked up a nice lunch. She made fried steak, potatoes, okra, and biscuits with Gummy Bears. Come over and eat with us."

With the rehab center in her rearview mirror, she sighed. "Sounds inviting, but I'm worn down. I just left Crosby at rehab, and I'm on my way to San Antone to deliver fresh evidence at the crime lab. Not in the mood for food. Hope you understand."

"Yeah, sure. Maybe see you at the chili cook-off this evening."

Crosby's hands separated the curtains in his room. As he stood in front of the window, his reflection mirrored in the glass. When Marla's truck turned out of the rehab lot, he hustled quietly down the hallway and slipped out the back door.

✦

At the crime lab, Marla shoved the gearshift into park and cut the engine. She'd been to this building too many times. Half of the structure held the medical examiner's office and the morgue, the other half was the crime lab. It had a light on in the lobby. David Weidman said he would wait for her.

She climbed up the concrete stairs and knocked on the glass door. Within seconds, he pushed the door open and motioned her in.

"Thanks for staying here, David. You didn't have to do this."

"No problem. My wife and kids are out of town, and I'm not in a rush to eat leftovers. Besides, anything I can do to help Crosby, I'm all in." He gazed at the three paper bags she held. "These are what you want to be processed?"

She held them out for him to take. "Only the broken handle tonight. I feel like these are from the Kinsey murder. I know DNA takes longer, but I was hoping for a match on the prints tonight."

"We can do all three. The DNA department can remove the super glue tomorrow with acetone, and it won't bother the DNA." He took them and strolled down the hall to the fingerprint room. "Becky said she would stay and register the evidence. Want something to drink while we're waiting? Water, Coke, Dr Pepper?"

"DP would be nice."

"Got something special for you. Follow me."

They entered the employee break room, where an antique Dr Pepper machine and a cold box stood against the wall.

She rubbed her hand across the top of the machine. "These look new."

"The director here is a descendant of Charles Alderton, the inventor of Dr Pepper. He trades out machines with the Museum in Waco every few months. The box holds water bottles." He grabbed one and twisted the top off. "And the machine holds only DP. No money needed, just pull a bottle out."

She slipped one out and stuck the cap under the bottle opener. It popped off, releasing a fizz. It tasted better than ever.

"Does Crosby like Dr Pepper?"

"Not as much as alcohol and pills." She took another gulp.

"Right. Being a hero has its handicaps." He drank from the water bottle. "Rumors are floating around you need help."

She held her hand up. "We're managing it. These fingerprints will help move it forward."

"Don't need to stick my nose where it doesn't belong, but have you thought about bringing in the Texas Rangers? This is what they do."

"Thought about it. Chief says no." She placed the empty bottle on the table. "Thanks." Walking out of the break room, she headed back down the hallway.

After the secretary entered all the information into the computer, David slipped on gloves and opened the sacks containing the handle, hunting knife, and a hammer head. "This is a cool machine." He opened the cyano-acrylate fuming box. "Super glue vapors stick to fingerprints." After a few minutes in the chamber, ridges and whorls appeared on the handle. "We have prints. I don't see any on the hammer head or the knife."

David ran them through the database, and Marla's spirit lifted. They waited. To kill awkward time, David asked again how she found the handle. She had almost finished telling him the story when the computer sent a response, James Kinsey.

Marla turned away and plopped down in a plastic molded chair against the wall. Her eyes welled. She ran her fingers through her hair. "You couldn't make it simple for me?"

"Sorry?" David asked.

"The fingerprints on the handle are the victim, not the perp. It couldn't be easy and leave someone else's print." She coughed. "Damn it."

"We'll do the DNA testing tomorrow. We might find something."

She stayed in the chair with her elbows resting on her knees, exhausted and despondent. The Hildebrandt Police needed a lucky break, and the murderer wouldn't allow it.

David looked back and forth and cleared his throat. He shook his head. "Sorry."

"Damn." She stood and traipsed around the room. "What in the hell am I doing here?" Her cough returned. She pulled the inhaler from her shirt pocket, sprayed once, and inhaled deeply. She coughed several times. Her heart rate jumped. She sprayed another and inhaled, but blew it out immediately. "Damn." She fell to her knees and coughed hard again.

David slipped the gloves off. "Sometimes, when people aren't used to the smell, it makes them cough."

She bent down, hands on her knees, and screamed, "Damn it! Damn it to hell!" She coughed hard again and rolled to her side.

"Do I need to call for an ambulance?"

"No!"

David had his phone in his hand. "Are you sure?"

Slowly, she rolled to her hands and knees, then tried to stand. David grabbed her elbow and helped her up.

"Shit, I can't believe this. Not one besides the vic? The bastard wore gloves when he killed Mr. Kinsey, didn't he?" She looked at David. "Right?"

"That's the likely scenario, but we have the hammer head and knife for DNA testing."

"Why am I here? I'm a small town cop in a quiet town," she stomped her foot on the floor, "with a serial killer wandering the streets. I've got an alcoholic, oxy addicted husband, a chief who is wacko with or without pills, and a brother who's... shit, whatever." She kicked the chair across the room. "Why, damn it?" She grabbed the chair and slammed it on the floor several times, then threw it against the wall. "Why me? I don't want this. I don't want any of this!" She charged down the hallway, shoved the glass door wide open, and disappeared down the stairs.

Chapter 30

A heavy mist rolled in from the west of the city, defying the sun's warmth. I-10 rush hour traffic dropped to turtle speed. A thousand headlights bloomed underneath the dusk. A quarter-mile away, a green overhead sign revealed the FM 404 exit, a two-lane road that snaked through trees and hills to Hildebrandt. Not Marla's favorite route, but better than watching a semi forgetting to slow down in her rearview mirror. She hopscotched lanes and grabbed the exit.

Outside of the city, the mist thickened. Visibility dropped from half a mile to a hundred yards. Backing off the accelerator, Marla slowed to 45 MPH. This drive would take twice as long as usual. Headlights glared across her windshield as they streamed by.

She turned the radio off after several country songs and tapped the call button on her steering wheel. It rang.

"Yeah. What?" Searcy announced.

"Were you at Crawdad Creek with the rest of us?" She heard a pop on the phone. "What was that? Are you okay?"

"Yeah, yeah. I'm good. Shooting grackles. Too damn many of them around here."

"Don't do that. They're protected in Texas."

"Not on my property, they're not. I know they want in my house."

"Shooting with what?"

"Piece of shit pellet rifle."

"Okay. Stop and put the gun down, then go get your pills."

"Too busy. The leader is telling others to jump branches. He's making me miss. I need my shotgun."

She ran her fingers through her hair. "No shotguns. I'm not hanging up until I know you took *two* pills."

"Only supposed to take one a day."

"You probably missed yesterday's pill. I'm waiting."

There was another pop.

"Got that bastard," Searcy said. "All right, I'm going."

Her fingers drummed on the steering wheel while she waited. "Pops? Answer me."

"Okay, took two. Why'd you call?"

"I'm heading out of San Antonio after dropping the hammer and knife at the crime lab. I wanted to let you know there were no fingerprints on the handle. The perp wiped them clean."

"Well," Searcy sighed. "We'll get him. *You'll* get him. I have faith in you."

She glanced toward the navigation screen like it would emphasize her point better. "Bullshit. I don't know what I'm doing."

"I need help with these damn birds. Where are you?"

"Leaving San Antone."

"Why?"

"Shit," Marla mumbled. "Never mind, I'll be back in town in a bit and come by and check on you."

"Don't come to my house."

"Why?"

"Are you in fog?"

She heard another pop. "How do you know about fog?"

"Why do you think all the grackles are in my yard? Damn fog ran them off. Are you on I-10?"

"No, FM 404."

Searcy cleared his throat. "Why 404? That's only two lanes and longer. Go back to I-10."

Marla crept up on a small set of taillights on the edge of town. "I'm almost home."

"I said, I-10. Now!"

Two bright headlights jumped out from the murk in a bull run toward her. "Oh, shit." She turned her head to the side, winced, and closed her eyes. The tractor-trailer zoomed by in a second. "I have to go. Call you later, and no shotguns." She flipped the emergency lights on, hoping idiots charging down the road would slow down.

Searcy tapped the red button on his phone and sighed. The background picture on his phone had Marla, Logan, and him smiling. "You're right. You have no idea what the hell is going on."

The fog thickened to whipped cream, dropping visibility to ten yards. The automobile ahead of Marla drifted to the right shoulder. An off-road pickup with aftermarket tires and suspension roared past. A deer stood on the right shoulder, its head up, with eyes glaring. The car veered left, crossing the middle line and then swerved back to the right.

The wild animal jumped in front of Marla's truck. She slammed on her brakes and felt the safety belt pull against her chest. The deer disappeared into a white hole.

"Damn deer. Not interested in playing tag with a hundred-pound tick bag."

The brake lights lit up from the car in front of Marla and turned into the Tinsley Electric Substation. It was a small SUV with a Channel Ten News vinyl wrap around it.

"Smart. Pull off and wait. Smarter than me."

◆

Rebekah Farmsdale's fingers gripped the steering wheel of the Channel Ten News SUV while driving on a two-lane road. Headlights clawed through a thickening mist. Her fingertips pulled the headlight switch forward and cut the bright to low beam. At the same time, her eyes jerked between the rearview mirror and windshield, hoping to avoid any vehicle barreling down on her. She would have only a second to decide which way to go. Veer right, veer left, floor it, slam on the brakes. This was stupid. She wanted to turn around and head back home, but potential fame drove her forward.

Icy spider legs climbed up her neck. Her finger tapped the temperature button up and spun the fan knob to high. From under the dashboard, a blast of heat shot out around her feet and up her legs. She felt like she was sitting in a rolling coffin.

In her rearview mirror, red and blue emergency lights flashed. She looked at her speedometer: 40 MPH. "I'm not speeding, and I'm not stopping."

The fog thickened. Headlights jumped out and charged forward like snowballs on fire. Rebekah slowed, drifted to the right, and looked away from the glare. Off-road tires on a hopped-up pickup truck roared past her.

She looked up. Two small reflections on her right came out of nowhere. Her foot shifted from accelerator to brake. Her hands tightened. Five feet from the edge of the road, a deer stood like a statue. She whipped the wheel left, then right. Her head bounced against the side window. Through the rearview mirror, Rebekah watched the deer jump across the road in front of the vehicle with the emergency lights.

She felt sweat on her neck and a chill throughout her body. Her hand flipped the heater fan to low and then glanced at the navigation system screen. GPS showed the destination was eight hundred yards away.

Headlights streaked across Tinsley Substation, a ten-foot chain-link fence surrounding electrical equipment on a concrete pad half the size of a football field. In the center of the substation, a single yellow light on top of a thirty-foot metal tower dimly lit the concrete pad. Rebekah pushed the turn signal down. Orange flashed against the fog as she turned. Behind her, red and blue swirled in the mist. The police truck sped by, continuing down the road.

Gently pulling in, the tires rolled over gravel. Rebekah stopped behind the substation, just as the man said on the phone call an hour ago. Headlights shined on onion stalks in a large open field. She held her fingertip against the stop engine button and imagined the praise she would receive after interviewing the Number Killer.

With the motor off, the headlights went dark, and the onions disappeared. She opened her door and her cheetah print, high-heeled ankle boot stepped on the ground. Standing next to the car, her hand tapped the phone in her back pocket before closing the door. Transformers hummed like monks in an Abbey.

She zipped her dark blue North Face jacket up to her neck, then bent down and pulled the bottom of her jeans over the top of the ankle boots.

A dog barked in the night, announcing to the world something was wrong. The field echoed snorts and grunting.

Her hand swept the side of her purse and grasped the five-inch long deer antler tip and tugged; the quick release chain snapped apart. She had carried it on the side of her purse since college days when a drunk frat boy cornered her and put his hands where they didn't belong.

She called out into the fog, "Hello? I'm here to meet someone."

Looking to each side, she backed up against the car. "Maybe this wasn't a clever idea." In her other hand, her thumb squarely rested on the panic button of the fob. She called out again, "Hello? If no one is here, then I'm leaving."

She scoffed at herself. "Stupid. What the hell am I doing here?"

Near the substation, a single noise sounded out like the swish of a boxing glove hitting a heavy bag. Her front tire made a thump and went flat.

"Oh, shit."

Chapter 31

Marla returned to the station and flipped the light switch on. Despite the murders, everyone had gone to the Hildebrandt annual chili cook-off festival.

She stood beside the corkboard. Her finger brushed across the images of Ethan and Willie. "I promise, boys. We'll find who did this."

On the center of the wall hung a blank piece of paper for an unsub, or unknown subject. "And who are you?" Her fingertip followed lines of string connecting each victim. Over the last few days, it grew like a spiderweb. She had to stop this craziness.

Logan texted her. *Lots of fun here. Great chili. Saved one for you.*

She grabbed the coffee carafe handle and spun the cold black liquid. Her thoughts went to Crosby. He would happily drink this tomorrow or the next day.

There was no one at her home, and Marla didn't want to be alone without Crosby. An overhead fan spun, pushing air across her face. She strode to the windows and closed the blinds. Remembering the hole in the boat made by a sledgehammer and wondering if any of Kinsey's hair or blood was stuck in the aluminum shards, she'd decided to return to the impound tomorrow with a magnifying glass. Until then, she turned her PC on, and it booted up at the speed of snails. The HPD logo flickered a few times before it lit up on the monitor. She held her fingertips over the keyboard, expecting them to type the answer to everything.

The station phone rang, and she answered, "Hildebrandt Police."

"Marla!" Logan yelled into his phone, with people laughing around him. "You didn't answer my text." A Brad Paisley cover song played in the background. "You have to come out here."

"I'm not in the mood. Too much work to do on these murders."

"Listen, sis. Everyone is here, and everyone is carrying a sidearm. I mean every parent and every grandparent. There is no killer here at the festival."

Marla laughed. "That doesn't surprise me a bit."

"If you don't come out, someone, I don't know who will let the air out of your tires every day for a week. And leave a present on your truck seat. A very smelly present."

She smiled. "All right. Heading out now. See you soon."

Rebekah Farmsdale flashed in her mind. The Channel Ten SUV turned at the entrance to Tinsley Substation. Thought the news agency would send her to the festival, but that's not on the 404. She picked up her phone and typed Rebekah's name on the contact list. Nothing. She didn't have it. "I'll see her somewhere tomorrow."

❖

Rebekah pushed the panic button on her fob. Headlights and taillights flashed; the horn blared into nothingness. She turned to run when a bullet punched against the side of the car. Another drilled into the metal behind her. She stopped, put her hands up, and hit the button again. The silence was heavy. "Okay, okay. You got my attention."

Ten yards away in the fog, a gray outline stood still. Every hair on her arms and neck shot to attention.

His right arm swung gently, holding a pistol twice as long as it should be–a suppressor.

She lowered her shoulder, and the purse slid to the ground while her hand tightened around the deer antler. "My name is Rebekah Farmsdale, and I'm with Channel Ten News. Did you call me and tell me to meet you here?"

Out of the opacity, a gray shape trailed closer and turned black, all black, with a ski mask, gloves, and jacket. Rebekah changed her focus from the gun to his face. His eyes burned like hot coals.

Her fingers wiggled on the antler. "What can I do to help you get your message out to the public?"

A deep malefic sound bellowed, "You think you can help me? You want to make me famous?"

She thought he was trying to hide his real voice, but something was familiar. Slipping the fob into her front jeans pocket, she bent down to her purse, pulled out a small recorder, and held it in the air. "You called me, remember?" She pushed the record button and placed it next to her on the car roof. "You want to talk here? That's alright with me. Are you the Number Killer?"

He aimed the pistol at her chest.

"Wait. I'm here to help you."

The gun spit once.

She raised her arm for a second as plastic shrapnel exploded around her head. She pulled her hand back quickly and looked at the roof. The recorder had disappeared. "All right," she said, an octave higher. "All right. No audio. How about we talk, and I take notes?"

"Drop the weapon," he said.

The voice was somewhat familiar. She turned her right shoulder away from the man and tried to hide the antler tip. "I don't know what you're talking about. I'm not carrying a pistol." Her hand tightened. "Let's get back to why I'm here. What happened in the church?"

She watched the gun barrel aim back at her.

"Drop the deer antler," he said.

She released it, and it clattered to the ground. "We've met before. Where?"

"Hey, what are you doing here?" A voice called from the direction of the substation. Three men wore high-visibility yellow and orange striped vests. "This is private property. No one is allowed here."

The man in black spun around and dropped his arm enough to hide the gun behind his leg. "Who are you? Nobody works here."

The one in the middle adjusted his plastic safety helmet that sat on top of gray-streaked hair. "Came out to work on the grid." He looked at the woman and then back at the man. "Ma'am, do you need help?"

Rebekah waved her hands in the air. "I'm sorry for the intrusion. We'll leave at once."

They kept walking toward her.

She held her palms out. "Please, stop." She glanced at the gun. "We're on our way out, so you can go back to work. Please go back to your truck."

"Miss, are you alright?"

The gun barrel raised chest high toward them.

The one talking said, "Whoa, buddy. Hold on."

She bent down and grabbed the antler from the ground. "Let them go, and I'll bring you back to the news station. We can do an extensive interview, on camera or off. Your choice."

Two suppressed shots hit the TEX ELEC employee in the chest. He dropped flat.

She raised her hand to her mouth. "Oh, God, no."

The other two ran sideways. The gun swept left to right, firing into the grayness until the slide slammed back. Hidden moans bellowed, crying for help.

The man snapped open a knife from his pocket. The fog cocooned around his body.

Rebekah jumped into her car, started the engine, and slammed the shifter into reverse. The vehicle roared backward. She had no idea where anything was, the exit, the fence, the men on the ground. She slammed on the brakes and shifted to drive. The vehicle jumped forward, and she spun the wheel. A bullet pierced the door, and fire seared through her leg, spewing blood from her thigh. She screamed. The car bounced across rows of onions and stopped.

Her side window shattered. Glass spewed over her. Instinctively, she raised her arms to protect her face. She felt the door rattle and realized he was trying to open the locked door. "Leave me alone." She swung the antler tip and punctured his forearm. She screamed when glass cut her arm and hand.

The door flung wide open. He yanked a fist full of hair and pulled her from the vehicle.

She grabbed his wrist with one hand and furiously swung the antler into the air with the other. "No! No! Stop it." Her nails dug into his hand, trying desperately to separate his fingers from her hair.

He dragged her over the gravel, then lifted her to her feet. "You said you want to make me famous."

"Get away from me." She stabbed his chest.

His eyes alighted back at her. "That won't go through my jacket."

She jammed her boot into his crotch and dropped him, then hobbled toward the field. The fog consumed her.

Chapter 32

Marla went to her locker and changed into street clothes, a plaid shirt, jeans, and a denim jacket. Before she left the station, she returned to her desk and typed Channel Ten News in the search bar of her computer, rolled to the bottom, and tapped the *Contact Us* link. She called the 24-hour hotline. "This is Hildebrandt Police Officer Adams, and I need Rebekah Farmsdale's cell number." After a few more questions from the news station manager, she wrote the number down and called. The phone rang.

"Hello, this is News Investigator Rebekah Farmsdale. I am unable to answer my phone at this time. Please leave a message, and I will call back as soon as possible. Thank you."

"Rebekah? This is Marla Adams. Were you on FM 404 and turned into the Tinsley Substation? Just calling if you need anything in town. Call me back."

◆

Rebekah ran as fast as she could down a row between the onions. The heel of her boot caught some roots, and she tumbled across the dirt. Rolling onto her back, still holding the antler, she pulled out a shard of glass from her palm, and blood spurted on the dirt.

A voice from her left called out, "Rebekah Farmsdale will make me famous."

She jumped up and fell again. The heel of one shoe had broken off. She pitched both boots at the voice and ran. Animal grunts came closer.

"What the hell is that?"

Gray nothingness hid everything. Her thigh swelled, turning her pants into a Vise Grip with each pounding pulse.

The man yelled, "Rebekah Farmsdale, make me famous."

The voice was closer. Tears clouded her eyes. She pulled her phone out from her back pocket to call 911. Marla Adams left a voicemail. She punched the name and called back.

A black mass lunged at her from the side and landed on top of her. The phone flew from her hand. "Get off me!" She stabbed the antler at the man. He yelled, then ripped it from her grasp. She felt a slap across her face. Feeling for the antler on the ground, her hand brushed across the onions.

"You so desperately want to make me famous. You want to be famous."

The screen on the phone lit and a voice called out, "Hello. This is Marla Adams."

His boot heel slammed against the screen, and the phone went dark. He stood above her, blood dripping from his forearm onto her blouse. "Get away from me." She threw a dirt clod and hit him in the head. She kicked his knee with her barefoot and then clawed away over a row of onions.

He grabbed the bottom of her coat and pulled her back towards him. He wrapped his arm around her waist and said, "Enough."

"What do you want?" She frantically kicked and swung her arms in every direction. "Stop. I'm begging. Stop."

He yelled as her nails dug deep into his forearm.

His fist slammed against the side of her head. "To hell with you, news girl."

She looked blindly in the fog, reaching in every direction for something, anything. She kicked at his ankles.

He swung her around and slammed her on the ground, landing next to a metal pole sticking out of the earth with zip ties and a chain beside it. It knocked her breath away. Animal grunting sounds were closing in.

Struggling for words, she screamed at him, "Wait, I can help you." She dug her heels into the dirt, trying to escape. "I'll do whatever you want."

"I want you to stay here and die."

She jumped up to run, but he grabbed her foot and flipped her on her head. Her chance to escape was gone.

She blurted out the only thing that came to her. "No, you can't do this. Everyone will know who you are."

His face still covered. "How's that?" He wrapped the chain around her ankles and zip-tied it closed.

"I left my phone in the car. It's connected to the radio, and it's recording everything out here and going to the cloud."

"That's a lie. I broke your phone."

"I have another one, a news phone. I know who you are. Let me go, and I won't say anything."

He rolled her onto her stomach and zip-tied her wrists behind her back. "And who am I?" He pulled a bottle from his pocket and cracked open the cap.

She felt syrup pour on her head and body. "What are you doing?"

"Feral hogs like maple syrup."

She spat the gooey liquid from her lips and then heard his knife click open.

"They like onions and meat."

He bent down on one knee. With his face next to hers, he removed his ski mask. "Now you know."

"No, wait." She twisted her hands, trying to loosen the zip tie.

He wrapped his fingers in her hair and pulled her head back. "You wanted bright lights and fortune, but instead, you got fire and brimstone."

She jerked at the cold steel point against her neck. She cried, "Please stop. Oh, God, please help me."

"They like bloody meat."

Chapter 33

On the edge of Hildebrandt, pickup trucks of all flavors lined the frontage road. Texas flags and chili cook-off banners buffeted in the air with temporary tents, propane heaters, and strings of overhead lights populating the open field. It seemed every adult carried a sidearm while the kids carried a plastic bowl and spoon.

Marla pulled into an empty spot, climbed out, and adjusted her Stetson hat. Music blared in the distance. Strolling to the entrance, she waved at a family leaving. It was bedtime for the kiddos.

A woman stood in the ticket booth and wore an enormous smile. A hand-painted sign next to her said, 'Ten Dollars, please.' Brittney Caudwell, a Hildebrandt Elementary School teacher, said, "Hi, Marla. So glad you came." She slid a map of the area across the counter. "We color coded it this year. Some booths have different chili heats. Green for mild, yellow for medium, red for hot," she chuckled, "and black for, I warned you." She pointed to the center. "Drinks are here. Water is free. Got to buy soft drinks and beer. No milk this year, so be careful."

"No milk for me. I'm not going for the black stuff, but I hear there's a new entry of meatless chili."

"You better hurry. Everyone is surprised, and people want seconds."

"I'll try it, but more interested in Jack Reed's tent. Last year, he returned from an African hunt and cooked amazing wildebeest and gazelle chili pots. I wanted to buy a gallon of each and freeze it."

Odors of cooked cayenne powder, hot peppers, onions, tomatoes, and meat circled in the air. Strolling between tents, she tried a few. Some were hot, some not, and some people flat out lied when they said it was medium.

A beehive of gossip buzzed around her. Where's Crosby? They're having problems. One or both are cheating. Drugs, alcohol. Is Hildebrandt safe with her family in charge of the police department? Half the people stared, and the other half pretended she was invisible.

The tent ahead had to be Eileen and Ron's. A banner flapped in the wind:

VEGAN CHILI CAN BEAT YOUR MEAT,

flapped in the wind. There was no one behind the table. Several small bowls stood ready on the counter. Marla picked one and tried it, wondering what the chunkiness consisted of.

Eileen trekked back to their small trailer, with Ron ten feet behind. She unlocked the rear door and swung it open.

"I can't believe these people." Eileen opened another twenty-pound box of vegan meat. "We are going to run out of food before this ends."

"You were so right. This stuff is great. People are flocking to it."

"Take this box to the tent, and I will bring the sack of tomatoes and onions." She glanced at another box. "Do we still have enough spices in the tent?"

A voice from behind them asked, "What's in that veggie meat?"

Eileen and Ron spun around. Logan stood a few feet from her, holding a bowl.

Eileen smiled. "Hello, friend. Hope you're enjoying the festival."

Logan scooped chili into his plastic spoon. "Pretty good this year. Have a close friend who entered the competition. He has the best this year. You should try it."

Ron closed the trailer door and snapped the lock closed. "We don't eat meat, but thanks for the invite." He nodded at Eileen to move toward the tent.

"Why don't you be normal and eat meat?"

Ron eased between Logan and Eileen. "We are normal. Why don't you back off?"

Eileen leaned toward Logan and placed her hand on his shoulder. "Your friend cooks with exotics, right? Why don't you bring a few bowls of his chili to our tent, and we'll have a small taste-off. Let people try both and they decide." She eyes Searcy fifty feet away, heading toward a tent. "We could invite the police chief."

Logan trudged down the hill, back toward Cindy. When Marla snuck up behind Logan, Cindy snickered. With both hands, Marla clamped onto his love handles. He jumped, and chili flew into the air. Cindy and Marla laughed.

"You scared the crap out of me." He looked at Cindy. "Did you see her coming?"

Marla brushed the back of his shoulder. "You're fine. I'm paying you back for the last twenty years of whatever."

"Well, I think I should contact HR. I'm being bullied."

"Bullied?" Marla asked. "Are you going to mention the reason I barely touched you?"

"If I have to. Mrs. Lopez in HR would like to know you hit me while on duty."

"Denise Lopez? She and her husband come to our house and have dinner about once a month. She's been close friends with Crosby since high school. Why don't you come over some night and explain it to her after dinner?"

"Oh, yeah? Rumor is Crosby was 'friends' with almost every girl in high school."

Marla stuck her finger near Logan's face. "You need to be real careful what you say next."

"I mean, rumor is, he was friendly to everyone. Nice guy spreading his friendliness to all the girls."

"And he married me."

"Yeah." He pointed at the bowl on the ground. "What about that?"

She paused. "Come on." She patted his butt. "I'll buy you a bowl and a beer."

He looked at Cindy. "See that? She hit me again."

"I'm glad the two of you made up," Cindy quipped back at them.

She noticed Logan's knife holder on his belt was empty. "Where's your knife?"

He tapped the leather holder. "Don't know. Must have dropped it somewhere."

"Dropped it? When?"

"How the hell do I know? It's gone. Maybe at the house."

"Where's Pops?" Marla asked. "He's here every year?"

"Not this early," Logan said. "The Chief comes around nine or ten."

"You don't have to call him Chief when not at work."

"He likes it. You should call him that."

"He's Pops. He's always been Pops. I've called him that since I was, I don't know, since forever. I can't call him Searcy or Chief. He's Pops, and he'll never be anything else to me." She glared at Logan. "You think calling him Chief is going to make things easier around here? It won't. He was Pops to you until you took this job in Hildebrandt. I'm your sister, and I think you should call him by his name, not a rank in the police business."

"Sometimes I don't want you to be my sister. How about that? It's not going to kill anybody if I call him Chief or Searcy."

Cindy gently touched both their shoulders. "All right. There's no reason to argue about a name. Can we just get another bowl of chili and move on, please?"

Marla slapped her hat against her leg. "I'm suddenly not hungry." She can't get a break. Murders piling like logs on a fire. Rampant gossip. She aimed her hat at Logan. "You need to call your father by his name."

"Oh, come on, Marla. I'm not liking you so much right now."

Marla raised her hat above her head. "Jeez, I'm leaving. There's a lot of work left to do and none of it being done here."

She climbed into her truck and cranked the engine. The navigation screen showed a missed call from Rebekah Farmsdale. "Damn." She pulled her phone from her back pocket and read the same thing. Tapping the recall button gave her the same response as before. "Hello, this is News Investigator Rebekah Farmsdale. I am unable to answer my..." Marla disconnected the call. "Can't go home without Crosby." She headed back to the station for the night.

◆

The phone rang, and Marla shook the cobwebs out of her head. Sunlight peeked through the closed blinds at the station. Reaching across the desk, she answered on the second ring. "Hildebrandt Police Department."

"Found you," Searcy said. "You're not answering your cell."

"Left it in the truck."

"Someone called 911 about a dead person near Horton's Creek in a hole, naked and mangled. Letters carved in a tree trunk. Be ready. I'll pick you up at the back door in five."

She slammed the phone back on the cradle and stepped to the window. Her finger pushed the metal blinds down. A blazing sun screamed back at her. She let go, and the blinds snapped back. "Damn it, Crosby. I need your help." Her hand swooped the pistol off the desk while she rushed toward the back door.

Searcy lowered the passenger window. "Hurry up. We got to go."

Marla climbed into Searcy's truck and buckled the seatbelt. The emergency lights on the roof and grill flickered red and blue and the truck roared over a narrow asphalt road toward Horton's Creek. Marla sat on the passenger side and stared at murmuration of starlings moving in ebbs and flows. The patterns changed every second; folds, curves, dragons with tails, a long cross. Her eyes widened when, for a second, she saw the shape of an arrow pointing in the direction the pickup truck headed. The ten thousand flapping wings roared over them and disappeared.

She turned back to Searcy. "About last night. Are you feeling any better?"

Searcy yawned. "What are you talking about?"

"I called you. You were shooting grackles in your backyard."

"I was wondering why there were dead birds on the ground this morning."

"You don't remember shooting the birds? What about me calling you?"

Searcy stared straight ahead. "No."

"When I called, you said to avoid the fog. How did you know about that outside of town?"

"What in the hell are you talking about, girl? Don't go psycho on me."

"Me? Psycho? You take your meds every day, and you won't be so... neurotic, psychotic, bullshitotic." She leaned her head against the window as the sun climbed through distant clouds, then raised up just as quick. "Did you take your meds this morning?"

A light wind swirled through a leafless apple orchard. Searcy turned off the pavement to a long, straight path. Fifty yards ahead, another police unit awaited them on an incline of a hill with their emergency lights on. An officer stood next to two teenagers who sat quietly on the dirt. Barren apple trees butted up to them.

Searcy stopped the truck and took a flashlight out from his console. They quickly climbed out of his vehicle, and Searcy headed toward the boys while Marla rushed to the apple tree near the hole in the ground.

The tree trunk was wide with two letters carved on it: NK. She thought, *Number Killer?*

Rebekah Farmsdale had made this person famous. Marla slipped on gloves, then her fingertip rubbed the carved letters, feeling, looking, hoping an answer would jump out from the bark.

Like the last crime scene, the perp wanted to announce his presence, his murder, his accomplishments. She knew the killer sets a stage. It meant something to him.

"Marla," Searcy said. "Do you recognize either person in the pit?"

"Either?" She stood. "There's more than one?"

Marla stepped past the two boys to the pit and looked down. Someone had dug a rectangular hole with a large pile of loose dirt next to it, just like a hole in a cemetery ready for burial, except twice as deep. Bright green paint had splattered across two naked bodies. She didn't recognize the man or the woman.

The sun warmed the cool morning air. The boys sat quietly, wearing running shorts and Hildebrandt high school sweatshirts with their legs bent and heads between their knees. Both held their phones in their hands.

Searcy bent down to address the boys. "Hi, Michael. Hi, Jonathan. What are you boys doing out here?"

"We were jogging, sir, just like every morning."

Searcy glanced at the boy's phones in their hands. "Take any pictures of the hole?"

They both shook their heads. "No, sir," Jonathan said. "That would be ...kinda creepy."

Searcy stood up and turned to Marla. "These are our two best runners at Hildebrandt High, Michael and Johnny Barron." He twisted back to the boys and gently pulled on their arms. "Alright, up you go."

"Mr. Searcy," Michael said. "We were jogging, just like every morning. We didn't do nothin' wrong." He shoved Jonathan's shoulder. "We stopped to see why there was a fresh pile of dirt on the hill. This is the first time we saw this hole. I promise."

Marla leaned over with her hands on her knees. "What time do you run?"

"We get up every morning at five, lift weights at home, then run," Michael said.

"What about school in the morning?"

"We drive to school, then run our route. The principal lets us change clothes in the gym."

"When was the last time you ran by here?" Marla asked as she rechecked her watch.

"Yesterday." Jonathan looked at Michael. "I told you we should have run down by the substation this morning."

Marla looked around for a shovel or something to dig a hole, then swung back to the boys. "How often do you run down this road?"

"We mix it up," Jonathan replied. "Sometimes we run the same for two or three days, and then we switch to a different route."

"How many routes do you have?" Marla asked.

Michael looked at Jonathan and raised his shoulders. "I don't know, a dozen or so."

"If we ran to the substation like I said," Jonathan barked back, "we'd be in class right now." He looked at Searcy. "Are we in trouble?"

"No, of course not." Searcy patted both boys on their shoulders. Logan and Larry Keyman stopped behind Searcy's truck with their lights flashing. When both doors opened, Searcy motioned Larry to come over.

"Yes, sir, Chief."

"Officer Keyman will take you boys home. We want you and your parents to come to the station later today and give a statement. Larry," Searcy said, "lights and siren off."

Logan held a grocery size paper sack. "Give me an update," he called out as he adjusted his bandage around his forearm.

"What happened to your arm?" Marla asked.

"You need to be nice to me." He held the sack out toward Marla.

"What is it?"

"The vegan chili. It's not too bad."

She closed her eyes and shook her head. "Thanks. Forgot to eat last night."

Searcy pointed at Logan's arm and asked, "What happened?"

"Butch and I played a little too hard last night. The damn dog got too excited and chomped down on my arm."

"Did you see Doc or the vet?" Marla smirked while she put the sack on top of Searcy's pickup hood.

"Funny, Sis. Yeah, antibiotics and a salve."

"You need to keep that covered," Marla said. "I have gauze and tape at the house if you need more."

Searcy motioned for all to come to the pit. "Two bodies are down there, naked. Can't tell yet who they are."

Marla peered down the side of the hole. "Whoever did this didn't want them to climb out. It's deep, and the sides are straight up."

Searcy pulled at his coat while aiming the flashlight into the pit. "All that movement you see around the bodies is not good."

"What do you mean?" Logan asked.

"Looks like a dozen or more rattlesnakes down there," Searcy said.

"Wrong time of year for snakes to be out. It's too cold." Marla looked around. "Whoever killed them had to pull snakes out of a den and drop them down there. Dangerous."

Logan leaned over and looked down into the pit. "Tell you what, sis," he said. "Why don't you go down there and fast draw on all the snakes, then see who the bodies are?"

She smiled while grabbing his wrist close to the bandage. "Why don't I wrap a few rats around your neck, throw you in, and then shoot?"

"Enough," Searcy said. "You two have been at it since birth. Cut the shit, would you?"

"How did the snakes get there?" Marla asked. "That pit is at least fifteen feet deep and had to be dug with a digger. Who has a digger around here?"

"Who has a digger?" Logan quipped back. "Every farmer and rancher within a hundred miles of here has a front loader and a digger in their barn."

Larry stepped between the feuding siblings and glanced into the hole. "The bodies kept the snakes warm for a few hours." He shook his head. "Now they look like they aren't moving too fast. Probably more of them under the bodies, trying to stay as warm as possible."

"Good point," Searcy said. "Hadn't thought of that."

"Somebody had to throw the snakes in the pit," Marla turned away. "Was it before or after the couple went in?"

"Need to take some pictures of the bodies before we move them," Searcy said. He pointed at Logan. "Get me your fishing rod from your truck."

Logan bunched his brow. "Fishing rod? What are you talking about.?"

"Don't give me any bull. I know you go fishing while *ON THE JOB*."

Logan looked around with his hands up. "It's called surveillance. I'm blending in with people while checking for suspicious activity around the lake."

"So? Go get it." Searcy said.

"Sure. It's in my truck bed. What do you need my rod for?"

Without answering, Searcy walked to his truck with the light-bar still flashing red and blue in every direction. He opened the glove compartment and pulled out a GoPro, returned to the pit, and waited.

"Pops," Marla said. "When did you buy a GoPro?"

"Don't call me Pops on the job. Remember the big drug bust nine months ago? It was in the guy's car. After the conviction, I put the camera in my truck. Used it a few times to video crime scenes."

Logan handed the rod and reel to Searcy. "Yeah, me too. I use this for police work just like Chief uses the camera."

Searcy looked at Marla. "See, he calls me Chief." He streamed the GoPro to his phone, then wrapped the fishing line around it and lowered it to the bottom of the pit. He handed the phone to Marla. With the camera hanging from the fishing line, they all squeezed around Searcy's phone.

The dead man lay to the left of the woman. Flat on his back, his torso twisted, and legs bent like he was running, the middle of his upper right arm bent at a 90 degree angle. His face turned toward the woman, who was as swollen as a ripe pumpkin. There were multiple snake bite marks on her face. The woman, also on her back, faced back toward the man with her elbows bent and her hands covering her breasts.

A snake slithered over the woman's neck and down her torso, smearing lines of blood on her arms and legs. Both had green paint splattered across their bodies.

Logan slipped back from the crowd and found a square piece of paper next to an apple tree. It had Marla's name on it.

"Damn." Searcy zoomed in on the camera screen. "That's Eileen Lieb and Ronald Abrams."

Marla looked bewildered. "Vegan chili. Someone killed the two who made the meatless chili after the festival last night."

Logan stood again and held out his hand. "Marla, found something next to the tree for you."

She spun around. "What?"

"An envelope addressed to you."

She hesitated before taking it from his fingers. *I. Don't. Want. This.* The words OFFICER MARLA ADAMS were printed on the front with a black felt marker. Her fingers fumbled, trying to pull the paper from the envelope. She shook her head and moaned. *I don't want this.*

She unfolded the page and glared at each word. Her ears roared, claws dug inside her lungs.

YOU DROVE PAST AND LET HER DIE!

She looked up at Logan and said, "Where did you find this?"

"Over there, leaning next to the tree trunk. What's it say?"

"Tinsley Substation." She wadded the paper and kept it in her hand.

Searcy asked, "What about Tinsley?"

"Rebekah Farmsdale drove in front of me last night. She turned, and I thought she was the smart one."

The squad car with the two boys backed down the hill. Marla ran and waved frantically. The vehicle stopped, and she opened the back door. "You said the substation? Do you mean the Tinsley Grid?"

"Sure," Jonathan replied.

"What about last night? Was anybody there last night?"

"I don't know. You're scaring me."

Searcy followed her down the hill and pulled Marla away. "What is wrong with you? These are kids. You can't talk to them like that."

She closed the door, took her phone from her back pocket, and tapped redial. "Hello, this is News Investigator Rebekah..." She disconnected the call. "We need to go to Tinsley right now."

Chapter 34

Sirens wailed down FM 404. Red and blue lights scraped treetops along the road. A low slung fog lingered between tree trunks. Tires from Searcy's dually truck slid to a stop at the entrance of the Tinsley Substation. Several cars stopped in defensive positions.

Last night's witch's brew hovered over the ground, lingering, hiding evidence. Marla slipped on a vest with the word POLICE across the back.

In front of the substation, the top half of a bucket truck with a TEX ELEC logo looked like it floated on a cloud. Transformers buzzed electricity through long-distance wires.

Searcy directed officers to the truck while others bypassed the substation to the back.

Marla spotted a small SUV around the back with the roof and windows visible, the rest of the vehicle hidden in the mist. She slowly drew her weapon. Her heart pounded against her vest. A chill in the air crept into the cuffs of her sleeves while sweat dripped down her collar. Marla calculated her steps, heel then toe; weapon pointed directly toward the SUV. Other officers on either side of her moved in stride. On the side of the car, she read the top half of the words CHANNEL TEN NEWS. Her nerves were on high alert, expecting someone to jump out and fire at them. Twenty feet from the car, her foot hit an object. Marla closed her eyes and didn't want to know if it was Rebekah. She whimpered as she bent down. Her hand touched a boot, fingers glided over a bumpy sole, thick stiff leather, and shoestrings. It wasn't Rebekah's, it was a work boot. She slid her fingers up the cool, stiff leg—dead.

"I have a body on the ground."

An officer to her right called out, "Body here."

She inched closer toward the car and noticed it stopped at an odd angle. Her foot hit something else. Her heart jumped into her throat. She warily reached down again. Her hand brushed across leather. She lifted it above the mist and glanced at a woman's purse with a single set of tire marks across it.

Ten feet away, the driver's side window was broken and the door partially open. She rushed to the car and swept the inside with her weapon.

Strands of dark blue nylon were stuck in the broken window. Shards of glass spread across the seat and floorboard, with visible blood on the door panel.

Another officer called out, "I see a metal pole in the field."

The mist rolled like waves in an ocean between rows of the onion field. She spun around and crept forward toward a pole stuck straight up in the air next to a mangled mound. Cautiously, she crept down a row. Her pistol swept across the knee-high fog.

She stopped. The mound wasn't dirt. It was a body. A bloody, mutilated body.

Marla's knees jelled. She told herself as the lead investigator, she couldn't pass out—couldn't fall down—don't cry.

Shredded bloody clothes were spread in every direction. The body laid on its side with the stomach shredded open, and the guts eaten. Wrists zip-tied behind the trunk with most of the muscle gone.

Marla lowered her weapon and stared.

Searcy caught up to her. "Oh, Jesus. Hogs."

She bent down on one knee and picked up the news logo ripped from the jacket a few feet from the body.

Her pistol barrel lifted the chains slightly, one end wrapped around the pole and the other around mangled ankles. She checked what she could for numbers carved anywhere. There were none.

Searcy slowly lifted Marla up off her knees. She pressed her face against his shoulder and wrapped her arms around him. "Please. I don't want to do this anymore. I want to go home. I want Crosby at home with me."

Another officer held a phone with a broken screen.

She pushed away from Searcy. "I want to leave all this shit, leave Hildebrandt, leave the force. Don't you see? I'm no good at this. You put me in charge, and people are dying." She wiped her palms across her eyes. "Four dead. Today!"

Searcy patted her on the back. "I know, but we have to find him." He looked at the mutilated body again. "We have to stop him."

She shoved him back again. "You don't understand. I could have stopped this."

He shook his head. "No, you couldn't."

"Yes. I could have. Last night, driving back from San Antonio, in front of me was an SUV, and it turned into Tinsley. I saw the news logo on the car." She pointed. "That car. It was Rebekah." Marla rubbed tears from her cheeks. "She turned here. This place right here." She scoffed and brushed hair away from her face. "I thought how smart that person was getting off the road and out of the fog. She wasn't getting out of the fog; she was meeting the killer. In her opinion piece on the news, she wanted to meet with him." Marla raised the crook of her elbow to her mouth and coughed repeatedly. She sighed. "I should have turned in and followed her. I should have... I could have killed that murdering bastard last night." She coughed again. "Damn it. I'm leaving. Going home. To hell with all of you." She glared into Searcy's eyes. "I DON'T WANT ANY OF THIS."

She retreated down the row of onions when Searcy called out, "You came with me, and I can't leave the crime scene yet."

She spun around and held out her hand. "Give me your key."

"Hold on."

"Give me the Goddamn key."

He dug into his pocket and pitched it to her. "All right. Be careful."

She trounced back toward the truck. When she passed Rebekah's car, she stopped and stared at words written across the windshield with a grease pencil.

SHE BEGGED FOR IT

BEGGARS DON'T DESERVE NUMBERS

Chapter 35

Early the following day, Logan opened Searcy's office door. "I called the electric company yesterday. The office manager was helpful. He said all the substations have cameras high on a pole to catch intruders and vandals. He asked me to come to the back door and would let me watch the video of that night. I'm heading there now. Want to come?"

"Sure." Searcy logged off his computer. "Fog was heavy around here. Don't suppose we can see much."

Logan glanced behind him, then closed the door. "It was a quick deduction of Marla from the paper."

"Meaning?"

"She picked out Tinsley awfully fast, and she knew where on the property to look. Like she had been there."

"What do you think you're going to see on that video?"

"Hoping to find a recognizable car or truck, or woman."

◆

The road into San Antonio took forever. Marla dodged fast moving cars and slow semi-trailers on I-10. Tall streetlights shined bright light on the highways. Random lights inside glass skyscrapers lit the black sky. Her sunken eyes begged for sleep. Her shoulders, heavy with guilt.

She tried not to think of Rebekah's smile while volunteering. Both she and her mother helping the community. The town failed her. Marla did as well.

Four hundred yards ahead, an MVA, motor vehicle accident, left one car upside down and the other with the trunk shoved into the backseat. She slowed and flipped on her emergency lights. Two Texas DPS units were there, along with an ambulance. A trooper waved to her.

Marla obliged by rolling down her window. "Looks like you have everything under control. Need anything?" she asked.

"People think this road is the on ramp to a NASCAR race."

She nodded toward the wreck. "More like a demolition derby."

He scoffed. "Right." He glanced at her door with a Hildebrandt Police logo on the side. "You got a mess over there, Ma'am. The Rangers might be an excellent choice for that."

She tight lipped a smile and nodded. "Thanks, but Chief Searcy thinks he can solve it."

"Hmm." He tapped the side of her truck. "What brings you here to the city, Officer...?"

"Adams, Marla Adams. And I'm in town to see Dr. Berghoff at the Bexar County Medical Examiner's office."

"Bergy? Nice guy, a little eccentric with the white hair and 'stache, but he knows dead people inside and out."

"I've gotten to know him a little too well."

"I would think so. Good luck to you, Officer Adams."

A few minutes later, Marla turned into the Medical Examiner's lot with only a few cars parked near the entrance. A few hours too early for the 9-to-5 employees to show. She waved her badge at the security officer and headed straight for the morgue. If Rebekah was here, she didn't want to see the body, or what was left of it.

The all too familiar odor of sanitized death penetrated her nostrils while passing the corridor marked Crime Lab where David Weidman worked.

"You Give Love A Bad Name" by Bon Jovi blared from a Bluetooth speaker as the door to the morgue closed behind her. The same stainless steel tables used for the previous victims now held two more bodies with arms and legs bent from rigor mortis. She heard silent screams for help.

Dr. Berghoff sang the words in harmony to the song. He came out of the sterilizer room with clear bags of medical instruments in one hand and a large Styrofoam cup in the other. He nodded at her. "Good morning, Officer Adams. I love that song." He sang the lyrics off-key. "My favorite line is about shooting someone in the heart." He held the cup in his hand and chuckled. "Breakfast of Pathologists." He slurped something red up the straw. "We seem to be seeing each other a lot."

"Good morning, Dr. Berghoff." She smiled as she pulled the strings of the mask behind her ears. "Don't get me wrong, you're a nice guy and all, but I don't wish to see you on a regular basis."

He chuckled. "Perhaps we should try to exchange Christmas cards once a year." He placed all the instruments next to the dead woman. "Haven't done much, just a quick external review."

For him not looking behind her shoulder for Crosby told her he recognized she was alone.

"Crosby couldn't make it this time."

"Yes, the haboob of gossip already swept through the office." He pointed back at the two bodies. "You know it's not required for you to be present. You can leave anytime you feel the need."

"I know." She cleared her throat. "I'm ready."

"First of all, I can tell you these are connected to the other killings."

"I was afraid of that. Did you find numbers?"

"Yes, and more." He slipped on a pair of blue gloves, then handed her a pair. "Did you know the victims?"

Usually, a corpse was flat like they were quietly sleeping. This time, the sheets looked deadly alive.

"Not well," she said. "Eileen Lieb was an attorney in town and could be as mean as a junkyard dog or pat children's heads and hand out lollipops."

He pulled the sheet halfway down to the waist. Green paint covered most of her trunk, arms, and face. "Small woman, perhaps sixty or sixty-one inches and one-hundred-twelve pounds." He touched several swollen places. "Over twenty snake bites."

"She's twisted like a statue," Marla said.

"Rigor mortis and cold storage. It's been about a day, and the muscles are softening." He pointed to the arms. "These abrasions are where a rope was tied around her wrists and then around her trunk. The rope held the forearms close to her breasts." He lifted one stiff elbow slightly. "There is paint between her breasts and the arms. My guess is, she was alive when thrown down into the pit. The killer poured the paint on her, then she moved her arms around, thus, paint all over her. If she were already dead, there might not be paint where skin-to-skin touched."

He held a long pair of forceps that looked like massive needle-nose pliers. He lifted the skin around the nostril. "Blowflies again, but this time, the eggs have not hatched. It takes one-to-two days for them to hatch. The cooler the weather, the longer it takes."

He pointed to her face marked with dried blood on her cheek. "Remember that. I'll show you why in a second." He touched the back of the body's shoulder. "Would you mind?"

Marla rolled the victim to the side and revealed what she expected. "He's a sick son-of-a-bitch."

Dr. Berghoff said, "Numbers 1 and 6 are cut into her back and not straight. There are thick blood lines below the cuts. Looks like she jerked from the pain. She had to still be alive when that happened." He pointed at the bottom of the scapula. "A single puncture hole from a bullet here on the left and another on the right. Blood poured into her lungs. She coughed and vomited when blood filled her trachea to her mouth. Her last few minutes of life were terrible; sliced, shot, then thrown into the pit. She was alive, coughing up blood and being snake bit."

"Have you determined the angle of the gunshot?"

"Only an estimate." He pointed the large forceps at a bullet hole in the back. "The angle of the right wound looks like she may have been standing when shot, and the projectile line looks horizontal with an exit wound in the chest, therefore, shot in the back. The left gunshot has the exit in front and angled as if she twisted from the first bullet hitting her. I need to probe the wounds and open the trunk to confirm."

"Two exit wounds?" Marla asked.

"Yes, two."

"That means there are two bullets out there somewhere. Did the perp shoot Eileen before or after he dumped her in the pit?"

"The preliminary angle suggests she was shot in the pit. The bullets could be buried in the ground down in the pit?"

"I'll look. What about the male?" Marla asked.

"Only an external review, as well." He pulled the sheet down to mid-chest and touched two slight burns on the neck. "Taser marks here to the right posterolateral neck."

"Tased, not shot?"

"Both. Shot in the left side of the head. No exit wound. You want to see the damage to the scrotum and penis?"

"Is this a sexual molestation case?" Marla asked.

"I'll let you decide. Ready?"

She nodded, reluctantly. "Sure, go ahead."

He pulled the sheet to the victim's knees. "Need to do a complete dissection of this area, but, as you can see, the scrotum looks like a black softball."

Marla's stomach churned, then she coughed several times.

"Not sure if he was hit in the groin or damage from snakebites. I'll find out."

"What about paint and numbers on him?"

Dr. Berghoff nodded as they walked around to the other side. "There were areas where paint did not cover the skin. I think he was dead when paint splattered over him. But the number, same thing, 16 on the back. These were straight. The killer probably practiced on her, did him second, or did him after being tased and shot."

"Time of death?" Marla asked.

"Early rigor, cold in the hole; just a few hours before you found them. "Marla glanced at her watch. "Early yesterday morning?"

"Sounds likely."

"If you don't mind, I'm heading out before you... start cutting. I have one thing to do in town before I head home."

"It's going to take a little extra time to finish the autopsy working around the rigor. I'll type up my prelim report the day after tomorrow and email it to you. The final toxicology report won't be for several weeks."

Marla left the parking lot and headed for the Food Pantry near the Alamo. She couldn't help but think about both Rebekah and her mother helping at the homeless shelter. The least she could do was drive by and give a donation in their names.

The morning sun lit the horizon as she pulled into the slanted parking spot across the street from the Alamo. This was not the shelter, but the office. She wasn't surprised that a homeless shelter wouldn't be in the middle of a tourist trap. The front door was locked. Lifting a mail slot on the wall next to the door, she slid an envelope with a check and a note inside before heading back to the pickup.

Hundreds of birds started chattering. Marla stopped in the center of the empty street and listened. Starlings lit on every tree branch and all along the top of the Alamo roof line. She strolled through the middle of the intersection. As if every bird looked at her at the same time, in unison, they flew into the sky. Wings fluttered like a million clapping hands. The black cloud performed a ballet above the buildings, turning and folding on itself.

She touched her holster when, for a fleeting second, the murmuration changed to the shape of a pistol before charging toward the empty sky.

Chapter 36

Marla opened the Crescent's front door, revealing a blackened room with dim lights over pool tables. She stood still for a few seconds to adjust to the darkness.

Moon waved at her. "Officer Adams...come in, sit down."

She sat on a stool at the center of the bar. "Moon, why is it always dark in here?"

He wiped down the bar in front of her. "When it's dark, people drink more," he leaned forward and whispered, "and I can water down the drinks." He leaned back. "Cosmo for the lady? Want to talk about Eileen and Ron?"

"Moon, I'm in uniform, and it's eleven in the morning. How the hell did you get that information? I left the morgue and drove straight here."

"You think your father is the only person who knows everyone in town? I'm the busiest bartender in the county, maybe the state. I know everyone, what they're doing, what they did, who they did, and what they're going to do, whether they're alive or dead."

After her eyes adjusted to the dark a little more, she looked around the room. "Father Jules is here." She watched him sitting at a table with several people surrounding him before she turned back to Moon. "If that's true, tell me everything about him?"

"Him? I think that might take about three Cosmos, and we don't tell Crosby what happens afterward. He's got eleven more days in the slammer, right?"

"Rehab, not the slammer."

"Whatever you want to call it. I still won't tell Crosby what happens between us after those three *free* Cosmos."

Marla chuckled. "I'm a happily married woman. But...if Crosby left me and all the other guys in town ignored me, then we'll see what might happen."

"Now you're just teasing with me. Okay, come back after five, and the first Cosmo is on the house."

Marla's smile disappeared. "How long has Father Jules been here?"

Moon leaned his elbows on the bar. "Hmm, about an hour. He used to struggle to get people to talk to him. It seems he's become a popular man with all the killings. All souls want to be saved in the foxhole."

"No place better than a bar," Marla retorted.

Daylight burst across the room as the front door opened. Two women charged in. "Moon, baby," the blonde said. "two double vodka tonics."

"Sandy, you're looking extra hot today," Moon said.

"That's so sweet. When you bring those drinks, sit down and make us laugh."

Marla smiled. "Excuse me, Moon, but it looks like both of us have work to do."

Father Jules continued to talk as he glanced at the police officer approaching him. He turned back to the three young girls across the table from him. "You see, God has a plan for each of us. He wants you to follow that plan. Come to confession tomorrow and tell God your sins."

Everyone around the table looked at Marla in her uniform when she stopped next to Father Jules. He glanced over his shoulder. "Officer Adams. Come join us."

"I will, but just the two of us." She swept her hand above everyone's head. "All right, find another table, please."

Chair legs scraped across the wooden floor as each person dispersed.

"Mind if I sit down?"

"Not at all, Officer Adams. I would enjoy your company."

"I want to ask you a few questions."

He took a sip of his red wine as she sat next to him. "How may I help you?"

Marla looked at the almost empty glass. "Want another before we start?"

"No, thank you. One is enough. Someone is always gracious enough to buy my wine for me when I come here, and I don't want to take advantage of people's goodwill."

Marla nodded. "Where were you last night?"

"Here, like most nights. I was trying to save a few souls."

"And when did you leave?"

His finger slowly spun around the rim of the glass. "That I'm not sure of. Can I help you with something?"

"You can tell me where you were from ten last night to seven this morning."

"Ten until seven? I think I might have left this establishment about midnight."

"Midnight? Are you sure? I can always check the video cameras."

He took a small sip. "I'm not sure of the time. You see, I don't wear a watch. God is not interested in being on time, and neither am I."

"You don't have a regular time for church services? People come and go as they please? You, also?"

"No, of course not. We have scheduled times for our services. For that, there is a clock in my church office."

"Yes, your office. The place where Crosby and I met you and talked about the first murder in town. Now we have multiple crime scenes and multiple deaths. Father, can you confirm your whereabouts during each of the murders?"

His lips pressed against the wine glass and took the last sip. He gently put the glass on the table and said, "You remember, I left for a few days after the terrible murder in my church."

"I do remember you leaving," Marla said. "Remind me where you went."

"Am I a suspect for these murders?"

"Should you be?"

◆

Marla swung by the station and stopped at the evidence/equipment room. "I need to check out the metal detector for a few hours."

Billy Singleton stood behind the Plexiglas. "Sure. I got it hanging on the back wall. Be back in a sec."

Another officer approached from behind and opened the door. A minute later, he returned, pressing his cap with the police logo on his head. He nodded to her as he closed the door. "Almost forgot this."

Billy returned with a bag marked HPD METAL DETECTOR. He opened the door and leaned it against the wall near her. Returning to his desk behind the Plexiglas, he slid her a piece of paper. "Sign here, and it's all yours."

She scribbled a quick signature, then slid the strap over her shoulder. "You left the door unlocked."

"I know. Mark called and said he forgot his cap. I told him I would leave it unlocked in case I wasn't at the window. Glad I did. He was in a hurry."

"Need to keep this door locked at all times."

Billy nodded. "Sure thing."

✦

Marla's truck stopped close to the crime scene of Eileen and Ron. Yellow crime scene tape wavered in the wind surrounding the hole and mound of dirt. Rebekah's body flashed in her mind.

Marla swept the metal detector over the ground in a semi-circular fashion. It didn't take long for the machine to beep. She pulled the garden trowel out from her back pocket and dug up a rusted penny. She pitched it away. After fifteen minutes, there were no further beeps.

Looking down the hole, all she saw was green paint and dead snakes. "Damn. I don't want to go down there." She zipped the metal detector back in the bag and laid it near the hole. Behind her, an empty apple grove stretched across the horizon. She pulled an extension ladder out from the back of her truck. After dropping the trowel into the hole and sliding the ladder down the side, she paused for a moment. "Don't like rattlers." She swung the strap around her shoulder and climbed down the steps. Grabbing the shovel handle, she chopped each snake head off, just to make sure they were dead. None moved.

The snakes felt like garden hose rolling under her boot. It didn't make any difference if they were dead. When her hand touched the smooth, cold walls, she could almost hear Eileen's and Ron's screaming, begging. There could be no escape from angry, coiled snakes. A square of blue sky stood above her head. No one could climb out. Her skin crawled.

It didn't take long for the detector to beep. Her boot pushed a dead snake aside. When she began digging with the trowel, it only took a few inches to find both bullets. She dropped them into an evidence bag and sealed it.

The ladder rose in the air, scraping and banging against the side of the wall. Marla turned away as chunks of dirt dropped on her head.

"Who's out there? Bring that back."

Marla felt the walls close in, her grave while alive. She drew her pistol and fired toward the blue sky.

"Hey, Sis. Just having a little fun."

Marla leaned against the wall and forced herself not to cough.

"Don't shoot me. I'm lowering it back down."

The ladder slid against the dirt wall, and a leg stabbed the middle of a snake. She rushed up the steps as quickly as possible.

Logan held his arms out like he was expecting a hug. "See, everything is wonderful."

She dropped the metal detector on the ground and smiled. "Funny." Her fist hit him right in the gut, and he fell like a lead balloon.

Curled in a ball on his side, he moaned, "All right, not so funny."

She held her hand out to him. "Get up. I didn't hit you that hard."

He rolled onto his hands and knees, then jumped up and swung at her. She stepped back and watched him fall again.

"You have done that same move since grade school. You finished?"

"Yeah, yeah, yeah. I came out here to help you, and, instead, you beat the crap out of me."

She held her hand out, and Logan reluctantly grabbed her arm and stood. She noticed his knife holder on his belt was still empty. "Find your knife?"

He tapped the leather holder. "Still haven't found it."

Marla's phone pinged–a text from Searcy. *Where's my damn truck key?*

"Jeez. It's Pops. He can't find his keys. Be a good little brother and take these bullets to the Bexar County Crime Lab. Hand them directly to David Weidman." He winced when she patted his stomach with the back of her hand. "Only him."

Marla placed the detector in the back of the bed and then started tapping a reply on her phone. She erased it. Texting him back and forth would take too long, calling would be better.

Searcy answered his phone. "Where's my damn keys?"

"Maybe it's on the kitchen counter." He was on the max dose of his antipsychotics, and it still seemed not enough. There were three phases in his sinusoidal life, pleasantly normal, rocket burning highs with ricocheting ideas, or buried deep in gloom. She started her truck and drove toward his house. "I can be there in a few minutes to help."

"NO! I don't want you here. Don't you dare come to my house. Nobody goes inside my house."

"Don't shoot any grackles." Marla turned right onto Main Street and then left to Sweetbrier Road. A few minutes later, she pulled in behind Searcy's truck. The front door to the house was wide open.

She entered and peered into the foyer with newspapers strewn across the floor and couch. The television paused at what looked like a scene of an incendiary bomb exploding. A prescription bottle laid sideways on the coffee table with Searcy's fob next to it. She picked up the bottle and the fob.

A rancid smell came from the kitchen. The cabinet doors were open, and every glass Searcy owned stood dirty on the countertop. She touched the warm Mr. Coffee carafe. The on-light was off. In the left basin of the sink were squirrel guts with two fresh hides in the right.

Marla raised her arm and coughed several times. She pulled out the inhaler from the shirt pocket and squirted two sprays into her lungs.

"Did you come here to steal my hides?" Searcy said.

His hair shot in every direction. The top two shirt buttons were one hole off. He rushed to the sink, turned the faucet on, and sprayed the hides. "Need to keep these wet."

"Pops, I came by to check on you." She poured coffee in the cleanest cup she could find from the sink and put a double dose of the medication in her hand.

"You mean, steal."

"Take these, Pops." She placed the pills in his palm, then handed the cup to him. He sipped his coffee, swished it in his mouth, and swallowed.

Marla grabbed a plastic grocery bag and scooped up the squirrel remains. "Why did you skin these?" She knotted the bag and rinsed the basin.

He spit the medication back into his hand. "They were here to rob me. Steal my clothes and money. They were going to take my coins."

Marla tilted the mason jar of dimes and quarters on the kitchen windowsill. "Listen to me, Pops. Squirrels can't take this. It's too heavy. They want acorns, and nuts, and seeds."

"No. There's more out there, and they want my money; they want everything." He pointed at the sink. "Showed them who's boss."

Searcy tore open the plastic bag, reached in for a bloodied squirrel, and smeared it across the front of his shirt. He rushed out the back door, held his hands high, and yelled, "This is my house! You can't take my money. All this is mine, not yours, mine."

"Pops, come back inside." She gently laid her hand on his shoulder. Sometimes you have to let the craziness just pass. "How about you go take a shower and put clean clothes on? I'll make you breakfast or lunch."

Forty minutes later, the dishwasher rumbled, bacon sizzled, and slightly burnt bread popped up from the toaster. Searcy entered into the kitchen wearing a clean uniform.

"You look much nicer." Marla slid the bacon and eggs onto a plate and placed them on the table. "Ready to eat?"

He sat, then grabbed the knife and pointed it toward her.

She focused on the knife point. "Pops, pick up your fork and eat."

He slid the fork under the fried egg and laid it on top of the toast. "What are you doing here, Marla?"

She scooted a chair back from the table and sat across from him. "You called me to come find your truck key."

He took a bite of egg and toast, then swallowed a large gulp of coffee. "No, I didn't. What are you doing in my house?"

"That's the only reason I came here." She stood, grabbed the carafe, and poured more coffee into his cup. "I'm glad I did." She looked around. "This place is a mess." She wheeled back to Searcy. "I emptied the trash cans, and the dishwasher is full and running. Everything is much cleaner."

Searcy swept the plate and cup off the table and across the room. They shattered into pieces. He stood, and the chair fell and bounced on the floor. "I said, why are you here? You taking whatever those damn squirrels don't get?" He trounced out from the kitchen and punched the side of the refrigerator, leaving a dent the size of his fist. "I'll take care of this." He turned into his bedroom and slammed the door shut.

"Pops, take it easy. I'm leaving."

Behind the door, she heard the only thing a metal snap-click could come from; his 12-gauge double-barrel shotgun opened and closed. She drew her service weapon and stepped back into the bathroom next to the bedroom. The doorknob twisted, and the door bounced against the wall. Searcy charged forward.

With the shotgun level to his shoulder, he fired. A blast shattered the television. "You damn squirrels can't steal from me anymore."

Behind him, Marla swept his feet, and landed on top of him. The butt of her pistol hit Searcy on the back of the head.

"Damn it, Pops." She shoved the shotgun away from the semi-conscious man. "Take your damn pills." Searcy groaned on the floor. Marla bent down to his head. "You hear me? Every God-forsaken day. Take your pills."

Her phone rang with *Crime Lab* on the screen. While sitting on top of Searcy, she answered, "Hello?"

"Marla, this is David Weidman at the Bexar County Crime Lab. I am deeply sorry to call you this late, but I couldn't call Crosby and I must contact someone."

Her hand pushed down on Searcy's head. "I'm sorry about when I was there fingerprinting the handle."

"Totally understandable. I hope I'm not bothering you."

She reached to the back of her utility belt and lifted the handcuffs out. "No, just having a little family time with my father." With one hand, she snapped the cuffs on his left hand and right ankle, then pitched the key on the kitchen floor. She noticed blood on his nose. *Sorry, Pops.*

"I need something cleared. How many bullets were fired in the church?" She stood. "Two."

"You only brought one here?"

"Right. We didn't find the bullet shot through the victim. It went out the window. You have the one fired into the Bibles."

"Someone from the Hildebrandt Police Department brought in two more bullets."

"Yes, that's right. Eileen Lieb was shot twice."

"I immediately ran these through the system, and I have double and triple and a million times checked. Absolutely certain of the findings."

"Of what, David?"

"Those striations match the bullet from Roberto Sardino's pistol. The same gun from the church shooting."

"That's impossible. We have that gun locked up in our evidence room."

◆

Marla stormed down the station hallway and stopped at the evidence room. There was no one on the other side of the Plexiglas, so she knocked twice. "Anybody in there?" She pounded with her fist. "Hey! Someone better answer."

Larry turned the corner and stopped next to her. "What are you doing?"

"I need to check a piece of evidence."

"What evidence?"

"The gun from the church shooting. I need to see it."

"Okay. I'm sure Billy is back there somewhere."

A voice behind them called out, "Can I help you?" Billy slipped past them with a soft drink can in his hand. He opened the door and closed it behind him.

"Did you leave the evidence room unlocked again?" Marla asked.

Billy shrugged his shoulders. "Only for a few seconds. Is there something I can get you?"

Marla cleared her throat. "You are in deep trouble for leaving."

"I got thirsty. Big deal, a few seconds."

She looked back at Billy. "I need to check the pistol from the church shooting."

He took a drink from the can and then waved them back. "Come in."

She turned the knob and looked at Larry. "He didn't lock the door." She pushed through with him behind her and twisted the dead bolt thumb turn to the lock position.

"Should be right here in this bin." Billy pulled it from the shelf, but the bin was empty.

Marla rubbed the back of her neck. "We have a missing weapon, and it was used on Eileen Lieb."

◆

A few hours after the sky blackened for the night, Marla turned on the barn light before she strolled over to her favorite horse and hugged its neck. "Daisy Bell, I hope your day was better than mine." She reached for the brush on the ground. "Do you get lonely out here in your stall?" She brushed the mane a few times. "Me too. My stall is empty tonight. I need that big man of mine to get back and help take care of all this. Hell, take care of me." The horse whinnied. "Hmm, I think you might be right. Should I bring your man over here? You and Blackie might make a ruckus and tear up the stall. Do you like it sometimes a little wild and crazy like I do?" The horse whinnied again. Marla laughed, then brushed the side of the horse. "We should wait until tomorrow, and the two of you head out past the trees, so no one is watching." Daisy Bell nodded her head. Marla laughed. "I'm going to have to wait a few more days for my stud." She rubbed her hand on the horse's head. "You think he's worth it?" The horse whinnied again, and she smiled. "Me too."

Back in the house, Marla poured two fingers of tequila in a glass. She tilted the bottle. "No more of this when Crosby comes home. Might as well get rid of it tonight." She trudged over to a dining room chair and sat crossed-legged. "Bullets from the same gun. A stolen gun. What the hell am I doing?" Papers spread across the table. "Thirty-seven, thirty-five, eighteen, and sixteen. What do they mean? Is Logan right? Add the numbers and there are seven, eight, nine, and ten." She sipped from the glass and combed her fingers through her hair. "Seven, eight, nine, ten; seven, eight, nine, ten. What do they mean?"

She dropped her feet to the ground. "Four scenes and six murders. Do I add these to this mess?" She gazed at the numbers again. "Now I have four, six, seven, eight, nine, ten. Is that something?" She took another sip. "Wait. Is it only four murder scenes or six? What about Tinsley and Montenegro? Is it six victims or do I count eight with Rebekah Farmsdale and Rector Sudvaric? They didn't have numbers carved on them." She shook her head. "Do I count four or six scenes, six not eight victims? Maybe it's six, seven, eight, eight, nine, ten. Wait, what about the electric company employees? Were they a diversion? Collateral? Do I count them?" She finished the tequila and banged the glass on the table. "Maybe I don't have a damn clue what anything is."

Chapter 37

When entering rehab, Crosby surrendered all his personal possessions, but he convinced Marla and the administrator to leave his truck on the back lot. During his one-hour break from daily scheduled activities, he would attach his new off-road lights on the front bumper. The administrator kept the fob with the rest of Crosby's locked items.

Crosby stood quietly in his room, waiting until the shift changed at eleven o'clock. The parking lot lights hung like fixed drones aiming balls of light at employee vehicles. They scurried to their cars, with most heading to Moon's Crescent Bar. Crosby climbed outside through his room window, snuck to his truck, opened the toolbox, and reached for his spare fob. The unopened off-road lights box sat in the back seat. After the engine started, he slipped out a burner phone from under the seat, flipped it open, and dialed. "I'll be there in ten." He snapped the phone shut and dropped the gearshift to drive.

Crosby would recognize Searcy's truck in an instant, so Searcy left his vehicle at the station and drove an impounded car. Parking at the other end of the rehab parking lot, he watched Crosby drive away. Every police vehicle had GPS, and a red dot moved down the street on Searcy's iPad. He followed a half mile behind Crosby.

A few minutes later, Crosby stopped at a downtown alley entrance and rolled his window down. Leaning against the brick wall with one foot, a thin man wearing a backward Astros cap flicked his cigarette butt to the side and looked both ways. Searcy stopped a block away.

Crosby hung his elbow out the open window. "You got what I need?"

The drug dealer nodded slowly and ambled to the truck. "I got enough oxy to take care of you."

Crosby held out his hand with two folded hundred-dollar bills between fingers. "Listen, my third night in a row picking up ten. How much more you got?"

"Enough."

"Don't like buying from someone I don't know. What's your name?" Crosby asked.

"You want the stuff?"

"I'm in the rehab center, and I can be your new middle-man to thirty or forty more people just like me."

The dealer stared at Crosby for a while. "I can manage it." He reached for the folded money.

Crosby bent his fingers away. "That would be a lot of pills. I want a two dollar cut from every pill sold."

"Too much. A buck apiece, but you buy a hundred."

"A dollar now, but more when I get you bigger numbers," Crosby said.

"All right. How many you want?"

He felt the small clear bag with ten pills. "I'll take a hundred tomorrow. Can you get it?"

"Yeah, sure. I can handle a hundred."

"Got to be getting them from somewhere besides here. San Antone, Dallas, Houston?"

The dealer snapped the money from Crosby's fingers. "Yeah, maybe."

"A hundred pills tomorrow, and I keep a hundred dollars from the sale."

❖

On his iPad, Searcy watched Crosby drive past the Catholic church.

Crosby slowed as he watched Father Jules park his vehicle near the outside entrance to the church office. "Why would he be in the church after midnight?" Crosby asked himself. After stopping across the street and killing the engine, he opened the small bag of oxy and chewed two and then, from the console, he pulled out a long-range PIR, passive infrared motion detector, and placed it on his dashboard. Crosby's eyelids became heavy as he slumped down in his seat. Winds swirled, and the truck shook like a baby carriage. The weatherman was right. It would rain buckets tonight.

With Crosby's truck stopped, Searcy closed the iPad and drove back to the station.

Two hours later, the motion detector on Crosby's dashboard flashed yellow and beeped. Sitting up, Crosby rubbed his eyes while a salvo of rain beat against the roof. Father Jules' car turned left from the parking lot. Water flowed down the curbs.

Staying a safe distance away, Crosby followed with the headlights off. Rain sheeted the windshield, wind shoved the truck side-to-side. Jules' car stopped at a red light. There were no other cars in sight. Nevertheless, Jules waited until it changed to green before turning onto Franklin Drive toward the outside of town.

Ten minutes later, the car turned into the muddied driveway of the same old Pearlman's house as before. Crosby stopped more than a hundred yards away and parked. As quick as Father Jules could run through the rain, with the satchel around his neck, he jetted to the front door. Water splashed with each step. Moments later, a dim light moved around in the house; a flashlight.

Through the relentless rain, Crosby caught an outline of another pickup truck a hundred yards to the other side of the house. He raised the binoculars to his eyes and adjusted the focus on the truck's windshield. A small lighter flicked on and lit a cigarette. It was Logan.

He watched the bright red glow of the cigarette from his binoculars. Seconds later, it flew out past the window to the ground.

Logan's door opened, and he ran through the rain to the front window of the house. Cupping his hands around his face, he peered in, then ran around the side to the back of the house.

Inside, rain leaked through the roof. "You hear that?" Father Jules whispered.

"What?" another person asked.

A boot clomped on the wooden back porch.

"That."

Logan kicked the back door open and then stepped in with his gun drawn. Father Jules stood there with a considerable sum of cash in his hand.

"Collecting for the church, Pastor? Hands up."

"Officer, this must look strange to you."

Logan scoffed. "This don't look strange. Two hogs fucking in a mud pit looks strange." He aimed the pistol at Father Jules' chest. "This looks like a crime. Drop the money and put your hands up."

"No, I don't think so."

The rain lashed sideways, partially blocking Crosby's view of the house. A flash of light and a gunshot came from inside. "Damn." Crosby leaned across the front seat, opened the glove box, and pulled out his S&W 9mm pistol. Checking the magazine, he snapped it back in. He opened the truck door, and a waterfall of rain pummeled his face and clothes.

The front door banged open; Father Jules charged outside to his car with the satchel still around his neck. His tires spun as he reversed, then raced down the unpaved road past Logan's truck.

Crosby charged toward the house. He stopped and knelt under the front window. His head bobbed up to see inside. Everything was black. An engine revved from the back side of the house. An older pickup tore past Logan's truck and disappeared down the road.

Crosby kicked the front door and charged through, yelling, "Police!" He swept the house, but Logan was gone. He sent a text to Logan. *Where are you?*

Ten minutes later, Logan replied. *Saw you at the house. Get your ass back to rehab and leave my stakeout alone. Got the priest in my sights. Don't text back.*

◆

The next morning, Crosby sat in the rehab's administrative office. He turned his wristwatch toward him for the third time in five minutes. The secretary sat behind a desk, typing on her computer keyboard. Printed in black stenciling across the door next to her was Paul G. Harland, Ph.D. Rehabilitation Counseling.

"Ma'am, I have a class to attend in ten minutes. Can this wait?"

Her eyes shifted from her screen to Crosby. With a plastic smile, she said, "I suggest you stay right here, Officer Adams. The doctor will see you when he is ready." The phone on her desk rang. "Yes, sir, I'll send him in."

She hung up the phone and looked back at Crosby. "You'll make your class after all. He will see you now."

Crosby entered Doctor Harland's office. Pictures of family, friends, and politicians hung on the wall. Dr. Harland sat behind his dark stained oak desk and motioned Crosby to sit in the chair in front of the desk. "Sit, Mr. Adams."

Crosby sat down. "Thank you, sir. Is there something I can help you with?"

"As a matter of fact, yes. We run a program based on trust. You trust us to produce a program that will teach you about sobriety, and when you leave, people trust you to stay sober."

"Yes, of course. That is precisely why I am here."

"Is it?" Dr. Harland stood from his chair and gazed out the window. Patients slowly strolled along the garden paths. "You trust us to do our job, but we need to trust you." He turned back to Crosby. "Your job is to follow the program we have scheduled for you while staying focused and sober." His finger slid his glasses off his face. "Mr. Adams, you have not been following the program."

"I believe I have. I am, sir. I go to every class and take part in all my scheduled activities." Crosby swung his arm out and looked at his watch. "In fact, I need to be in class right now."

"Don't worry about that. I can give you an excuse for your absence." Dr. Harland sat down again and slipped his glasses back on. "I was talking about the rules."

"Rules? I have followed the rules. I study, go to class, interact, and I've been in no confrontations. Almost had to break one up before the 'help' came in and separated the two."

"Right. What about the rule where you must stay on our campus while you are going through our program?"

Crosby sat back in the chair. "Sir?"

"You can't figure this out? Mr. Adams, you're a smart man. A cop, right? You read the rules. I'm sure there are many rules you must follow in your line of work."

Crosby uncrossed his legs and then recrossed them. He scooted back against his chair as far as possible. "Come on, Doc. Tell me what I did."

"Do you remember where you were the last three nights?"

"Oh." Crosby looked down. "Yes, of course. I didn't think the staff would catch me being gone."

"The staff," Dr. Harland replied. He turned his laptop toward Crosby, which showed him sneaking out the kitchen window one night and the back door two nights. "I guess you haven't noticed. We have CCTV everywhere, including the kitchen. We ran the videos back each night you've been here, and you did this the last three nights. Mr. Adams, you need to tell me where you went."

"I am very sorry about that, and I promise this won't happen again," Crosby said.

"Did you sneak out and go to the bar? Did you drink alcohol during those times while gone?"

"No, sir. I just needed to get out. A breather. Smoke a cigarette."

"We allow smoking in designated areas 24/7. I don't believe you."

Crosby uncrossed his legs again and leaned his elbows on his knees. "All right, you caught me. Can I tell you something in a doctor-patient privilege?"

"I'm not a medical doctor, but go on." Dr. Harland reached for his pen.

"I run several catfish lines at the lake. I don't have a commercial license, so that's illegal. You can't put lines out and catch thirty or forty a night. I know the game warden, and he doesn't look at the area where my lines are hanging. I have done this for years, selling fish to the restaurants at a discount rate. They don't say anything, and neither do I. You know, supplement my income. A cop's salary in this town isn't enough to pay the bills. That's where I was the last three nights—pulling catfish from the lake and selling them. No booze, no bars. Promise."

The doctor raised his eyebrows. "Catfish. And are you doing this every night?"

"No. It depends on the weather, moon, wind... stuff. The first night, the lines were full, so I went back the next night. Last night there were only a couple, so I don't need to go out for a few more nights."

"You think you are leaving our facility again at night?" He sat back in his chair. "Let me be clear; if you leave again, there will be no reason for you to return. You're done. Understand?"

"Doc, that's income..."

"No second chance. You leave. You're gone. Mr. Adams, time for you to go to your class."

Chapter 38

"Come on, slide down the roof and jump," Julian whispered in front of his girlfriend's house.

Mia looked out her second-floor bedroom window and down at Julian. The moonlight cast a shadow of him across the front yard. "You have ball practice and I have cheerleading tomorrow morning. It's almost past nine o'clock. I'll get in trouble. I don't want to miss the game."

"Let's walk over to the Dairy Queen and split a milkshake."

She looked back at her bedroom door. There were no lights under the threshold. She spread pink lipstick on her lips and slipped the black pepper spray bottle into her back pocket. So far, Julian's been nice to her. Sliding to the edge of the roof, she jumped into his arms.

"I didn't bring any money," Mia said.

"I got some." Julian held a twenty-dollar bill in his hand. "Mowed Mister Bigham's yard today after school. He's always a good tipper."

Gray clouds crept past the moon. Brown and yellow leaves rustled in front of them as they walked down her street. Mia crossed her arms to warm herself.

"You cold?"

"A little."

"Here, put my jacket on."

Mia's eyes widened as she pretended not to notice Julian taking his Varsity Letterman jacket off. He slipped it over her shoulders. "Better?"

"Wow. Yeah." Mia's grin spread across her face. "Better."

They sat next to each other at the Dairy Queen with a milkshake and two straws between them. Mia glanced at each person as they walked by their table; her smile couldn't hide her feelings.

"Are you warm yet?" Julian asked.

"Hmm, yeah, almost."

"You should put your arms in the sleeves."

Mia pulled her straw away from her lips. "You want me to wear your jacket?"

"Maybe, if you want to. You don't have..."

Mia grabbed his cheeks with both hands and landed a big kiss on his lips. She quickly slipped her arms through the sleeves. "I do. I mean, yes, I'll wear your jacket."

The last of the milkshake slurped through their straws. The manager informed them the store would close in five minutes. "Is it ten o'clock already?" Julian patted her hands. "Let's go."

"Go where?"

"Across the street and down to the park. Can you stay out a little longer?"

Her face hurt from the constant grin. "I'll go anywhere with you, Julian."

Mia forgot about the chilly weather as they walked arm-in-arm. They turned down from the street to the grassy knoll of the park.

Julian's phone dinged. He read the text from his father. *Are you with Mia?* He aimed the phone toward her, and they both chuckled. He texted back. *Why?*

She's not in her house and her father called the police.

We want to be together. Got milkshake, now at park. Will bring her home soon.

Marla's truck had pulled in front of Julian's house. She stood on the front porch, and Julian's father showed her the texts. "Sorry that I must check on you and all. Another officer is with Mia's parents right now. They are pretty unhappy."

"I'm so sorry, Officer Adams. I don't think Julian has ever done anything like this before. He's smitten with this girl."

"Understand. We've all felt like Romeo and Juliet in high school."

"They're juniors in high school." He snickered. "When Julian gets back here, I'll ground him until he graduates."

"Nevertheless," Marla said. "We have a murderer somewhere out there, and they need to be home. Do you know which park?"

"Across the street from Dairy Queen."

A shadow crept between bushes in the park and followed the two teenagers strolling arm-in-arm, oblivious of the world around them.

Julian looked for a secluded place for them to stop and sit and, if he's lucky, lie down. "We can stop on the other side of that building, away from the chill."

"Anywhere with you." Mia wrapped his letter jacket around her and felt warm and safe. She hung onto his arm, planning never to let loose. Her head rested against his shoulder as she lock-stepped toward wherever he wanted to go.

Branches rustled to Julian's right. While changing directions toward the overhead lights along the concrete pathway, he sent a text on his phone.

A boy wearing worn Wranglers and a black cotton beanie stepped out from a tree shadow and stopped the two teenagers in love. "What are you two doing here? It's late and a school night."

Mia's eyes opened wide and squeezed Julian's arm tighter.

Julian held out his hand. "I know you, Wesley Reed. You work at Hildebrandt Machine Shop."

"So."

"We're walking. Leave us alone."

"You're in my park," Wesley said.

"Not your park. This is a public park," Julian snapped back.

Another voice came from behind the two.

Julian spun around and glared at who he expected. "Figured your buddy, Cooper Jackson, was close by."

Cooper held an empty quart-sized beer bottle by the neck. "It's *my* park at night."

Julian stood in front of Mia. "We got no money. I don't even have a wallet on me."

"That looks like a right nice jacket you got on there, little girl. Bet that would keep me warm tonight." Cooper flipped the beer bottle in the air and caught it by the neck. "Shouldn't be out with a killer on the loose."

Wesley unsheathed a knife on his belt and aimed it at Julian. "Carving numbers on the bodies after they're dead." He looked at Cooper. "What number should we put on them?"

Mia reached into her back pocket. "I'll scream if you get any closer."

"Give me the jacket."

◆

Julian's father's phone dinged with another text. *Help, Dad*. He showed Marla the text. She ran to her truck and sped away as red and blue lights swirled in the air. Minutes later, her truck jumped the curb and bounced through the empty park. Brakes slammed tight, and the vehicle slid sideways. She jumped out, scanned the grass with her flashlight, and picked up a varsity jacket on the ground.

"Julian! Mia! Where are you?" She ran to the park benches. Her flashlight darted across each one. "Julian! Come on out. Mia!"

Her light skimmed under the branches of waist-high bushes. The light stopped on a pair of black and white Converse shoes.

"Julian? Is that you?"

Marla's eyes caught something running at her from the side. Arms wrapped around her, and they both fell to the ground.

"You damn crazy cops!" Julian screamed. "We almost died out here."

Marla boxed both of Julian's ears and flipped him over her shoulder, then picked him up like a rag doll.

"Where's Mia?"

Julian pointed to the bushes while she came out.

"Why did you ask for help?" Marla asked.

"Two guys stopped us." Julian looked around for his jacket

"They said they were going to carve numbers on us."

"Where are they?"

"One of them grabbed Mia by the wrist and pulled her away. I tried to shove him, but he was too damn big. He turned to hit me, and I kicked him in the balls. Mia sprayed something in the other one's face, and we ran into the bushes. That's when your truck slid down here. Are you crazy?"

Marla exhaled deeply. "No. I don't know. All this is crazy."

Mia wrapped her arms around Marla's waist. "I'm sorry. We were just having fun."

"Did you know these two?"

Julian glanced at Mia and back to Marla. "Wesley Reed and Cooper Jackson."

The young girl looked around the grass. "Where's my jacket?"

"I don't think they're the killer. They're too stupid." Julian swiped his jacket from Marla's grip and place it over Mia's shoulders.

◆

After dropping the teens back to their homes, she called Searcy on his phone and over the squelch box in her truck. No answer. "Come on. I need help with this."

"Grand-mamma," Marla glanced at her watch, 11:19 PM.

"Grand-mamma here."

"Wesley Reed and Cooper Jackson attacked two teenagers in the park. Both perps nineteen years old, approximately six-foot, two hundred pounds, and brown hair. Have units check their houses and video game rooms. "

"10-4. Will send info out to all units."

She called Searcy again with no reply. She found his truck on the police GPS system moving down Main Street.

Calling Logan had no response, either. "Damn, the one time I really need you, little brother, and you don't answer." She typed Logan's truck into the GPS. It was at the abandoned Pearlman house. "Maybe Cindy knows what he's doing."

At almost midnight, Marla turned onto Logan's driveway to a bleak house. Her silhouette marched across the headlight beams. She wiggled the locked doorknob. Cindy must be asleep. Walking around the house to the carport revealed what she expected; Logan's truck was missing. She touched the hood of Cindy's car under the carport. It was cold.

The wooden fence gate to the backyard was open and their dog was not in the yard.

They keep this closed for the kids and dog.

Marla's eyes swept the backside of the house. The door was open. Her heart raced. She pulled her service weapon from the holster and pushed the door wide open. Entering the house, she yelled, "Cindy? Are you here?" Turning on her flashlight, she crept past the kitchen and down the hallway. The first door was to Logan and Cindy's bedroom. Her flashlight breezed across the empty bed. In the children's beds, Pokémon stuffed animals sat quietly, staring back at the flashlight.

After she turned on the living room lights, that's when she saw trouble.

Bloodstains on the carpet. A broken lamp, family pictures splayed over the floor. Blood splattered the wall. Whose blood? Logan's? Cindy's? The girls?

She called Cindy's phone; it rang under the couch. Her hand swept for it. The sides felt wet, with bloody fingerprints smeared across the screen.

Marla jumped when her phone rang. "Oh, Jesus, hell." She reached into her back pocket. "Hello."

"Are you trying to call me?" Searcy asked. "I'm sorry about what happened earlier. I promise to take all my meds. All the squirrels are gone, and the birds stopped talking. Forgive me?"

"I don't care about that now. Where's Logan and Cindy?"

"I don't know. Date night somewhere."

"And the twins? Where are they?"

"You sound upset."

"No shit!" Marla looked at her phone, then put it back to her ear. "Where is everybody?"

"The twins are spending the night at one of their friend's houses. Logan and Cindy wanted some quiet time together without two girls crawling all over them. I'm sure everything is fine."

"Bullshit. I'm at their house, and there's blood on the floor and walls. The living room is torn to pieces."

"Blood? Call the emergency room and see if they are there."

"I'm heading there now."

Marla's truck slid to a stop next to the ambulance entrance of the emergency room. Rushing up the ramp, her hand pounded against the doors. The hallway was empty, with no one in sight.

"Hello! Anyone here?"

An ER tech stepped out of the employee break room, swallowing the food in his mouth. "May I help you?"

"Has Officer Logan Searcy or his wife come in this evening?"

"No, ma'am. We've had only four people since I started my shift at midnight." He rapped on the wooden molding of a door twice. "Quiet night so far."

"Anyone here now?"

"Just me and the nurse," he opened the radiology door. "And the rad tech. Oh, and Dr. Sanborn earlier."

"How earlier?"

The tech pointed toward the central part of the hospital. "Should still be at the nurse's station. He delivered a baby."

She darted down the hall, where a few nurses moved from room to room. When Marla grabbed a clipboard and banged it on the countertop, everyone stopped and stared.

"Has anyone seen Officer Logan Searcy?"

Each shook their head, then went back to their duties.

Marla called out, "Dr. Sanborn." She coughed several times. "Where are you?"

He came out of a room and slipped two blue gloves off his hands. "Marla?" He pitched them in a waste can. "What are you doing here?"

"I'm looking for Logan and Cindy. They..." Her lungs spasmed and coughed. She turned away, pulled the inhaler from her pocket, and took a breath.

"Are you alright?" He slid a chair closer to her. "Here, sit. Let me listen to your chest."

She slipped the inhaler into her pants pocket. "Don't have time for that." She inhaled deeply and coughed again. "Do you know where Logan or Cindy are?"

"No, but you need to come see me in the office for that cough."

"Dr. Sanborn, we have an active crime scene at Logan's home, and it is probable there are injuries. Could you please keep the ER staffed until the day shift comes on? We do not know how badly we may need you before this night is over."

"Anything for you. Keep me informed."

Marla rushed out past the emergency room doors and headed for her truck. She opened the driver's side door and pushed the button on the radio mic. "Grand-mamma. Is Logan at the station?"

"Not sure."

"Have someone look."

Grand-mamma returned in less than a minute. "Negative."

"He's not answering his phone," Marla said. "GPS has his truck at the old Pearlman place, and there's blood on the floor of his house. Send a team to his truck and another with a forensic kit to the house."

She closed the cab door and pushed the on-engine button. When Marla's cell rang, UNKNOWN lit the screen.

"Hello?"

"Marla, It's Crosby."

"Crosby? Oh, Crosby." The truck engine started. "Crosby, I miss you. Please leave rehab and help me." She laid her head against the steering wheel. "I need you with me."

"I miss you too. I can't leave. Just a few more days, and everything will be back to normal."

"Normal?" Marla sat straight. "Nothing will ever be normal again."

"Why? What happened?"

"Haven't you noticed? There are dead people everywhere, and now..." she sniffed and wiped a tear away, "Damn it," she yelled. "I need you back here. I can't do this alone."

"Dr. Harland won't let me out again until graduation day."

"What do you mean, again?"

"I uh... They stopped me a few nights ago when I was outside for a smoke."

"How did you get outside? I thought they did a lock-down at night. And you don't smoke."

"I was outside with new friends, and they were smoking."

"How are you calling me from the rehab center? It's nighttime. Are you in your truck?"

"A friend's phone. He snuck it into rehab."

"Leave rehab right now and come back to me."

"I just wanted to say that I miss you and will see you soon."

"I hear another person. Is there someone with you?"

"I have to go."

"Where are you?"

She lost the connection. Marla pitched the phone on the passenger seat, shoved the gearshift to drive, floored the accelerator, and charged toward the rehab center.

His vehicle should be there. He wanted to see it every day. Like a favorite horse tied to a hitchin' post, it comforted him. That was a mistake.

Marla pulled into the lot and slammed on the brakes. "Damn it." She hit the steering wheel with her hands. "Damn it to hell."

Crosby's truck was missing.

She ran to the back side of the building and used her flashlight to tap on his window. No answer. "You son-of-a-bitch, don't you dare be him."

When the glass broke, the alarm blared in the night. She shoved the curtain to the side, revealing an empty room.

"When I find you, Crosby Adams, I'm going to kick your ass."

She tapped the GPS system on her navigation monitor. Crosby's truck was not anywhere close to the rehab center. It was at Horton's Creek, the last murder scene.

The truck's digital clock changed to 3:00 AM. She jerked the shifter to drive. Tires spun and rocks spewed across the ground. Her head hit the roof when the truck bounced over speed bumps. She slammed on the brakes and snapped the seat belt in place. Seconds later, the engine roared, sirens blared, and the speedometer needle swooped past the 100MPH line as her headlights and off-road rooftop lights brightly lit the narrow road. Trees dashed by.

The town had changed. Happy. Touristy. Fun. Ribbons of roads drew people into festivals, music, and food. There's nothing left but faded black tarred roads leading to tombstones. A cloud will forever hang. Not the same town, the same feel. It's all gone wrong.

She turned toward Horton's Creek as a mass of floodlights and head-lights rushed across an open field. The truck climbed up the hill and stopped at the crest next to the freshly covered ground. It looked like a burial site.

The full moon threw gray shadows of apple trees. About seven or eight-hundred yards away through the grove, bright lights glimmered.

She shut all her truck lights off and grabbed the binoculars from the glove compartment. Headlights flickered on and off when someone walked in front of them. It was a single person moving. She pitched the binoculars in the passenger seat and drove slowly between the rows of trees toward the other truck.

Two hundred yards away, she saw a white muzzle flash. Her truck's radiator hissed steam. She slammed on the brakes, swung her door open, and jumped out. A bullet pierced the windshield and shattered the back glass. She reached across the dashboard and flipped the emergency and headlights back on. The truck was the same color as Crosby's. With the mic in her hand, she called out, "This is the police. Drop your weapon and put your hands on your..."

Two gunshots hit her headlights. She aimed at the back tires and re-turned fire as the truck drove away.

Marla raced toward the scene, skimming her flashlight beam across the ground. A red hot branding iron head laid on top of a portable butane burner. Next to an apple tree, a man and a woman lay naked with blunt force trauma to the side of their heads with blood matted in their hair. The woman's foot was under the man's trunk like she was pushing him away. The number 3 inside a circle was branded on their chests. Marla turned the man's face towards her. She backed up; her hands squeezed her temples hard. Her throat tightened; she couldn't breathe. White noise filled her ears. It was Logan and Cindy.

Chapter 39

Red and blue lights flickered like a snake for a half-mile down the frontage road. The line turned onto the whitewashed gravel trail in the cemetery. Police vehicles stopped, and the emergency lights went dark.

Logan wasn't Jewish or Muslim, but he liked the idea of burials within 24 hours. Get it done and over.

A few yards from the burial site, a single guitarist sat on a three-legged stool as a young woman sang *Amazing Grace*. With only a few hours' notice, it seemed all of Hildebrandt had come to Logan's funeral.

Searcy, Marla, and Crosby sat beside the casket covered in roses and tulips. Each of them held a single long stem rose. The brass buttons on their uniforms glittered in the sunlight. Behind them, Logan's two children sat in their chairs and held each other's hands. On each side of them were Mayor Pichler and his wife. Marla spun around and angrily scanned the crowd.

Crosby leaned toward her. "Who are you looking for?"

"Someone out there killed Logan, and he's in the crowd gloating." She spun in the other direction. "I'm looking for the one person, not tearful, not sad; just standing and staring, emotionless. Where are you, you son-of-a-bitch?"

Crosby's hand touched her arm. "Turn around. We'll find him."

Marla wiped a tear with the back of her hand. "Makes no sense. A cop killer will bring more attention." She grasped Crosby's wrist. "Does he want more attention? Not just local, Hildebrandt attention. He wants Texas or national attention." She laid her hand on Crosby's thigh. "Maybe Pops does need to call the Texas Rangers on this. A cop killer. A serial killer.

He'll lose this. The Rangers will take this from us, and we'll be on the back row like clueless oglers."

"Let's get past today." Crosby looked straight ahead and tapped the back of her shoulder twice. "Then we can focus on what this person wants."

Marla swept a string of hair behind her ear. "I know what he wants. He wants to kill people. I want this guy more than anything else. I'll hunt this bastard down until he's dead."

Searcy leaned toward Marla. "You two shut your traps. People are staring at you."

Marla felt the murderer reveling in the publicity. "I need to find Logan's killer." She leaned toward Searcy. "You know he's out there. He's watching us."

Searcy sat firmly, hands resting on his legs. "Later. Now is not the time."

Marla's eyes shifted around the crowd. "He's here. I feel it."

Crosby's hand gripped Marla's thigh. "Later."

She stared back. "There's nothing *you* can do. You decided to get drunk again and take drugs and almost killed yourself. You must go back and finish five more days of rehab while this town is going to shit. That badge you're wearing depends on the doctor releasing you."

"I'll be back next week, and I'll start kicking up the investigation."

Marla pushed Crosby's hand off her thigh. "You damn well better be here, but this case is mine. Logan is dead, and I want the bastard who did it."

Mayor Pichler leaned in behind Marla and Crosby. "Did I hear you say you are bringing in the Texas Rangers? Will you call today?

Searcy twisted around and glared at the mayor. "We are burying my son. Give him respect and be quiet...sir."

Marla stood from her metal folding chair with her arm stretched out. Her finger arced across the crowd. "I know one of you did this. Which one of you?"

Both Crosby and Searcy grabbed her arms and pulled her back to her chair. "Shut the hell up," Searcy said.

She stared at the casket. "Which one of those people behind me killed my brother?"

Searcy wrapped his arm around her shoulder and pulled her closer. "Marla, stop. This is a funeral."

She pushed away and glared at Searcy. She said in a loud whisper, "I know what the hell this is, but we've got a crazed lunatic killing people, carving them up like sliced barbecue. I found a branding iron next to Logan. He was branded like cattle."

The mayor leaned in again. "And that is why we need more help."

The music stopped. The Hildebrandt First Baptist Church preacher opened his Bible and read several passages.

Tears ran down Marla's face. It was time to do the rose. Her legs felt like jelly. She couldn't stand. She didn't want to stand and place a flower on her brother's casket. Crosby loosely held onto her elbow and helped her up. The two steps to the casket felt like it was a mile away.

"Logan, I promise to find him for you. Believe me, that is all I want in the world." She laid the rose on top of the casket, and it slid across and fell into the hole. She scoffed. "Looks like I beat you again. Something I have is already six feet under." She laid her palm on the casket. "I promise, I will put someone else six feet in the ground."

◆

After everyone gave their condolences at the cemetery, Crosby and Marla left in her rental car. He pulled into a spot near the rehab center front doors and killed the engine. Marla sat limp in the passenger seat while her head leaned against the door. Her hand half-pounded the dash. She didn't say a word.

"I'm supposed to check back in," Crosby said. He opened his door. Her hand swung around and locked onto his wrist like a Vise-Grip.

A tear clutched at the corner of her eye while she stared out her side window. "Where were you when you called me last night? The same night, Logan and Cindy were killed."

His other hand reached around to her shoulder. "I think you need to back away from this investigation. It's too close to you. Friday is graduation, and I can take over."

She released her grip and shot out the passenger door, trouncing around the backside of the car as the heels of her hands rubbed tears away. Crosby stepped out and closed his door. Marla's hands pinned Crosby's shoulders against the vehicle.

"You didn't answer my question. Where the hell were you last night?"

His arms gently wrapped around her waist. "Today is Monday and graduation is Friday. Four more nights without you. Nights are what I struggle with. I can manage the days, the activities, classes, group sessions, but I can't stand being here at night. I miss you. Pick me up Friday at noon, and we can leave. We will get this guy, I promise."

Marla's lips tightened as she looked around the parking lot. "Where's your truck?"

"Stolen."

She fixated deep into his eyes. "When?"

"Sometime yesterday."

"In my report, I stated the perp's truck was the same color as yours. And now yours is gone?"

"You think my truck was at Logan's crime scene?"

Marla pushed a little harder on his shoulders. "Can't rule that out, can I?" She remembered the police GPS configured the area of his truck near the scene. "I checked this morning before the funeral, and the GPS couldn't pick up your truck. Where is it?"

"I wish I knew."

"Did you report it stolen?"

"Not yet. Things have been–busy lately."

She stepped back. "Busy? As in, how to put puzzles together, or write poetry, or some other bullshit you do in that building? Someone stole your truck, and you didn't.... When were you going to report it?"

"Today, after the funeral. Don't worry about my truck. Insurance will cover it." He gently put his hands on her waist and pulled her toward him. She leaned her forehead against his. He spoke into her ear. "What about Logan's kids? What are they going to do? What family is going to take them? You, me, Searcy? Cindy's parents live in Timbuktu. We'd never see them again. You need to help with Logan's children."

"No." She shoved him away from the car. "My job is to find the killer before he does it again," she opened the car door, "and you need to go back and finish your cross-stitching. I'll be back on Friday." The door slammed shut. The seatbelt clicked. "Don't you dare disappoint me."

Crosby watched the car turn onto the road and disappear. His burner phone vibrated in his sock.

✦

Marla called Dr. Dr. Berghoff on her cell while heading for the police station. "Doc, I want to thank you for coming in and doing the autopsy last night. Above and beyond, sir." Her lips sealed onto the Primatene Mist before she inhaled two squirts. Her breath stammered.

The doctor cleared his throat. "I'm deeply sorry for what happened, Officer Adams."

"Can you give me the COD?"

"The cause of death was cardiac arrest from a stun gun. They each had taser wires attached to their bare chests and necks. Both had blunt force trauma to their heads. Not enough to kill them, but enough to render them unconscious."

He paused for a few seconds. "I am looking at the pictures of the crime scene. Something caught my eye. The victims were stripped of their clothes while unconscious and put in position. There are scrapes on the legs and sides from dragging them on the ground."

She heard paper shuffle over the phone.

"In the photographs, are the bodies exactly as you found them? Nobody moved them before these pictures were taken?"

"No. I did not move them. Why?"

"The image of both naked and on the ground may be a coincidence," he said. "Logan Searcy is leaning against a tree trunk. Cindy Searcy is facing the other way with her foot against his side." He paused again. "Are you positive these are their positions at the scene?"

"I'm driving, so I don't have the pictures in front of me, but I remember the crime scene. Yes, Logan was naked and leaning against the apple tree."

"Have you ever been to the Sistine Chapel at the Vatican?" Dr. Berghoff asked.

"Doc, come on. I live in Hildebrandt. What do you see?"

"This looks as though the two were posed like Michelangelo's *Creation Of Eve* fresco, which is in the center of the Sistine Chapel ceiling."

Chapter 40

Two o'clock that afternoon, Marla entered the squad room of the police station. Everyone's eyes shifted to her, then immediately looked away. No one spoke. She stared at the images of Logan and Cindy on the wall. Dr. Berghoff was right. It was no accident. They were posed like Adam and Eve. Marla pulled the pushpins from the photos on the wall and removed them. One by one, she meticulously pushed the pins back into the corkboard and dropped the photos on her desktop.

She took a deep breath, held it for a few seconds, and exhaled, then grabbed the back of her chair and flung it against the wall. It bounced twice on the floor with a leg snapping off. The broken chair laid sideways. Her boot stomped the armrest, breaking it in two.

Every eye focused on her. The room stood silent. She reached for Crosby's chair and drug it across the floor, wheels clattering. She sat at her desk, then flipped her computer on, typed Michelangelo's Sistine Chapel, and tapped the image of *The Creation of Eve*. Holding the crime scene picture next to the monitor, she stared at the resemblance. Her stomach flipped from the two images. Adam was lying down against a tree, just like Logan. Looking the other way was Eve emerging from Adam's body, his rib, just like Cindy. God was there in a flowing robe. *I didn't see a robe. Where the hell is the robe? Did I stop the killer from completing the scene? Logan was a pawn in someone's sick mind.*

Searcy charged through the squad room and aimed directly toward his office. He nodded at the broken chair across the room. "Somebody make some coffee and get that crap off the floor." He opened his door and paced into his office.

Marla printed the image on her screen. Taking the crime scene photo of Logan and Cindy from her desk, she walked by the printer, snapped up the printout, and hustled to Searcy's office. Her knuckles rapped on the door.

"Leave me alone."

Marla entered and slammed both pictures on the desk in front of him. "Look at these. Do you know what these are?"

"I don't want to look at anything." Searcy pushed them off the desk.

Marla picked the two pages off the floor and slapped them back on the desk. "This one is a painting, a fresco. It's Michelangelo's *Creation Of Eve.*"

"What in the hell are you talking about?" He sat in his chair for a second, then jumped back up and paced again.

She leaned over the desk. "Dr. Berghoff told me that Logan and Cindy were positioned like Adam and Eve in this fresco. The fresco is on the ceiling of the Sistine Chapel." She straightened her back. "I knew little about that place, so I looked it up on the computer. Michelangelo painted nine frescoes on the ceiling. Well, he painted more than that. A bunch more other stuff on the ceiling. It took him years to do that."

Searcy jumped in front of her face with arms spread wide. "Marla, you're rambling."

"Logan and Cindy are positioned just like Adam and Eve."

Searcy sat down and leaned back as far as the chair would go.

"Adam and Eve, Pops. Adam and Eve."

He stood and slammed his fist on his desk. "I heard you, Adam and Eve. I don't want to look at this today. I can't look at Logan that way." Searcy stood and paced back and forth. His fingers raked through his short hair. He groaned like an angry bear and flailed his arms. "That crazy doctor in San Antonio told you this? It's got to be him. How did he know about the painting? He told you about it. Maybe the doctor killed them, moved them like statues, and that's how he knew. He set the whole thing up. The Sistine Chapel? The doc slipped up and told you what he did. Criminals do that."

"Whoa, Pops. Slow down."

"I've seen pictures of that place. How did the doctor pick that one painting out of all the murders?"

"Pops, I don't know."

"Because he did it." Searcy's arms pointed to his office ceiling. "How many pictures do you think I could paint on my ceiling?" Searcy pointed from one end to the other. "I could get a hundred, or two hundred, maybe three hundred. Yeah, that's it. I'll paint three hundred little tiny-ass pictures, and that doctor can confess where he plans to kill the next person."

Marla touched Searcy's arm and gently pulled it down. "Pops, sit down, please." She held his hands. "I'm sorry I brought it up. Sit, please."

He groaned, then plopped down in his chair and pointed at the ceiling again. "I can do that. Come back tomorrow. I'll paint all those pictures."

Marla squatted in front of Searcy and gently patted his knee. "We need to look at the crime scene pics again of all the other murders. Were these victims positioned in the same way as the paintings?"

"You think we have a killer that likes Michelangelo and wants to copy his paintings with dead people?" Searcy shook his head. "That's insane."

"That would be a very educated killer."

Searcy leaned from his chair. "Like a doctor."

"This is something, Pops. This is a legitimate clue. I must follow this."

Marla sat in the county library computer room and typed 'Sistine Chapel' on the screen. Three books popped up, two on Michelangelo and one on the building itself. She quickly grabbed all three and sat down at an empty table.

After forty-five minutes of searching through the three books, Audrey, the librarian, appeared next to Marla. "I am so sorry for what happened to Logan and Cindy."

"Thanks." Marla quickly nodded at Audrey. "I need some help."

"Sure. whatever I can do to for you?"

"I'm trying to find some information about the Sistine Chapel and the frescoes that Michelangelo painted. These three books are not enough information. They all say the same thing."

"Marla, unfortunately, that is all we have. Is there something you want to know?"

"I need to know as much as possible about everything."

Audrey chuckled. "I think it's wonderful you want to read more about Michelangelo. He was a fascinating man."

"Do you think there is more at the San Antonio library?" Marla asked.

Audrey sat down across from Marla. "If you're willing to go there, I know the auxiliary bishop at the Archdiocese of San Antonio. He spent some time at the Vatican when he was quite young. I'm sure he could answer all of your questions. Let me call him."

✦

Marla sat in the office of the Archdiocese of San Antonio, staring at an ornate 11x14 inch gold picture frame on the wall with a photograph of a man in his late forties or early fifties. A bronze rectangular nameplate was under the frame with the name, Auxiliary Bishop Raymond Medina. His photo was much better than the ones inside a folder on her lap. She wondered if it was proper to bring photos of dead people in a church.

The window blinds were open, revealing a manicured garden. Marla watched a bird jump from tree limb to limb while her right leg would not stop bouncing.

The woman sitting behind the desk in the office read a Bible while slowly chewing gum. She glanced at her desk computer when it dinged twice. "The bishop will be here in a minute."

"The bishop or the auxiliary bishop? I'm here to meet the auxiliary bishop? I'm not ready to meet the boss of this place...establishment... sorry, church."

The woman smiled. "He's called an auxiliary because he helps in this archdiocese, but he's still a bishop."

Marla nodded. "Okay." She popped all her knuckles again when footsteps in the hallway grew louder.

A well-groomed man wearing a black shirt and pants with a white tab collar appeared from the open doorway. He extended his hand toward Marla. "Hello, I'm Bishop Raymond Medina. And you are Marla Adams?"

She stood and shook his hand. Thankfully, Audrey had told her the title she should use to address him. "Your Excellency, thank you for meeting with me so quickly."

"Audrey is one of my favorite people. I have missed her since she moved to Hildebrandt. She mentioned you had questions about the Sistine Chapel."

"Yes. Many questions."

He motioned her down the hall. "Let us go to my office."

They both sat in high-back chairs with a small round table between them.

"I'm guessing, because you are a Bishop, you know everything about the Sistine Chapel."

"We are taught much about it, and I have personal experience there. As a young man, I volunteered to help with the restoration in the 1980s."

"Mary said you were there. Doing what?"

"Mostly apprentice work, carrying things, helping with moving items in and out of the building. I was trying to decide if I was going to dedicate my life to the church."

"How long were you there?"

"I stayed for two years in 1987 and 1988."

"This restoration ended when?"

"It ended in 1989. I learned much about the process of cleaning dirt and soot from the ceiling without damaging the fresco, as well as the painter's craft in revitalizing them to their beautiful presence people see now."

A lady entered wearing 1950s style cat eyeglasses and a conservative Sunday going to church dress. She carried a small tray with two cups of tea and four shortbread cookies.

"I hope you don't mind. This is the one vice I can't give up. Hot tea and cookies in the afternoon." He handed Marla a cup and saucer.

Creation of Eve. I looked at the pictures again and agree. I'll admit, I don't know much, if anything, about Michelangelo. I'm a Baptist, so I studied nothing about the Vatican or the Sistine Chapel. All I know is what I read early this morning. I have pictures, gruesome pictures, of the victims at their respective crime scenes. This person or persons must be caught and sent to jail. I personally would string the perps up and let them hang for everyone to see." She cleared her throat, remembering she was inside a holy place. "Excuse me, Your Excellency. Would you mind looking at them and tell me if these remind you of anything about the paintings in the chapel?"

He sipped his tea and then bit a nibble of the cookie. "Man can do terrible things to one another. Since Adam and Eve left the Garden of Eden, man has sinned. All of us sin." He reached across the plate and placed his hand on Marla's. "God has the power of forgiveness, and you must ask for forgiveness of your sins. Allow justice to oversee this. Do not, yourself, delve into hatefulness or vengeance." Lifting his hand from hers, he glanced at the folder she held. "I'm ready if you are."

Marla handed it to him. After slipping reading glasses on, he studied each picture. For several agonizing minutes, she watched his face cringe, but continued studying each image intently. These were pictures she preferred no one saw.

Medina closed the folder. "This can only be a personal opinion, not an official reply from the church."

"Yes, of course."

With one finger, he clasped the corner of his glasses and slid them off. "I see a pattern."

Electricity shot straight up Marla's spine. Her fingers clamped tightly onto her thighs. "Okay...what?"

"After Audrey contacted me, I printed photographs of the nine frescoes you mentioned." Bishop Medina held Marla's images in one hand and reached under the chair for his and then pointed toward the middle of the floor. "Shall we?" He bent down on his knees and spread his photos of the frescoes in a line. He had numbered them one to nine.

Marla watched as he placed the murder scene images under frescoes five to nine. She stood. She wanted to walk out, walk away, and run like hell to any place besides there. Instead, she bent down next to him. Her hand rubbed across the floor below frescoes one to four, with no photo underneath them. *Will there be more murders?* Her heart jumped in her chest when he spoke.

"Your murderer is extremely specific. He has a plan, and it seems he has studied the ceiling of the Sistine Chapel quite thoroughly. Each murder scene is similar to a fresco represented in the Book of Genesis, and he is killing people in an orderly fashion."

His finger drew an imaginary rectangle around the images. "This is the building, if you will. Inside, the altar is to the left where the Pope speaks." He put a cookie against the imaginary left wall. "The entrance into the chapel is here, on the right side." He placed a second cookie against the imaginary right wall. "Michelangelo painted nine large frescoes in order of the Book of Genesis. Three frescoes are of the beginnings of heaven and earth. They are closest to the altar. Three of the beginnings of man are in the center, and three on the right, near the entrance, are of God's anger and punishment."

The hair on her arms shot to attention. "There are no victims under the first four frescoes." Her eyes teared as she looked for hope. "Not yet."

His hand swept to the far right. "At the entrance is the ninth fresco." He tapped his finger on the picture of John Walker's body and the matching fresco. "Your murderer is following the images in reverse order."

He placed his glasses back on. They rested halfway down his nose. "The ninth fresco is *The Drunkenness of Noah*. I won't go into a full history lesson, but in the Bible, his three sons found Noah drunk and naked. Two helped cover him with a sheet. Thus, the tube down the man's throat and wine poured in it suggests the drunkenness. The man, naked and wrapped in a sheet, is a display of Noah himself."

She folded her arms and squeezed tight.

"The second murder represents *The Sacrifice of Noah*. Noah was not sacrificed, but rather, Noah and his family sacrificed a ram to God for their surviving the Great Flood. In the eighth fresco, the intestines were removed and placed in a fire." He pointed to the murder scene of Mr. Kinsey. "The position of the man and the animal in this picture and the fresco are similar."

Marla rubbed her face and wiped the salty smell of sweat from her forehead. "Sick. The man is sick. He has to be."

His finger tapped the seventh fresco in line. "*The Flood or The Deluge* clearly has a picture of a boat nearly capsized with too many people and leaning to the side, a tree at the water's edge, just like the two leaning over the side of the boat and the stick near the water's edge."

"Crosby, my husband, a fellow police officer, heard the perp while in the process of killing both teenagers. We almost caught him."

"The sixth fresco is *The Temptation and Fall of Adam and Eve*. God recognized their sin of eating the forbidden fruit and they were forced from the Garden of Eden." He stopped and looked at Marla. "I read one of the two killed was an attorney, and they cohabited outside of marriage."

"Yes, that is correct," Marla said. "By the way, what about the numbers on them or any of them? Do they mean anything in the Book of Genesis?"

"I don't think so. Each of the numbers, 37, 36, 18, and 16 do not correlate to anything in Genesis."

Marla's lips tightened. "Right. Thank you. Go on if you would, Your Excellency."

"Adam and Eve were not married and were not intimate in the Garden. There was no sin until they ate from the Tree of the Knowledge of Good and Evil. After they left Eden, they married and had children. There are some who say that Adam and Eve asked, debated, or argued with God—asking for his forgiveness, wanting to stay. There's a correlation to what an attorney does in their job. They debate or argue their side." He pointed to the snake in the fresco picture. "The snake, or Satan, convinced Eve to bite into the forbidden fruit. Snakes in the pit fit well with that thought."

"The two were found in a pit next to an apple orchard," Marla said. "the forbidden fruit."

"An apple orchard?" He slipped the glasses off, held them with two fingers, and leaned back on his haunches. "Your killer knows what he is doing." The glasses slid back on his head and then he leaned forward again.

He touched the fifth fresco. "Within this image, there are two sets of Adam and Eve, the happy, youthful set on the left near the tree and the second set to the right where they have been banished from the Garden. As you can see, they look older and distraught on the right. I'm going to guess the two victims in the pit were physically attractive people, but their faces and bodies were swollen and grotesque after multiple snakebites. Just as in the fresco, a before and after scene."

The Bishop adjusted the last crime scene picture in front of Marla and himself. "I understand these victims were close to you. Your brother and your sister-in-law?"

Still on her knees, Marla looked out the window. Sunlight warmed her face. She reluctantly nodded. With words just above a whisper, she said, "Yes, it's them."

His hand rested on her shoulder. "I am deeply sorry for your loss. They are at peace with God." He turned back to the images. "Your doctor is correct. They are almost in the perfect position for *The Creation of Eve*."

Marla stood and walked to the chest-high window. Her lips tightened as tears welled in her eyes. She put her elbows on the windowsill, dropped her head down, and sobbed. "Logan, I'm sorry. I didn't mean any of that crap I ever said to you." She lifted her head high, sniffed away tears, and turned back toward the bishop.

"I can see you loved your brother. I'm sure he's forgiven you. As part of your own healing, remember to forgive yourself."

Chapter 41

B etween wooden slats, early morning sunlight speared through the barn. Rows of white lights cut across the darkness, horse stalls, and Marla. Her mouth felt like sawdust climbed inside and grew. She rubbed her face to wake up; the empty tequila bottle rolled down the haystack and came to rest against her head. Daisy, her horse, neighed in the stall. Marla looked around, remembering she was in the barn last night trying to kill the pain of Logan's death. And Crosby in rehab. And her father's peculiar kind of crazy. And everyone in town talking about her failing to find the murderer. She rolled over on her elbows and knees and slowly stood. With each heartbeat, it felt like an anvil clanged in her brain.

When she exited past the barn door, a bright morning slapped her across her face. She squeezed her eyes shut while her stomach churned. She forced herself not to vomit and leaned against the barn. Jet engines burned miles above her, leaving morning contrails strung across the pale blue sky like silver bullet streaks. She envied the people going somewhere, anywhere. A burnt orange ball slowly rose above the horizon, needling through tree canopies. Leaves stood at attention in the windless morning air. Each heartbeat pounded behind her eyes, competing with the high-pitched shrill in her ears.

After a hot shower and breakfast, she sat on the porch wooden bench and sipped her coffee. A few leaves laid on the six wooden steps. A green carpet of ryegrass spread across the field between the house and barn. There were no deer this morning. The chickens weren't out of the coop; unusual. They should be looking for something to eat. The horses neighed in the barn.

Twenty feet in front of the house, a cougar the size of an overgrown German Shepard slinked across the grass. It stopped. Silver-dollar-sized eyes stared at Marla.

Sitting still, her hand slid to her hip, but her service weapon was in the kitchen. Her fingers tightened around the mug handle. She watched the cat's feet almost slide across the grass toward the house, now only twenty feet away from her. It could jump over the wooden rail and be on her in two seconds. Its head lowered slightly. The front shoulder muscles seemed to expand to twice their size. Marla felt the concentration, the focus within the cat. The coffee mug in her hand might as well be a pebble. Its lips quivered. Bright white pointed teeth revealed what would be a quick death. The front paws rose from the ground, the back leg muscles bulged. It shot into the air. Marla swung the mug, and coffee sprayed across the wooden porch. She dove and covered her head.

Nothing happened. She sat up and looked. The cougar pranced away with a rabbit in its mouth.

Her breath faltered. She crawled a few steps past the door, then rushed to the kitchen. Her hands shook while grabbing a small glass from the cupboard and pouring tequila. She drank it in one gulp and did it again. It burned straight down to her stomach. Her body shook; she dropped to the floor, rolled onto her back, and laughed and cried.

She jumped to her feet when the phone rang. SEARCY was on the screen. "No." She grabbed her pistol from the countertop. "Stop calling me." She glared at the phone. It rang again. "Leave me alone." Her finger slipped behind the trigger guard. "Stop it. Stop it." It rang again. She slid the pistol across the countertop and grabbed the tequila bottle, smashing it against her phone until it stopped ringing, then pitched the bottle through the window above the sink.

Screaming, "God damn it!" she fell to her knees. "I'm sorry, Logan. I'm sorry. I should have saved you." She bent down into a ball and covered her head. "Why is this happening? I'm sorry for everything."

Crosby's phone in the bedroom rang. It rang again. She ran to the bedroom and saw Searcy on the screen. She answered and yelled, "Leave me the hell alone! Stop calling me. Do you hear me? I said stop."

"We found Crosby's truck," Searcy said.

Her eyes opened wide. She quickly stood, the motion in her head took an extra second to catch up. "Where? I need to see it."

"Get off I-6 at mile marker 359. That's Hendrix Road, then turn right and go 2.7 miles. Turn right, and it's a half-mile down the dirt road."

"How did you find it?"

"Anonymous call. The wrecker is on its way."

"Anyone injured?"

"Just get here."

Marla's head spun, thinking of a thousand reasons for Crosby's truck to be there. None of them made sense. Eighteen minutes later, her rental car stopped behind Searcy's truck. Crosby's truck was on its side, down in a deep ditch. Clifton's Wreck and Tow Service was painted on the wrecker's door. With the winch hooked on the truck's doorpost, a metal cable retracted as the winch motor whined. The truck's tires bounced back onto the dirt road, revealing heavy damage to the front end, hood, roof, and bed.

She looked in the cab. The navigation system in the center of the dash and the rearview mirror were missing. That was why she didn't find the truck again. Someone deliberately removed the GPS system.

Searcy stepped behind her. "Looks like someone lost control and rolled it on its side. Didn't see anyone in the cab, so he must have climbed out and ran off."

"Blood?" she asked.

"No visible blood, but we'll luminol it thoroughly."

"Did you dust it for prints?"

"They're taking samples now."

Marla walked over to the wrecker driver since they know what happens in a wreck before anyone else. "What do you think, Cliff?"

He raised his shoulders. "Looks a little funny." He pointed to the tire tracks. "They're straight and then they turn into the ditch."

"Okay. What does that mean?"

"No tire slide. It doesn't look like it was going too fast and lost traction. It just turned into the ditch."

"You mean someone did this intentionally?" Marla bent down near the back dually wheels and noticed no bullet holes in the bed or wheel well. It wasn't his truck at the crime scene.

"Did Crosby have a problem with the original truck bed?" Cliff asked.

"What do you mean?"

"The bed is a different color." He pointed to the cab and the bed. "See? This truck is a 2015 model, but this is not the original bed. I think it's three or four years older."

Marla stared at the bed. "I don't see what you mean." She coughed a few times. "Hold on." She pulled out the inhaler from her shirt pocket and shot two breaths into her mouth. A few seconds later, she inhaled deeply. "Sorry. Okay, go on."

"You okay, Marla?"

"Yeah, yeah. Damn weeds. Must be a particular one out here." She held the inhaler up. "Primatene Mist has epinephrine in it. The other asthma inhalers don't work as well for me."

He turned back to the truck. "Look." he rubbed the paint with his fingertips. "The finish on the bed is duller. Like it's been sitting out in the sun longer."

"You're saying this is not the original bed? Where did it come from?"

"Probably came from a wrecking yard."

"What are you two talking about?" Searcy stepped closer.

"This truck bed is not the original," Cliff rubbed his hand across the side of the cab and bed. "Different paint."

Searcy did the same. "Hmm. Didn't see that." He glanced toward Marla. "Why would Crosby get a different bed?"

She remembered the darkness, a pickup driving away. She fired toward the back tires as it escaped from Logan and Cindy's crime scene. "I wasn't sure if I hit the truck."

"Your report stated you fired at a pickup." He shoved his finger against her shoulder. "You didn't say it was Crosby's."

"I didn't know." A gust of wind swirled around them. Her lungs spasmed. She leaned forward, hands on her knees, and coughed. "How the hell do I know whose truck it was?"

"Your drunk-ass husband has a different bed on his truck. You want to take a guess why?"

"No."

"Hard to explain bullet holes in your vehicle. He went out and bought another bed and put it on. After that, he wrecked it and made it look stolen. Except he didn't think about sun-beaten paint."

"Crosby's in rehab. How can he do all that?"

"All of a sudden, your screwed-up, drugged-out husband is suspect number one." Searcy threw his arms up in the air and walked away. "I'm checking this out."

Cliff stood silent.

"He's crazy." She squeezed two more times on the inhaler. "Pack it up and send it to Jerry's Body Shop."

Between shallow breaths, she wondered how many times Crosby escaped the rehab center and where he went. She tapped the rehab number on her phone, but the line was busy. She coughed harder.

"Marla, you okay?" Cliff asked.

"Sure. You get the truck out of here."

Marla hurried to her car, using her hand as a support against the hood, and opened the driver's door; she laid across the front seat and reached for an EpiPen in the glove compartment. Her fingers pulled the blue safety cap off and pitched it onto the floorboard. Jamming the orange-colored end against her thigh, she felt the prick of the needle penetrate her skin. Her hand held it firm against her thigh for ten seconds and then threw the pen on the floorboard next to the blue cap. Her body buzzed.

Crosby crossed her mind. Back in Montenegro, his body, full of alcohol and opioids, laid motionless on the motel bed, with no heartbeat. Three EpiPens, two Narcans, and her CPR saved his life. *Is it my fault all these people are dead?*

Chapter 42

L ater in the morning, Marla drove the rental car into Jerry's Body Shop and stopped next to her repaired truck. The garage doors were up, and Jerry's legs stuck out from under a car.

He watched two black boots come closer and stop next to his automotive creeper. Sliding out from under the car, Marla stood over him in her uniform.

"Hey there, Officer Adams. Your truck is all fixed; new headlights, windshield, back window, and radiator. Had to put new hoses on the engine, one was punctured. It's best when you replace one, you replace all." He slipped a red rag from his back pocket and wiped the top layer of black oil off his hands. "Keys in the cup holder, and don't worry about the bill. I'll send it to the station."

"Thanks, Jerry. Where's Crosby's truck?"

"It's in the back. He messed that thing up pretty bad. The whole right side needs replacing." He opened the metal door to the dirt lot behind the building. "What happened?"

"Stolen. Not sure who, yet. We're waiting for fingerprints."

He pointed toward the left side of the lot. The dirt puffed up around their boots with each step. The mangled truck sat alone in the corner, with its grill pointed toward the twenty-foot tall metal fence like it was embarrassed.

She rubbed her hand across the driver's door and down the side of the bed. "Jerry, can you see the difference in the paint?"

He squatted down, so the door was even with his eyes. "Sure. Not original. What happened?"

"Don't know," Marla said. "Anyway, could you find out when and where he purchased this bed?"

"Only if he bought it from a place that had part records. You know, a retail business, not an individual. I can call my buddies at wrecking yards close by, check a few websites. Call FedEx, UPS if they shipped something that big to town."

She bent down, looked under the truck, and felt a bolt that held the bed to the chassis. "Look at this. Can you tell how long ago this was replaced?"

He felt the bolt, then went to the other side and did the same. "They're new. No rust. Not even any mud or dirt caked around them. I think this happened recently."

"How recent?"

"A few days, if that many."

◆

Less than an hour later, Jerry leaned back in his faded wooden office chair at his shop with his phone in hand.

Marla sat in her truck at an intersection. The ring startled her. She answered, "Adams here."

Jerry sat up. "I got lucky and found a pickup, the same color."

"Where?"

"A buddy from a wrecker service in Hondo towed a 2012 Dodge Ram 3500 dually pickup to the owner's house after he hit a deer. Tore the front up pretty bad."

"Know where he towed it?"

"A house about 4 miles east of Hondo. He sent me a picture of the worksheet. I'll text you a copy with the address."

"Got his name?" Marla asks.

"Ronnie Travis."

"Thanks, Jerry. I'm heading in that direction now."

◆

Marla's truck veered a slow right turn onto the two-lane asphalt lined with thick tree trunks and soaring branches. Dark, irregular shadows covered the road. An open spot to the side of the road had wide muddy wheel ruts where someone had done multiple donuts. Beer cans and broken furniture scattered across the weeds. A straight line of telephone poles held miles of black wire topped with birds. She passed over a dry creek bridge and glimpsed at a sad looking house with multiple stages of amateur repairs sat alone on a plot of dirt. Stopping at a single mailbox that stood next to the road, Marla rolled her window down to read the name on the mailbox, TRAVIS. She turned down the dirt pathway toward the house about a hundred yards away. A weather-worn Chevy pickup in as bad a shape as the house sat near the front porch. It had to be over thirty years old. The house was twice that. She honked her horn several times, expecting someone to come out, but no one did.

After angling her truck back toward the dirt road, just in case, her hand slipped the magazine out of the Glock handle and snapped it back in. She holstered her service weapon.

An old-school screen door not fitting flush moved slightly with the wind. Her boots clunked on the dried slats of the porch. The partially open front door had a hole the size of a boot heel next to the broken door handle.

"Hello." She kept her fingers resting on her weapon. "Anybody home?" Her throat twinged and held back a cough. *Not now. I don't have time for this.* She slipped the inhaler from her shirt pocket, squeezed, took a breath, then placed the inhaler back. She knocked on the screen door. "Anyone home? This is the police." *Like I have any jurisdiction here.* She slowly opened the screen door and pushed on the front door. The hinges snapped off, and the door banged onto the floor. Dust swirled. A fly buzzed near her ear; her hand swatted the air. "Police. Anybody here?"

Her spine steeled with a familiar iron tainted odor hovering in the air. She slipped her weapon out of the holster. The living room was clean and straight. Stepping left to the kitchen, she caught a glimpse of a body, face down, sprawled across the floor with several cats chewing on the arms. "Get!" They screeched and scattered. Her stomach cramped; she forced vomit back down.

The bloated pale green body laid in a coagulated blackened pool. Flies buzzed around the mass of blood matted in the scalp hair.

The kitchen back door was open. The ground was flat with no grass, or flowers, or bushes; nothing but dirt, two lifeless trees, and a pillaged Dodge pickup with the front-end smashed and no bed. Thirty feet away perched a truck bed, alone, with bullet holes in the side.

After the sheriff arrived at the house, she interviewed him as much as he did her. The wreck happened over a month ago, and Mr. Travis advertised pickup parts for sale on Craig's List.

Whoever bought the bed probably killed Travis, and Logan and Cindy, and everyone else. Marla asked the sheriff to inform her of any unexpected fingerprints, but that would be too easy.

Marla turned back onto the road. *Did Crosby come here and take the bed? How could he get back to rehab after he wrecked the truck?* Her chest tightened. She shook the inhaler and squeezed twice. Nothing. She shook it next to her ear. There was no liquid in the container. She pitched it on the floorboard, pursed her lips, and tried slowing her breath. The hiss of tractor-trailers barreling down the highway brought her focus back. Merging into traffic, she touched a phone number on her Bluetooth.

"Dr. Sanborn's office."

"Marla decided to throw her weight around. "This is Hildebrandt Police Officer Marla Adams. I need to see the doctor. Meet me at the back door in twenty-five minutes."

Marla paused at the back door of the family medical clinic. A scattering of flattened cigarette butts lay on the ground five feet from the door. A driver waved as the car drove around the back of the clinic. Marla smiled and waved back. She knocked on the metal door. A few seconds later, a young woman pushed the door open wearing a blue scrub top, pants, and white shoes, and a nameplate with SUZIE SANBORN, LVN STU-DENT. Marla thanked her, slogged down the hall, and caught a glimpse of Dr. Sanborn coming out of a room. His bright smile helped. He gave her a one-arm hug across her shoulders and pointed to the only room with an open door. He promised it would only be a few minutes. That probably meant an hour.

Sitting in the metal and fabric chair, she rested her elbows on her knees with her head in her hands. *Where is Crosby right now?* She coughed, then tapped her empty shirt pocket.

Dr. Sanborn entered the room. "Marla, you look stressed." He watched her rapid breathing. He tapped the patient table with the flat of his hand. "Up here, young lady."

She swooped her hair back from her forehead and stood with an uneasy balance.

"Whoa there, girl." He grabbed her elbow. "What's up?"

She sat on top of the table. "My lungs. They're bad, and the inhaler isn't working anymore."

"Which inhaler?" He looked in her EMR, electronic medical record. "I don't have you using an inhaler."

"I use Primatene Mist."

They spoke for another fifteen minutes, him more than her. After checking her blood pressure and pulse, he listened to her heart and lungs. Opening the door, he said, "Come with me," and pointed to a nurse. "Estelle, take Officer Adams and do a pulmonary function test." He put his hand on Marla's back, and in a faint voice, he said, "I expect this to come back normal. After that, let's talk about what's going on. Okay?"

Twenty minutes later, Marla sat in the same room, the same chair. Dr. Sanborn returned while holding a basket of candies and cookies.

"Here. This is for you." He handed her the basket. "I can't take this." He tapped his stomach. "My diabetes."

Marla unconsciously grabbed it before she thought to say no.

"Mrs. Garcia, lovely little woman, she brings a basket of homemade cookies every time she comes here. We have baskets piled high in the break room. Eat one. They're better than a shot in your eye."

"I would hope so." She bit into a warm chocolate chip cookie. "Wow, these are fantastic. She needs to sell these."

"Feeling better? You look better. Chocolate chips always help."

Marla finished the cookie. "Um, sure. I guess so."

"Your pulmonary test was normal, nothing unexpected." He sat on the stool and turned in front of her. "You don't have asthma or allergies, Marla. I have always suspected this would happen with your family history. You have anxiety, and the Primatene makes it worse."

Her hands tightened around the arms of the chair. "No. No, I don't!"

"I know, with your father having his problems and you telling me about your mother before she left your family. Mental disorders of distinct types can run in the family."

She shot up from the chair. "I'm not crazy." Her hand swept everything off the countertop.

The clanging of metal trays and plastic containers filled with tongue depressors hitting the floor brought hard knocks on the door. The large chrome door handle moved down as the door cracked open.

Dr. Sanborn stopped the door with his hand. "I'm good, Estelle. We're both good."

I'm the goddamn sane one in the family." The heels of her palms wiped tears off her cheeks as she stared back at him. "You understand what I'm saying? Someone has to be clean." She leaned her head against the wall and touched her empty shirt pocket for the inhaler. "I've got too many things going on, the murders, Crosby, Pops... Logan." She stood up, ready to walk out. "I need to go. I've got work to do."

Dr. Sanborn stood and held up his hands. "I can't stop you from leaving, but I want you to stay."

Her voice pitched an octave higher. "Well, I don't." She stepped next to the sink in the corner of the room and slid down to the floor. "No. I have too many things. Too many things going on." She clutched the sink and pulled herself up quickly. "I'm leaving." Her head spun; vision tunneled. "Oh, damn."

Marla opened her eyes, only to see bright fluorescent lights above her. She felt a blood pressure cuff release its grip around her arm. "What happened?" she asked.

Dr. Sanborn stood next to her while she laid on the patient table. "You hyperventilated and passed out. I have something for you. Better than chocolate chips."

With a deep sigh, she capitulated. "All right, fine. What are you giving me?"

◆

The pharmacist slid the paper bag toward Marla. He explained all the required medical literature to her, which flew over her head. She nodded her acceptance and reluctantly slipped the credit card into the processor. Walking toward the front door, she rolled the bag tight against the pill bottle, and held it like she was holding a dumbbell. She felt like a dumbbell.

In the car, she ripped open the bag and stared at the label. "Duloxetine? What the hell is that?" She pulled the product information sheet off the bag. It had a litany of side effects. "Oh, great. Is this going to fix me or kill me? Drowsiness, seizures, headaches, all kinds of stomach shit. Not good. Wait, no, no, no, decreased libido? Sorry, doc. That is not happening." She looked near the bottom of the list. "Hmm, weight loss. Okay. If one is good, then two are better." She popped them in her mouth and drank the rest of her cold coffee.

Chapter 43

Marla's phone rang next to her bed. She reached for it and her brain screamed not to move. The worst hangover in years, and without alcohol. The ringing became louder. She rolled off the bed to her hands and knees and touched the speaker button. "Huh?"

"Did you go back to the beach?" Searcy asked. "Where have you been? I've been calling you for hours."

Her palm wiped her forehead, hoping the hangover would miraculously disappear. "Not feeling good. I need to rest a little longer."

"And where the hell is that drunk husband of yours?"

Her bottle of duloxetine had spilled over her nightstand. She scooped them up and counted 26 of the 30. *How did I take four?* "He's still in rehab."

"Someone called me and said he was in town, not in rehab. Get down there and find him."

◆

Six ibuprofen and a bucket of coffee later, she banged on the locked front door of the rehab center. She hit it again. "Open up. This is the police."

The deadbolt unlatched, and the knob twisted. Marla shoved the door open, revealing an older woman in blue scrubs.

"Can I help you?" she asked.

Marla pushed through the entrance. "I need to investigate Crosby Adams' room. Now."

The woman closed the door and latched the deadbolt again. "I'm sorry. Our clients are not allowed visitors at this time."

"This is not a social visit. I need to see if he's in his room."

The woman scoffed. "Of course he is. No one is allowed out of their rooms after dinner."

"I'm not leaving this place until I see him." Marla motioned toward the hallway. "Show me which room."

A minute later, the woman tapped on Crosby's door. "Mr. Adams, I'm very sorry to disturb you…"

Marla stepped in front of her and opened the door to reveal an empty room and an open window. "Damn it."

The woman looked behind the door. "I'm sorry. I don't know what to say."

"I do." Marla charged toward the entrance. "You have a problem at this facility."

Tapping her shirt pocket for the inhaler, it wasn't there. *Dr. Sanborn said deep, slow breaths. No more Primatene. When are these pills supposed to work?* She drove off to find him. Turning a country song on the radio down, she yelled, "Come on, Crosby. Show your face."

◆

An hour later, headlights crept into the parking lot, swung into a spot at the far end, and darkened. Two rehab employees, Rigo and Dax, climbed out of a dark green Fiat. Crosby opened the back door and glanced around and then all three slinked between cars and past shrubs behind the building.

At the other end of the lot, Searcy climbed out of his truck and walked to the compact car. He tapped the microphone on his radio. "Grand-mamma. Need a license plate check on a dark green Fiat." A minute later, she replied with the information he needed. Rigo Childress owned the vehicle. Searcy placed a GPS tracker under the fuel tank. He noticed the passenger door unlocked and slipped a listening device under the seat.

After driving the streets and alleys all night looking for Crosby with nothing to show for it, Marla stopped at the station. She wasn't heading home with no one to greet her, so she dismissed the night shift. The empty squad room felt like a mausoleum. Marla's eyes shifted from one victim's picture to the next. She whispered, "Someone tell me what all this means. Each number means something to the killer. Why did he do this?"

Marla's desk phone rang. She reached for it while still staring at the wall. "Police department."

"Officer Adams?"

"Yes."

"This is Carter Barkley at the bank. I normally would not call you over a bank matter. In fact, I probably shouldn't, but with all that has been going on in town, I mean, you know, the murders and all. I called Father Jules at the church office and his cell phone with no answer from either. It's probably nothing... I'm sure he will call me back... but..."

"Mr. Barkley, it's the middle of the night."

"I have insomnia and some nights I come to the bank and work."

"Get to the point, please."

"The St. Juan Diego Catholic Church account has been emptied."

"What do you mean, emptied?"

"If there is a withdrawal of over ten-thousand dollars, I get a notification. The church account came up, but I was gone this afternoon. I should have been here. I should have made it where I had to clear any transaction."

"How much money, Mr. Barkley?"

He cleared his throat. "Someone must have hacked into our site and entered the church building account. This was for the expansion planned next year. We were going to double the church capacity."

"How much money?"

"I, we have been looking at this, trying to figure out how this happened. Someone transferred the funds to an unknown account. We contacted our IT company, and they have been trying to find where it went."

"Mr. Barkley, how much money?"

He cleared his throat again. "Over three-hundred-thousand dollars."

Marla sat in her chair. "When?"

He waited several seconds to answer. "We did our due diligence, internally, and now I am contacting the police and the regulatory institutions."

"When, Mr. Barkley?"

"Two minutes before three o'clock."

"Church money is gone, and you can't contact the priest. You think he stole the money? Is that what you're saying?"

"I cannot be sure of that. Father Jules had the authority to withdraw funds but needed a second signature for any amount over ten thousand dollars."

"And who can co-sign?"

"Mrs. Woolham, our secretary for forty-two years, and Mayor Pichler."

"You said Pichler?" Marla shook her head. "This was electronic, not a paper check, right? Do you need a second signature on an electronic withdrawal?" Since the priest came to town, all hell had broken loose. Homicides, stolen money, and now he's disappeared. "Never mind. It makes no difference, paper or not. Thank you, Mr. Barkley. Please come to the station after nine this morning and fill out the necessary paperwork." She ended the call and stared at the board on the wall.

The phone rang again. "Police department."

"Officer Adams, this is the secretary at the San Antonio Archdioceses. Bishop Medina would like for you to see him. He said he thinks he can help."

"Does nobody sleep anymore?" Marla tapped her shirt pocket for the inhaler and coughed. She concentrated on slowing her breaths.

The secretary replied, "I'm sorry, ma'am, but it is eight o'clock."

Marla glanced at her watch. Hours had passed. "I can be there in forty-five minutes."

She slammed the truck door shut and flipped the emergency lights on. The back tires spun forward. The truck bounced over the curb, and the engine roared down the street.

Charging down the highway, red and blue lights flickered out from the grill and roof of her truck. Headlights and taillights flashed in unison. Forty minutes later, the truck turned into the Archdioceses parking lot. Her hand tapped her empty shirt pocket. A bottle of duloxetine in her pants pocket had replaced the inhaler. "Thirty milligrams are not enough today. Sorry, Doc. I need more." She pulled out another from the bottle, popped it into her mouth, and drank from the water bottle. "Okay, this better be good."

The richness of the entryway brought peace, even for a minute. The beauty was a definite benefit to working here. A lady on the other side of the desk smiled and pointed toward the hallway. Bishop Medina's feet bounced down the hall with his hand stretched out. His smile gave her hope.

"Thank you, Your Excellency. I hope you can help."

Medina shook Marla's hand. "I have pondered over this since you left. I have additional information." His hand pointed toward his office. "Please."

The tea set and cookies sat on a table between two chairs. A foldout table stood in the corner with several pages on top.

"I hope you don't mind the tea and cookies. Remember my vice?"

Marla smiled. "I was hoping for it."

"Please sit." He poured tea into her cup. "I have been praying for these poor souls. The numbers carved into them, and the two branded must have felt unspeakable terror." He sipped his tea. Marla followed his lead. "You mentioned numerology last time," Medina said.

"Oh, Your Excellency, I apologize for that. My brother mentioned it."

"Yes. Of course, I don't believe in that, but I believe in mathematics. There are many celestial phenomena, much of what God has done, can be explained by numbers." He bit into his cookie and sipped more tea. "I have studied these numbers against the Book of Genesis and the Sistine Chapel frescoes. I believe there is a pattern to your numbers and a prediction of the future."

Marla drank the rest of her tea in one gulp. "Right. Would you show me?"

Bishop Medina stood. "This is all about numbers from here on."

They stepped to the table. Bishop Medina said, "The rectangular table represents the Sistine Chapel. Inside, the altar is on the left side, and the entrance on the right." He lay nine photographs of Michelangelo's paintings on the table side by side. Each printed with the name of the fresco at the top of the page. A square, yellow sticky pad and a spiral notebook sat at the edge of the table.

"Remember the order of the frescoes?" he asked. "They are directly related to the chapters in the Book of Genesis. The first chronological fresco, *The Separation Of Light From Dark*, is closest to the altar, here on the left. The last fresco, *The Drunkenness Of Noah*, is near the entrance, here on the right. These murders are happening in reverse order, right to left. The first murder stood for *The Drunkenness Of Noah* and told in Genesis 9:21." He took the yellow pad and pencil and wrote 9+21=30. "Thirty, not thirty-seven, which was carved on the man in the church, but the word Genesis has seven letters. If you add seven, you get thirty-seven."

He wrote just below, 7+9+21=37, then pulled it off and stuck it on the fresco image.

Marla rubbed her forehead. "Thirty-seven equals the Genesis verse for the fresco?"

"Yes, and he did that with each body," Medina replied. "The second murder represented the next fresco in line, *The Sacrifice Of Noah*, Genesis 8:20. The victim had thirty-five carved in the skin." On the yellow pad, he wrote 7+8+20=35 and stuck it on the picture.

"The third murder represented *The Deluge*, Genesis 6:5, with the number eighteen carved on one body." He wrote 7+6+5=18.

"The fourth murder represented *The Temptation and Fall of Adam and Eve*, Genesis 3:6, with the number sixteen carved on the bodies." He wrote 7+3+6=16.

"The last murders, represented by *The Creation of Eve*, Genesis 2:21, were branded with a thirty." He wrote 7+2+21=30.

"Thirty?" Marla asked. "I thought the brand was a three." She hesitated, then said, "It wasn't a three in a circle. It was a three and a zero."

"Yes, thirty."

"I'm sorry, Your Excellency. I know he's a sick fu..." Marla cleared her throat, "a sick man, but this will not get him caught."

"I didn't understand myself until I studied a little more. Then I looked at the summation numbers."

He took the spiral notebook from the table's edge and wrote the numbers in a column.

37

35

18

16

30

"I added the two numbers together."

3+7=10

3+5=8

1+8=9

1+6=7

3+0=3

"If I remember, the first murder happened about 1 AM." He changed the 10 to 1+0=1. "The second murder happened about 8 AM. The third at 9 AM. The fourth at 7 AM. Do you see the pattern?"

She flailed her hands in the air. "No. No, I don't."

"The number on the body? It's the time of the murder." Reaching for the next image, he said, "*The Creation Of Adam* is found in Genesis 1:26." He wrote 7+1+26=34=7.

"7 AM?" Marla asked. "But what day?"

He smiled. "There's a sequence."

"What do you mean?"

"There's a murder every three days."

"Oh, crap. I never picked up on that clue."

Medina tapped the pencil on the pad. "I believe your next murder will happen at seven o'clock tomorrow morning. He knows what time he will kill, and so do you."

Chapter 44

"Pops!" Marla yelled. She dodged desks in the police squad room like ski moguls. Her breaths were rapid from running from her truck. She stopped for a few seconds and then yelled, "Pops, I got it!" She banged on Searcy's closed office door and opened it. The room was dark. She spun around and glanced at the victim's wall, then a quick scan across the desks. Everyone's eyes stared at her. "Where is he?"

"He left to buy more coffee at the store," Larry said. "He should be back any minute."

Searcy tracked into the squad room with a small paper sack under his arm. "What's up?"

Marla rushed him and slapped the sack away. She grabbed his shirt and pulled him toward her desk. "I got it. I got it all figured out. You won't believe it. It's wild." She pushed his shoulders down, and he plopped into her chair.

She explained what the Bishop had said. How each victim's position was the same as a fresco on the Sistine Chapel, with the numbers carved standing for the book of Genesis, chapter and verse, and the time the murder happened. Each one, clear as day; 1 AM, 8 AM, 9 AM, 7 AM, and 3 AM.

Larry tapped the victim's board. "Marla, we're not sure what time the second murder happened since he was dead for so long. It could have been at night."

"That's right, but all the others we are sure of. Oh, I almost forgot, there's a pattern of days between the killings. Every three days, Walker, Kinsey, Willie and Ethan, the snakes in the hole, and...three days... three days later..." She stopped and rubbed her eyes. "He killed Logan and Cindy. That was two days ago. Tomorrow is day three."

She stood and held her arms out wide. "I came straight from the Archdioceses to here. Nobody else knows about this outside this room." Marla glanced at her watch. "It's four o'clock. We could have this whole thing wrapped up in fifteen hours. The murderer doesn't just randomly kill someone, he takes hours to set things in order. We need to look now. Everyone be vigilant. Every unit needs to be on the streets, keep your eyes peeled, and *please*, call out *anything* suspicious.

Chapter 45

C rosby sat alone at the rehab center dining table when two CNAs, Certified Nursing Assistants, wearing gray scrubs, stopped at his table. Rigo had blond hair just below his ears, and Dax had black hair to his neckline. Rigo stopped next to Crosby, who kept eating.

"This afternoon," Rigo said.

A dining room attendant stopped his pushcart next to Crosby's table. "You finished with that?"

"You got any dessert?" Crosby leaned back.

"Dessert." Dax pointed at a small empty plate. "You already had dessert."

Crosby shook his head and scoffed. "Right." He looked up at the attendant. "I forgot about the dessert. I was hoping for some *cake*."

The dining attendant nodded. "I'll bring it to your room later."

"That would be great."

Rigo watched as the attendant left. When out of hearing distance, he turned back to Crosby. "Dessert? What the hell is wrong with you? Don't get flaky on me, man. You passed the test with a hundred pills. The boss has a thousand, and we need to wrap this up today."

"Sure, today is the day. A thousand oxy pills." Crosby stood. "I'll meet both of you at the back door in fifteen minutes." He strolled down the hallway and high-fived a nurse before turning into his room.

A few minutes later, there was a knock on Crosby's door. The dining room attendant entered and closed the door behind him. He held a wrinkled sack in his hand toward Crosby. "This takes me off your list."

Crosby flipped the sack upside down on his bed, and a Ruger LCP 380 pistol dropped out. It was smaller than his hand. He checked the magazine, six bullets, and snapped it back into the pistol grip. "Deal. Not a word to anyone. Understand?"

The attendant scoffed. "I'll be glad when you're gone from here." He closed the door behind him.

Crosby watched the door close, then he pulled a backpack from under the bed and dropped the gun on top of ten bundles of cash worth ten-thousand dollars each, $100,000, and slid it back.

♦

Marla's Dodge truck sat quietly between two cars at the far end of the rehab parking lot. She sipped coffee from an insulated tumbler while reaching for the duloxetine bottle. She held it in front of her and reread the instructions. *Take one a day.* "Hmm." The bottle rattled back into the cupholder. Her eyes shifted to the clock: 4:27 PM.

♦

Crosby slipped on the black cotton hooded jacket and grabbed the backpack out from under the bed. Pulling the nightstand drawer out and placing it on the bed, he pulled his DEA badge and handcuffs taped to the back and then stuffed them into his jeans pocket. He cracked open the door. The hall lights were off, and it was quiet. He closed it again, opened the window, and stole outside.

Rigo smoothed his hair behind his ears. "You bring the money?"

"Don't worry about that. You just make sure the guy has the pills," Crosby said. "Where's your buddy?"

"At the place."

"Let's go." Crosby flipped the backpack over his shoulder.

They crouched down and snuck their way behind the shrubbery. A few minutes later, the Fiat engine started, and the car slowly rolled out of the parking lot.

Marla started the engine and kept the headlights off. Trailing the Fiat, it raced down the narrow road.

She picked up the mic. "Following a dark green Fiat heading east on FM 404."

Grand-mamma called out, "10-4."

"Are you calling from the rehab center?" Searcy asked over the radio.

Marla cringed at his voice. She's not supposed to be hanging around the rehab.

In the Fiat, Rigo's eyes glanced in the rearview mirror. "We got a pickup about four hundred yards behind us."

Crosby spun around and recognized the grille of Marla's Dodge truck. "Not good. You got this thing floored?"

"It's a Fiat, not a Porsche."

Crosby looked at the side mirror, then straight ahead. "See that dirt path to the right? Take it."

"Going too fast," Rigo said.

"Do it."

The Fiat's brake lights brightened in front of Marla. It turned hard right onto a dirt road. After flipping on the emergency lights and siren, she coughed hard before grabbing the mic. "In pursuit of the Fiat evading me. It turned south on a dirt road just before the Grun Fluss bridge." *What are you doing, Crosby?*

The Fiat bounced over rocks and tree branches. Rigo's hands tightened on the steering wheel. "Why is a cop after us?"

"I bet the Doc called the cops on us," Crosby said. "He caught me sneaking out once."

The road narrowed. Wild grass stood two feet high along the sides. The Fiat's small back tires slipped on the grass as it followed the curves in the road.

Rigo pushed back against his seat. "Where the hell is this shit path taking us?"

Crosby motioned with his hand. "We got this. I know where I am."

Red and blue lights streaked across evergreens. The road straightened, and Marla floored the accelerator.

Rigo's voice rose. "Getting closer. You sure you know where we're going?"

Marla's brain hurt. Her soul crushed. How was this going to end? What was Crosby going to do when everyone stopped? Would he draw his weapon? "Still in pursuit of the Fiat." She coughed again into the microphone. "The road's fading to thin ruts." She closed within fifty feet.

Her truck, sitting high, could manage scrub brush scraping the sides of her truck. The Fiat wouldn't survive a head-on collision with a tumbleweed. She yelled at the car. "Stop this, Crosby. Tell me why you are doing this?"

Crosby pointed ahead. "See the two trees a hundred yards away?"

"Yeah, the road's blocked."

"No. I've been here before. There's a large branch, broken off from the crown and leaning at a forty-five-degree angle across the road."

Thick scrub scratched the sides of their car.

"There's not enough room. I'm slowing down. I'm not dying for oxy pills."

"Step on it," Crosby said. "The truck is right behind us."

"There's not enough room. We'll crash."

Crosby pulled out the pistol and stuck the barrel to Rigo's head. "I said step on it."

The Fiat sped up and shot under the branch. He flinched as the left side mirror exploded off the car.

Marla slammed on the brakes and slid to a stop inches from the trees. The Fiat disappeared from her view. She opened the pill bottle and took another, then pushed the microphone button. "Lost contact. I believe Officer Crosby Adams is in the car."

"10-4," Grand-mamma replied.

"Marla?" Searcy called out on the radio.

"Here."

"What's your location?"

"Not sure, about a mile south of the 404. Where are you?"

Searcy watched a red dot move on his tablet, where he attached the GPS tracker on the Fiat. "I'm roaming the streets of Hildebrandt like everyone else. Meet me at the DQ parking lot in twenty minutes."

She cringed. "Okay."

Chapter 46

Wind gusts bounced an empty Styrofoam cup across a stripped cotton field. The Fiat eased down an open dirt road two miles outside of town near an abandoned cotton gin. Headlights spotlighted Dax with a cigarette in his hand as he sat on an empty metal barrel next to the road. He took a long draw and flicked the butt in the air. Crosby felt on edge, scalp buzzed, adrenaline escalated. He detected neither of them seemed anxious.

The Fiat stopped next to Dax. Crosby stuck his elbow out of the open side window. "Where's the guy?"

Dax pointed toward the building. "Be here soon. You got the money?"

"This is where the oxy is?" Crosby shifted in the small seat. "The buy, everything happening here?"

Rigo shifted to first gear and drove slowly. "You need to keep that pistol out of sight. He sees it, and the deal's over."

A tumbleweed rolled in slow-motion in front of the car, snagging onto others alongside the building. Corrugated metal panels squeaked. They both raised the windows up as dust swirled around them.

The car turned and stopped at an angle twenty feet in front of an abandoned pickup pushed against the outside wall, tires flattened and cracked. The raised hood revealed a wilted bird's nest of twigs and leaves on top of the carburetor.

Crosby climbed out of the Fiat and slid the backpack full of cash over his shoulders. Dax caught up with them. Crosby's fingers rubbed an official black and yellow county sign nailed to the door. It said CONDEMNED PROPERTY. He pulled the broken padlock off and grasped the door handle.

Dax stuck a gun barrel against Crosby's side. "We're not going in."

The wind increased as black puffy clouds crossed a nearly full moon.

"No? Where are we going?" Crosby asked.

"Drop the pistol," Dax said.

"Yeah, drop it," Rigo said, "and give me the backpack."

"Are you planning on killing a DEA agent?" Crosby asked.

"A what?" Rigo asked. He turned to Dax. "We're shit, man. Let's get out of here."

Searcy cut around from behind the broken down truck. "I had a suspicion you were DEA or FBI."

"Chief? What are you doing here?" Crosby glanced at an orange taser gun and remembered taser marks on the victims.

Searcy raised his left hand and pointed the taser. "I believe if these two boys took your backpack full of money and disappeared forever, I could never arrest them for all these murders."

"Wait, I didn't kill nobody," Rigo said.

"How do we know you won't come find us?" Dax asked.

"You're right. I should kill both of you and pin the murders on two dead junkies."

Dax swung his pistol toward Searcy, who quickly drew his service weapon and fired. Dax fell and grabbed his shoulder.

"Shit, man. You almost killed me."

"Stop your sniffling. I only grazed you."

Rigo dropped to his knees. "I won't talk. I can disappear forever. I promise."

"I'm tired of killing," Searcy said. "Go. Get out of here."

Rigo grabbed the backpack before helping Dax up. They jumped into the car and took off.

With his hands up, Crosby asked. "Now what? Are you going to kill a DEA agent?"

"No." Searcy fired the taser gun. "Need you as bait."

After Crosby stopped spasming, Searcy pistol butted the back of his neck and then duct taped his mouth, hands, and feet.

Minutes later, Searcy pulled his truck next to the church's side door. He dropped the tailgate, grabbed Crosby's ankles, and slid him down the bed. Flipping him over his shoulder, Searcy banged on the door. Simic opened it and pointed them to the altar. Searcy dropped Crosby on the floor. "Watch him." He handed Simic a taser gun. "If he acts up, shoot him again."

"I'm here for the coins," Simic said. "I'm not shooting anyone."

"Do what I said or you're next," Searcy said. "I'll be back. I have more business to take care of first."

Marla's mud-splattered truck sat in the DQ parking lot. Searcy's truck stopped next to her, and both rolled their windows down.

"Why are you paying so much attention to Crosby tonight?" Searcy asked. "We have other things to worry about."

"Why?" Marla snapped back. "Because something's not right about what he's doing. Did you know he was sneaking from rehab at night and doing... something?"

Between his legs, Searcy loaded another cartridge into the taser. "No, I didn't. We have bigger fish to fry right now. Forget about whether your husband is smoking dope, or buying pills, or whatever else he's doing." He looked down at his watch. "If your theory is right, something is going to happen tomorrow morning, and I need you on the south side of town."

"We need to find out what Crosby is doing," Marla said. "Is it related to the murders?"

"Are you saying he is a person of interest?" Searcy asked.

"No, of course not."

"If it makes you feel better, I'll send Larry to the other side of town to look for him. You get down south and call if you see anything. Like you said, this perp will set something up before it's time for the next killing."

Marla headed toward the south side streets with her windows down. A train's distant horn bellowed long and lonely. She wondered where it led. Would tomorrow be a happier day if she left all this behind? She thought of Crosby. *Where is he?*

◆

Wind gusts raked across trees with animals huddled under bushes. Carbon copy houses crammed together like cars in a Walmart parking lot. Thunder clouds rumbled, hiding the sound of footsteps in a backyard.

Draped in a black hoodie and gloves, Searcy skulked past the fence line. Boots stepped on thick fescue grass, leaving impressions trailing to the concrete patio. A wind chime clanged random notes. The back door lever turned, but the deadbolt was locked. His hand crept under a vinyl flap of the doggie door. Gloved fingers felt upward and twisted the deadbolt knob and pulled the lever handle down. His shadow slipped past the open door. Two cats scurried away.

A distant snore came from the back bedroom. A picture of a white-bearded man wearing a Santa Claus suit hung on the living room wall, the owner of the house, Samuel Chenier. Headlights moved outside. He glimpsed out the front window. Marla's truck drove steadily down the street.

A box fan hummed in the bedroom. Black curtains covered the windows. Searcy's taser gun scraped across the bedroom door; deliberate, callused. In the far corner, an upholstered recliner sat empty with an oxygen bottle standing next to it and a long oxygen hose snaking over worn carpet. Searcy heard a grunt to his left. The door shoved hard against him, and he fell back against the wall. Raising his hand, he pointed the taser. A baseball bat slammed against his arm.

"Get out of my house, you maggot," Chenier yelled.

Searcy fell as the bat hit him again. His foot swept Chenier's feet away, bouncing him hard on the floor. Chenier pulled the hood away from Searcy's head. Taser wires spit toward Chenier's chest.

❖

Searcy pulled to the back of the Flagstone Theater. He wrapped a steel chain around the back door handle. His truck engine roared, tires spun, and the chain uncoiled like a striking snake. The solid metal door snapped off the hinges and bounced down the parking lot.

❖

Marla drove past a few porch lights brimming with false security. She stopped at an intersection and gazed at her phone weather app, showing heavy rain approaching in five minutes. Her truck eased down Fannin Street again. When she'd driven by earlier, a house on a corner looked different. This time, the garage door was up.

"Grand-mamma to Marla."

She answered, "Here."

"Neighbors of 3301 Fannin Street reported loud noises."

"I'm close by." Marla stopped two houses over as tiny raindrops prickled her windows. She snapped the mic button down. "Send all units for assistance. No lights or siren."

"10-4," Grand-mamma replied. "And Marla, we're in a tornado watch."

"Damn." She looked up at the black clouds. "Need cross-reference of the owner of the house, ASAP."

Seconds later, the clouds opened, sheets of rain rolled down her windshield and pounded her roof and hood. She reached behind her back seat for her rain jacket. Grand-mamma responded with the owner's name.

One unit approached moments later. Marla called out on the radio, "Headlights off." The vehicle with wipers at full speed stopped in front of the house. She zipped up her jacket and opened her door. A waterfall slammed against her. She waved her arms and motioned Eddie Mayfield, the newest HPD officer on the force, to the backside of her truck. "Where the hell is everyone?"

"Steve caught his hand in a table saw this morning. Darren's wife is in labor. They both left for San Antonio a few hours ago."

"And Larry is on the other side of town looking for... just... he's there searching," Marla said. "So, it's you and me?"

Ethan wiped his face. "Guess so. For a while."

"Okay. Grand-mamma said this is Samuel Chenier's house. Do you know him?"

Ethan yelled against the rain, "Yeah, I know him. He plays Santa Claus at the Christmas play every year?"

"Right. I haven't seen him since last Christmas." The fresco of The Creation of Adam flashed in her brain. God had a long, flowing beard. "Does he still have a long beard?"

"Saw him last week." Ethan tried to block the rain with his arm. "Long, curly white beard."

Rain pounded their clothes. Marla wiped her face. "You take the front door. I will take the back. Keep your eyes open. If this is the killer, he might disappear in this downpour."

Marla opened the wooden gate fence. Lightning crackled across the sky. Recently planted pansies stood flooded across the back patio. A pergola hovered over chairs with plastic still wrapped around the cushions. Rain poured into the house through the open back door. She tapped the mic on her shirt. "Ready?"

Ethan called out, "Ready."

"Go." Marla charged through the back entrance and yelled, "Police! Everybody on the floor." She swept the living room and entered the hall. She wondered why Ethan didn't come in. Clearing the bathrooms and closets and then the two bedrooms, she found a baseball bat next to a used taser cartridge on the bedroom floor. "Ethan? Where are you?"

Larry entered the front door with his pistol raised. "Marla, you good?"

"Yeah. Where Ethan?"

"You're not going to like this."

"What?"

"Officer Mayfield is dead."

"What?" She walked toward the front door.

"I found him on the porch. He's dead."

Marla stopped. "How did you know to come here?"

"Larry stumbled with his answer. "I... it was on the radio. Grand-mamma said the address."

Marla pointed toward the door. "You first." On the edge of the porch lay Mayfield, eyes staring blankly, with his throat slashed and a knife punctured through the center of his vest. She knelt next to him and checked for a pulse, a useless effort.

Larry went back inside. "Have rolls of partially used duct tape behind the couch. And a dining table with only three chairs."

Her radio squelched on her belt. Grand-mamma asked, "Do you have Zoom on your phone?"

Marla looked puzzled. "Yes. Why?"

"A silent alarm went off at the back door of the Flagstone Theater. At the same time, an anonymous phone call said for you to join a Zoom meeting."

"I don't have time for a Zoom."

"The caller said, Now."

"What kind of meeting?"

Marla's phone dinged. It was a Zoom request. She touched the blue hyperlink, and it opened. She and Larry watched. "Oh, God, help us."

The Zoom site showed Samuel Chenier's arms and legs duct taped to a chair with more tape across his mouth and beard. Eyes red and wet. Pupils wide.

Marla looked back at the dining room table with a single chair. The killer was here, and she missed him. "Shit. The theater, Larry. They have to be there. Let's go."

Rain careened sideways, twisting between houses. Her truck u-turned and charged down the road. She snapped the mic button down. "All units to Flagstone Theater. Hostage situation." She remembered Officer Mayfield saying there were no other officers on duty.

Windshield wipers sloshed back and forth. Tires sprayed sheets of rain in the air. Emergency lights danced across the wet intersections. Marla glimpsed at a set of headlights coming from the right. She changed the siren from a wail to a high-low. "Stop, you idiot. Don't you see me coming?" A Channel Ten News van turned at the intersection, heading toward the theater. Rebekah flashed in her mind.

A river flowed down the street and swirled into a churning mass at the next corner. The van stopped and the backup lights lit.

Marla slammed on the brakes and called out on the radio, "I can't get through the intersection. The water's too high. Backup and turn at the side street."

Marla narrowly squeezed her dually between the cars lining both sides of the streets, missing them by inches. Larry followed, his red and blue lights swirling in the air. Curious people stared outside from their homes.

She sped past the temporary lake, then charged down Main Street. One block ahead, glaring neon lights proclaimed the majuscule lights of the Flagstone Theater. Marla headed into the rear parking lot. Emergency lights raked against the building.

The back door lay on the ground with a chain wrapped around the door handle. Inside the building, lights blazed down a single hallway. Samuel Chenier's muffled voice bellowed from an outdoor speaker.

She tore out of the truck and swept away hair soaked against her face. Racing to the outside wall, she leaned against the entrance where a door once stood. Larry caught up to her. They snaked down the hallway and entered the auditorium. Stepping onto the stage, she checked behind the curtains. Larry swept rows of empty seats. There was no one.

Water pooled around her from her wet clothes. To the side stood a small television on a metal rollaway shelf. From the speaker, a distorted voice laughed. "Everything you thought was going to happen was wrong." The screen lit with Samuel Chenier sitting in a chair, his shirt ripped open, and mouth taped shut. His eyes were wide with terror.

The voice spoke again. "Marla Adams, you are the evil one who murdered your brother. Who sheds the blood of others shall themselves shed blood."

A laugh bellowed out from a speaker on the other side of the stage. Marla swung her pistol at the noise. It's not time, she thought. The murder wasn't supposed to happen until seven tomorrow morning.

She turned back toward the television. A man stepped in front of the camera, his back to the lens with a blood-stained bandage wrapped around his forearm. "You have failed him, Marla Adams." He ripped the tape from the bearded face.

Chenier screamed, then begged, "Please, let me go—"

The bandaged forearm raised in the air. A taser gun aimed toward the man.

Chenier's expression flattened. His eyes focused on the gun. He raised his chin slightly and then leaned forward. "You go to hell."

The gun fired; wires shot into his chest. He screamed and spasmed in the chair. The picture froze.

Marla stared at the screen. Chenier wasn't wet. Behind him, a Santa Claus picture hung on the wall. She remembered the picture in the house, next to the fireplace. They were never on this stage. This is a video made in Chenier's living room.

Marla jumped through her skin when her phone rang. She pulled it from her pocket and answered, "Adams here."

The distorted voice spoke. "You think you know when death will come? Too soon for you, and someone has died tonight. God moves quickly when he does his best work."

Chapter 47

Standing on stage, Marla called her father, with no answer. Rain pummeled her as she ran to her truck. Her clothes stuck to her skin. Opening her door, she climbed in and then reached for the police radio mic.

"Pops, reply immediately." No answer. She called out again, "Chief Searcy, where the hell are you?" No answer.

She called Crosby on her phone. "This is Crosby Adams. Please leave—" She hung up. "Shit."

Her fist pounded the dash with each word. "WHERE. THE. HELL. IS. EVERYONE!" She grabbed the radio mic again. "Larry, head back to the house and check it out again."

Larry replied, "Roger, 10-4."

She drove out into the street and stopped. With the wipers slinging water away and rain pounding the roof, she listened to the distorted man's voice in her head.

She called Grand-mamma on the radio. "Is Chief Searcy at the station?"

"I'll check." A long minute later, Grand-mamma replied, "He's not in the station, and his truck is not in the lot."

Marla threw the mic on the passenger seat and charged for his house. Tires splashed muddy water across his front yard. His truck was not there. She unlocked the front door and entered a dark room smelling like dead animals. With her elbow over her mouth and nose, she called out in a muffled voice, "Pops, you here? Where are you? I need your help." She turned the living room lights on. The cluttered house had trash piled high and dirty dishes stacked on the floor. She opened windows and let air and rain in. Shuffling through fast-food wrappers and potato chip sacks, past the couch, she opened the bedroom door—bed covers scrambled into a jumbled heap in the center of the mattress.

She entered the kitchen. *Good God, not again. Leave the poor squirrels alone.* A chemical smell hung in the air. "Pops, you back here?" A two-by-three foot animal skin lay on the breakfast table. A bucket of milky water on the floor with bottles of tanning ingredients sat on the countertop, and guts, brains, and bones in the kitchen sink. She held back a cough, then opened the back door to let in more air. What went through his screwed-up head that said it was okay to tan leather in the kitchen?

She clutched his brown-tinted prescription bottle on the countertop and started to leave until she found the key to the safe sitting next to a green sticky notepad. He always kept the key on a key ring in his pocket. The hall closet door was ajar with the safe inside. She never knew what he kept in there; never looked—never allowed to look.

She wiped her hands dry on a cup towel and then dropped in front of the safe, placed the key in the lock, and turned it. There were only two items, a drawstring money sack and a single folder. The heavy bag clinked when she placed it on the floor. The folder had staples across all four sides and equations written on the front of the folder.

~~500x1000=500,000~~

~~750x1000=750,000~~

~~1200x1000=1,200,000~~

Marla glanced at the front door and then back at the folder. If she gently pulled the back of the staples out, she could open it, then close it by pushing the staples back through the holes and bending them back down. Pops would never know. She caught herself hyperventilating. With closed eyes, she imagined opening the folder.

She jumped when the radio on her belt squelched. Brushing her hair from her face, she answered, "Adams here."

The blunted Grand-mamma's voice said, "Marla, the rehab center called reporting Crosby missed his bed check."

Marla stared at the folder again, then out the front window. Crosby and someone else ran from her a few hours ago. Was he buying drugs? She tapped the mic. "I'll head to the center in twenty minutes."

With slow, gentle manipulation of the staples, she opened the folder. The first thing which caught her eye was paper money, several 100,000 Lira bills with BANCA D'ITALIA printed on the bottom.

A yellowed Italian newspaper dated 27, Aprile 1988 laid behind the paper money. She pulled her phone out from her pocket and opened the Google Translation app Crosby had loaded days earlier. She read the Italian news article clippings. Four young men worked as volunteers at the Sistine Chapel restoration program in Vatican City. They disappeared from the site after a thousand coins were reported missing—six hundred 1958 Vatican City Pope Pius XII 100 Lire gold coins and four hundred 1959 Vatican City Pope John XXIII 100 Lire gold coins.

Marla's fingers separated the drawstring on the money sack, reached in, and dropped a handful on the floor. They were the same as the one the Montenegrin Rector gave to Crosby. The one Searcy took and never gave back. She understood the equations, the value, $1,200,000.

Behind the news article was a faded photo of four men standing outside a campground with their shirts off and smiling. Each had a square yellow and white tattoo on their chest. The name Roberto Ducati was written under a young Simic, Mark Everett under a young Rector Sudvaric, and next to Everett, William McCleskey under the face of John Walker without scars.

Logan discovered John Walker as a PI with an alias of William Mc-Cleskey. At the time, it meant nothing to her.

The fourth name stood out with the name written in bigger letters–Edwin Searcy. "Pops?"

Another newspaper clipping from Cleburg, Alabama, dated June 9, 1996, told the story of a house fire with two victims, William and Mary Lou McCleskey. Their six-month-old infant survived the fire. Paper-clipped behind the article was a confirmation letter of adoption of Marla Mc-Cleskey with a name change to Marla Searcy dated March 6, 1997. McCleskey was Walker, her blood father, but he didn't die in the fire.

The rain pounding on the windows and roof had stopped. Truck tires crunched gravel in front of the house. Frantically pouring the coins back into the sack and shoving all the paperwork into the safe, Marla snapped it shut with the key still in the lock, then partially closed the door as it had been. She adjusted her wet shirt and holster as Searcy entered his house.

"What are you doing here?" He looked at his watch: 6:08 PM, fifty-two minutes until 7 PM.

Marla pushed her damp hair back and bent down to pick up the prescription bottle. "Thought you needed this. Just came to help you out.

You know, the medicine." Her hands trembled as she twisted the cap, then poured one tablet into her palm. "Here, take this." She held her hand out as she noticed his clothes were dry.

Searcy took the pill from her palm. "Good idea. Not sure if I took one yesterday."

She stared at the bandage on his forearm. It was the same as the one on the man in the Zoom video. "What happened to your arm?"

He ignored the question, pointed toward the kitchen, and moved past her. "Just need some water from the kitchen faucet." He glanced at the sticky pad on the countertop. The key was missing.

"You know, Pops, I got a report that Crosby is missing at the rehab center. I'll meet you back at the station."

He drank a few gulps of water and set the glass down. He mumbled to himself, "Not seven yet. It's not time for her." He leaned, stiff-armed, against the counter. "Hold on." He pushed away. "I know all about him sneaking out, buying drugs. Possibly more." He stepped next to the closet door and pressed his hand against it.

A thunderbolt clapped inside her brain when the door latch snapped shut.

"I think he's the serial killer," Searcy said. "Makes sense, a perfect alibi. Crosby's confined in rehab, except he's not. He snuck out and back in with each murder. Come into the kitchen, and let's figure out the details." His hand slid down to the doorknob.

"Pops, I'll see you at the station. I need to find Crosby. Perhaps there is something I, we missed."

"You think you missed something?" He twisted the doorknob and opened the door. His right hand moved to his holster. "Did you have enough time to find what you were after in here?"

"Pops, your clothes are dry. Everyone went to the theater during the rainstorm. Why are you not wet?" She took a step back. "We don't need to do anything crazy."

"Crazy? You think I'm crazy?" Underhanded, he pitched the pill toward her.

She batted it away like a fly in her face. A curtain of understanding opened inside her. "You don't take those, do you?" She dropped the pill bottle; tablets scattered across the floor.

"No. Never did."

"Why fake the craziness?"

"Craziness? You mean schizophrenia? My psychosis? Backup plan. If things go sideways for me, hard to sentence a crazy man to death. I'd rather spend my life in the nuthouse watching Wheel of Fortune every day." His finger tapped twice on the closet door. "Did you see what you wanted in the safe?"

"You were friends with William McCleskey, right?" she asked.

Searcy's grin widened only on one side. "I haven't heard that name in a long time. Over twenty years."

"You and your friends stole the coins in Italy."

"I believe the statute of limitations for theft has come and gone." He shook his head and laughed. "Don't think you have the authority to discuss what happened in Italy."

Marla's trigger finger bristled. "The house fire in 1996 wasn't an accident. It was a double homicide. You killed McCleskey and his wife, then stole the coins from him in Alabama. Except you *didn't* kill him. He showed up in town as John Walker, didn't he?"

"You think I killed all those people?"

She came inches closer and pulled out her handcuffs. "You're under arrest."

He gut punched her, and she fell to her knees. The cuffs rattled in her hand. Groaning on the floor, she squirmed away from him.

"Why kill the McCleskeys and take me?" Marla asked.

"I wanted the coins, and your mother wanted children."

"She was not my mother. Mary Lou McCleskey was."

"Have to admit, I thought McCleskey died in the house fire. Instead, his wife was having an affair, and the dead man was her lover, not her husband. Didn't know it until Walker confessed to me just before I killed him in the church."

"You killed Walker, McCleskey? My father." She pushed up from the arm of an overstuffed chair, but Searcy shoved her back to her knees.

"I am your father."

"Bullshit. You murdered all those people." She pointed at the bloodied bandage wrapped around his left forearm. "That's the bandage in the Chenier video." She quickly stood before he could push her back down. "Is that from Rebekah Farmsdale's broken antler tip at Tinsley?"

Searcy drew his weapon.

Marla responded in equal time. Two pistols pointed at their targets five feet from each other.

"Didn't want to kill her. She didn't want to die, but she stuck her nose too far in the rabbit hole."

Legs trembling, she sat on the edge of the chair. Her arm holding her pistol dropped to her side. "And you killed Logan, your own son."

"He came close to breaking this case wide open—hell of a smart guy. You, on the other hand, I picked you to run the investigation because I never imagined you figuring out anything. Scared of your own shadow. Followed Crosby like a lost puppy dog for years."

She glanced at the closet. "All this? Why?"

"There's a connection between Walker and me, so I needed a misdirection. Thought it was a good idea with more killings."

Her gun slid back into her holster. "Are you going to kill me, too?"

"Always had a soft spot for you."

"I don't care anymore." She shoved his shoulder back. She felt the barrel against her chest. "You think you're sane? You're fricken psychotic. No one in their right mind thinks killing more people is a good idea."

"It's what needed to be done."

She took a step back. "When were you going to stop?"

His eyebrow rose for a second. "It got to be a game. I figured one more."

"Simic... Roberto Ducati? Why is he here?"

"I'm impressed. You have finally connected all the names," Searcy retorted. "He came to buy the coins from me. He doesn't know it yet, but I'm stealing his money and keeping the coins."

With a capitulating voice, she asked, "Did you kill Crosby?"

"He's not dead. Need an insurance policy. I have him, and if you want him alive, you need to let this go."

"No." She drew her weapon again. "Give me Crosby."

He scoffed. "You're not using that on me."

"Lower your weapon, Mister Searcy."

He motioned to her. "Give me your phone, and I'll let you talk to him."

"I don't trust you."

"Just pull it out."

She yelled, "It's in the truck." She focused on the barrel aimed at her. Distant thunder rumbled outside.

He smiled while staring straight into her eyes. "Have your vest on?"

Her fingertip moved across the trigger. "Why?"

"To finish this game correctly, you have to die at 7 PM."

An explosion ripped through the room as he fired his pistol, hitting her center chest. Marla stumbled backward and over the chair to the floor. His foot skidded her pistol away.

After ripping the radio off her belt, Searcy patted her pants pockets for her phone. She didn't lie to him. It wasn't there. He stepped back into the kitchen and grabbed the notepad and pencil. "You want this game to end?" He wrote on the pad, dropped it in front of her, then swung open the closet door, opened the safe, grabbed the money sack, and charged out the front door.

Her truck tire flattened with a gunshot. After opening the driver's door, he took her cell phone from the cup holder and pistol-whipped the police radio and GPS monitor screen.

Marla coughed and rolled onto her side. Her face wrenched from the chest pain as she heard a motor roaring away. She read the note.

Chapter 48

Searcy's truck screeched to a halt at the side of the church. He blew the horn long and loud, then jumped out of the truck. His fists banged on the metal office door and yelled, "Open up!"

Simic shoved the door open. "I don't like this. I came here for one thing."

"I don't give a shit what you don't like." Searcy shoved Simic against the wall. "You're coming with me."

"Bullshit," Simic said. "I told you all I want are the coins, and now you've involved me in these murders."

Searcy rushed from the office and looked behind the altar and ambo, or podium. He shoved chairs aside before running back into the office. "Where's Adams?"

Simic pointed at his mirror, then toward the hallway. "On the monitor, I saw Mrs. Nagly park her car. Thank God she's slow. I had to hurry and move him. Seeing a cop sprawled on the floor might look suspicious."

He grabbed Simic's shirt and backhanded him. "Where is he?"

"The kitchen."

"You left him alone? Untied? Taser effects don't last long."

He ran past the altar, down the hallway, and swung the kitchen door open. Crosby was flat on his back, with hands and feet zip-tied and tape across his mouth. His eyes burned with a vengeance.

Simic caught up to him. "You left me the taser, so I shot him again."

Searcy pulled Crosby's hands forward and lifted him over his shoulder. He glared at Simic. "I'm heading out of town. Do you want the coins? Get in the truck." Searcy marched in front of the pews and out the side door. He rolled Crosby over the side of the truck bed. Landing with a hard thud, it knocked the wind out of him. Face-to-face, Sam Chenier's dead eyes stared at him—motionless.

As the truck careened forward, Crosby felt like a thousand killer bees stinging every muscle in his body repeatedly as the truck bounced hard on the dirt road. Taser wires still stuck in his chest. His wrists ached from the zip tie.

The feeling in Crosby's fingers slowly returned. He cringed as he pulled the wires out of his skin. The truck hit a pothole, and his body jumped a foot in the air, landing hard on the metal bed. Crosby groaned in pain. Chenier rolled on his stomach and face.

There were no sharp corners to cut the zip tie. Crosby squirmed on top of the dead man and swung his arms around. His fingers grabbed the side of the truck bed. If he could swing his legs around, he might be able to roll out of the truck. Crosby's boot hit the top of the bed. July fourth sparklers shot straight up his leg. His taped mouth muffled his scream.

Searcy's eyes shifted to his side mirror and watched Crosby's fingers hugging the top of the bed. A boot slapped over the edge. He smiled and said, "No, you don't." He jerked the steering wheel hard, then back again.

Crosby rolled and hit the other sidewall and screamed in frustration.

Searcy's teeth clenched, lips quivering. He laughed, then yelled out the window, "You are not stopping me! I will make Hildebrandt shake to its bones."

Simic's left hand rested on the satchel in his lap, hiding the 9mm pistol he held between the seat and the door. "I'm not here for your crazy shit killings. I'm only here to buy those coins. Besides, a fourth of those are already mine."

Searcy cackled. "You relinquished ownership years ago."

"You told me the price is $500 each. It took gambling, extortion, and stealing from the church, but I got the five-hundred-thousand." Simic tapped the satchel. "I want them now."

"I don't give a rat's ass what you want. The price has doubled. A thousand apiece."

"No. We agreed on half a million."

"Not anymore. All or nothing. I want a million."

Simic tore off the white tab on his collar and pitched it to the floorboard. "Why don't I kill you and take the coins?" He swung the pistol around and aimed it at Searcy's head. "Give me the coins."

Searcy looked toward Simic and slammed on the brakes, throwing him hard against the dash. The satchel slid to the floor. Searcy reached for a pistol inside the door panel as Simic raised his weapon. A flash exploded in the cab. The truck's front tire dove into another deep pothole, bouncing Crosby and Chenier against the metal bed.

◆

The truck slid to a stop in front of an abandoned barn. Simic held his bleeding wrist. "You shot me, you asshole. Give me the coins and I'll get out of here."

Searcy jammed the gearshift into park. "Stay here." He opened his door and looked at Crosby in the back of the truck. "Get out." He ripped the tape off Crosby's face.

"You just electrocuted me, hog-tied me, threw me all around in the truck bed, and now you want me to get out?" He pushed himself to the opposite side of the bed. "No. I'm staying here."

Searcy shot a hole into the bed. Crosby jumped and said, "All right. Fine. I'm getting out."

The tailgate dropped, and Crosby scooted to the edge until his feet hung down. "Now what?"

"Stand up."

"Can't. My arms and legs are still numb." He held his hands out in front of him. "Cut these zip-ties."

Searcy flicked his pocketknife open and cut the leg zip-tie. As soon as he cut the wrists free, Crosby wrapped his arms around his captor and both fell to the ground. The pistol fired. Crosby rolled away after he reached into Searcy's pocket and lifted his phone. "All right, I give up. You got me." Crosby rolled to his elbows and knees and slipped the phone into his pants.

Crosby felt the gun barrel against his neck. "Don't give me any more shit, Mr. DEA agent."

"What about Simic?" Crosby asked.

"He's in the cab bitching about me shooting him in his wrist."

A single hole had pierced the back glass, and there was no movement in the cab. Crosby sidled around to the right side of the truck. Simic leaned forward against the dashboard with a bullet hole in the back of his head.

"He's dead," Crosby said.

Searcy laughed. "Shit happens." He slid Chenier to the end of the tailgate and flipped the dead man over on his shoulder. "Pick the bastard up and carry him." He nodded at the satchel. "And leave that in the truck."

Crosby swung Simic's leg to the outside, dropped the dead man's feet to the ground, and lifted the body over his shoulder. A stream of blood oozed down Crosby's shirt and pants.

Chapter 49

After Marla changed her flat tire, she glanced at her watch: 6:27 PM. The Creation of Adam. Genesis 1:26. 7+1+26=34=7. She was right about the seven, but it would be PM, not AM. Someone is dying in thirty-three minutes. Her truck turned off SH 216 and roared down a narrow gravel road.

Gray and black clouds stretched across the horizon in the east. Miles away, rumblings in the sky declared atmospheric trouble.

She gave up trying to miss a thousand potholes and let the truck rock like an out-of-balance washing machine. She begged the broken radio to fix itself. Her finger touched the note stuck on her dashboard.

BARN
COME ALONE OR CROSBY DIES.

There's only one barn he meant, the Briscoe Barn. The owner died over thirty years ago and left it all to the family in the estate. Nobody ever came to collect. Searcy said he wanted to buy it one day, but he didn't have the money. He always had the money—gold coins in the safe.

The bipolar sky threw a violet and orange sunset at her driver's window while ominous clouds to the right rolled toward her like soldiers gathering for a second assault. A deceitful, musky odor filled the air. A hard rain was coming...maybe more.

Her truck swerved and charged toward a wet field with an abandoned barn five hundred yards away. Her tires slipped in the mud. Searcy's truck sat at the entrance with the headlights and taillights still on, both doors open and the tailgate down.

After stopping behind his truck with the diesel engine humming, she drew her pistol and rushed to the right side of his cab. It was empty. She reached for the radio microphone on the dash, but the coiled cord was cut.

Blood splayed across the passenger seat, dashboard, door panel, and the ground. Next to the open passenger door was a V imprint from a shoe print. *The priest is here.* The infamous satchel lay on the floorboard. What was so important to him? She opened it to find bundles of 100 dollar bills. Thousands, no, hundreds of thousands of dollars were in it. She pitched the satchel into her truck.

A wind gust lifted her partially wet hair above her shoulders. Black monstrous cotton balls grew in the sky as a chill whipped through her body. "Crosby, where are you?"

Opening the back door of her truck, she slipped on the camo patterned hunting vest with a short LED Maglite in one lower pocket and a handful of glow sticks in another. She zipped it over her tactical vest, then slid the Model 97 shotgun off the seat. An army metal ammunition canister sat on the floorboard with a partial box of #00 buckshot 12-gauge shells, and two full 9mm magazines. She loaded six into the shotgun magazine tube, then did something she hadn't done in a long time. After racking the pump handle, which loaded a shell into the chamber, she stuffed another in the magazine tube—seven, not six.

She placed a seventeen-round 9mm magazine in a vest pocket and another in her back pants pocket, then jammed the small Glock 26 with a full ten-round magazine behind her belt at the small of her back. Marla grimaced, then tapped her standard police-issued Glock 17 pistol in the side holster. "Not enough for this son-of-a-bitch." She hustled around her truck and opened the passenger front door. She opened the glove box, clutched her .45 caliber Smith &Wesson semi-automatic, and stuffed the barrel inside the front of her pants. Marla pressed her finger against the indentation from the bullet in her tactical vest. She hoped this was enough firepower.

A deserted wooden monolith with gaping, weather-beaten slats stood before her. The time was 6:42, eighteen minutes before 7. Bishop Medina was right.

This is when it will end.

❖

Her sore chest ached more when she pushed the shotgun barrel against the door. Rusted hinges squawked, announcing her presence. Air, heavy with mold and hell, rolled past her head. The wide open barn had enormous neon orange and green-colored graffiti sprayed with psychotic images high on the walls. A massive vinyl copy of the Sistine Chapel enshrouded the ceiling. *I don't give a shit what he thinks. The man is not sane.*

To the far right side, near the wall, wooden stairs climbed to a second floor with no railing. Dried, weathered posts held the precarious upstairs wooden floor. They creaked with the wind, like everything else. Hay bales and tires piled on top of each other sat next to forgotten machinery and could easily hide a man. Decades of brown leaves, weeds, and dried hay, a foot thick, had accumulated across the dirt floor.

A sound came from the back, a cackle called for her.

She bent down on one knee and raised her shotgun to her shoulder. "Edwin Searcy, give yourself up." Nothing but silence. She didn't expect a response.

In front of her, shoe prints in the hay led toward the other side of the barn and behind a hay thrasher.

Where are you?

She needed her inhaler or three more crazy pills right now.

Someone, years ago, stacked twenty paint cans against a wall. Marla crept forward with boots crunching dead leaves until she felt a click under her foot.

A whooshing sound came closer. She turned. A pendulum swung two paint cans from the roof toward her head. She fired the shotgun, blasting the cans and spewing paint into the air.

Down on her knees, her hand rested on the paint-splattered shotgun.

"What is this? A game to you? A carnival ride?" She jumped up and swung the shotgun barrel around. Brown paint dripped down her hair. "Come on, Searcy, or should I say, McCleskey's murderer. Show yourself."

An office with no windows and battered sheetrock stood out from the back wall. It looked like an addition after the original build. Several holes the size of a sledgehammer head pockmarked the wall near the door. *Did he do that before or after hitting Mr. Kinsey?* An orange spray-painted arrow pointed to the doorknob. She felt Satan's fingernails claw the back of her neck.

She rushed toward the office, leaned against a wall, and almost fell when the drywall cracked at the baseboard. One entire wall dropped to the ground. The room was small and dank, with no ceiling. Sticking out from the floor, an open metal door leaned back. She entered the room, turned on the Maglite, and aimed the shotgun barrel at the hole. Concrete steps angled downstairs. Sweeping paint away from her face, she leaned forward. She manipulated a glow stick between her fingers and the flashlight, snapped it, and pitched it as far back into the abyss as possible.

"You forgot I was here," Searcy said from behind. He hit her wrist, and the Maglite fell to the floor. Grabbing her by the neck and belt loop, he shoved her downstairs. The door slammed shut behind her.

She rolled down the steps and heard a lock snap closed behind her. The stench of stale air, mildew, and decayed animals made her cough. It was surprisingly warm in the hole. She pitched glow sticks on the floor and held one above her head. Trash piled knee-high in each corner, with no furniture or canned food in sight. The walls were cinder blocks, not concrete. This was not a bomb shelter. It was for surviving thirty minutes while a tornado ran above your head.

Leaves shuffled; she thought rats or opossums, neither good to have cornered in a dark room. On her knees, her other hand swept across the floor, hoping to find the shotgun. She touched cold metal. Her fingers wrapped around the barrel.

The leaves moved again, then stopped. This time, the noise rattled. Marla jumped back as the snake, as wide as a water hose, lunged across the glow stick toward her. It hit her in the chest and retracted for another attack. She shoved the barrel against the head. "Die, you son of a bitch. Die, and goddamn everything in here." The end of the barrel twisted on top of the snakehead until the rattle stopped.

Her diaphragm froze. A vice-grip clamped around her chest. She dropped to her hands and knees, and the shotgun bounced away. *No. No. Not this way. Can't die here. Crosby, where are you?*

Her stomach spasmed. She drew in a hard breath, fell to her side, and screamed, "Goddamn you. Let me out!"

She stood and drew the pistol from her waistband and fired until it wouldn't. Bullets shattered the door handle and round holes of light infiltrated the room, but the door stood in place. She pitched the empty pistol on the ground and racked the shotgun. A snake rattled behind her. She swung around and aimed at the noise. Thoughts of ricocheting buckshot bouncing a thousand directions in a small room changed her mind. She spun and fired at the doorknob. The buckshot blew a basketball-sized hole through the door, and it burst open. Another rattle came from near the stairs. Quickly racing up the steps, she snatched the Maglite. She brushed her hands over her clothes and touched something protruding—a broken tooth pierced the center of her hunting vests. "Damn snakes."

A small mirror with desilvered black spots hung on the wall. She wiped partially dried and stiffened paint off her face, and leaves and trash stuck to her clothes and hair. She knew how a scarecrow felt.

Chapter 50

M arla charged out of the demolished room and aimed the shotgun toward three pickup truck cabs which sat like a row of rusted bread boxes. Crouching down, she closed in on the front cab, then knelt, listening for a clue. She racked the pump action, the spent shell ejected and bounced on the floor.

She rushed past one cab to another. A stench of old iron and copper hit her square in the face—coagulated blood. The smell had become familiar. She buried her nose into her elbow as she peeked around the rust bucket. A wooden staircase led to the second floor with a dozen squirrels frozen in place, lined up head-to-tail on the bloodstained handrail, looking like they were climbing upstairs, one behind another, except for a nail punched through each skull. A swarm of flies buzzed the staircase. *Does he hate every squirrel in the world?*

She aimed the shotgun upstairs when she heard a laugh. His boot shoved a man off the floor above her. In a second, she dropped to her elbows and knees and covered her head. The body bounced off the stairs twice and knocked her sideways. She pushed and shoved the hundred and fifty pounds of whoever off of her.

Sanguine fluid saturated the dead man's hair and scalp with his shirt and pants bloodied over disfigured arms and legs. She rolled the body over. It was Simic. She cried out, "Stop this, you son-of-a-bitch!" Her hands wrapped around the bloodied head. She slowly lowered the eyelids. Her shirt sleeve wiped tears from her face.

Vinyl coverings, like the ones in the church office, splayed across the wall next to the staircase. This time with neon painted exaggerations; smiling joker red lipstick over mouths, green tongues long and curled, and orange horns projecting out of God's head. Spray-painted yellow and red arrows pointed upstairs, daring her to follow.

Marla clenched her jaw; her neck tightened, she tried to swallow the lump in her throat. Her thoughts raced up the steps.

Boots clomped above her from one end of the second floor to the other. "Come on, girl, let's get this over."

Wind gusts rattled slats against themselves as black clouds advanced above her. The temperature plummeted. A barn owl flew inside and perched on a high beam.

Marla stared at the bird. "What do you see up there?"

Her hand wrapped around the pump action of the shotgun. She cringed when the wooden steps creaked against her boots. Searcy, or Chief, or Pops, or whatever the hell he wanted to be called, was waiting for her.

Adrenaline raced through her arteries. The reek of mildew returned. Her lungs tightened, and she choked back a cough. Reaching the top of the stairs, she put her back to the wall and wanted to charge through, shattering everything with #00 buckshot, screaming at the top of her lungs. Instead, she stood paralyzed.

Thunder rumbled louder overhead. Prophetic clouds killed the last of the outside light.

She scanned the room with her Maglite. More psychotic paintings. Abandoned cobwebs in corners sprayed green. Her light swept across five biblical vinyl coverings nailed onto a row of hay bales. All one theme, one repetitive fresco, the next Sistine Chapel painting, the next murder—The Creation of Adam.

Her pupils widened; hands trembled.

A single purple light bulb on a long black wire hovered over the center of the second floor. Next to it, a disco ball slowly spun.

Large hooks attached to thick chains hung from the roof and swayed in the wind. To the side, a wooden desk covered with dirt and bird droppings stood alone.

Three towers of hay bales piled on top of each other looking like Jenga blocks. *Which hay bale are you behind, you sick bastard?*

Something caught her eye, one fresco out of place with a man leaning against it and something over his head. Crouched down, she rushed toward the man. It was Samuel Chenier with a rusted chain wrapped around his neck. His face, swollen and blue, eyes bulged almost out of their sockets.

A zip-tie clamped around his right wrist, positioning his arm over God's arm on the fresco. Another zip-tie wrapped tight around his index finger covered God's finger and pointed toward Adam.

He made Chenier God. Searcy was filling in a jigsaw puzzle. Was Crosby to be Adam?

She shined the light on the fresco. Adam looked different with a large, open zip-tie stuck through the neck and a smaller at the wrist. Black paint streaked down the scalp and circles around each pectoralis muscle—a shoddy attempt at drawing a woman's hair and breasts.

This was not for Crosby. It was for her. Searcy was making The Creation of Marla Adams.

A moan came behind Chenier. Crosby kicked a hay bale. Duct tape covered his mouth, hands zip-tied in front of him and the left side of his face, swollen and bruised. A chain wrapped around his neck.

Marla laid the shotgun down and pulled the tape off. "Where is he?" she asked.

"Get out!" he yelled. "It's a trap."

The purple light illuminated overhead and brightened the neon paint. Loud circus music screamed from the four corners of the roof. The disco ball shot a thousand erratic lights across the walls and roof.

From a crossbar above Marla, a chain spun through a hoist. The rusted chain around Crosby's neck tightened, his body shot up in the air, toes stretching to reach the floor. With his wrists zip-tied in front of him, his fingertips struggled at his neck. Carnival organ music shrilled in the air. Marla wrapped her arm around Crosby's legs and tried to hold him up. She drew her service weapon from the holster and fired into the three hay bales across the barn. Crosby gagged and struggled with the chain around his neck. She fired at the disco ball, shattering it into pieces.

A heinous laugh blared across the barn. "You have a choice. Will you save him or kill me?"

"Come out, you freak."

"You should have stayed my little girl. Because of you, all these people are dead."

The music grew louder. The chain pulled Crosby higher, making his toes dangle inches above the floor.

Lightning ripped across the sky. Sonic booms exploded outside. Sheets of icy rain blew through the walls and onto the speakers. Sparks jumped into the air, and the music stopped.

Marla fired at the hoist. It snapped in half and Crosby dropped to the floor, with a row of metal chains rattling beside him. She fired again, the light bulb exploded, and blackness enveloped the barn again.

The pistol's slide locked backward. She fumbled for the magazine in her vest but dropped it on the floor. Her hand swept for it. Her fingers touched the shotgun barrel.

Crosby groaned as he lay twisted on the floor with the chains still wrapped around him. Marla dropped to a prone position and inched toward him as the rain beat against her back.

"You must pay for that," Searcy said.

A jolt of electricity shot through the chain around Crosby's neck. He screamed as his body winced in pain.

"Slide the shotgun out to the middle of the floor. You don't want me to hit Crosby with electricity again."

"Stop it." She swept the wet hair from her face, then swung the shotgun and fired into a hay bale tower. It fell backward. Searcy wasn't there. He had to be behind one of the two towers left.

Electricity shot through the chain. Crosby convulsed.

The vinyl covering on the roof filled with rain. On her hands and knees, Marla yelled, "What do you want?" Her lungs spasmed and coughed.

"To leave with the coins, with no witnesses."

"You killed Logan for gold coins."

"Not just a few coins, a million dollars' worth. After tonight, they jump in price. Ever heard of the dark web?"

Marla inched toward Crosby as she tried to listen to where Searcy was hiding. "No. Tell me about it." Thunder rolled in the darkness above her. She slipped her knife out from her belt sheath and sliced the zip-tie around Crosby's wrists.

She had to keep the lunatic talking. "How did John Walker track you down after all these years?"

"I still have friends in Vatican City. They told me the church hired Walker to quietly find the coins, but they didn't know he was McCleskey. I knew he was coming for me."

Crosby loosened the chain around his neck and turned toward Marla, trying to speak in a low raspy voice, "Phone in my pocket."

Marla felt around Crosby's shirt and pants. "And what about Simic? Father Jules? Why did he come to town?" She pulled the phone from Crosby's pants pocket. She swept rain off her face and pushed 911.

"911, what is your emergency?"

From behind hay bales, Searcy called out, "He called me from Europe and said he had a buyer willing to pay five-hundred-thousand in Dallas for the coins but would only deal with Simic. We had to get him a new identity so he could come to America."

"You, as Chief of Police, brought Father Jules into town illegally with falsified immigration papers." One hand held the phone while the other swept the floor for the dropped magazine. "Why are we at the old Briscoe Barn outside of town?" Lightning streaked across the sky. She laid the phone down, sat up, and rapid-fired the shotgun twice at the hay towers. The metal wire around a bale sparked and set the bale on fire.

"What the hell are you doing? You're going to burn the place down."

She could feel him losing control. "Why did Simic kill the Rector in Montenegro?"

"How did you know that?"

"I'm a cop. Cops know stuff. Tell me more about Simic."

"He was a hothead. That wasn't supposed to happen in Montenegro."

"Why did you kill Simic?"

"Greed. What else? I wanted the coins and the three hundred thousand dollars he stole from the bank."

Chilled rain changed to sleet while flames ravaged the hay and climbed the walls.

A voice called out from behind the bales. "What are you doing with Crosby?"

"Nothing. Let us leave this barn." A thousand ice picks hit her face. She gazed at the roof and the vinyl stretching from water. She fired the shotgun twice, water plunged on top of the hay bales where the floor flooded, and the phone screen went blank. *Damn.*

Crosby tried loosening the chain. Electricity shot around his neck again. He screamed as his body seized on the floor.

"Not going well for you, is it, my dear daughter?"

"I'm not your fricking ass daughter. Go. Get out. You leave us now, and I will let you walk down those stairs and disappear forever."

"Why would I do that?"

"You have the coins and Simic's cash. There's nothing else here for you."

"Can't leave my masterpiece without filling in all the characters. You are my last one."

Lightning streaked overhead, seconds at a time. The rain stopped. Thunder roared. Tornado.

A strip of shiny metal reflected next to Chenier's body. She reached for the lost magazine next to the dead man, shoved it in the pistol, racked it, and rapid fired toward the fallen towers. Red rings exploded from the barrel.

From the corner of her eye, muzzle flashes appeared.

The blow hit her hard and heavy. Two fastballs in the chest. Her head hit the floor; stars floated in the blackness. The barn spun. Her tongue thickened, throat tightened. The Maglite rolled from her hand across the floor.

Above her, lightning bolts streaked across the splintered roof. Her clothes felt like a hundred-pound blanket. Her face, neck, arms—too wet, too cold to move. She winced and closed her eyes as sleet bounced onto her face.

Just leave. Take your coins. Leave us alone.

She tried to say it out loud, but her lips wouldn't move. Bright lights flickered above her closed eyes. Heavy footsteps, even-measured, came toward her. She turned her head toward the paced sound and forced her eyelids open. Searcy appeared between lightning flashes. Rain beat against his wide-brimmed hat. Against her back, she felt her small Glock pistol.

She cried out when he stepped on her hand. He bent down on one knee, his face inches from hers. "I need a print and blood. Remember the dark web? You'll be famous. Every news station in America will have you on their screen. Small town cop almost catches the man who stole from the Vatican. *Almost* catches the man." He snapped open his pocketknife. "Walker, your daddy, had a nasty cut on his face. Maybe you should too."

She closed her eyes and turned away. She mumbled, "Maniac."

His hand grabbed her jaw. "You thought you were going to win." He leaned back and sliced off a square of her pant leg. "With your blood on the coin, those sick bastards on the dark web will pay me two, maybe three thousand dollars for each coin. And I have a thousand coins in my truck."

Marla screamed as the knife sliced across her calf muscle. Tears filled her eyes. *Crosby, help.*

Searcy soaked the cloth in the blood. Thunder exploded again. Lightning strobed behind him as he put the torn fabric in his shirt pocket. "Some of these nuts buying the coins will check your DNA. Needs to be yours."

Struggling for breaths while flat on his back, Crosby pulled the chain off his blistered neck and weakly swung it at the man's legs.

A boot slammed into Crosby's stomach. "Don't mess with me, you little DEA, piece-of-shit."

Marla turned toward Searcy and saw the utter depravity of his soul.

He wrapped the chain around her ankles. "You, Marla, my dear sweet, stupid *adopted* daughter, need to be taught a lesson and put in your place where you belong—in my masterpiece."

An electric motor clacked on and hummed. Sleet battered her face as she rolled over. Her ankles lifted into the air while dirt and hay scraped across her face. Fingertips touched the shotgun butt as her body upturned.

Searcy's boot shoved Crosby onto his back. "It's seven o'clock. Time to die." A red flash spewed from the gun barrel.

Upside down, Marla watched Searcy break a hay bale in half and rip out a handful of dry hay. He flicked his lighter; a small red and yellow flame lit the hay.

He felt the shotgun barrel against his side and twisted around toward Marla. His lips stretched into an evil grin. "Well, now. What are you going to do with an empty shotgun? I drop this, and the place burns with you and Crosby inside. Will you die from smoke inhalation," he pointed his pistol at her, "or should I shoot you and let you hang like a dead bat?"

Her vision returned; the fog lifted. "I have one left."

"No. I counted. The 97 carries six in the mag tube, and you fired six." He pitched the flaming hay on the broken bale. "I've decided you will die upside down."

"You're staying with us," she said.

She swung the shotgun away and fired at the railing. The wooden stairs crashed to the ground.

The recoil spun her in circles and swung her backward. She dropped the shotgun, pulled the pistol stuck behind her belt, fired, and broke the chain.

She bounced hard on the floor. Searcy had disappeared. Firing into both towers until the slide locked back, she heard a thud on the first floor.

Near her, Crosby moaned. Blood gurgled from his throat. She holstered her weapon, then grabbed Crosby's shirt at the shoulder and rolled him on his side.

"Stay with me, Crosby." She moved his hand to the bullet wound in his chest. "Push on this. Push as hard as you can."

The fire grew six feet tall, smoke billowing through the roof like a pyre. Her lungs tightened; the cough came back. She wished for the rain to return.

The wind speed increased. She stood to help Crosby and had forgotten about the cut on her leg. She screamed and fell. Groaned, trying to stand again, she called out, "Come on, big boy. We need out of here."

Crosby crawled to his feet while his right arm wrapped around the back of her neck. Vicious flames grew along a wall. "How are we getting off the second floor?" He looked up at the last hoist hanging from the roof and pointed. "There. We can wrap the chain around ourselves and lower down to the ground."

"No counter-balance weight," she said.

The rain stopped like flipping off a light switch. Searcy came out from behind a bale with his pistol aimed at her. "Neither of you are leaving the second floor."

Marla's eyes widened. She tried to hold Crosby up. He felt weak.

"You thought I fell backward to the first floor?" Expansive flames swirled and climbed up the walls. "Hoping I was dead?" A smile stretched across Searcy's face. "A hay bale can make a big noise when it hits the ground."

Wind swirled, wood creaked. The fire roared in delight as it gorged itself on timber and hay.

"All right, you win." She twisted slightly to the right, away from Searcy. "Go, leave us, leave town. You got what you wanted, you greedy bastard. Sell your damn coins and never come back."

Her hand slipped the pistol from the holster and held it behind her back. Crosby watched the empty magazine pop out. She tapped her back pocket with the gun barrel. He slid the mag out and snapped the other into her pistol grip. She slowly holstered the weapon with the slide still back.

A cloud of smoke hovered above their heads.

"You know too much, and you're both cops. I could never be free while you're alive." He turned directly in front of Marla, twenty feet between them, and holstered his gun. "I've already put two in your vest. The next one goes in your forehead."

"Wouldn't be much of a fast-draw contest with me holding Crosby."

"Won't be a contest at all. I watched you fire your gun at the bales." He pointed at her gun with the slide rearward. "This time, I know you're empty."

A train horn roared outside, except there were no tracks for miles.

Marla yelled above the noise, "I'm not empty!"

"I saw the slide go back. You're empty."

Crosby released her neck and sat down hard on the floor. She turned face-to-face toward Searcy. He glanced at her pistol as she snapped the slide forward.

"Amateur move, Officer Adams, pressing the slide release and making me think you have a bullet in the chamber. I thought you were better."

Burning boards from the roof broke free, floating to the ground. The floor beneath their feet shook. Marla's finger touched her holster. Her vision widened as she glanced at his hand easing toward his pistol. Lightning flashed behind Searcy. Thunder exploded. The train noise charged closer.

They both drew and fired. The roof ripped off—lightning shrieked above—walls exploded. The second floor gave way as Marla fell backward and grabbed Crosby's leg. They slammed against the ground.

Wind speed skyrocketed. The walls around the tornado shelter had blown away. A rusted truck cab flew by and crashed against a tractor. A fifteen-foot-long chain swirled like a broken propeller in the air, shredding anything in its way. The train horn turned into a screaming jet engine.

She wrapped her arms around Crosby and rolled down into the shelter. Air pressure squeezed against her ears. A bomb exploded above their heads. The cinder blocks cracked, and a cloud of dust and dirt surrounded them. They wrapped their arms around each other and held tight.

Chapter 51

The wind stopped. Nothing moved. A musty smell of moldy hay suf-
fused the black air. She wondered what the world looked like above
her. Then again, she didn't. The only sounds were her shallow breaths.

Wood cracked above her. Footfalls clambered.

"Marla," Larry called out, "we got your 911 call."

Flashlights swung across splintered boards, broken hay bales, and twisted
metal. Searcy's truck laid upside down where a barn once stood. Her truck
had twisted around a tree trunk.

"Marla! Where are you? We got here as fast as we could." Larry shoved
boards away and looked into a mangled truck cab. "You in here? Talk to
us, Marla. Say something."

His light swung between branches of a broken tree limb stretched over
a glowing green hole in the floor. "Anyone down there?" He aimed his
flashlight down the hole and froze.

Marla sat cross-legged, staring blankly at Larry. Crosby lay on his side
with his bloodied head in her lap, pushed against her ribs. His eyes closed.
Her left hand repeatedly brushed Crosby's hair from his face. Her right
hand gripped a pistol with the handle resting on her thigh and finger firmly
on the trigger.

Larry yelled to the others topside, "Down here! She's inside a shelter."
He mumbled, "Thank God, she's alive."

He rolled the tree limb away from the entrance and stepped down the
stairs. His flashlight scanned the dirt walls. Scattered green glow sticks on
the floor revealed five rattlesnakes with their heads blown off. He bent
down on one knee in front of her as his flashlight aimed at her pistol.
Larry's other hand gently wrapped around the barrel. "You don't need this

anymore." He lightly tugged on the gun. Her hand tightened. "Marla..."
he inhaled deeply, "you're all done. You did your job. You can let go now."

Her bloodshot eyes; unmoving, unblinking. Black soot and dirt covered
her face, wet lines streaked down her cheeks. Her grip snug around the
pistol handle, with a finger on the trigger guard.

Larry glanced at Crosby, who wasn't moving. Blood had soaked his shirt
and pant leg. "Is it okay if I check on Crosby? He's bleeding."

Her grip eased. Larry slipped the pistol from her hand and slid it across
the floor. He shined the flashlight on her chest. The hunting vest had three
round burn marks in the center. "Marla? You've been shot."

She didn't answer. Instead, she continued to brush Crosby's hair and
stare straight ahead.

"Marla? Are you alright? Talk to me."

With her head still and eyes fixated straight ahead, her fingers touched
the three holes in her vest. The corner of her mouth raised. She whispered,
"He's fast."

Boards shifted above them. A voice called out, "EMS is here." A flood-
light aimed down into the shelter. Crosby's eyes looked up.

❖

Three hundred yards from the barn, the police found Searcy's mangled
body with a bullet hole in the center of his neck. As miracles happen, the
bag of coins and the satchel stayed inside Searcy's truck.

In 1998, Pope John Paul II denied the robbery with a statement that
no one has ever robbed the Vatican. After the recovery of one thousand
gold coins in Texas, the Vatican reemphasized there was no robbery. The
Hildebrandt City Council sold them and used the funds for families of the
deceased.

Crosby explained his actions as a DEA agent to Marla. After recovering
from the gunshot wound, he returned to the Austin field office for his next
assignment.

The DEA offered her a job, as did the Texas Rangers, and the Hildebrandt Police Department as the new Chief. Marla stood next to her new
truck in front of the police station and looked back at the front door once

more. She turned away, climbed into her truck, and headed to San Antonio to join the DEA and Crosby.

THE END

About the Author

Patrick Hanford has lived in Texas most of his life. He graduated from the University of North Texas, Texas College of Osteopathic Medicine and recently retired from family medicine after more than thirty-five years. He interjects his past experiences of daily medical clinic life throughout his stories.

His passion for reading and writing has progressed to published short stories and now his first novel.

He lives with his wife, plays golf, walks in West Texas wind, and travels from one end of Texas to the other visiting children and grandchildren.

Acknowledgments

I took bits and pieces of many small municipalities to make the fictional town of Hildebrandt, Texas. San Antonio, Bexar County, and the Alamo are real, but most everything else is not, as expected in a fiction novel.

I want to thank the Lubbock and Slaton Police Departments for their information. The drive-alongs were very informative.

To the golf buddies and friends who read my first novel and pushed me to have the next one as soon as possible.

To the cotton-gin co-op managers. Even though I didn't use a cotton gin in the last scene as initially planned, I will keep their information and use it in the future.

To the Write Right Critique Group for their many different views and ideas.

To Audrey Mackaman and Cameron Chandler for being outstanding editors.

To Jody Smyers Photography for the fantastic book cover.

To KJ Waters for her everything in putting this into print.

To Sharon for supporting, ignoring, and helping me on a daily basis.

Please visit my website at www.patrickhanford.com. You can find me on social media at:

Facebook: PatrickHanfordauthor

Instagram: @patrickhanford.

Twitter: @patrickjhanford

If you'd like to receive the first few chapters of my next book, please sign up for my newsletter on my website. I'll share occasional updates on my writing, upcoming releases, sales, and special offers.

Made in the USA
Monee, IL
04 May 2023

33005458R00167